GAMBLING ON A SCOUNDREL

SHERIDAN JEANE

To my parents, Joe and Winnie Ferguson, who had the foresight to name me Sheridan Jean because they thought it would look great on the cover of a book someday. Talk about a self-fulfilling prophecy.

PINK'S TEA SHOP

Mayfair, London, 1861

FRENCH TART STEALS BLISS'S BLISS

The imaginary headline Temperance Bliss conjured from her fears mocked her as she hurried along the refined streets of Mayfair.

Tempy brushed a tear from her cheek with the back of her glove, hoping any passers-by would assume it was a drop of rain. Her other hand clutched a letter pressed tightly against her corseted waist.

She needed to compose herself. One simply didn't comport oneself this way in Mayfair. It wasn't done. Lifting her chin, Tempy erased all signs of emotion from her face. The best way to regain her composure was to focus on honing her imaginary headline. Perfecting it always helped calm her.

BLISS BETRAYED BY FRENCH TART

Slightly better, but still not quite right. Still not catchy enough.

How could Ernest undermine her in her moment of triumph? "I'll always be here for you," he'd said. But now...

She lifted a handful of her full, bell-shaped skirt to keep it from dragging through any of the puddles that had the temerity to form on the otherwise pristine sidewalks of this exclusive section of London.

Everything would be better once she reached Millicent. Her friend would know what to do. She always did. Millicent had the advantage of age and wisdom, although she probably wouldn't like hearing those qualities ascribed to her.

Until then, Tempy'd keep working on that headline.

FRENCH WENCH BANISHES BLISS

That was more like it. Short and catchy. Plus, it worked with both meanings of "bliss."

As Tempy rounded the street corner, she spied her destination, Pink's Tea Room. She glanced up at the clock tower overlooking the square. Her punctual friend would likely already be sitting at one of the cozy tables.

She peered through the tea shop's large window with its overly cheerful red mullions dividing the panes of glass and quickly spotted Millicent Kidman. Her friend wore her signature ostrich feather hat perched atop her graying upswept hair. It made her look like some sort of species of exotic bird.

Millicent poured steaming liquid into her cup. A second pot sat before the empty chair across from her at the four-person table. Wasn't that just like Millicent, to mother her on the rare occasions they were able to meet?

As Tempy focused on the little white teapot that awaited her, a sense of comfort washed over her, allowing her chest to relax. Finally, she found herself able to stand more upright.

Millicent would help her make sense of all this.

Tempy maneuvered her way between the tables toward Millicent who looked up at her with a welcoming smile, but it quickly froze when she caught sight of Tempy's face. She kept silent only long enough for Tempy to lower herself into the chair opposite her.

"My dear, what's wrong? You don't look yourself," Millicent said, keeping her voice low as she glanced around for possible eavesdroppers.

Tempy pressed her lips together, unable to bring herself to speak. What if that wretched reporter saw how upset she'd become and decided to write about it? Even now, she could feel the pressure of fresh tears threatening to spill out, so she mutely handed over the letter.

Millicent peered at Tempy thoughtfully and then rummaged around in her reticule, extracting a small pair of reading glasses. She dropped her head a bit as she slid them on and turned away from the room so that the wide brim of her hat concealed her face from most of the other patrons. She'd only recently started using eyeglasses to read, and she seemed self-conscious about them.

Millicent quickly scanned the letter, letting out a "humph" and frowning. Upon finishing it, she removed the glasses and peered at Tempy. "So, he's gone and found someone else, has he? And he can't be bothered to tell you in person?"

"He *is* in France. Telling me in person would be quite a challenge." She pressed her lips firmly shut. Why was she defending him?

Millicent didn't even pretend to look forgiving and instead uttered another "humph."

"He's bringing her back to London with him tomorrow, along with her parents." Tempy envisioned arriving at the dock without the foreknowledge that this letter provided. What if she'd greeted him there only to have him rebuff her and thrust the French woman between them? How appalling. "At least his letter spared me the humiliation of meeting her as they disembarked the steamship."

"You'll forgive me for being blunt, but the least he could have done was not ask someone to marry him while still being promised to you."

Tempy felt the blood rush to her face. "It's not...I mean, we weren't officially engaged."

"Don't be foolish. Everyone assumed the two of you would marry, including him. And he couldn't be ignorant of the effect this news would have upon you. And yet, he has the gall to ask you to...Now let me get this straight." She slipped her glasses back on and glanced at the letter. "'...treat Clarisse like a sister and welcome her into your heart'?" Her voice ended with a squeak of outrage.

Upon hearing those words, Tempy's chest began to tighten again and she glanced around to see if anyone had overheard.

Thankfully, they hadn't. A white aproned waiter approached, but Millicent caught his eye and waved him away.

Perhaps Tempy would wake up and realize she'd accidentally stumbled into one of those opium dens she'd read about. An opium-induced hallucination would be vastly preferable to this.

But no. This was reality.

Tempy slumped back in her chair. Or at least, she slumped as much as her tight corset and the tiny chair would allow, which was very little. After a brief moment, she sat upright again to relieve the uncomfortable pressure on her ribcage. Then, she forced out the question she'd been agonizing over all morning. "Am I so unlovable? After all, Father never really cared about me and I have no friends other than you and Ernest. And now I don't even have him. Is there something wrong with me?"

"Unlovable? You? That simply isn't possible," Millicent said, shaking her head vigorously. Her hat looked as though it were readying itself for flight with the way she sent its ostrich feather fluttering from side to side. "Please don't measure your worth based on your father's values. He was only interested in things, not people. His view of life was an extremely limited one."

Tempy wanted to believe her. Really she did. But the evidence proved otherwise. Father had lavished his attention on Bliss Railways, on his employees, and even on other railroad men, but he'd been indifferent toward Tempy. He'd displayed the odd flash of interest in her at times, but it was always fleeting. She'd never fit in at home, and eventually she'd come to realize that she didn't fit anywhere in London society either.

She shook her head. "I need to face the reality of my situation. The upper class might turn a blind eye to one or two eccentricities, but I have entirely too many of them to be found acceptable. Between my father's involvement in business affairs, my unwanted notoriety, and my unfeminine interest in journalism, I'm a pariah."

"You're wealthy. That will make up for any so-called eccentricities you have."

Again, Tempy shook her head. "It's not as though I've suddenly been found acceptable since Father's death. He might have left me with a large inheritance, but he made no friends when he was still alive. He was brash and untitled and he thumbed his nose at the peerage. Even worse, he didn't even have the decency to inherit his wealth. He *earned* his money."

Logically, therefore, Tempy should have been able to fit comfortably into the middle class, but her wealth and notoriety made her an outcast there as well. Who would risk associating with a woman whose name frequently could be found in the newspapers? They might find themselves mentioned there as well.

"Then they are all idiots."

Tempy's eyes widened for a moment at Millicent's choice of words, and then she smiled crookedly. She took a fortifying sip of Darjeeling oolong tea, breathing in its subtle floral and citrus notes. A proper cup of English tea served as an excellent tonic for low spirits, but even better was Millicent's staunch defense of her. The anger and hurt roiling within Tempy began to subside.

Millicent, still watching her carefully, gave a satisfied nod. "I'm glad to see you're recovering some of your aplomb. But I feel I must remind you that we arranged to meet today for an entirely different reason. We're supposed to be celebrating your triumph."

A waiter serving a nearby table set down his tray with a clatter, startling Tempy and giving her a moment to recall why a celebration might be in order.

"Triumph?" Tempy sipped her tea. "I haven't even written the article yet." She cleared her throat. "I'm hardly triumphant."

"Of course you are, my dear. How many other women did Charles Dickens ask to write an article for his newspaper? Hmm? My guess is none, so by rights, simply being offered the project is cause for celebration."

A bubble of pride rose within her. "You're not far off the mark, but I'm sorry to disillusion you. He's also having Eliza Lynn Linton write an article. Hers will be on pauper girls and work-houses." Tempy set her teacup back on the saucer with a slight clatter of china.

"That's why I've always liked Mr. Dickens. He's such a forward-thinking man who isn't at all afraid to give talented women an opportunity to write. I'm quite proud of you, dear. We *should* celebrate."

"Celebrate?" Tempy tried to force a cheerful smile, but failed miserably. She let out a sigh. "I'll try. Of course I'm thrilled about this opportunity. It's what I've dreamt of for so long. I can hardly believe it's happening. It's just...well...," she swallowed, "I can't stop thinking about Ernest."

Millicent covered Tempy's hand with her own and gave it a comforting squeeze. "Of course I sympathize with you, darling. And I don't mean to push you. But you must remember, you're hardly the first woman to have her heart broken by a man. In

London alone, there must be thousands of hearts breaking even as we speak."

Imagining all that pain welling up throughout the city did nothing to ease her heartbreak. Instead, it caused the band around her heart to tighten, so she tried to focus instead on Millicent's words.

"The offer to write this article has placed you at an important crossroads in your career," Millicent continued. "You need to seize the rare opportunity Mr. Dickens is offering. You can't let your emotions prevent you from completing this assignment. That would only serve to support all of those naysayers who believe that women aren't constitutionally suited to the workplace. Remember, there are other women who will follow in your footsteps, and you owe them your best work."

"I wouldn't dream of abandoning the article." Did Millicent think she'd quit on writing the same way Ernest had quit on her? *Never.*

But she wouldn't quit on Ernest either.

"I *will* complete it. I promise." She shot her friend a look of grim determination. "But there *is* something you can do for me." And Millicent wouldn't like it.

"Anything. Tell me what I can do."

"Help me win back Ernest."

Millicent's jaw dropped and then she quickly clamped her mouth shut with a clack of her teeth. "Win him back? But why?"

"I can't bear to lose him." There it was. As simple as that. Even considering living without him made her chest tighten. The thought of being alone...

"But my dear, after what he's done to you, he's hardly worth keeping. You deserve a man who values you for who you are. And Ernest Lipscomb is certainly not that man if he's willing to treat you so shabbily."

Tempy twisted her dainty handkerchief into a ball. "It's not just Ernest," she said in a soft voice. "If I lose him, I'll be losing his entire family too."

"Surely that's not so. The Lipscombs have been like a second family to you for years. They'd never cast you off."

"But they'd *have* to if he marries her, don't you see? Imagine how awkward it would be to have me hanging about on the fringes of their family events: at Ernest's wedding, or as they announce that they are expecting their first...," her voice broke, "their first child. It would be terrible both for them and for me."

"Then move on. You have other people in your life. Your happiness doesn't depend upon Ernest."

"I do? Who? Of course, there's you, but you're gone most of the time, so who else?"

"Surely your life isn't so restricted."

"You aren't here often enough to know what my life has become, and I must admit, I haven't wanted to talk with you about it on those rare occasions that we've met. But think about it. What other decent woman is willing to befriend me? I'm beyond the pale with most of polite society. On those rare occasions when I'm invited to some ball or other event, it's painfully obvious that I'm welcome solely because of my money. The only women who dare speak to me are the mothers of desperate young men who absolutely *must* find a wealthy bride in order to save the family estate, or some such rubbish. Each of those mothers makes it painfully clear that I must stop writing as soon as I marry her darling son."

"I hadn't realized," Millicent murmured, looking stricken.

Tempy rolled the balled-up handkerchief between her palms so that it began to resemble a pale cigar. "I receive fewer and fewer invitations over time. At this point, only the most desperate mothers even consider me as marriage material. Don't you see?" she asked, looking directly into Millicent's eyes. "If I lose Ernest and his family, I won't have anyone left who cares for *me* rather than my money. I absolutely must win him back. He's the only one who accepts me for me. Writing and all."

Millicent's brows dove into a deep V. "But Ernest says they're engaged. He's bringing back this Clarisse person along with her parents to meet his family."

"I'm certain that once he sees me, he'll come to his senses. What Ernest and I share goes deep. This woman must have bewitched him somehow, and I refuse to simply whimper and let him go. I plan to fight for him. If that French woman knows what's good for her, she'll stay on her side of the English Channel."

The corner of Millicent's mouth twitched. "Well, at least you're beginning to sound more like the Temperance Bliss I've always known. You're forever fighting lost causes and convincing the world to conform to your wishes. Your father called it stubbornness, but I call it passion. I don't want to give you false hope, but I must admit, if anyone could win a man back by sheer force of will, it would be you."

Those words teased a smile from Tempy's lips. "You make me sound like Don Quixote. I don't know if I should be flattered or offended."

Millicent's smile looked rueful. "I didn't mean any offense, so please, be flattered. If only for the sake of an old woman."

"Stop that," Tempy said. "You're barely fifty. That's hardly 'old'. You're quite lovely."

Millicent gave the smallest of shrugs. "Have it your way. But these reading glasses make me feel ancient," she said, nudging the offending bits of glass and wire with her index finger so that they slid under her saucer. She poured more tea into her cup. "Enough about me. In your note you mentioned wanting to interview people at a casino, but I'm still unclear as to why."

"Yes. The article." She needed to learn more about how casinos operated. She'd had the seed of an idea when she'd first mentioned wanting to visit a casino to Millicent, but at the moment she couldn't seem to wrap her head around it.

A flash of sunlight glinted off a raised teacup at a nearby table, and Tempy became aware again of her surroundings. The soft, gentle murmur of voices would normally feel soothing, but not today. Instead she felt exposed. Shattered.

"Oh, Millicent, I feel much too scattered right now to be able to focus on my article. Ernest's letter has pushed every other thought from my mind. Couldn't we meet again tomorrow for tea?"

"I'm sorry, Tempy, I wish I could indulge your sensibilities, but today is my only opportunity to meet you. I need to leave town again on business. Why don't you start by telling me why you need access to a gambling hall?"

Tempy suppressed a sigh of disappointment and soldiered on. She lifted her teacup from the saucer as she gathered her thoughts and once again ignored her surroundings. "Let me explain the context of my assignment first. You see, Wilkie Collins wrote a story that Mr. Dickens is publishing in his newspaper." She took a small sip. It was rather tepid, so she set it back down. "Mr. Dickens plans to include news articles and editorials in his paper that focus on issues raised in the story."

Tempy picked up the white teapot with a steady hand and added more tea to her cup to warm it. "In an upcoming installment, Mr. Collins reveals the heroine's father led a dissolute life, gambling and marrying an—," she cleared her throat, "inappropriate woman."

She took a tentative sip as she paused. Ah, that was much better. Much hotter.

"I'm to write an accompanying editorial piece that looks into gambling and casinos from a woman's point of view and examines the effects that gambling has on families. I'll need to do research." She paused, looking at the letter lying on the table.

"Stay focused on the topic at hand," Millicent said in a tone as tart as unripe berries. "I invited a dear friend to meet us here. He happens to own a gambling hall, and he'll be the perfect resource for your article. With his help, you'll be able to learn everything you need to know about gambling in London."

"He's coming *here? Now?*" Tempy's eyes widened. Immediately, she smoothed her hands over her damp hair and then tucked a loose strand into place. She must look terrible, with puffy eyes and a red nose.

"You look fine. Stop fussing."

At least she'd remembered to wear a hat today. That was yet another reason she didn't quite fit in with society— she frequently forgot to follow its rules. It was too bad her hat was so small that it couldn't conceal her face. Perhaps she should bring veils back into fashion.

Ha! As if anyone would follow her fashion lead.

Millicent's gaze flickered toward the entrance behind Tempy. "I see him arriving. I'm sorry, Tempy. I meant for it to be a pleasant surprise."

Tempy let out a groan. Knowing Millicent, she should have expected something like this. But to be completely honest with herself, if Ernest's letter hadn't just arrived, she'd have been thrilled to meet the owner of a gambling hall.

Come to think of it, even though Millicent had connections all over town, she'd never mentioned knowing the owner of a gambling hall. Tempy opened her mouth to ask why, but stopped when she noticed the way Millicent's face seemed to glow as she watched the man approach. Was that a look of pride on her face? Why should this "dear friend" elicit that kind of a response? Tempy's inner journalist sat up a bit straighter.

She resisted the urge to look over her shoulder and observe the man. That would be quite rude, and her former governess would have been horrified if she'd seen her behave so improperly. Imagining that old harridan's critical gaze upon her, Tempy schooled her features.

Since she couldn't observe him as he approached, Tempy bided her time by imagining how the man would look. He'd probably be a bit older than Millicent, perhaps in his late fifties or early sixties. As the owner of a gambling establishment, he probably looked rather elegant, with a bit of steel in his spine. Yes. And since he'd be used to running things and giving orders, he'd have that commanding, privileged air about him. Perhaps with a bit of oily charm, like a salesman or confidence man.

"Lucien. Thank you so much for joining us," Millicent said as the man's shadow fell across their table.

Tempy raised her head to look up at him and found her neck craning. Her eyes widened in surprise. My, but he was tall, wasn't he? And not old at all. She judged the broad-shouldered man to be around thirty, with thick, dark hair and a rather attractive smile.

She glanced at Millicent, noting the glint of pride that continued to shine in her eyes. And the gambling hall owner's expression reminded her of a child hoping to please a favored adult.

Why would this man, whom she'd never met in all the time she'd known her friend, care so much about pleasing Millicent? Of course, her friend often had that effect on people. Even Tempy frequently found herself trying to win her approval.

Seeing this endeared him to her.

But when those pale blue eyes turned to focus on her, his doting attitude disappeared. It was replaced by one of calculation that caused the hairs on the back of Tempy's neck to stand on end. He was taking her measure, and he seemed to see much more than she wanted to reveal.

Feeling exposed, Tempy became aware of Ernest's letter still resting on the table. She darted a hand out to sweep it up and then tucked it into one of the large pockets in her dress, hoping the movement looked casual, as though she were simply clearing off the table.

Millicent seemed unaware of the change that had come over

the man. Smiling with delight, she said, "Tempy, this is Lucien Hamlin, the proprietor of Hamlin House. Lucien, may I introduce my dear friend, Miss Temperance Bliss. She's the writer I've been telling you about. Please join us."

"It's a pleasure to meet you," Mr. Hamlin said formally. He pulled out the chair to Tempy's left. His long, slim fingers smoothly unbuttoned his black frock coat as he sat, allowing the bright scarlet fabric of his waistcoat to peek out. Satin, she would wager— and a wager would be appropriate given the man's occupation.

She'd heard of Hamlin House. It was a grand Mayfair gambling hall that catered to the wealthy sons of the peerage. Their motto was 'the best of the best,' or some such trite rubbish.

Tempy's lips felt tight as she forced a smile. "I'd like to offer my thanks as well, Mr. Hamlin. It's very kind of you to take the time to meet with us. I must admit, Millicent has taken me quite by surprise by inviting you to join us."

Tempy's late governess would have approved of Mr. Hamlin's erect posture. Tempy might have been wrong about most of her other guesses, but she'd been right about the steel in his spine. What was the name of that famous Spanish steel, finer than any other? Toledo? Yes, that was it. A spine of Toledo steel. Strong and hard, with just the right amount of flexibility to keep it from breaking.

Everything about the man seemed elegant and commanding. But there was also a faint weariness in his eyes, as though they'd seen too much in this world, and not enough of it had been good.

Despite his veneer of sophistication, Tempy sensed a deep power and menace in the man, and it made her mouth go dry. The meek and cautious part of her wanted to flee from him, but the inquisitive part of her was intrigued and wanted to learn more. This man was nothing like her sweet and unassuming Ernest. Of that she was thankful.

But wait. He wasn't *her Ernest* anymore. He was someone else's

Ernest. Some evil French woman who'd stolen what was rightfully hers.

Tempy felt her lower lip quiver, so she pushed Ernest from her mind. She couldn't think about him right now if she wanted to maintain this facade of normalcy.

Millicent glanced at Tempy and her eyes widened. She must have detected Tempy's momentary lapse of composure, because she immediately jumped into the conversation with a great deal of animation.

"Ah, yes. I must admit, I didn't tell Tempy I'd invited you here today," Millicent said, as she touched Mr. Hamlin on the shoulder in an apparent attempt to keep his gaze focused on herself rather than on Tempy. Then she made a great show of calling their waiter to the table so that Mr. Hamlin could order tea.

It didn't take long for Tempy to compose herself. Even so, there was something disconcerting about this man. Was it because he was a gambler?

"I understand that you're the founder of Hamlin House," Tempy said.

"Yes. I opened it about ten years ago."

"I've heard it's a beautiful establishment." Her fingers itched to hold her pen and pad. This would be a perfect opportunity to take some notes.

"You've never been there?" Millicent asked. "You really must visit. It's quite lovely."

Oddly, Mr. Hamlin said, "Yes, you must," while at the same time shaking his head "no." She suspected that his body was showing her his true opinion on the subject. He wore a slightly pained expression. Apparently, he really didn't want her to visit Hamlin House, but he was too polite to contradict Millicent's suggestion.

Well, that was too bad. For him.

"Thank you, Mr. Hamlin. I believe I'll take you up on that

generous offer." She continued to watch him as he frowned, but he said nothing.

An awkward silence fell over the table. Perhaps it would be best not to push Mr. Hamlin further on the subject of visiting his gambling hall. It was apparent that he'd already regretted his polite agreement now that she'd used it as an invitation.

Tempy chose to make a tactical retreat from the topic and glanced at Millicent. "You mentioned you're leaving London...," she prompted.

Millicent nodded. "There's an issue at one of the steel mills, and I need to meet with my manager there. Apparently, there's some trouble with their coal supplier, and I need to intervene."

"What type of problem?" Tempy asked. "Is it with transporting the coal? If so, perhaps I can speak to someone at Bliss Railways."

"No. It has to do with the quality of the coal. They aren't sending us what we need in order to heat the furnaces to the correct temperature. But thank you, though. You've been quite generous in helping me smooth over problems in the past."

Tempy glanced at Mr. Hamlin and then back to Millicent. "Forgive me for asking, but it appears that you've known one another for a number of years. How is it that we haven't met before this?" Tempy knew she was being forward, but really, Mr. Hamlin's seemingly close bond with Millicent left her confused, to say the least.

"Oh," Millicent said, looking slightly chagrined. "I must admit, I've broken a promise to your father by introducing the two of you. He didn't approve of having his young daughter exposed to..., now how did he put it..., 'the more scandalous aspects of society.'"

Mr. Hamlin arched his eyebrows. "I'm scandalous, am I?"

"You're quite the scoundrel," Millicent teased. "Don't you read the newspapers?"

"Lies. All lies." He glanced at Tempy as he said this, giving her a pointed look.

His expression confused her for a moment, but then, with a flash of comprehension, she suddenly grasped the source of his antagonism. The man must be worried about what a journalist might write about his establishment. "I assure you, Mr. Hamlin, that not all newspapers are the same," Tempy said.

"That's the only reason I'm sitting here, Miss Bliss. Well, that and my respect for Mrs. Kidman. I've never found myself lambasted in *All the Year Round* for owning a gambling hall. I hope that continues to be the case."

Tempy felt a fiery blush rush to her cheeks and raised her chin. "Mr. Dickens doesn't print a scandal sheet. You have no cause for concern on that account."

Mr. Hamlin frowned at her response. "But you understand why I might worry, don't you?"

"Of course. But I can assure you that you and your establishment will not be the focus of my article. I'm interested in the ways that gambling affects women and families in general. Not in you or your gambling hall in particular."

He still didn't look convinced. The chill emanating from him was almost palpable. He must have been the victim of a great deal of bad press over the years.

Millicent cleared her throat. "Speaking of the news, have either of you ridden on the new horse tram on Victoria Street?" Trust her to try to soothe the growing awkwardness.

"As a matter of fact, yes," Tempy said, switching to the new topic with relief. "I tried it only a few days ago and found it most convenient. Why are so many people against it?"

"It's mostly due to the fact that the rails they laid on the street stick up above the road surface and cause problems for every other vehicle," Mr. Hamlin said.

Millicent frowned. "They should use one of the newer tramway track designs that cuts grooves in the street and then places the rails inside the grooves. Then everyone else who uses the road wouldn't be so terribly inconvenienced. One of my steel mills produces them, and they've been quite successful."

"Oh, no," Tempy interrupted. "All of this talk about 'track' just reminded me." She pulled a small watch from the pocket of her dress. "I have a last-minute appointment to meet with Mr. Dickens, and then I need to hurry off to another one to speak with Father's lawyers. They want me to sign some business papers concerning the railway." She pushed the button on the edge of her watch and the cover popped open. "I'm late," she said, and rose to her feet. "I do hope you'll excuse me. I look forward to visiting your casino."

Mr. Hamlin quickly stood up as well, and Tempy had the distinct impression that he wanted to say something more, but then he pressed his lips together and nodded.

"It was a pleasure to meet you," Hamlin said, and for a moment she wondered if he might actually mean it. There was something in his expression that hadn't been there before.

Tempy blushed slightly as she made her good-byes, keenly aware that his gaze still lingered upon her.

❧ 2 ❧

POOR LITTLE RICH GIRL

Lucien watched Miss Bliss as she hurried toward the door of Pink's Tea Room. A strand of her chestnut brown hair had fallen from its tight bun, and her hat was a little lopsided. She'd probably lose the thing in a stiff wind.

Even so, she was a pretty little thing, although not the type he normally would have noticed. She was intelligent too. But compared to the glittering women who walked into his gambling hall each evening, she was a mousy little ingénue. So why did he find her so intriguing?

Miss Bliss posed an interesting conundrum. She'd seemed upset about something when he'd first arrived, but whatever it had been, she'd recovered. Even so, there was something about her that seemed fragile. It made him want to protect her.

He didn't like that. Stray feelings such as these were bound to land him in trouble.

It wasn't until he felt the touch of a hand on his forearm that he realized he was still standing and staring after Miss Bliss.

He slowly sat back down. "Tell me. Who, exactly, is that young woman?"

Millicent's face froze, and then became expressionless. "Whatever do you mean?"

"Don't pretend you don't know what I'm asking you."

She arched her eyebrows in a quizzical look that oozed innocence.

"She's the daughter of that railroad man who died last year, isn't she?"

"What does that have to do with anything?"

Lucien sighed with exasperation. "Isn't she the 'poor little rich girl' from the newspapers?"

Millicent scowled at him. "I'm surprised at you, repeating such a hurtful epithet. And after you've been shredded by the newspapers so mercilessly in the past. It's not her fault that idiot, Earl E. Byrd, has decided to harass her through some scandal sheet. I shouldn't have to tell *you* not to believe everything you read." She picked up her teacup and took a sip, but her hand trembled slightly.

"Are you saying that the stories he prints about her are false?"

"They all have a grain of truth about them, but he paints her in a most unfavorable light. You'd never recognize his version of events if you'd been there in person."

Lucien frowned. "I suppose she and I have something in common in that respect." He continued to stare at Millicent, trying to detect any deceit. Was she trying to play on his sympathies? "Are you saying you have no other motive in introducing us?"

She lifted her chin. "I've been entirely aboveboard with you. I'm not sure I know what you're driving at with these questions. I wanted her to meet you because she needs access to your establishment to write that article."

Lucien leaned against the back of his small chair. It was a fussy piece of furniture with a tiny, round seat. It might not be well suited to a large man, but at least it didn't feel as though it might break. "I've already agreed to allow her to visit Hamlin House, despite my reservations. She can come by early one day before we open and I'll explain how the gambling hall operates. I'm certain she'll gather enough information for her purposes."

Millicent frowned at him, and a little divot appeared between her eyebrows that only came out when she was especially annoyed. "You know as well as I do that she needs more than that," she said, setting down her teacup without making the slightest clatter. "She has to be able to speak with your patrons, or at the very least, to observe them."

"Absolutely not," Lucien said, surprised that she'd press him on this point. "I can't have reporters coming in and interrogating my guests."

Millicent held up her hand to halt his flow of words. "That's not what I'm proposing. She doesn't want to divulge information regarding your patrons, but simply to observe their behavior."

"I can't risk it," he said, regretting that he had to refuse her. But he knew he was making the right decision. "I'm sorry, but this isn't what I agreed to do."

"But Lucien, this is too important," she said, her voice pleading as she placed her hand back on his forearm. "You simply *must* help Tempy. Writing for Mr. Dickens's newspaper is an enormous opportunity. One that she desperately needs. Especially now that her idiot of a fiancé has abandoned her." Millicent's eyes widened and her hand flew to her mouth. "Oh, no. I didn't mean to say that."

"Is that why she was so upset?" he asked, leaning forward. That would be quite a blow. No wonder Miss Bliss had seemed upset when he'd first arrived.

Poor little rich girl indeed.

Millicent looked pained, obviously torn between her reticence to gossip about Tempy's private life and her need to convince him to help. Finally, she leaned closer to him and spoke in a low voice.

"I'm not sure how much you've already read in the newspapers, but her father died last year and she has no remaining kin. Even when he was alive, that father of hers rarely paid her any notice."

Lucien nodded. He'd heard about the man's death, and the rest didn't surprise him. The late owner of Bliss Railways had been renowned for his obsession with trains and the railroad industry. According to the news stories he'd read, the man often forgot he even had a child.

"Tempy's governesses and tutors always kept her busy, but when she was able, she'd slip away to visit some neighbors, the Lipscombs. They were the closest thing she had to a normal family. She and their son, Ernest, became friends, and over time everyone assumed they'd marry. It would have been a convenient match for both of them. They frequently discussed their future together."

"And now he's broken it off?"

"She received the letter from him only this morning. It was very dismissive."

"A letter?" Lucien snorted. "Then she's well rid of him."

Millicent frowned. "Normally, I'd agree. But Tempy is different. Because of her father, she's had few close relationships in her life. And the few she had ended tragically. Her mother died when she was just a child, and then there was a string of nurses and governesses that always failed to please Mr. Bliss. Her last governess stayed with Tempy for a couple of years, and Tempy grew attached to her, but when she died, she left a hole in Tempy's life. After her father's death, she clung to the Lipscomb family as though they were a lifeline."

"She has no other friends?"

"No. Her interest in journalism has caused many women in society to avoid her, but she isn't willing to give it up, and I respect her for that." Millicent took a deep breath and held it for a moment before exhaling it as a soft sigh. "She's usually completely composed and focused, but Ernest's betrayal has been a terrible blow. I wish she could understand that she's better off without him. I never thought he was the right man for her."

"I sympathize with her. Really I do. I know how hard it is to have no family and to be completely on your own." Hadn't he been in a similar situation when his own father had died? "But she has you."

Millicent glanced away. "I wish that were true, but with all of the demands of my steel mills, I'm not in London very often. We correspond through the mail, but that isn't enough. I want to do more for her. That's why I need your help. Her work means everything to her. She's already sacrificed so much for it, and it's important to me to help her with this article. Mr. Dickens has offered her an amazing opportunity, and she can't let it slip through her fingers. I need you to let her visit your gambling hall and talk to your patrons."

Lucien shook his head in frustration at not being able to grant Millicent this one request. "Everything you just told me makes me even more reluctant to put my place of business at risk. What if someone learns of what she's doing and decides to write another article about her, vilifying Hamlin House as well? I've already had enough half-truths turned against me. What if I'm accused of fleecing the 'poor little rich girl'?" He shook his head. "No. I can't risk it. I simply can't afford any bad press about my casino right now."

Millicent narrowed her eyes. "Right now?"

Lucien mentally kicked himself. Millicent was far too clever. When she'd inherited her late husband's steel mills, everyone had assumed she'd sell them. Instead, she ran them at an even greater profit because of the improvements she'd made to the manufacturing process. She produced a higher-quality product than any of her competitors. Millicent said she did it by hiring the right people for the right positions. That was something Lucien had in common with her. They both understood that a person's worth didn't come from their birthright. It came from hard work and ingenuity.

She grinned at him, obviously pleased that she'd caught him out.

Lucien didn't respond, but waited to see what card she'd lay down next. She'd already tried playing on his sympathies, but he knew she'd have another trick up her sleeve.

Millicent played the waiting game and sat back in her chair to observe him. Finally, she said, "You seem unusually worried about public opinion, which is unlike you. I think you've decided it's time to set aside your checkered past and move on to something a bit more respectable. You've decided to accept the responsibilities of that title, haven't you?"

He sighed. "Stop trying to read my mind. It's annoying. And just for the record, I haven't reached a decision yet." He pushed his hair back from his forehead. "You're wrong about my motives. This is *not* about respectability. It's about necessity. Having an earldom doesn't interest me in the least. Nor do I care what those titled profligates think of me. But I *do* care about the property I stand to inherit. They can keep the title."

"But the title and the lands are intertwined. You can't have one without the other. I know how much you resent your grandfather, but he's dead, and the title of Earl of Cavendish is yours no matter what. You can choose not to use it, but you're still the earl."

"I hate giving him the satisfaction of having that title continue. Blood meant everything to him. Except for my father's, that is. Grandfather was convinced he'd sullied the line by marrying my mother."

"Don't be foolish. Your grandfather is dead. He'll never be satisfied about anything ever again. This is simply about your pride, and before now, I've never seen you so easily swayed by something so illogical."

Lucien paused to think as he poured tea into his cup. "I have good reason to resent the man. He detested my mother for being French, and he never had any use for my father. He said Father was 'boring as a stick' when he wouldn't become yet another dissolute Hamlin."

Millicent patted his arm, probably in an attempt to calm his rising ire, but he sipped his tea, thereby shrugging off her touch.

"Who nicknames his son 'Stick'?" Lucien asked, his voice rising in indignation. Some people at a nearby table glanced at him in alarm, so he lowered his voice as he continued, "The only reason I'm inheriting is because there's no one left alive with a better claim. My father's two older brothers both drank and whored themselves to death without ever bothering to worry about an heir."

Millicent looked at the other table. Apparently satisfied that the people there were no longer listening, she glanced back at Lucien and said, "At least you're fortunate in that neither of them bore the same low opinion of your father that your grandfather did."

Silence stretched between them. His uncles may not have hated his father, but neither had they helped him. They'd been much too interested in gambling and horse racing to be bothered with their boring brother, Stick. Or with Lucien. "They never acknowledged me," he muttered, scraping his thumbnail at a loose thread in the weave of the starched, white tablecloth.

"But they never denied you either. As demonstrated by the fact that you will now inherit the title of Earl of Cavendish."

"An entailed title that can't go to anyone else," he muttered.

"With estates and untended lands all over England." She furrowed her brow. "I'm not an expert in these matters, but I believe only an act of Parliament could relieve you of your title. Why would you even want to go to such lengths? Perhaps your best revenge will be to enjoy your inheritance. Was it four houses you'll inherit?"

"Five estates. And that hunting lodge. Oh, and the dowager house. Plus the houses in London and Bath."

"And the mines. Don't forget the mines. It all makes for an impressive income. Why not accept it?"

"Because taking it turns me into a hypocrite. I've made my money off of wastrels like my uncles for years. How can I use this title and join their ranks?"

"Lucien. I'm surprised at you," she said with mock severity. "Why on earth would you want to become a wastrel? After all, you've already perfected the role of the scoundrel." She took a sip of what, by now, must be cold tea. Lucien knew she did it to try to hide the grin on her face. It didn't work because he could still see the curve of her lips from behind the teacup.

He smiled at her teasing tone. He knew that Millicent loved it when she landed a good jab in a verbal sparring match, and that had been a solid hit.

"It would be a shame to throw all of that aside," she continued in a gentler tone. "I quite look forward to seeing you revitalize all of those estates."

He frowned. "I just returned from Shropshire. It's criminal, the way my grandfather let things fall into disrepair. Neither he nor my uncles have done anything to manage that property in years. They owned so much that it still provided them with a good income, despite their neglect. But most of the people whose livelihoods depend upon maintaining those estates are suffering. Many have already left to take manufacturing jobs. The towns are suffering."

"It won't be your problem if you were to turn the lands over to the crown," she said, in a nonchalant tone. "I'm not certain it's even possible, mind you, but if you could, you'd be able keep your gambling hall and maintain your current lifestyle. Hamlin House is so popular that you could continue to take your profits and live extremely well. You could stay here in London and do as you please."

He frowned. "When you put it that way, you make it sound as though I'm doing the same thing my grandfather and uncles did. That I'm turning my back on my responsibilities." His expression turned sour. "You like playing devil's advocate, don't you?"

"Perhaps," she said tartly. "But that is hardly relevant. What would your father have done?"

He didn't have to think about his answer. He already knew it. "He would have wielded the power that came with his new title and instituted the changes he'd envisioned for so many years. He loved everything about those estates. That's why grandfather thought my father was a stick-in-the-mud; he preferred caring for the land and the people to gambling and drinking in London."

"There's a little bit of both of those men in you. The hard-working man and the gambler who loves to play the odds."

Lucien shook his head. "You're wrong there. It was never that I loved to play the odds, it was only that it was so easy for me to win at it. My mind simply works that way." Lucien never took credit for his skill at making quick calculations. He'd been born with an amazing facility with numbers, and early in life he'd understood that when it came to gambling, the house would always win. The odds were stacked in its favor. That's why he'd opened the lavish Hamlin House.

"And does that other life appeal to you? The one your father wanted?"

Lucien looked away from Millicent and gazed out the red-mullioned window at the front of the tea room. It was raining again. "Father took me to visit each of the estates when I was a boy. He said I needed to understand our family's history. During our trips we'd do various tasks that would help the community."

"Such as?"

He shrugged. "We'd do different things in different regions. Sometimes we'd shore up dams or thatch roofs. Other times we'd help with controlled burn-offs up in the moors...whatever was needed." He glanced back at Millicent. "I feel a connection to the people in those communities. A responsibility."

Millicent gave him a level gaze. "These are the words of a man who has already made his decision. You're planning to sell Hamlin House, aren't you?"

Lucien released a mock-sigh of defeat. "Yes," he said, and shot her a wry smile. "And that's why I can't risk having a reporter stirring things up. She could scare away my patrons, or worse, my buyer."

Millicent leaned forward. "But you *must* help Tempy. She can't wait. She has a deadline to meet, and she needs access to Hamlin House."

"I'm sorry, Millicent, but the answer is still no. It isn't just about me. I have to look out for my patrons— my employees too, and having a reporter come in now is too risky. What about my staff? What about my buyer? It would be reckless of me to risk sabotaging my own business while trying to sell it to him. I won't risk it."

Millicent sighed and leaned back in her chair. "I can't say I'm surprised, but I *am* disappointed. I have to leave town for a short time, but if you change your mind, please send word to me. Tempy isn't reckless. She'd never do anything to harm your establishment."

"And neither would I."

3

MISS LIPSCOMB BEGS
THAT YOU RECEIVE HER

BLISS BOMBS

She'd lost everything.

Well, perhaps not everything. At least, not yet. But it could happen.

It was hard to find anything positive about this day. Most of it had been a disaster. First, Ernest sent that horrible letter. That was enough on its own, but then she'd met the irritatingly smug Mr. Hamlin who distrusted all journalists. His dislike had been palpable.

The one good thing to come of the day was that he'd agreed to allow her to visit his gambling hall.

But then, when she'd arrived for her meeting with Mr. Dickens, it was to discover that he'd rescheduled it for the day after tomorrow. Apparently he'd sent a note to her house, but since she was out, she hadn't received it.

Tempy had also stopped by to speak with her father's lawyers and sign some papers. What was supposed to have been a minor matter turned into an ugly fight when they condescended to her and tried to browbeat her into signing something she didn't understand. Instead, she'd taken the papers with her to read rather than signing anything.

She'd never been very tractable when someone tried to bully her.

Even so, today was one of those days when, over and over, she'd been given the message that she wasn't good enough.

Wasn't clever enough.

Wasn't loved enough.

She tried to look on the bright side. There must be a bright side, right? At least she had slid all the way to the bottom. Things couldn't get much worse, could they?

Yes, said a tiny voice at the back of her head.

She ignored it.

It was time to start climbing back up. She could do this. She had to. Nobody else would come save her from the disaster her life had become, so she needed to save herself.

On the positive side, she'd been able to obtain Mr. Hamlin's consent to visit his casino, so that, at least, was under control.

And Millicent would be able to advise her regarding those lawyers. Tempy would need to meet with her once she'd returned to London again.

So Tempy's first order of business was to deal with Ernest.

She peered at the letter in her hand as she resumed pacing through the large sitting room again.

"*My dearest Tempy*," it began. Didn't that suggest that he still cared for her?

"*I hate to surprise you this way*." When she'd read it earlier, she'd thought she'd detected a slight nuance that suggested that Ernest had been coerced into writing the letter, but now she couldn't be certain.

She'd read it so many times that the words didn't even make sense to her any longer. They all ran together on the page like little crooked-legged spiders.

Tempy plopped onto the uncomfortable custom-made blue silk sofa that Father's decorator had chosen for the room. She particularly disliked its carved, dark mahogany arms. She'd discovered that those curlicues on the arm rests could be quite painful when one bumped one's elbow against them.

She sat only for a moment, and then propelled herself back to her feet to begin another circuit of the room.

She strode toward the closed double doors, and then made a sharp left to circle around the matching pair of equally uncomfortable pale blue chairs. Next, she paced toward the side table where Father's pipe collection still remained on display, and then she continued on her path past the longcase clock with its huge pendulum swinging the beat of time.

Tempy carefully ignored the tall mirror next to the clock. It was not her friend today and kept insisting upon showing her glimpses of a slim, pale, dark-haired harridan every time she came near it. She completed her circuit by crossing in front of the sofa, but she didn't pause in her pacing.

She really ought to put Father's pipes in storage. The stale scent of tobacco lingered in that part of the room, even after a year of disuse. But the pipes carried too many memories— or perhaps it was more that they were the only truly personal items remaining of her father's life.

He'd always been obsessed with growing his railroad empire and had expended little effort in cultivating outside interests, including an interest in his only child. His one weakness had been those stinking pipes. He'd been smoking one when his heart had given out. The black stem of his favorite rosewood pipe had been clamped between his teeth when the housekeeper found him. That particular pipe was now gone. Tempy hadn't wanted it back when the mortician had offered it to her. Instead, she'd had him buried with it. It seemed fitting. So here his collection sat, in homage to his memory.

She scanned Ernest's letter, looking again for his arrival date and time. The ship would dock tomorrow at ten o'clock.

The butler opened one of the double doors and stepped inside the room. "Miss Bliss, Miss Lipscomb begs that you receive her."

Tempy gasped softly. Ernest's sister was here? Thank goodness. Perhaps Emily could shed light on this tangled mess. "Send her in."

Tempy hurried over to the dreaded mirror in the hope that she could put herself back into some semblance of order. Her eyes widened at the sight that greeted her. How had she managed to smudge ink across her cheek? She glanced down at her hands, noticing the purplish-blue stain on the knuckle of her right index finger. It exactly matched the ink on the envelope from Ernest, and when she looked back into the mirror again she realized that, oddly enough, it clashed with the green in her eyes.

With a sigh, Tempy tucked the letter into her pocket and removed her handkerchief. She rubbed away the offending ink spots, gave her face an evaluating stare, and then tried to rub just a bit of color into her pale cheeks.

It didn't help.

The door opened and Tempy turned to greet Ernest's fifteen-year-old sister.

Emily took a tentative step into the room. The petite blonde's gaze sought Tempy's like a drowning child clutching at a rope. Her eyes were red and puffy, and as she rushed toward Tempy, she pressed a handkerchief to her mouth, stifling a sob. "Oh, Tempy. How could he? He's ruined everything. I wanted *you* to become my sister, not some French girl."

Tempy stopped herself from taking a step backward in an attempt to avoid Emily's unexpected display of emotion. People simply didn't *hug* Temperance Bliss. They kept their distance.

She'd assumed that Emily had come here to comfort her, but apparently that wasn't the case. Instead, the girl wanted to be the one being comforted. But then again, Emily had always loved melodrama.

"I'm sure there must be some sort of mistake," Tempy said. Hadn't she been telling herself the very same thing ever since she'd received the letter? A mistake. It had to be a mistake. "He needs me. He needs my steadying influence."

"But he sounds so sure of himself," Emily wailed. "In his letter to Mother and Father, he says she's everything he's ever wanted in a woman. That she's his Venus, come to Earth."

A sharp pain shot through Tempy's forehead, leaving a deep ache in its path. She turned her back to Emily and groped for a seat on that blasted sofa, bumping her knuckles painfully against its carved arm.

Venus? She sat down.

In her distraction, she began to slide off the slippery, over-stuffed seat cushion, and barely managed to keep from falling to the floor.

Emily's eyes widened and she hurried to sit next to Tempy, reaching out to grab her hand. "I'm sorry. I never should have told you that. It's just that I've never heard him talk that way before..." She looked chagrined. "That sounded bad. I mean, except for when he talked about you." Her voice faltered at the obvious lie.

She'd never heard Ernest make a similar declaration about her. She pulled her hand away from Emily's grasp. "Did he really call her his V-Venus?"

"Of course not. I'm certain I was mistaken." This time, Emily's lie sounded smoother and more believable. She was improving.

Tempy waved away the words so that they wafted toward Father's smelly pipes, where they belonged. "I've been formulating a plan," she said. "I've decided to meet his ship when it docks tomorrow."

"Oh! But you *can't*," Emily said, making another grab for

Tempy's hand and missing. "*She'll* be with him. How can you speak with him while she's there?"

"That's why I plan to wait near the spot where the porters stack the luggage after it's been unloaded. Surely she won't follow him when he goes to collect it."

Emily shook her hands as though she were trying to flick away something distasteful. "Won't that make you appear desperate?"

"But I *am* desperate. I've never been more desperate in my life. She's taken *everything* from me."

"You blame *her*?" Emily asked incredulously. "But you should be blaming *him*. *He's* the one who led you on. *He's* the one who's being unfaithful."

"Stop it. You aren't helping." Tempy pressed her hands over her ears. "I won't have you speak against your brother. What would Mother say if she heard you?"

"Mother? Are you certain, under the circumstances, that you should still be calling her Mother? Perhaps you should refer to her as Mrs. Lipscomb now."

Tempy's jaw went slack as the logic of Emily's comment hit her. If things kept going this way, all she'd have left would be Father's nasty, stale pipes. This couldn't be happening. "Emily! Don't say such things."

"I'm sorry. I'm not very good at this, am I?"

At offering comfort? Tempy couldn't think of a polite response, so she said nothing.

"Oh, Tempy, what will you do now?"

Tempy shook her head. That had been the question she'd been asking herself all day. "Whatever it takes. I refuse to let that woman steal my entire future away from me. I can't allow it. You'll help me, won't you?"

"I'm so sorry, Tempy. I wish I could. But Father says it is best we make a clean break of it with you. He doesn't want to complicate things for Ernest and his bride."

A cold, tight band squeezed Tempy's chest. "So I'm to lose

your friendship too?" she managed to whisper. "The only real family I've ever known is casting me out?"

Emily didn't meet her gaze as she nodded. After a moment she looked up. "Perhaps we can meet for tea from time to time."

"Tea." Tempy was vaguely aware that the single word she uttered was devoid of emotion as what remained of her world crashed down around her. When she opened her mouth again, she tried to imbue her words with a bit more feeling. "You'd take tea with a social pariah? That might not be wise. You know it will end up in the newspaper. What would your father say to that?"

"Don't say such things. You know we've never believed all that rubbish they print about you in the papers. We know the *real* Temperance Bliss."

Did they? How could they, when even *she* didn't know the real Temperance Bliss?

4

SPINNING A WEB

❦

Lucien pushed open the ornate oak and cut-glass door of the Crown and Feather pub and entered the dark interior. Even though the sunlight streamed in through the diamond panes of the cut-glass windows, the interior remained dark, thanks to the stained oak paneling.

At lunchtime, the owners of the various nearby shipping offices would fill the room to capacity, but even at mid-morning, disembarking passengers frequently made the Crown and Feather their first stop. Lucien wasn't able to come here often, but he was familiar with their routine.

Lucien ignored the chalk board listing the day's special, having already detected the rich aroma of shepherd's pie. That, and a glass of ale, would carry him through the day.

He glanced around, looking for a shock of graying hair, but he quickly ascertained that John Snowden hadn't yet arrived. Lucien sat at one of the clean oak tables so that he faced the door, and then he settled in to wait for the man.

Lucien ordered drinks, and a waiter delivered the two glasses of ale moments before John Snowden limped into the pub. The tall, muscular man's cane thumped against the floorboards as he approached.

"Impeccable timing," Lucien said.

"A habit in which I take great pride." John's chair let out a loud creak as he carefully settled his large frame onto it. Lucien couldn't help but wonder how he would have fared sitting on one of Pink's Tea Room's chairs yesterday. It wasn't that the man was fat. Far from it. But anyone as tall and heavily muscled as John would cause a piece of furniture to creak, if only in general complaint at the unusually burdensome task expected of it. Hearing the sound, John shifted in his chair, apparently testing its sturdiness. Satisfied, he settled back and stretched his bad leg out under the table, accidentally kicking Lucien in the process. "Move your feet. You're taking up all the room under there."

Lucien shifted in his chair and moved his feet to one side. "Are those boats or are they shoes? If you weren't a giant, you wouldn't have this problem."

"I'll have none of that from you, little man. It's not my fault everyone else is so small. You've no call to be casting aspersions. Giants are evil creatures, and I'm far from evil."

Lucien chuckled. John was the only man in the world who would have called him little. "How's the knee?"

"Better some days, worse others. I'll wager there's a storm coming. I can feel it."

"I don't think I'll take that bet, but I'm impressed that your knee can predict the weather."

"Gaining the ability to forecast rain was a bad trade. But at least I still have the leg. That's more than I can say for some. Those bloody Maori are fierce fighters. New Zealand might be beautiful, but I'll die happy if I never lay eyes on it again."

"Is it true the Maori tribesmen are cannibals, or were the newspapers just trying to paint a lurid picture?"

"It's true enough. I never heard that anyone was proven to

have fallen victim of cannibalism when I was there, but rumors always flew whenever a soldier went missing."

A chill ran down Lucien's spine and he twitched his shoulders to shrug it off. "I can see why. People couldn't help being jumpy in that situation." He took a sip of his ale, and its bite helped wash away the lingering eerie sensation. "Do you miss military service?"

"No." John took a healthy swig of ale and smacked his lips, obviously savoring it. "Don't get me wrong. I loved it when I was doing it, but glad I'm done. I like having good ale, and I like my life here in England. But I'd like it even more if I owned a casino."

And there it was.

John had broached the subject of the casino without prompting, just as Lucien had hoped. "You're still interested?" Lucien asked.

"What can I say? I like being in charge, and I like the thrill I get when taking risks. Owning a casino is perfect for me. This railroad business I'm in simply doesn't suit." He studied Lucien's face. "Is that why you asked me here? Are you finally ready to sell?"

Lucien smiled at the man's forthrightness. "You're good at reading people. You probably *would* be good at running a casino. When did you suspect?"

John let out a bark of laughter. "When I received your note. Why else would you want to meet me on a Friday morning? You're never out and about this early."

"Why else, indeed. I don't want to give you the wrong impression." Actually, that was *exactly* what Lucien wanted to do. He'd learned years ago to always play his cards close to his chest. "I'm not ready to sell, but I'd like to explore the possibility. Are you certain this is what you want? I know your brother won't be pleased if he hears that you're considering this."

"Good. He's never approved of me before this. There's no reason to change that. I'd hate to disappoint him by doing something conventional. It might shock him so much that he couldn't produce an heir."

"I thought he already had a son." Lucien swallowed the rest of his ale. When the waiter offered to bring him another, he waved the man away.

"The little Viscount of Oswell? He's a sickly child, but yes, he's the heir. No one holds out much hope that he'll live to a ripe old age, so my brother wants a spare. An heir and a spare. That's the saying for a good reason."

Lucien's grandfather once had an heir and two spares. He'd been so prolific that he'd been willing to toss aside his youngest son for marrying a French girl. And now that half-French grandson had inherited the old man's title. The thought brought Lucien a grim sense of satisfaction. The entire situation had just the right amount of poetic justice. For the first time, Lucien felt himself warming to the idea of inheriting the title.

He wanted the estates. And now, he was beginning to realize, he even wanted the title. But first he'd need to sell his casino. Running it required his full attention, and he wouldn't have the time for it once he began managing all of his new estates.

He shot John a level gaze. "I'd like to make an appointment for you to come out and look over my establishment. You can examine my books, interview the staff, and observe our practices. But please, don't mention anything to my employees unless and until we've reached an agreement. I don't want to worry them needlessly."

John nodded. "That sounds perfect. How about Monday? One o'clock?"

"That works for me."

"And I might try my hand at your tables tonight for one last time before we begin this process."

Lucien grinned. "I'd be happy to take some of your money. The house always wins."

5

PILES OF LUGGAGE

೩౫౬

Tempy would have to leave without her carriage.

Again.

It served her right. All she'd needed to do was tell one of her upstairs maids to wake her by nine. But no. She'd been so certain that she wouldn't sleep all night that she hadn't thought it necessary. She'd been right, in a sense. She hadn't slept all night. But as soon as sunlight had hit her bedroom window, she'd finally given in to exhaustion.

Tempy hurriedly selected a dress and called in one of the maids to help her with her corset.

The maid began tugging at the corset strings, pulling them tighter and tighter.

"Ah, stop." Tempy tried to take a deep breath, but couldn't.

"Sorry, miss, but this dress is the one with the narrowest waist. Should I choose a different one?"

Blast. "No, I'm late as it is. This one will do."

Once Tempy was dressed, she checked herself in the mirror. She did look quite fetching from the neck down. Unfortunately, there wasn't much to be done for her pale face or the dark rings under her eyes. Only sleep would improve her pallor.

As Tempy rushed through the foyer, Harris, the butler, held out a dark reticule and a hat. "Funds to pay your driver, Miss Bliss."

"Thank you," Tempy said. "I'd nearly forgotten." She crammed the hat onto her head, barely paying any attention to it.

Harris didn't say anything, but gave a discreet dip of his head. He always thought of everything, even when she didn't.

A worn-looking black hansom cab stood at the bottom of the front steps, waiting for Tempy as she hurried out the door. Apparently, one of the footmen had managed flag it down and have it waiting for her, which was a relief.

Tempy did her best to keep her full skirts from brushing against the large, dirty wheel as she climbed into the cabin of the cab. Once inside, she put her hand into the reticule and blindly felt for the bills and coins she knew would be there. Yes, there they were, along with her pen-and-ink set and a slim bound notebook. A journalist should always be prepared, and correctly recording pertinent facts was an essential part of the job.

The driver, his long gray hair hanging loose and blowing across his grizzled face, closed the box at the front of the carriage without glancing at her. She didn't like the feeling of being locked up until someone else released her, but she knew it was necessary because the boards would protect her skirts from the mud and muck that would surely be tossed up against the front of the little box by the horse's hooves. At least the upper part of the cab was wide open, and that eased her niggling sense of claustrophobia.

The cab made good time as it stuttered over the rough roads on its way toward the docks. Was it her, or was this ride rougher than usual? When the carriage hit another rut, her teeth clacked together. Tempy sighed. Perhaps she could find a newer hansom for the ride back. This one had a distinctly unpleasant odor about it. There should be plenty of hackneys looking for passengers at the docks. She could find one a bit more comfortable for her ride home.

Tempy's stomach groaned. When had she last eaten anything? Not this morning, and she'd skipped her evening meal. It must have been at tea yesterday. She remembered that there had been sandwiches on the tray, but she couldn't remember eating any. Perhaps she'd stop at a tea room on the way home. In fact, if things went the way she hoped, maybe Ernest would even join her.

Tempy's clutched at her reticule. What if this didn't work? What if Ernest was entirely under that woman's spell? But no. He couldn't be. Tempy was certain that as soon as his gaze met hers, he'd remember their plans for a future together. He'd remember what they had meant to each other.

He had to.

It took the driver two tries before finally depositing Tempy at the correct dock, and by then, she had scooted so far forward on her seat that she was in danger of falling off it.

Once the driver brought the hansom cab to a complete halt, Tempy passed her payment to him through the small trap door above and behind her head.

The wind gusted, briefly clearing away the musty odor of the docks as Tempy tipped her head back to peer at the ship. She clamped her hat to her head with one hand to prevent it from being whipped away by the stiff breeze, and briskly repositioned her hat pin to secure everything more firmly.

Ernest's ship, the SS *Spofield*, was a large steamship. Tempy much preferred the older sailing ships. They were so much more beautiful and graceful, but the steamships were much faster and more reliable. Sailing ships were rarely seen these days, which seemed a shame. Father had always droned on about the superiority of the steam engine and the inevitable march of progress.

Apparently, the *Spofield* had just docked, and Tempy watched as a steady stream of porters contributed to the growing piles of luggage at the base of the gangplank. Steerage passengers were already leaving the ship, carrying their own bundles, but it appeared as though the first-class passengers were waiting to disembark until after their luggage had been unloaded.

Tempy found a safe place to stand near the growing piles of bags and boxes, and she peered at the ship, scanning the deck for Ernest, but saw no sign of him. Of course, there were so many men on board wearing black frock coats and stovepipe hats that it would be difficult to spot him, even with his bright blond shock of hair. Even such distinctive hair wouldn't be of much use in identifying him while he wore a black hat.

As Tempy picked her way through the piles of luggage, she congratulated herself on how prudent she'd been in deciding to find Ernest here. She could spot him as he walked in a line down the gangplank and then track his progress as he led the porters to his bags.

Tempy's stomach growled again, and a woman standing nearby glanced at her, showing surprise when she realized that Tempy had produced the noise. The woman blushed and said, "It's a lovely day, isn't it?"

Lovely day? Tempy glanced up in surprise. The bright blue sky was dotted by fast-moving clouds, and the temperature was rather pleasant. She nodded at the woman. "Yes, quite." Such a beautiful day seemed to suggest that good things would happen today, and Tempy's spirits lifted.

The woman turned back to her examination of the ship. After a moment, she tut-tutted. "Will you look at that. Young people these days. That pair should be ashamed of themselves. Why, he's holding her much too closely. If she were my daughter, I'd box her ears, I would."

Tempy couldn't see the couple in question since a loose strand of her hair was covering her eyes. "What makes you think they aren't married?" she asked. After tucking that errant lock back in place, Tempy glanced up at the ship again. She quickly located a man with his arm encircling a woman's waist. Their backs were to her, but based on their closeness and the way the man's hand lingered low on the woman's back, the two seemed quite enamored of one another.

"Why, because she's wearing such pale colors. She must be unmarried."

That made sense. Once married, a myriad of colors became available for women to wear, and most eschewed the pastels they'd been required to wear as debutantes. Tempy glanced down at her own pale green dress trimmed with forest green piping. If Ernest went through with his plan to marry his Venus, she'd be obliged to wear these pale colors for quite a long time.

"The vicar says there should be enough space between two people for you to pass a glass of red wine between them without spilling a drop. Well, these two would never pass *that* test, I'll tell you that."

The woman they were discussing turned her head to the side, providing Tempy with a clear view of her lovely face. She was quite stunning, and quite unlike most English beauties. She had full lips, dark, wavy hair, and large brown eyes. There was something about the woman that was both lush and mysterious. Tempy glanced at the man accompanying her. His face was still obscured.

But it didn't matter. Tempy would recognize him even if he wore a canvas bag over his head.

It was Ernest.

When the temptress—the *Venus*, she corrected herself—shifted her head and revealed Ernest's face, his besotted expression caused Tempy to gasp.

"Oh my, isn't she beautiful?" The busybody's voice now oozed treacle as her former disapproval vanished like a shadow at noon. "They must be newlyweds. See how in love they are?"

Tempy didn't want to look...couldn't *bear* to look. She had to get away. This had been a horrible plan.

A cab. She needed to find a cab.

As Tempy prepared to escape, she took a quick step backwards and banged her heel hard against something quite solid. Her upper body kept moving while her feet remained locked in place, forcing her to lose her balance, and her momentum caused her to topple over backwards.

With horror, Tempy saw her frothy white petticoats billowing up as she went sailing over a trunk. With a hollow thump, the back of her head made contact with the wooden dock.

And then there was nothing.

❧ 6 ❧

STUMBLE

L ucien stepped out of the dim interior of the pub and into the bright London sunlight. The brisk wind blowing along the Thames tried to snatch his top hat from his head, and he grabbed it just in time to keep it from tumbling down the dock.

The stench of the Thames wasn't as bad this year as it had been in the past. Ever since the Great Stink in 1858, engineers had been working to improve London's sanitation. On a day like today, with gusting winds and a bright blue sky, the aroma of the river was quite tolerable.

Lucien walked briskly along the river to clear his head as he reexamined the next steps in his plan. As he had expected, John still wanted his casino.

Very much so.

John hadn't even tried to disguise his interest. That was one of the things Lucien liked about him. He was straightforward and honest, and those were admirable qualities in a man. Now the question was, how could Lucien encourage John to move quickly?

Lucien needed to propel his buyer toward a decisive action, and it would be best if he did it before news of his new title became common knowledge, because once that bit of information was out, people would assume he'd want to sell the casino and would feel free to offer him amounts well below its actual value. Of course, they'd do so in the guise of doing him a favor. As if gouging someone was ever a kindness.

As he slowed his pace and strolled down the dock, Lucien swiftly sorted through his options. Once he included John's continued interest in owning the casino in his own calculations, Lucien was able to play out a number of scenarios before choosing the option that would best achieve his desired outcome.

Hurrying this deal along shouldn't be a particularly difficult task. He simply needed to create a sense of urgency for his buyer, and the best way to do that would be to let him believe that he had competition.

Even though that wasn't the case.

Lucien had built Hamlin House from nothing, and selling it felt like cutting off his arm, but it was for the best if he wanted to ensure that it remained strong and had a solid future. So he would only sell it to the right man, and he'd already decided that John Snowden was that man.

Content with his new plan of action, Lucien came to a stop and turned to walk back toward the pub. His coachman, Higgs, should be waiting somewhere nearby with his carriage.

Lucien glanced over toward a group of people standing along the dock. They appeared to be waiting to greet the passengers from a steamer ship that had just arrived.

The steerage passengers were hurrying off, hefting their baggage and keeping a sharp eye on their belongings. The docks were a favorite haunt for pickpockets. The area was riddled with grubby little children who'd slit your throat just as readily as they'd pick your pocket.

Lucien wondered briefly about Miss Bliss and then paused. What had caused her to suddenly pop into his thoughts?

He turned and looked again at the people on the docks. Yes. There she was. He must have recognized her without being aware of it. What a strange young woman. A journalist, moreover. How outrageous. But Millicent held her in high regard, so there must be quite a bit more to her than he'd seen so far.

Lucien was about to continue on his way when he saw Miss Bliss step backward and stumble over some baggage.

Lucien sprinted toward her. He was too far away to break her fall, and he winced when, even at this distance, he heard her head slam against the dock with a thwack. He wove between the dock-workers, porters, and passengers, trying not to hurt anyone as he rushed to Miss Bliss's side.

An older woman was fussing over her, pulling Miss Bliss's skirts to rights so that her limbs would be hidden from view.

"Miss? Miss? Oh, my goodness." The woman looked around, and her gaze landed on Lucien as he hurried toward them. "Oh, thank goodness! She fell, and I don't know what to do about her. Do you know her?"

Lucien nodded as he knelt beside Tempy. Her eyes were closed, but she was breathing. The fall must have knocked her unconscious.

"Oh, thank goodness," the woman repeated. "I was afraid she was here alone. My son is coming down the gangplank just now, and I can't linger, but since she has you, I don't need to worry." She turned away and hurried off.

Lucien looked back down at the young woman who was now in his care. He picked up her gloved hand and squeezed it. "Miss Bliss. Can you hear me?"

She breathed steadily, but her eyes didn't open. With a sigh, he scooped his arms under her back and knees as he prepared to lift her from the dock. As her skirts shifted, he noted a reticule that had been hiding under them. He eyed it for a moment and then picked it up as well. It was probably hers.

Lucien shifted the slim burden in his arms so that her head rested comfortably against his shoulder. He noted that her small black bonnet had a long hat pin securing it to her chestnut hair, so he didn't need to worry about having it blow away in this wind. He did, however, need to take care that he didn't get jabbed with the thing.

He wished he could see her eyes. He hadn't noticed their color yesterday, and now he wondered. Would they be brown? Green? He guessed green, as green eyes often accompanied hair that had a hit of red, as hers did.

She smelled of lavender. He'd always been partial to that sharp, clean floral scent. It reminded him of summertime and the lavender fields he'd tramped through in Somerset when he'd visited there as a boy.

People made way for them as Lucien carried Miss Bliss toward the road. He looked around, wondering if he should walk back to his carriage or hail one of the hansom cabs waiting to pick up passengers. The decision was simplified when he recognized the sharp whistle emitted by his coachman, Higgs.

The carriage pulled to a stop right in front of Lucien. Higgs jumped down from his perch and hurried to open the carriage door. "I saw you scoop her up, sir, so I came as fast as I could. Who is she? Is she badly injured?"

Lucien hadn't told any of his employees about his new title yet, so they hadn't started *my lord-ing* him. He'd need to decide how to handle that, now that he intended to accept the inheritance.

But that wasn't important right now. "She's an acquaintance, and I don't know how badly injured she is. All I know is that she fell and she's unconscious. I'll take her home and send for a doctor." A thought struck him. "Blazes. I don't know where she lives. I suppose I'll have to take her to Hamlin House."

With Higgs's assistance, Lucien settled Miss Bliss on the seat and squeezed in next to her. He cradled his arm around her small shoulders and tucked her head against his chest to keep her from being thrown around on the drive. Higgs shut the door with a snap, and then Lucien felt the carriage shift as the coachman climbed onto the driver's seat.

The carriage had been traveling for a while when Lucien heard a soft sigh. Miss Bliss's gloved hand, loose in her lap, shifted. She raised it and slid it across his chest. Her fingers opened like a little white starfish and rested there for a moment as she turned her face toward his. Her eyelashes fluttered, tickling his neck in a pleasant manner.

And then she froze.

The hand that had been resting so softly against his chest suddenly pushed against it, and she thrust herself toward the far side of the carriage seat. She winced as the back of her head bumped against the side of the carriage. She rubbed at the lump that must have developed there, and a look of comprehension came over her. She relaxed slightly.

Her gaze focused on Lucien and her brows furrowed. "Mr. Hamlin?"

"None other."

She glanced at her surroundings. "This is your carriage?"

He nodded.

She gingerly touched the back of her head again. "It seems that I owe you my gratitude along with an apology."

"Apology? Why?"

She sat up straight and began checking her clothing, making small adjustments here and there. He couldn't tell what she was doing, but she looked more neat and composed once she was done. She really was quite fetching. "For requiring any assistance in the first place. I apologize for making such a ridiculous scene."

"Think nothing of it," he said. "I'm glad I was there to help." With the sunlight shining into the carriage, Lucien could see that her eyes were green, just as he'd guessed. Green with little flecks of gold. "Our mutual friend highly recommends you, and I trust her judgment."

"You can't know how much that relieves me. You've been quite kind."

He waved her continued apologies away. "I didn't know where you lived, so my coachman is taking us to my casino. Would you prefer an alternate destination?"

"I'd prefer my own home," she said, and then rattled off her street name.

As soon as she said it, Lucien realized he'd already known where she'd lived. Everyone knew about the Bliss residence and the enormous statue of a train that Mr. Bliss had erected in the green space across from it.

Lucien opened the small window and leaned his head out. "Higgs, we'll take the young lady home." After repeating the location, he pulled his head back inside and closed the window. "We'll have you there in five minutes. Mayfair is a very pleasant part of town."

"Yes. I've always found it so." She shifted in her seat to look out her window, and he watched her profile as she chewed at her bottom lip. She frowned and glanced at him. "Why do men cheat?"

"What?"

"I said, why do men cheat?" She stared at him, clearly expecting an answer.

"Because they like to win, and because they are greedy. Is that what your article is about?"

She looked at him blankly. "What? No. Not that kind of cheating. The other kind."

The other kind? "You mean, men whose affections wander?"

She nodded.

"Ah. I suspect this has something to do with that letter you snatched from the table yesterday. Is that what brought you to the docks today? A man who you believe cheated you?"

She looked away and turned a deep shade of pink. "Certainly not. How absurd." A haughty look curled her upper lip into a charming sneer, but her face seemed unaccustomed to making that sort of expression. She couldn't maintain the look for long and her features soon relaxed. "I need you to answer my question. I'd like a man's point of view."

Lucien shrugged in that Gallic way he'd perfected. It had never failed to annoy his grandfather. With fingers splayed, eyebrows raised, and lower lip jutting out just slightly, he communicated his disavowal of any knowledge regarding the subject at hand. "Perhaps he was bored. Perhaps he wanted to feel better about himself. I don't know the man."

"There is no man. This is purely an academic question."

"Ah." It was obvious that she was lying, but Lucien saw no reason to argue the point.

Miss Bliss leaned closer to the window. "We're almost there. I recognize this street." She noticed her reticule on the seat and picked it up, giving him a grateful smile as she slid its string handle around her wrist. "I never thanked you for allowing me to visit your casino."

"Think nothing of it," he said, pleased that he could offer her this bit of assistance. "As I explained to Millicent, it's no problem to have you visit and interview the staff when we're closed."

"Closed?" Miss Bliss's voice squeaked. "But that won't do at all. I need to observe people while they're gambling. How can I do that if I come in when you're closed?"

He shook his head. "That's as far as I'm willing to bend. I can't allow you to bother my patrons. They come to Hamlin House to relax and enjoy themselves and I don't want a reporter vexing them."

"Oh, but Mr. Hamlin. It isn't like that at all," she said, twisting the fabric of her reticule with white-gloved hands. "If you'd allow me to explain, I'm sure you'd change your mind."

Lucien didn't like the expression on Miss Bliss's face. She looked desperate, and that couldn't be good. The moment the carriage pulled to a halt, Lucien darted forward and opened the door.

He'd rather not be trapped inside the carriage with this woman in her current emotional state. He had the distinct impression that he'd just dealt Miss Bliss an unexpected blow, and it left him feeling like a cad.

Lucien jumped down from the carriage and turned to face her through the open door. "This happens to be a particularly inopportune time for a reporter to visit." He took her hand and helped her step down from the carriage.

As Miss Bliss's foot touched the pavement, she stumbled slightly, and Lucien immediately wrapped his arm around her waist so that she wouldn't fall. As soon as she regained her footing, he withdrew his support.

The door of her stately home flew open and a man who appeared to be her butler hurried outside. Relief washed through Lucien. The sooner he could turn Miss Bliss over to someone else, the better.

Despite his obvious concern for his employer, the butler shot Lucien an expression of shocked disapproval. Apparently he wasn't accustomed to seeing his mistress arrive home in the company of a strange man. That only served to confirm Lucien's impression of her as an ingénue.

"Please assist Miss Bliss," Lucien said brusquely, taking a step back to distance himself from her. "She had a fall and hit her head. She might be concussed."

The butler paled and rushed forward to offer his arm for support, but Miss Bliss hardly seemed to notice him as she stood rooted to the ground with her gaze fixed on Lucien.

"Please, Mr. Hamlin. You don't understand. If I can't visit your casino, I won't be able to write my article."

Lucien frowned as he shook his head. "Under different circumstances I might have allowed you access, but it's not possible right now."

"But you're the owner," she said, her brow furrowed with confusion. She pressed her hand against her forehead. Did her head ache? "Surely you could allow me to visit. You're in charge of everything that happens at Hamlin House."

"That's the point, Miss Bliss. I *am* in charge." He bowed slightly and touched the brim of his hat. "Good day, Miss Bliss."

Although he'd done the right thing for his casino, that didn't keep him from feeling as though he'd kicked a helpless child. It took a great deal of fortitude for him to ignore Miss Bliss's continued pleading and climb back into his carriage, but he did.

As the carriage moved down the street, the sound of her voice faded in his ears, but it continued to echo in his heart, leaving him feeling like the worthless cur his grandfather had always believed him to be.

MR. DICKENS

❦

Tempy's breathing became labored and it rasped in her ears, drowning out all other sounds. The ground slid under her feet as she hurried down the hill.

Gravel.

Now she could hear it crunching and rattling as bits of it skittered downhill ahead of her, racing her to the large expanse of water below.

The steamship was there, preparing to depart. She knew her father was already on board. Why hadn't he waited for her at the house? Why had he left without her?

Tempy could barely make out his figure as he stood on the deck of the ship and gazed uninterestedly at the shore.

At her.

Still running toward the ship, Tempy threw her hands up and began waving frantically, trying to draw his attention.

At first, Tempy was afraid her father didn't notice her, but then his gaze drifted up to focus on the hill.

On her.

Thank goodness. Father wouldn't let the ship depart without her.

But then she noticed a flurry of movement among the dockworkers. With a jolt of panic, Tempy realized that they were casting off the lines that kept the ship tethered to shore.

"No!" shouted Tempy. "Wait for me!"

Despite her shouts, nobody else on board the ship turned to look at her. Her father's gaze didn't alter. He continued to stand without moving, watching her run toward the ship.

Tempy pushed herself to move faster. She was desperate to narrow the gap. Desperate to reach her father. But her burst of energy didn't help. No matter how fast she ran, she couldn't close the distance between them.

A glimmer of water appeared between the ship and the shore.

It was leaving.

Leaving without her.

"Father, don't go!" Tempy's voice was the only sound that existed, and it seemed to reverberate around her. It grew, becoming a boom that should have left everyone aboard ship deaf.

But her father turned his head away from her, as if responding to another person's voice. She saw a flicker of motion next to him and then Ernest was there, standing with her father, with his bright blond hair fluttering in the breeze.

"Stop!" she shouted. "Don't leave me here all alone!" But this time, her voice didn't seem to have the same strength. It was as if the air itself swallowed the sound, muffling it in a featherbed.

Her father gestured in her direction and Ernest spotted her. He grinned broadly and waved at her.

He waved goodbye.

Then Ernest's family gathered around him, all waving cheerfully at her.

How could they look so happy? So excited? "Don't go!" she shouted, tears welling in her eyes. "I want to go with you!"

Ernest's sister, Emily, looked confused for a moment. Had Tempy's pleading words reached her? Emily seemed on the verge of saying something to Ernest, but her mother pulled her away. Emily turned her back on Tempy and allowed Mrs. Lipscomb to draw her inside the ship's cabin.

The breadth of water between shore and ship grew larger and larger. By the time Tempy reached the water's edge, no one was there. The workers had all disappeared. In fact, the dock had disappeared as well.

The ship was shrinking in the distance. Tempy couldn't make out the faces of the people standing on deck any longer, and when she looked around, she realized she stood alone on the shore of an uninhabited island.

"Help!" Tempy cried. "Won't someone help me?"

Tempy heard the splash of oars and turned to see a stream she hadn't noticed before. It emptied out into the ocean not far from where she stood. There was a man in the little boat. Actually it was little punt, like the ones she'd ridden along the Thames.

With a glimmer of hope, Tempy ran toward it, but she wasn't fast enough because the stream became a river as it reached the ocean and the little punt picked up speed. It almost seemed to fly past her, and in just a moment it was bobbing in the ocean, just yards away from her.

"Help me!" she called to the oarsman.

At the sound of her voice, the man turned to look at her, and Tempy was shocked to recognize Mr. Dickens.

He'd help her. Of course he would.

"Mr. Dickens, I need your help," she said as politely as possible. "Could you please row me out to that ship? My father and my fiancé are on it, and I need to join them."

Mr. Dickens smiled broadly. "I can do even better," he called back. "I'll lay a path for you."

He reached into the bottom of the boat and pulled out a sheaf of papers. Licking his forefinger, he plucked the top sheet from the stack and carefully laid it on the surface of the ocean. He then grabbed the oars, pulled on them to move the boat a little farther away from her, paused, plucked another sheet from the stack, and laid it on the water. "There you go!" he shouted, clearly very pleased with himself. "I'll lay the path and you can walk there yourself."

Tempy stared at the rectangle of paper floating on the flat, waveless ocean. "But how? Won't I sink?"

"Sink? Why would you sink?" Mr. Dickens asked as he let another sheet of paper drift down and land on the water.

She would, wouldn't she? She reached out her foot to test the solidity of the paper, and the white sheet sank beneath the water. "It won't hold me."

"You have to commit," Mr. Dickens said, speaking slowly as though talking to a rather slow child. "Just step on."

Tempy inhaled sharply and held her breath for a moment. She slowly released it as she closed her eyes and placed her foot on the paper...

...and sank like a stone to the bottom of the ocean.

☙❧

TEMPY'S EYES FLEW OPEN AS SHE TOOK A GASPING BREATH OF air. She was in her room. In bed...not under the ocean. Even now, she realized that the heavy weight of the water pressing against her was fading.

Or rather, it was now centered on her chest.

She focused on a spot just a few inches above her breastbone where Osiris, her cat, was perched on her chest, his two front feet poking into her ribs just below her heart. He peered into her face with what seemed to her to be a self-satisfied cat smirk and bumped his forehead against hers.

She pulled him against her and pressed her face in his soft white fur. He permitted her embrace for only a moment, and then pulled away.

"I suppose you think it's time for me to wake up and pet you."

Now that his mission of waking her was complete, Osiris ignored her. He walked away, tail held high, and jumped to the floor.

Tempy sighed and then noticed that her face was wet. She must have been crying, she realized, and vaguely recalled something about trying to walk across the ocean on sheets of paper.

What an odd dream. And Mr. Dickens had been in it.

Tempy sat bolt upright in her bed. Mr. Dickens! She glanced at the clock on her bedside table. It was nine o'clock, she saw with relief. She flopped back against her feather pillows. She wasn't late. The meeting wasn't until eleven, which meant she had plenty of time dress and review her notes.

Her thoughts returned to yesterday's encounter with Mr. Hamlin, like a tongue worrying at a sore tooth. Yesterday her thoughts had bounced back and forth from Ernest's behavior on the docks to Mr. Hamlin's refusal to allow her to speak to any of his patrons. Whenever one topic became too painful or frustrating to ponder, she'd switched to the other, but she hadn't been able to find a resolution to either problem.

With the upcoming meeting with Mr. Dickens looming, Tempy could only think about finding a way to access Mr. Hamlin's casino. She had briefly considered visiting one of the other gambling halls London had to offer, but discarded them as all being too ordinary in comparison to Hamlin House. It would be as though she'd hobbled herself before beginning to write her article. Hamlin House was the premier gambling palace in all the city. If she wanted to write about the effects of gambling, she could hardly ignore the most popular and successful establishment in all of London.

She'd noticed Hamlin's reluctance to grant her access to his establishment when they first met at the tea room, but still, he'd said she could visit. What had happened during the time that had elapsed since then that had caused him to all but rescind his invitation? This had been the question upon which her worries had become stuck all day yesterday, and a good night's sleep had done nothing to move her any closer to understanding Mr. Hamlin's motivation. He was hiding something. She was certain of it.

Tempy glanced at her bedside clock again and let out a heavy sigh. She bounded out of bed and yanked at the bell pull to summon one of the servants. She'd made a point not to hire a lady's maid. After all, this house already boasted three upstairs maids, and any of them could help her with the few small personal tasks that needed doing.

After about a minute, one of the maids appeared. She was carrying a tray bearing Tempy's morning bowl of oatmeal and a teapot. She slid the tray onto a small round table in front of Tempy's bedroom window and then placed the silver egg-shaped tea infuser into the pot to allow it to begin brewing.

Another maid entered with a pitcher of water which she placed next to the wash basin. Both of the young women left the room, and Tempy settled onto the little upholstered chair by the table and began to eat. By the time her meal was done, she had also finished her mental preparations for her meeting with Mr. Dickens.

She discarded her dressing gown, and as soon as she'd slipped into her fresh pantaloons and shift, she pulled the bell cord again.

Tempy had already selected the dress she planned to wear today. It was a silk afternoon dress, the color of tea spilled on a white napkin. Crisply pressed pleats ran across the top edge of the high-necked top, and they continued down the side of the bodice where it would fasten with a row of small buttons along her waist at her side.

But first she needed her corset. Tempy chose a plain one, unhooked the row of fasteners down its front, and swung one edge of it around her back in a practiced move that allowed her to deftly catch the other end of it as it wrapped around her body. She aligned the row of silver hooks down the front of it and swiftly fastened them from just below her bosom to below her hips.

The same young woman who had delivered her tea slipped into the room. Tempy offered her back to the girl, who made quick work of the task of tightening the bindings. She alternated between tightening the upper and lower sets of corset strings as she pinched in Tempy's waist far enough so that the dress would fit.

"I think that will do," Tempy said, as soon as the corset felt right. She picked up the bodice of her dress and shrugged into it, testing the fit to ensure that the corset was tight enough. Fortunately, it fit perfectly on the first try, and the row of buttons easily slid into their buttonholes. Satisfied, Tempy thanked the maid who then retrieved the breakfast tray and departed.

Tempy donned the skirt and the voluminous petticoats that would give her the required inverted-tulip silhouette.

As the last step of her morning toilette, Tempy pulled her hair into a severe bun and fastened it with a handful of hairpins. She used a lot of them, knowing that she'd be losing them all day. This was the only part of her morning routine that lacked finesse, but she was inept when it came to doing anything more elaborate. Unfortunately, this was a talent that the upstairs maids were lacking as well.

Mr. Dickens wouldn't care. He wasn't interested in her ability to arrange her hair, but rather her ability to arrange words on a page.

Tempy's stomach tensed. What if she was wrong? What if he didn't like her writing? But he *had* to still like her writing, didn't he? She hadn't changed in that respect.

But what if he'd changed his mind? Just like Ernest?

She jabbed another hairpin in place, wincing as she scraped her scalp in the process. This was no good. She couldn't wind herself up like a child's clockwork toy. She needed to compose herself.

Headlines.

BLISS BUILDS BRIDGES

Hmm. Not a very good headline. Not very descriptive. It made her sound like she was engaged in construction work.

BLISS MEETS DICKENS

Still not good. Very flat. It didn't capture the imagination at all.

She'd need to work on this one.

She hurried out of her bedroom and down the stairs, making good time. Mr. Dickens's offices were less than two miles from her house

She arrived at the offices of All the Year Round about ten minutes before the time of her appointment. The dark building had a curved corner entrance at the intersection of Wellington Street and Tavistock Street. It was just off Covent Garden, and it had been pleasant to walk there this morning.

BLISS HAS GREAT EXPECTATIONS

Hmm...maybe.

A bell attached to the door rang as she pushed it open, and Mr. Dickens's secretary, a neat young man with short blond hair, looked up as she walked in. She introduced herself.

The young man glanced at a day calendar that lay open on his desk and slid his finger down the page. "You're early." He looked up at her disapprovingly.

"Yes."

"He's in a meeting. You'll have to wait." He gestured toward some empty chairs and then returned to perusing a sheaf of papers.

Tempy nodded and sat down in one of the wooden chairs along the wall. The office was on the ground floor and had large windows, so Tempy could watch people passing by on the street. It was a rather busy intersection, and Tempy was able to keep herself entertained by trying to imagine where each person who passed by might be going.

It wasn't long before the door to Mr. Dickens's office swung open and two men emerged. The first, a bearded man of about forty and wearing wire rim glasses, leaned heavily on a cane.

Tempy immediately recognized his round, boyish face. It was none other than Wilkie Collins, the man who had written the novel being serialized for *All the Year Round*. He was followed by Mr. Dickens.

Tempy watched Collins keenly as she rose to her feet. She'd

heard rumors that he was sorely afflicted with a joint ailment. Based on his stiff movements and his heavy reliance on his cane, Tempy realized that the rumors had not been exaggerated.

Mr. Dickens followed his friend out of his office as the two men chuckled over some shared jest. Mr. Dickens's gaze immediately fixed upon Tempy, and he paused. "Miss Bliss, I'm sorry if I kept you waiting," he said, and then stepped forward to greet her.

She smiled and held out her hand. "I arrived a bit too early. It's a pleasure to see you."

Mr. Dickens performed the introductions, and Mr. Collins smiled encouragingly at her. "I can't tell you how happy I was to hear that you will be writing for the newspaper," Mr. Collins said.

"The honor is all mine," she said, focusing on Mr. Collins. She noted that his pupils were oddly dilated. "I hadn't expected to have the opportunity to meet you today. I particularly enjoyed your book, *The Woman in White*."

Mr. Collins's round face brightened with an affable smile. "Why, thank you. I hope you'll find that you also enjoy *No Name* as you read the serialized version over the next few months." He glanced back at Mr. Dickens and then returned his gaze to Tempy. "I found it necessary to finalize a few details before leaving for Bath. It's my hope that the waters there will help with my affliction. I count myself lucky that my dear Caroline and her daughter will accompany me. Having close friends and family make afflictions easier to bear."

His words sent a sharp jab of pain through Tempy, and suddenly she envied this man, with his painful joints and his purported opium addiction and the love of his friends and family. "I couldn't agree with you more." And she would have that kind of love, too, as soon as she won back Ernest. She had to, because it was the only way she could have her family back. Well, Ernest's family, yes, but they would also be hers as soon as they married.

Mr. Dickens clapped his friend on the shoulder. "I think Bath is just the place for you. Take as much time as you like. You needn't rush back to London. If I have any questions, I can write to you."

Mr. Collins nodded. "Then I'll be off. It was a pleasure to meet you, Miss Bliss," he said, tipping his hat to Tempy and then stepping carefully out onto the street.

Tempy watched through the rectangular panes of glass as the man limped painfully down the street. She sent out a fervent wish for him to find some relief from his pain in the waters of the ancient hot springs in Bath. Many people had sojourned there over the centuries, so there must be some truth behind the rumors of its curative effects. She hoped so, for Mr. Collins's sake.

"Please, come into my office," Mr. Dickens said, waving his arm in a broad flourish. Like Mr. Collins, he was bearded, but Dickens favored a mustache and a rather wiry goatee. The warm brown of his beard matched his hair, but his receding hairline and arched brows left him with a slightly surprised air. Overall, he appeared to be a genial man, with a kindness about him that immediately put Tempy at ease.

She preceded him into the room and then sat on the chair next to his desk. Mr. Dickens's desktop wasn't cluttered. Far from it. Everything seemed to be meticulously arranged. In the bright sunlight shining into the room, she noticed surprisingly few dust motes. When she glanced at the papers on his desk, she saw he favored blue ink. An anachronistic quill pen rested on his desk blotter. These days, most people preferred metal nibs since quills required careful preparation, but apparently Mr. Dickens wasn't among them.

Mr. Dickens pulled out a low-backed wooden desk chair, causing its wheels to clatter on the hardwood floor. He sat and relaxed against its curved back. His pose was casual, with one arm draped over the unpadded armrest. As he observed her, he crossed his legs, rotating the ankle of his raised foot as though it had a kink in it.

"Have you decided upon a focus for your article?" he asked.

"I'm narrowing it down," Tempy replied. "A friend arranged for me to have access to an elite gambling establishment." She intentionally omitted the fact that she'd only been invited to go there when it was closed. After all, that detail didn't matter, since she'd already decided to ignore that particular restriction. "I want to understand the various effects gambling has upon the wealthy members of our society."

"Excellent. That will fit in perfectly. I can count on you to deliver it in two weeks?"

Tempy swallowed. Two weeks? How would she manage to write this article when she also had to find a solution to this problem with Ernest? But looking into Mr. Dickens's confident eyes, she realized that there was only one acceptable answer. Only one answer she could live with. "Certainly."

Dickens slapped his leg and grinned. "I knew I could count on you. Your reputation for tenacity and reliability precedes you. Have it here two weeks from this Monday. Or the night before, if you can manage it."

That gave her a couple of more days than she'd expected. An entire additional weekend. A knot of tension in her stomach that she hadn't even been aware of suddenly eased. This kind of opportunity didn't come often, and she was determined to impress Mr. Dickens with her writing, her timeliness, and her professionalism. This could lead to many more writing opportunities. Or to none at all if she failed.

And failure wasn't an option.

They chatted for a few more minutes, and then Mr. Dickens escorted her out, just as he had done with Mr. Collins. His show of respect was like a balm, and Tempy walked out of the doors of All the Year Round with her head held high and a bounce in her step.

Mrs. Jenkins, who lived two doors down from Tempy, was approaching with her daughter, Beatrice. Tempy had known them both for years, but not well. She smiled and nodded a greeting.

Mrs. Jenkins glanced up at the sign on the building Tempy had just exited and frowned. Then she let out a huff and grabbed her daughter by the arm and hurried them both past Tempy without even acknowledging her presence.

All of Tempy's good humor disappeared. Could she really blame the woman? After all, anyone who was seen speaking with her ran the risk of having Earl E. Byrd write about them in tomorrow's newspaper. And what kind of mother would let her daughter consort with a female journalist?

There was no acceptance here on the street from the privileged members of society. It could only be found inside the doors of All the Year Round with people who truly understood her.

And with Ernest's family.

A VISIT TO HAMLIN HOUSE

❦

BLISS BREACHES BASTION

Why did she even own a carriage if she never used it?

Tempy hadn't wanted anyone to identify her carriage during this visit to Mr. Hamlin's establishment, so she'd decided to hire a hackney. At least this one was newer and cleaner than the one she'd taken to the docks.

There'd been an article in the paper today by her nemesis, Mr. Byrd. Either he'd seen her at the docks yesterday or someone had told him all about it, because he'd informed all of London about her fainting spell. She only hoped the man wasn't following her now, but tonight's weather would make that task a difficult one.

It only took a few minutes to make the trip. The hansom cab swept through the low-lying fog that had rolled into London along with nightfall. She could see little as she gazed out into the street, but she marked the passing of the gas streetlights, and they helped to orient her in the otherwise formless landscape. Occasional gaps appeared in the mist, but she saw no one in those brief glimpses of Mayfair. She knew there were people around her, however, because their voices drifted through the night.

The hackney pulled to a stop inside one of those gaps in the fog, and it deposited her directly in front of the decorative marble edifice of Hamlin House.

Tempy climbed the steps toward the entrance, but her heart beat harder than was justified by those five shallow risers. She took a breath to calm herself. It wouldn't do to arrive looking nervous and out of place. Especially after she'd put so much effort into choosing just the right gown and mantle for her role this evening. Tonight, she was a lady gambler, out to enjoy an evening at the lavish Hamlin House.

After all, she didn't need Mr. Hamlin's permission to lose money in his establishment.

She tried to ignore the little voice that scoffed at her boldness, but it persisted in pointing out that Mr. Hamlin had very specifically denied her request to come here.

How was she supposed to complete her assignment without interviewing anyone? Mr. Hamlin would just have to accept her presence... if he even knew about it.

"What's the worst you can do, throw me out and make a scene?" she muttered to herself.

That was highly unlikely.

But there was still that lingering doubt that left her wondering if he might do just that...eject her from the premises and humiliate her in front of his patrons.

That would certainly provide fodder for yet another of Mr. Byrd's horrid newspaper articles that constantly nipped at her heels.

She didn't know if she could withstand any more emotional blows, but she also knew she had to try this. Writing the article was all she had left right now. Between her father's board of directors belittling her and trying to steal the railroad from her,

Ernest's defection, the loss of the Lipscomb family, the nameless reporter who kept targeting her, and her trepidation about writing this newspaper article, she needed to find some way to assert herself. She refused to allow herself to be placed in the role of a victim by everyone else in the world. She needed to take a stand.

Not that she'd given up on winning back Ernest. Of course not. But she'd realized today that she needed a much better plan than simply begging him to come back to her. She needed to make him *want* to come back.

And while she figured out how to do that, she'd keep working on this story for Mr. Dickens and poor Mr. Collins.

It was warm inside the casino, and with a footman's help, Tempy shed her mantle and checked it in the cloakroom. The foyer's dark granite floor reflected the glittering crystal chandelier above her, and the dark paneling gave her the immediate impression of both luxury and security.

Despite Tempy's relatively sheltered upbringing, Father had once allowed her to visit a gambling house with him. In Father's opinion, gambling was an abhorrent pastime and a complete waste of time and money. At the time, he'd said he wanted to show her the level of mania to which some men succumbed when they were caught up in the experience. She hadn't gambled that night, of course, and her father had only gambled enough to allow him to spend time with another railroad man who frequented the place. But Tempy had soaked in every nuance that night.

The first thing Father had done when they'd arrived was to provide a cashier with a letter from his bank to cover any losses, so Tempy had made sure to have one drawn up that afternoon. She found the cage where cashiers waited to hand out chips and then cash them in again at the end of the evening. She passed her letter of credit to the pale-faced teller sporting a splotchy beard. In exchange, he slid a box of chips through the small opening of his cage. The transaction was similar to one at a bank, and she was fairly certain that Mr. Hamlin had that idea in mind when he had designed the area. It was clever of him to play on the sense of solidity and security that banks engendered.

Tempy turned away from the cage and peered down at the small collection of round disks she'd just purchased for a rather substantial sum of money. No wonder people would lose so much. These little chips didn't look or feel like real money. It was like dressing up and wearing play clothes to look like Cleopatra or one of the fairies from Shakespeare's Tempest. It was separate from reality. Just a bit of pretend.

The chips seemed to come in three different denominations. Apparently Mr. Hamlin had them custom-made. Each ivory disk had the letters "HH" embossed on one side and a number on the opposite side. The plain ones had a "1," the ones with a blue rim had a "5," and the ones with a red rim had a "50" emblazoned on the back.

She kept most of the chips in the box, but she slid a few five-pound chips into her reticule. She wasn't sure why, but it seemed as though she shouldn't keep all of her money in one place. Lastly, she slid one fifty-pound chip down the front of her bodice. She'd seen a sophisticated-looking woman do that when she'd been to the gambling house with her father, and when the woman had produced the chip with flair, she'd caused quite a stir. Tempy wondered if she'd be able to duplicate the same effect at the proper moment.

Tempy planned to locate the roulette table. A place like this had to have a roulette table, didn't it? Most of the games were fairly complex. She was certain she'd never be able to look competent if she were to try to play anything else. Her lack of experience would be obvious, and she didn't want to draw too much attention to herself. She needed to blend in if she wanted to talk with the other patrons.

Once Tempy passed through the archway that led to the main gaming room, all thoughts of gambling fled, and she tried to mask her interest in the sumptuous surroundings. Potted palms dotted the room. There were no windows, only mirrors with ornate gilt frames where windows should have been, and the room was brightly lit with crystal chandeliers. With the mirrors reflecting the light, one could lose all sense of time in here.

She circled the gaming floor, absorbing everything. After mentally cataloging the thick dark red carpet and the heavy mahogany paneling on the walls, she pushed the room itself away from her consciousness and began focusing on the people within it.

They varied greatly in age, which surprised her. She'd assumed that gambling would be much more attractive to younger people, and although the majority of the patrons were young gentlemen, there were quite a few older people in attendance as well. Gray-bearded men wearing ebony dinner jackets dotted the room. And heavy-armed matrons with their necks dripping with jewels that sparkled in a kaleidoscope of colors sat among the tables, playing cards. A group of men, their eyes narrowed and glittering, stood around an oval table, shouting out numbers and strange phrases whose meanings Tempy couldn't begin to guess.

After a short time, Tempy realized that the mirrors would also make it difficult for a person to cheat by pulling an odd card from a sleeve or passing information to an active gambler. They'd never be certain they weren't being watched by the Mr. Hamlin's staff from some odd angle. There seemed to be a number of people in Hamlin House livery who were avid observers.

How interesting.

A woman in a dark blood-red dress sauntered by and slid onto a chair at a twenty-one table. Tempy watched her languid movements. The woman seemed to have all the time in the world. She smiled, and her laugh was lyrical and enticing. Every man at the table seemed entranced by her, but some hid it better than others. The ripple of excitement at the table was palpable. Tempy heard the woman's laugh again, like little silver bells all tuned in harmony, and she vowed to practice it when she was alone. There was something about the woman that reminded her of that conniving Clarisse, the witch who had stolen Ernest's heart. Was it her style or her grace? Tempy wasn't sure. What was it that both of those women had that Tempy *didn't* have?

The woman in red won, tossing her head back in an expression of exultation that exposed the long white line of her slim neck. Everyone at the roulette table took a moment to stare, and they seemed as pleased for her as she was for herself. How had she managed to gain their support and approval when most of them had lost money? How had she seduced every man at that table without even speaking to them?

As the woman sauntered away, her hoop-skirts swaying saucily as she moved, she swept past Tempy. A spicy scent of perfume wafted in her wake, and Tempy could see the diamond hairpins glittering in her dark, upswept hair.

Tempy followed her, trying to recreate the woman's gliding movements. She caught sight of herself in one of the mirrors long enough to see herself fail miserably. Then she glanced over to see a young footman watching her. He was clearly trying to hide his gap-toothed grin. When he realized he'd been caught laughing at her antics, he immediately schooled his features, but it was too late. She'd already seen him watching her.

She felt the heat rise in her face. She'd have to save practicing that saunter for another time.

What on earth did she think she was doing by playing around this way? She needed to remember that she was here with a specific purpose in mind: to research her article. To do that, she needed to talk to people, and so far, she hadn't spoken to anyone except that apathetic, pale-faced cashier.

She headed over to the roulette table that was farthest away from the overly observant footman. Perhaps changing her location would also change her attitude and allow her to start afresh.

A gentleman standing at the edge of the roulette table moved over slightly to give her a better view of the wheel. He smiled and nodded in greeting. "Well, hello. Fancy a bit of roulette?"

Having a stranger address her in public made Tempy uncomfortable, and she couldn't bring herself to respond. Instead, she set her box of chips in front of her and forced a tight smile before glancing away. "Eight," she said to the croupier, sliding two of her chips forward.

"A lucky number, I'll wager," the man next to her said, but she noted that he put his money on sixteen despite his words. She berated herself. Here was the perfect opportunity to speak to someone, and she couldn't move beyond her sensibilities of propriety to accept an offer of conversation.

The croupier spun the wheel and then set the ball spinning in the opposite direction around the outer rim.

"Is it usually this full on a Friday evening?" Tempy asked. Her voice didn't normally quaver like that, did it? If her governess could see her now...well, the poor woman would swoon. It seemed that she was doing quite a few things of late that would cause her late governess grief. She dragged her gaze away from the sight of the ball racing along the rim of the roulette wheel to glance at the man next to her.

"The crowd seems typical," the man said as he surveyed the room. "First time here?"

"No," she said. Too quickly, she realized. It came across as defensive and made her sound like a liar. Which she was. She heard the roulette ball lose enough momentum to fall, and it hit the wheel and started bouncing, searching for its eventual resting place. She turned to watch it and pressed her lips together. "Well, it's my first visit to Hamlin House, but not my first time at a casino."

"Then I'll stick close by. You're due for some first-timer's luck." The marble on the roulette wheel stopped its bouncing and landed in the slot marked "eight." "See?"

"Oh, oh!" She'd won. She'd actually won. "This is marvelous!"

She grinned, wanting to share the moment with someone, but when she looked up, she realized that the only person interested in her stroke of luck was the stranger standing next to her. Everyone else looked slightly annoyed with her. Tempy's excitement whooshed out of her like a sail that had suddenly lost a capricious breeze.

A sense of loneliness swept over her.

The croupier started pushing a stack of chips toward her, and her eyes widened at the size of the pile. "Oh, but that's too much, isn't it?"

The man next to her chortled. "You won 35 to 1. That stack looks just about right to me."

"Oh, my," she said faintly, trying her to recover the enthusiasm she'd lost, but failing. "I can see why people find this so much fun."

"Certainly." The man gave her a perplexed look.

Tempy gathered her winnings and stacked them neatly in her box, with the man at her elbow watching her the entire time. She reminded herself that tonight's excursion had a goal. A purpose. She needed to write that article for Mr. Dickens, and this man was perfect for her first interview. "Is that why you like to come here? For the thrill of winning?"

"Of course. That and to see my friends. And to meet interesting new people." He smiled again, revealing his crooked teeth, and looked at her pointedly. "And I find you quite fascinating."

She tried not to squirm under his gaze. "Do you come here often?" She immediately regretted the question. It sounded appallingly gauche to her. But perhaps he wouldn't notice.

His condescending expression told her otherwise. "Only a couple of nights a week. I used to go to Crockford's years ago, before it closed, but now I frequent Hamlin House and Templeton's."

Crockford's had been the first casino of any real significance built in London, and Templeton's had a rather staid reputation.

Did that mean this man was a bit of a traditionalist? But he didn't spend many nights at home, did he? "Are you married?" she asked, wondering what his wife thought of his lifestyle.

"What?" He sounded surprised by the question. "Yes, as a matter of fact."

Now she was getting somewhere. "What does your wife think about your frequent visits to gambling halls?"

At that, the smile left his face. "What is this? Do you know my wife? Is that why you're asking me all these questions?"

Tempy felt the heat rush to her face. How could she have asked such a personal question? And so quickly. She knew better than to push someone too fast in an interview. She could feel the opportunity to learn anything more from this man slipping away. "Of course not. I was just trying to make conversation."

"Questioning a man on his habits and his marriage," the man said, in a voice as icy as a February gust of wind, "is an odd way to pass the time. What is it you're really after?"

Tempy froze for a moment and then scooped her remaining chips into her container, preparing for a hasty retreat. "I'm terribly sorry if I've caused offense. None was intended. I hope you'll excuse me."

She turned, carrying her box of chips and moving quickly away. But the man reached out and grabbed hold of her upper arm, nearly knocking her chips from her hands.

"Just you wait a minute. I don't like this, and I want some answers."

Tempy tried to pull away, but the man held her firmly. How could she make him stop? Her gaze darted around the room, not sure where she could turn for help.

She caught the eye of the same gap-toothed footman who'd found her so amusing earlier. He was already crossing the room toward her, weaving his way between Hamlin House's patrons.

The young footman stopped just behind the other man's

shoulder. "Can I be of assistance?" he asked, gazing pointedly at the man's grip on Tempy's arm.

The man looked over his shoulder at the footman and then dropped his hand from Tempy's arm as though it had just transformed into a hot stovepipe. He didn't say a word but simply shot Tempy a withering glare. Then he turned his back to them and stalked off, heading toward the bar across the room.

"He appears to have been suddenly overtaken by a profound thirst," Tempy said, her voice quavering.

"Miss?" asked the footman. "Are you quite all right?"

"Yes," she said, pressing her hand to her rapidly beating heart. Her arm still hurt from the man's grip, and she wondered vaguely if she'd develop a bruise where he'd grabbed her. "And thank you. I'm not sure what I did that irritated that gentleman, but I'm relieved that you intervened."

"It's not just you. He tends to be irritable. I'm sorry that he bothered you. Please inform a staff member if you have any further trouble with him."

She nodded and looked down at her box of chips. They were rattling slightly from the little tremors that ran through her. She pulled the box more firmly against her stomach to hide the telltale movement. When she looked back up, the footman was gone.

What she'd really like right now was to find a quiet place to sit.

With not a small amount of relief, Tempy noticed a woman rise from her chair at one of the smaller gaming tables and gather her winnings. The woman headed toward the cashier, presumably done for the night. Tempy hurried toward the vacant chair and placed her hand on its back. She glanced at the other players at the table and asked, "Would you mind if I join you?"

"Not at all," one of the gentlemen replied.

Tempy lowered herself onto the chair, thankful that it had become available just when she'd most needed it.

"As long as you can play whist," he added, almost as an afterthought

Whist? She furrowed her brows. "I don't suppose you'd want to teach me?"

Based on the stony expressions the other players shot her, they did not.

This evening was not going well. Not well at all. With a sigh, Tempy collected her chips and stood. Her chair was filled, almost immediately, by an older woman who glared at her contemptuously. It was hard for Tempy not to look foolish as she beat a hasty retreat, but she managed to maintain a modicum of grace and composure as she walked off.

Why had she come here alone? It had been an absurd notion. She needed a new plan. Perhaps she could enlist Millicent to accompany her. At least then she'd have a friend by her side for support. Things were certain to be better if she tried this with a companion.

Tempy wandered toward the archway leading to the cashiers' windows as she tried to decide whether she should stay or cut her losses. Fortunately this evening wasn't a complete waste. At least she'd won something.

As Tempy stood in the archway, she caught sight of the couple standing at one of the cashiers' windows. The man had pale blond hair and the woman on his arm had her dark mass of hair artfully arranged so that curls cascaded down her hack.

But it was the man with the blond hair who caught Tempy's full attention.

Ernest?

Here?

But that wasn't possible. Ernest's family disapproved of gambling.

Then Tempy saw the expression of tenderness on his face as he looked down at the odious French woman on his arm, and her stomach twisted.

Wasn't it bad enough that the evil woman had snatched Ernest from her arms? Did she also have to come here and ruin her research for the article for Mr. Dickens? The woman was insidious.

Tempy stepped back through the archway and hid behind a potted plant, peering between the leathery leaves to observe the couple as they stood at the cashier's window.

Clarisse wore the latest in French fashion. Wasn't that just like a Parisian? Tempy glanced down at her own dress, which she'd been quite pleased with a scant hour ago. But now, looking at the lovely confection in pale pink satin and creamy lace, she discovered that she felt dreadfully out of style.

Ernest and Clarisse gathered up their chips and moved through the archway into the main casino. They were just inches away from her, but fortunately they were scanning the room, either looking for a game to their liking or for people Ernest knew. As they walked on, Tempy could see that Clarisse led the way, resting her hand lightly on Ernest's forearm as she guided him.

Tempy scooted a bit farther behind the plant, circling behind it as the pair moved on. She sidled around the large pot, trying to keep it between her and the other couple. It proved to be difficult to keep her wide skirts out of the couple's line of sight. Mountains of fabric must have been used to create her dress.

Once Tempy was on the opposite side of the plant, she realized that this was the perfect opportunity to make her escape. Ernest and Clarisse had their backs to her, and the cashiers' cage was right behind her.

Tempy took two quick steps backward and began to perform what she hoped was a graceful pirouette, but instead, she felt her shoulder bump into something that gave way behind her. She heard a tinkle of glass, followed by a crash, and then had the sudden sensation of cold liquid dripping down the back of her dress.

The footman she'd backed into tried to prevent the large silver serving tray she'd hit from toppling to the floor, but he lost the battle, along with his balance, and fell into her. This knocked her off her feet so that she landed on her seat in a froth of petticoats.

The round silver tray hit the floor with a clang, but it didn't land flat. Instead, it spun, its edges bouncing up and down and round and round in a crescendo of noise until it finally came to a painfully slow stop and ceased making such an incredible racket.

The entire casino was silent as Tempy climbed to her hands and knees. She glanced over her shoulder and then widened her eyes in horror as the two people she most wanted to avoid in this world tried to peer past the leaves of the potted palm to see what had caused the commotion.

It felt as though time stopped for an instant, and Tempy's gaze momentarily focused on the faint mote of dust that caught the light as it floated past her face.

Tempy turned away from the pair. At the same time, she grabbed the large silver serving tray from the floor and whipped it up to block their view.

She had to get out of here. What if Ernest recognized her?

Tempy lurched to her feet, keeping the serving tray raised to shield her from view, looking, she realized, just like a fallen knight lumbering to his feet after being unhorsed. Could this moment be any worse?

Tempy rushed toward the archway, only to find her escape blocked by a large man. She looked up, not wanting to meet his gaze, but what choice did she have?

She locked eyes with a very irritated-looking Mr. Hamlin.

Tempy nearly lost her grip on the silver platter, but then clenched it more tightly than ever. She couldn't squeeze past Hamlin without forcing him to one side, so she stopped short in her headlong rush to freedom.

When she gave Hamlin a look of pleading desperation, she was appalled to see the restrained fury on his face.

"Please," she whispered to this man whose anger seemed to radiate from him in waves of crimson and scarlet. "You must help me. Don't let him see me this way."

Did Hamlin's face soften, almost imperceptibly, at her words? Every atom of her being focused on the man, willing him to help her.

✣   *9*   ✣

ANGELS RUSH IN

⚜

This infuriating woman was a walking disaster. Every time Lucien saw her, she was in the midst of some emotional crisis.

But the pleading look Miss Bliss gave him seemed to thaw something inside him, allowing his heart to beat a bit more smoothly as bits of ice broke free. She seemed to have a great deal of faith in his ability to rescue her from this humiliating situation.

Perhaps too much faith.

Lucien wasn't certain from which gentleman Miss Bliss wished to hide, but he felt certain that it had something to do with her recent abandonment by her faithless fiancé. Despite wanting to remain uninvolved, Lucien couldn't bring himself to peel Miss Bliss's fingertips away from the edge of the cliff to which she now clung only to fling her back to the howling wolves below.

"Boothby," Lucien said, addressing the young footman who had suddenly appeared at Miss Bliss's shoulder, "would you be so kind as to gather the young lady's winnings from the floor?"

Boothby nodded and immediately turned away to fulfill his

task. Lucien then trained his gaze back on Miss Bliss, quickly gauging her level of panic. It was already too high, and he could tell that it was increasing with every moment that passed.

But why was she hoisting that enormous silver platter like a shield? Then, with a flash of comprehension, he understood. Of course. She was hiding behind it.

"This way," Lucien said, putting his hand on her elbow to escort her to safety.

Miss Bliss didn't move. Lucien exerted some gentle pressure, but she remained solidly affixed to that spot on the floor.

Lucien leaned closer to her ear and murmured, "Either come with me now, or face them alone." From his light grip on her arm, he could feel the tremor that his words elicited.

Miss Bliss kept her head down but gave a small nod. This time, when he put a little pressure on her elbow, she allowed him to escort her off the casino floor.

Lucien pulled a key from his pocket as he headed toward the locked door next to the cashiers' windows. He slid it smoothly into the lock and twisted it in a motion he'd made hundreds, no, thousands of times in his life.

But this was the first time he'd ever taken one of the casino's patrons into this area. It went against every rule he'd maintained over the years.

The cashiers looked at them, wide-eyed at this violation of his most sacrosanct rule, but no one made a comment. He frowned as he hurried Miss Bliss back toward the only other door in the cashiers' area. The door to his office.

Thumbing through his key ring, Lucien selected a second key that allowed him passage into his office. Once in the room, he locked the door behind them.

"Thank--" she began, but Lucien wouldn't let her finish.

"It takes a lot of audacity for you to come here when I made it clear that you're not welcome. Don't think you can presume upon me simply because we're both acquainted with Mrs. Kidman."

"But I..."

"There *are* no 'buts,' Miss Bliss. You are entirely in the wrong."

"Yes, I am."

"I--" He stopped. "You admit it?"

"Of course. This entire evening...no," she corrected herself, "I should say this entire *week*, has been one mistake or misjudgment after another. I don't know what's happening to me. I apologize for ignoring your wishes, but I felt so beaten down by everything that's happened to me that I simply had to do something constructive."

Someone knocked at the door, and when Lucien bade them enter, Boothby came in carrying Miss Bliss's tray of winnings. "I think I was able to retrieve most of your chips. One of the cashiers provided me with the amount that you'd withdrawn from your account, and I added your winnings from the roulette table. Unfortunately, some chips still seem to be missing."

"They're probably all here in my bag," Tempy said, bouncing her reticule by its strings so that her chips rattled against one another with a muffled clatter. "I wanted to hold a little in reserve."

She pulled the chips out and laid them on Mr. Hamlin's desk. "Thank you for gathering those for me."

Boothby poked at the pile of five pound chips with one finger, apparently counting them. "It appears that a fifty-pound chip is still missing," Boothby said. "I'm sorry I wasn't able to retrieve them all."

"Perhaps it's under one of the tables," Lucien said. He glanced at Boothby. "Ask the cleaning crew to look for it later. And thank you, Boothby."

The footman nodded at the obvious dismissal and then left the room.

"One?" Miss Bliss cleared her throat. "That won't be necessary." She flushed and pressed her hand to her chest. "It isn't missing."

She slid her index finger and thumb down the front of her bodice, and Lucien couldn't stop his eyes from widening slightly. What on earth was this woman doing? At the next moment, something came flying out of her bosom and smacked him in the forehead.

"Oh, my!" she exclaimed.

Lucien looked at the floor by his feet and saw the object that had struck him. A red-rimmed chip. The missing Hamlin House chip with his "HH" logo imprinted on one side.

He bent over and retrieved it, finding the small object still warm from its nest. Instinctively, his hand closed around the little disk that had so recently been on such intimate terms with Miss Bliss.

He didn't like the direction in which his thoughts were wandering, so he forced himself to relax and unclench his hand, but it wasn't easy. He couldn't quite bring himself to meet Miss Bliss's gaze as he approached her. He stretched out his arm and dropped the chip in her trembling hand, glimpsing the "50" on it before it disappeared in her fist. Where would she put it? His gaze crept back to her cleavage before he flushed and spun on his heel. He quickly retreated to his former position across the room. How could someone as seemingly innocent as Miss Bliss affect him at such a visceral level?

He shook his head, hoping to clear it, and forced himself to focus on the problem at hand. "What precipitated the scene I just witnessed?"

"I was clumsy," she said, quickly depositing the chip in her reticule. Lucien swallowed his disappointment and avoided glancing at her cleavage again. "I took a step backwards and bumped into a man carrying a tray of drinks. It was entirely my fault, I assure you."

"It seems that walking backwards is a problem for you."

She looked at him blankly.

"That's what caused you to fall yesterday at the docks." He couldn't keep the irritation from his voice.

"Oh, no, that wasn't it. You see, I had just seen my fiancé with his new fiancée, and I was in such a state of shock that I tripped."

He shook his head in confusion. "Did you say you saw your fiancé's fiancée? That can't be right."

"It certainly isn't," she said vehemently. "That little French tart is trying to steal my Ernest from me, and I refuse to stand meekly by and allow her to destroy our future together. She doesn't know me well if she thinks I'll..."

He interrupted, sensing a diatribe building. "How does that explain your presence here and the scene I witnessed?"

"Oh. But they're here. Both of them."

"You followed them?"

"No, no. You don't understand. I was already here when they arrived, and I didn't want them to see me, so I hid until I could leave without being noticed. But then I bumped into someone holding a tray, and..., well, you know the rest."

There was another knock at the door and it opened a couple of inches to reveal Boothby.

"Not right now," Lucien said. "I'm busy."

"There's a gentleman by the name of Snowden, sir," Boothby replied through the narrow opening. "Mr. John Snowden. He's asking to see you."

Blast it. Now? The woman's bad luck was beginning to rub off on him. He needed her to leave.

"Is he waiting?"

"He's at one of the roulette tables. He asked that you send for him as soon as you're free."

Lucien sighed. Good. He'd have a moment to move Miss Bliss out of his office. He glanced at her. "This is why I didn't want you here. I have business dealings I need to address with this gentleman, and you are a complicating factor. I need to move this transaction forward smoothly."

She blinked. "Did he say John Snowden?" Miss Bliss asked, her face softening as she said the man's name.

"Why? Do you know him?"

"He was an acquaintance of my father's. I didn't know him well, but he came to our house on business occasionally, and he was always kind to me. He'd recently left the army and had decided to enter the railroad business. I wonder what business he might want to transact with a casino owner."

Lucien stared at her blankly for a moment. This woman, with her odd sense of dress, her unusual interest in journalism, and her obsession with winning back a former fiancé, confounded him. He'd entirely forgotten that her late father had owned Bliss Railways. "I realize that this is an impertinent question, but if you're the daughter of a wealthy man, why do you bother to battle your way through life as a journalist?"

She sighed. "You sound just like my father. Why do people assume that a woman has no desire to do anything meaningful with her life? Men want to accomplish things and nobody believes that it's odd, so why can't women?"

"What about a family? A husband?"

Miss Bliss reddened. "Having a family does not preclude a rich, meaningful life. My mother died when I was young, and my father had little to do with my upbringing. Although I do not plan to pattern my methods of parenting on his example, he allowed me to see that nothing is impossible. It simply takes hard work."

He stared at this unusual woman, startled by her words. How odd to hear something he'd often said coming from the lips of another. Especially from someone so unlikely.

"And society?" he asked, suddenly quite curious. "I'm sure you haven't found it easy to follow this path and still be accepted there."

Miss Bliss sighed. "I haven't. You ask probing questions. Are you certain you want to continue doing so while Mr. Snowden is waiting for you?"

Lucien snapped his jaw shut. How had he allowed himself to become so distracted? This woman was trouble. But maybe..."Perhaps you could help me."

"With what?" She raised one eyebrow. "Closing a deal with Mr. Snowden?"

She was a perceptive thing, wasn't she? "Yes. That's the gist of it." He paused. Did he really want to tell her this? But if she were helping him... "I'm hoping to sell Hamlin House to him."

Her face went slack for a moment, and he could have sworn his announcement surprised her, but she hid her reaction so quickly that he wasn't quite certain he'd seen it. "Tit for tat," she said. "I'll make you an offer. We'll trade something for something. I'll help you woo Mr. Snowden so that you can sell him your casino if you'll agree to help me."

Could she? But what did he have to lose? If she really knew Snowden, as she claimed, then she'd be unlikely to destroy the man's dream of owning a casino. And perhaps she might be of some benefit.

"Deal," Lucien said. He hurried for the door and opened it, finding Boothby standing outside. "Please ask Mr. Snowden to join me, and apologize for keeping him waiting."

❧ 10 ❧

GOALS ALIGN

❦

Tempy's entire body relaxed, and until that moment she hadn't realized how tense she'd been. Not only had Hamlin allowed her to stay, but he seemed to have revealed his reason for not wanting her here. Could this be the secret Mr. Hamlin had been keeping from her? That he was selling Hamlin House?

When John Snowden's broad-shouldered form stepped through the door, the warm smile of greeting she sent him was sincere. After all, without his arrival, Hamlin may well have ejected her from the building for good.

Mr. Snowden's face registered astonishment at seeing her. "Miss Bliss? Good heavens, girl. Aren't you a sight for sore eyes. I haven't seen you in over a year."

"Not since Father's funeral."

Mr. Snowden leaned on his cane as he crossed the room, and the pressure of his weight on it left little divots on the oriental rug as he approached her. She'd forgotten how tall he was.

She gazed up at him as he took her hand in greeting, holding it gently in his massive one. His smile was warm and genuine. There was more gray hair sprouting along his temples than she remembered from a year ago. "I always enjoyed seeing you when you visited Father. How are things going with your railroad?"

She noticed a frown that crossed his face before he disguised it with an unreadable expression. "Well enough," he said with a shrug. "A bit dry. I miss your father's advice. He had a keen insight into that business."

"Can I offer you something to drink?" Lucien asked. "Do you still favor cognac?"

"I can always rely upon you to have a stock of the good French stuff," Snowden said with a nod.

That word again, Tempy thought. *French*. Just as she'd begun to relax long enough to forget about her problems with Ernest and that French tart, that word had jumped up and startled her like a child's jack-in-the-box toy.

She watched as the two gentlemen examined the label on the cognac bottle. They had a similar bearing about them, with their straight backs and broad shoulders. Their elegant evening clothes fit them both perfectly, and they were both relaxed and at ease in Mr. Hamlin's sumptuous office space.

The tall bookcases and large wooden desk were of the same mahogany as the paneled walls. And the red velvet curtains with their gold tasseled trim almost made her feel as though she were performing on stage in one of London's many theaters.

Tempy was pulled from her reverie when Mr. Hamlin halted next to her with a snifter of cognac in his hand. He didn't hold it the same way she'd seen her father hold a glass of wine. Instead, he cradled the bowl of the snifter in the palm of his hand, allowing the stem of the glass to protrude from between his fingers. He swirled the bowl, apparently warming the brownish liquid with the heat of his hand as Father always had. His pale blue eyes were fixed on hers and he wore an expectant expression. Had he spoken to her? "I'm sorry. Could you repeat that?"

"I was telling Mr. Snowden that this is your first time here at Hamlin House."

"Yes," she said, turning her attention to Mr. Snowden. "And I had excellent luck. I won on my first bet at the roulette table."

"You don't say. Black or red?"

"Eight."

Mr. Snowden's eyebrows arched as he pulled his head back in surprise. "Are you telling me you bet on a single number and won? That's astonishing." He took a half-step closer to her. "Perhaps I should join you for the rest of the evening to see if some of that luck rubs off."

"As much as I would enjoy that, I'm afraid I can't linger here. I already used up all of my luck. I had a mishap with a tray of drinks, and my dress is quite ruined." She turned slightly to show him the streaks of wine down the back of her gown, marring the pink silk.

"I'm sorry to hear that. You would have been a delightful companion." Snowden sounded genuinely regretful.

Mr. Snowden had always been a favorite of hers among Father's work associates. Of course, he was one of the few who saw her as an individual rather than as an extension of her father's railroad empire. That, on its own, endeared him to her.

"It seems that I've caught you at an inopportune moment," Snowden said. "Perhaps Lucien and I can have our chat after he's arranged for your safe return home." He shot Mr. Hamlin a pointed look and then jerked his head toward the door, indicating that Mr. Hamlin should join him over there. For a private talk, of course.

Tempy sighed. Mr. Snowden might have been happy to see her, but her presence in the casino was a different matter. If she were to hazard a guess, she'd say that Mr. Snowden didn't approve of her being here.

She needed to address this problem immediately, otherwise Mr. Hamlin might decide to reconsider the agreement they'd struck. "Mr. Hamlin very kindly invited me to visit his casino so that I can conduct some research for an article I'm writing. He has been most generous." There. Let Mr. Hamlin try wriggle out of their deal now that she'd announced it to Mr. Snowden.

Mr. Snowden's rigid posture relaxed, but only slightly. "I must say, that relieves me. I was afraid you might have turned to gambling since your father's passing. You've a fine mind, and I'm glad to hear you're doing something constructive with it."

"Thank you. That means a great deal to me."

"What kind of research are you doing?"

Tempy paused, not sure if she wanted to reveal the topic of her article. What if Mr. Snowden didn't want a journalist spending time in the casino he hoped to purchase? She glanced at Mr. Hamlin to see if he wanted to intercede, but he was no help at all. All he did was raise his eyebrows as if interested in hearing her response.

It would be best to be discreet. "I'm terribly sorry," Tempy said, "but I don't think it would be prudent to discuss it at this time. But as soon as it is, I'll be quite happy to explain everything to you."

"Oh? Now you've aroused my curiosity, Miss Bliss." He smiled at her indulgently. "I hope it doesn't take us another year before we meet again, but if it does, you'll have to tell me all about your research."

Tempy smiled and nodded.

"If you'll excuse me, I'll let you arrange for Miss Bliss to return home," Mr. Snowden said. He turned toward the door, but hooked his hand around Mr. Hamlin's elbow so that he had to walk with him. Even though Mr. Snowden pitched his voice low, Tempy could still follow their conversation.

Apparently, Mr. Snowden was giving Mr. Hamlin a dressing down for inviting her to the casino. She couldn't hear Mr. Hamlin's reply, but then she heard Mr. Snowden say, "...don't think I won't do everything in my power to defend her honor. Just because her father..." She didn't hear the rest of what he said, but she relaxed slightly. He wasn't worried because she was a journalist, but because she was a single young woman. That was a relief.

Mr. Hamlin patted Mr. Snowden on the back reassuringly, and then Mr. Snowden glanced back and gave Tempy a solemn nod before leaving the room.

Mr. Hamlin waited until the door closed behind the departing Mr. Snowden and then turned his attention to Tempy. He was frowning. "You managed that adroitly."

"Hmm?"

He raised a brow. "Telling John Snowden that I agreed to allow you to do your research here. You created enough of a mystery that he'll be certain not to forget it."

So he *had* noticed. That pleased her. "There's more to it than just the research."

"More to what?"

"There's something more I need from you." She licked her lips. "Don't forget, you already agreed to help me before we negotiated the terms."

"Do you mean that you want something more from me other than access to my casino?"

"Yes." She caught her lower lip between her teeth. "It's about my fiancé."

"Isn't he someone else's fiancé now?"

She shot him her most quelling look. "I don't appreciate your flippant tone, Mr. Hamlin."

He raised his hands, palms out and fingers splayed. "You're right. I shouldn't have said that. But how do you expect me to help?"

"I finally came to understand my underlying problem tonight. Men don't want this," she said, her hand sweeping down in a broad gesture toward herself. "They don't want solid responsibility and dependability. They don't want independent thought. They want that." She flicked her hand in the direction of the casino. "They want glamor and excitement. They want risk and the thrill of the chase. And that French woman is the type of person I need to become in order to win Ernest back."

Mr. Hamlin furrowed his brow. "Why do you want to win him back at all? If I'm not mistaken, he's the man you were hiding from in my casino just now, isn't he?"

"Yes."

"From first impressions, he seems a bit easily led, don't you think? Perhaps a bit weak?"

"He certainly is not weak!" Tempy stamped her foot, but the gesture was hidden by her full skirt. "How could you possibly come to that conclusion after seeing him from across a room?"

Mr. Hamlin gave that Gallic shrug again, with his hands splayed wide and his lower lip jutting out just a bit. She was beginning to dislike that shrug. It was much too *French*. "Perhaps I was mistaken, but the woman he was with seemed to be taking the lead."

This caused Tempy to pause. To her knowledge, Ernest had never even been to a casino before tonight. "I think it must have been her idea to come here, so he brought her," she said slowly. "Which serves to prove my point. Men will do anything for a woman like that. Like *her*."

"Not every man," Mr. Hamlin said, sounding a little defensive.

Her temper flared. Why did men always feel they had to defend one another against women? Even men who were complete strangers?

"Ernest will. And since that's what he wants, that's the type of woman I need to become. We made a deal, Mr. Hamlin. I help you sell your casino to Mr. Snowden, and in return, you help me. And helping me means allowing me into your casino, and it also means helping me become more... well, more like *her*."

Mr. Hamlin thrust his chin out. He was going to refuse, she could tell.

"Or, if you prefer, I could find Mr. Snowden right now and let him know that you're trying to manipulate him. It might not prevent him from ever purchasing your casino, but it would certainly cause him to take some additional time in making his decision, don't you agree?"

His only response was a slight tightening of his jaw.

"Or perhaps I could write an article..." she mused.

He flushed. "You surprise me. I had no idea you could be so unscrupulous."

She arched one brow at him. "'All's fair in love and war,' Mr. Hamlin. And this is both."

11

PATRON PROBLEMS

⌘

"I don't like being manipulated this way."

"It's not my fault you assumed too much. If you'd bothered to finish negotiating with me before you accepted the bargain, you wouldn't be in this situation."

That made him pause. She was right. He'd assumed too much when he'd made the deal, and that was unlike him. After all, her obsession with her former fiancé was no secret. "Fine," he said.

Her eyes widened. "Fine?"

"I've noticed that you have a habit of parroting my words." He held up his hands in surrender. "Yes, fine. I formally agree to your bargain since I already unknowingly did so."

Miss Bliss clapped her hands together in a flutter of applause. "Oh, thank you."

"Let's get you home. I'm sorry, but I have a casino to run and some of my responsibilities can't wait." He opened his office door and spoke briefly with Boothby. A moment later the young man returned with Miss Bliss's cloak and the news that a hackney had been procured for her.

"Tomorrow then?" she said.

He nodded his agreement, and she left.

Clearly, Miss Bliss wanted to begin work on this transformation of hers as soon as possible. The entire scheme seemed far-fetched, but Lucien would do his best to fulfill his part of the bargain. And to that end, he had an idea.

An excellent one, for that matter.

Lucien returned to the casino floor with a spring in his step.

Meeting that woman, he had to admit, had been a stroke of luck. Their deal would be mutually beneficial. Snowden clearly doted on the young woman, and she seemed to genuinely like him as well. Now Miss Bliss would be extremely unlikely to write anything that might harm his casino since doing so would hurt Snowden as well.

It only took Lucien a moment to locate young Boothby again. He'd come to rely on the abilities of this young man more and more of late. "She's gone."

"I should mention that she either said or did something earlier in the evening that upset one of the patrons. You can probably guess which gentleman it was."

"Our not-so-favorite earl?" Lucien guessed, referring to the Earl of Sherwood.

"None other."

"I'll bear that in mind. Over the next week or two she'll be visiting here rather frequently. Keep an eye on her, especially when the earl is around."

Boothby nodded. "One more thing. The Viscount of Avignon would like a word with you."

Lucien nodded. The young viscount probably wanted to arrange to use one of the casino's private rooms. Any member of his staff could handle that for him, but Lucien had found that most members of the peerage expected the owner of an establishment such as his to be at their beck and call. It fed their pride. "Is there anything else?"

Boothby hesitated. When Lucien cocked an eyebrow at him, he flushed. "Actually, it's Mme Le Clair, sir. She hoped you'd be able to speak with her tomorrow morning and she asked me to make arrangements."

An easy smile slid across Lucien's face. It was wonderful to see his new plan fall into place as though by fate. "Of course. As a matter of fact, she's exactly the person with whom I hoped to speak." Lucien studied Boothby's reddened face. "There isn't anything wrong, is there?" He glanced around the room to see if he could catch sight of Mme Le Clair.

"She's not here. She sent a note. I think she's hoping for your guidance in a personal matter. Shall I send her a message that you'll see her?"

"Of course. Tomorrow morning would be best." He paused, considering his next words. "I've known Mme Le Clair for many years and count her among my friends."

Boothby took a deep breath, visibly relaxing. "Thank you, sir. I didn't want to impose."

"It's no imposition at all. I'm sure she went through you simply because she wanted to ensure that her message wasn't overlooked." With a nod of dismissal, Lucien turned to go in search of the privileged young Viscount of Avignon.

After arranging for the young peer and his party to have the use of a private room, Lucien made his rounds on the casino floor, shaking hands with a number of patrons as he observed the workings of his casino and made small adjustments as needed.

Lucien noted the sour expression of the face of the Earl of Sherwood and the way he continually drummed his fingers on the bar. That did not bode well. The man had already created some sort of a scene with Miss Bliss, and based on his level of tension, Lucien could tell that another eruption was likely to occur.

Lucien murmured his concern to one of his footmen, and a few moments later a waiter brought the earl a tray of his favorite hors d'oeuvres, compliments of the house. The waiter lingered, ostensibly to ensure that everything was to the earl's liking, but more to fawn over the man and thereby soothe his easily bruised ego. Lucien had discovered years ago that the Earl of Sherwood loved this sort of treatment.

When the earl smiled, Lucien knew that the intervention had worked. He turned his attention back to observing his patrons, searching for the telltale signs of forthcoming problems so that he could avert them.

Dear Ernest and his new fiancée seemed to be on the winning side of things tonight, but Lucien wasn't sure if that was good or bad. The ones who won the first time tended to come back again soon. It was better for them if they lost the first night, and better for Lucien if they won. The odds were always on the casino's side, and eventually he'd recoup all of his losses.

An hour or two later, the crowd was beginning to thin, and the people who remained were in one of two categories. Either they wore jubilant expressions, or they appeared resigned to their losses. There were more of the latter than the former.

Fortunately, nobody appeared overly despairing. When John Snowden approached, Lucien was pleased to note that the man had had a successful evening.

"Is this how you plan to fund your purchase?" Lucien asked with a grin that mirrored Snowden's. "By winning your blunt from my casino? How do you expect me to be able to afford to sell it to you if you break the bank?"

"Funny. You're a funny man," Snowden said, thumping him on the back with the flat of his hand. "I have eyes in my head. You might lose a bit off me tonight, but you've mostly been winning. The house always wins."

"Aye. The trick is to keep everyone coming back for more of the same."

❧ 12 ❧

MEET BOOTHBY'S FRIEND

T he next morning, Tempy paced through the empty casino. She'd been careful on her way here, changing cabs part way here to throw off anyone who might be following her. The gas chandeliers that had been blazing with light last night were now dim. It was as though day and night had traded places here.

She tried to identify the exact location on the rug where she'd knocked over the tray of drinks last night. Nothing remained to mark the incident. Someone must have scrubbed the spot clean.

Tempy moved over to the table where she'd seen a group of men huddled the night before, shouting out strange phrases. It was a crabs table. Crabs was an odd word. Did it have something to do with the crabs one found in the ocean? She'd noticed Ernest standing there as well when she'd departed last night. She'd spent the morning reading about various casino games, so now she knew a bit more about crabs.

Tempy tried to make sense of the markings on the green covering on the table. One of her reference books mentioned that the Americans called the game craps instead of crabs. Why would Americans want to rename it? Especially to such an unpleasant-sounding word. Not that crabs was a particularly pleasant name either. Tempy mentally shrugged off the question. Despite reading about the game, she wasn't sure if she wanted to try her luck at it. She'd need to watch others play it first. But she'd have her chance over the next couple of weeks.

She took a couple of sideways steps to move to a different spot along the edge of the table and then stopped. Here. This was where she'd noticed Ernest standing last night when she'd left the casino. She placed her hand in the spot where she'd seen his resting on the edge of the long table.

Had he won or lost? Had Clarisse celebrated with him, or commiserated?

When the couple had arrived, Clarisse had been elegantly dressed, drawing the attention of every man in the room, just like the woman in red Tempy had observed. How did they both manage to command that kind of attention?

Tempy heard a door open in the otherwise quiet building, and then footsteps approached. Tempy turned and immediately recognized the young footman with the ruddy complexion from the previous evening. His name was Boothby. She smiled in greeting as she took a step toward him.

"Mr. Hamlin is ready to see you, miss," Boothby said, coming to a stop in front of her. But instead of turning and leading the way, he stood there without moving, in that way servants had when they had something they wanted to say. Their manner allowed you to either question them or ignore them. And Tempy could never resist asking a question.

"What is it, Boothby?" she asked. The young man stared at a distant point over her shoulder. Was he frowning slightly? It was difficult to tell in this dim light.

"Mr. Hamlin has another guest in the room with him, and he

plans to introduce her to you." He paused before continuing awkwardly. "She's not the sort of woman ladies normally meet."

"But Mr. Hamlin plans to introduce us anyway?" she asked, her curiosity snapping to attention.

His eyes widened as he met her gaze. "N-not that it is my place to criticize Mr. Hamlin's actions," he stammered. "I would never do anything of the sort. But I wanted you to know that the woman you're about to meet was a close friend of my mother's."

"Of your mother's? But why would meeting her be so unusual?"

"You'll understand soon enough, miss. But she's a good woman, despite what others might think of her. I just wanted you to remember that when you meet her."

She nodded. "I'll bear that in mind. Thank you." She would have said more, but Boothby spun on his heel and began to lead the way to Mr. Hamlin. She fell in behind the young man, trying to puzzle out his words.

Upon entering the office, Tempy virtually ignored Mr. Hamlin and immediately focused her attention on the woman. Since Tempy knew that she was Boothby's mother's friend, she'd expected to meet a working-class woman who was in her mid-forties. But this woman appeared to be younger than that, perhaps in her thirties. And she was most certainly not in the working class.

She was striking, but not beautiful, or at least, not in the traditional sense. Instead of having the light brown hair and pale skin associated with most English beauties, this woman had thick dark hair and a full figure with a narrow waist. But more importantly, she commanded attention in the same way that the woman in the red dress had last night. This woman's attire made her stand out, not because it drew attention to itself, but because it accentuated her every asset so perfectly. Her gown was well-made and conservative, but on her, it looked slightly more seductive than it would on any other woman.

Or did the aura of seduction come from the woman herself? In a flash, Tempy realized *what* this woman must be, and she nearly stumbled over her own feet. She was a member of the demimonde. She wasn't quite a courtesan since she didn't accept payment from gentlemen, but instead she was supported by a wealthy lover. As long as she was discreet, she remained marginally acceptable. And as long as she didn't mingle with the young single women of society, their mothers wouldn't ostracize her.

Here was a woman who understood how to manipulate a man. A demimondaine. And quite a successful one too, judging by her appearance.

This was exactly the sort of woman Tempy needed to meet.

"Thank you for joining us, Miss Bliss," Mr. Hamlin said. "I'd like to introduce you to Madame Le Clair."

The fact that the woman was French startled her. Clarisse Beaumont was French, and Tempy had suddenly developed an intense dislike for everyone from that country. But in this situation, she was willing to make an exception.

Tempy smiled broadly as she moved closer to the woman and offered her hand. "It's a pleasure."

Mme Le Clair hesitated for a moment, and then took Tempy's hand briefly in her own. She quickly withdrew it as though scalded. "*Enchantée*," she said, her eyes darting around the room and looking everywhere except at Tempy.

"I can't tell you how pleased I am to meet you," Tempy said. "I have so many things to ask you."

"Are you certain you want to speak with me?" she asked. Her French accent was faint. "If this were to become known, there could be dreadful consequences for both of us. People would assume the worst."

Tempy waived away the woman's concerns. "I'm sure it wouldn't be catastrophic."

Mme Le Claire fixed her with a cold gaze. "Never underestimate the cruelty of England's upper classes. Once your reputation is ruined, you'll have no way to recover. It would be like trying to put spilled milk back into a pail."

"That's why I arranged for you to meet in my office," Mr. Hamlin interjected. "Your reputation is safe here, and you can ask Mme Le Clair anything you want to know."

"I understand that it would be reckless to be seen together, but I promise I'll be discreet," Tempy said.

"Still, this might not be wise," Mme Le Claire said.

"Where should I begin?" Tempy muttered, more to herself than to the others. "There's so much I want to learn. Not only for my article, but for myself."

"Your article?" Mme Le Clair asked, stiffening. "Are you referring to a newspaper article?"

Tempy nodded. "I'm writing about the effects of gambling and casinos on women."

"I couldn't possibly allow you to use my name in an article such as that. I'm known for my discretion, and I refuse to allow my name to appear in print."

"Oh, my, of course," Tempy said. "I never meant to suggest that I'd mention your name. Everything would remain anonymous. I want to inform my readers, not titillate them with gossip."

Mme Le Clair shook her head. "I don't think I can take that risk."

"I promise, I won't put you at risk," Tempy said, reaching out to touch the woman's forearm. "Don't you see? We're both taking a chance by meeting with each other. After all, if I were to break my promise and reveal you as a source, I would be opening myself up to criticism as well. Oh, please, Mme Le Clair. I need your help. I can't do this without you."

The woman paused, looking doubtful. "You mentioned that you needed my help not just for the article, but for yourself. What did you mean by that?"

Tempy felt the blood rushing to her cheeks and she turned

away, putting a couple of paces between herself and Mme Le Claire. This was humiliating, but how could she get the help she needed if she wasn't willing to ask?

She glanced at Mr. Hamlin, embarrassed to have him witness the exchange.

When their eyes met, a look of comprehension crossed his face. He had been leaning against the edge of his desk as he observed them, but now he stood up straight, saying, "If you ladies will excuse me, there are some matters to which I must attend." He walked out the door, closing it behind him with a click.

"Lucien has a talent for discretion," Mme Le Claire murmured.

"That's good to know," Tempy said, and began pacing the length of the room. She wondered, briefly, at the woman's use of Mr. Hamlin's given name, but quickly squelched her curiosity since the question was irrelevant. "My personal life has been through a tremendous amount of upheaval recently, and Mr. Hamlin is aware of much of it." She glanced over at Mme Le Clair as she passed her. "I'm determined to make some changes in order to repair things."

"What sorts of changes?"

"Changes in myself." Tempy caught her lower lip between her teeth as she searched for the right words. "I've decided that I need to undergo a transformation in order to become the type of woman my former fiancé finds desirable. This," Tempy glanced over her shoulder as she made a gesture indicating her entire self, "won't do." As she neared the fireplace, she felt the heat emanating from it, and spun around to retrace her path toward a cooler part of the room.

"What is it you wish to become?" Mme Le Clair asked, as her gaze followed Tempy's movements.

"Someone elegant and in control. Someone more like you," Tempy said, gesturing toward the other woman. "Someone who *knows* what a man wants, or even better, knows how to *tell* him what he wants. That's what his new fiancée can do." Tempy increased her pace, taking longer strides. Moving this way helped keep her nervous energy under control.

"So you want to learn the tricks of a courtesan, do you? And you think I can teach them to you? That's a rather ambitious goal. And I don't think it's one I'm suited to help you with. I think you may have misunderstood who, and what, I am."

Tempy blushed. "I'm sorry. For someone who makes a living with words, you'd think I could speak more clearly. I'm sorry if I offended you. I did *not* assume you were a courtesan. But you have a lover, don't you? A wealthy one?"

Mme Le Clair didn't say anything, but continued to stare at her coldly.

"I'm sorry again. That was rude of me. But this is what I mean. It's why I need your help. I am unpolished and unable to make a man find me appealing, and I want to change. If you'd be willing to work with me...to help smooth out the rough edges..."

"First of all, you must stop pacing," Mme Le Clair said, pressing her fingers to her temples as she closed her eyes. "The way you dart about the room makes me feel as though I'm watching a game of lawn tennis, and I've always found that particular entertainment tedious."

Tempy stopped short, her insides vibrating with excitement. Was Mme Le Clair on the verge of agreeing to help her?

The woman let out a sigh and stared at Tempy. "That can be your first lesson. A lady always appears calm and restful. She never paces about. At least, not where a gentleman can see her."

Tempy's eyes widened. "You'll do it?"

The woman nodded. "But only as a favor to Lucien."

"Thank you," Tempy said, and rushed toward Mme Le Clair. "You don't know what this means to me."

"Slowly, slowly," Madame said, recoiling slightly. "You aren't in a footrace. A lady needs to appear to insinuate herself across the floor."

Tempy paused for a moment. How did one "insinuate" oneself? Then she began walking again in an exaggerated glide. "Like this?"

"That's slightly better," Mme Le Clair said, lifting her chin, "but don't move in such an obvious manner." She nodded when Tempy modified her stride. "Keep your shoulders even. Don't bob them from side to side."

Tempy made the adjustments, trying to eliminate any bounciness from her gait while simultaneously *insinuating* herself across the room. She looked around, but didn't see a mirror anywhere in Mr. Hamlin's office. She'd have to do something about that.

"Better." Mme Le Claire sank gracefully into a chair by the fireplace and focused her attention on Tempy in a rather intimidating manner. "Walk toward the door, turn, and come back to me."

Tempy followed the directions and watched Mme Le Claire for her reaction. "Is that better?"

"Yes, but keep your head level. You'll need to practice this at home. Place a book on your head and make sure it doesn't fall off. I assume you wish to progress quickly. Shall we meet daily?"

Tempy came to a halt and nodded, hardly believing her luck.

"I can't stay at the moment," Mme Le Claire said, "but I can return later this afternoon to resume your lessons. At that time, we will create a schedule for when we will meet over the next week." Then Mme Le Claire rose gracefully from her chair and *insinuated* herself across the office and out into the foyer. Tempy followed.

At the front doors of the casino, Mme Le Clair stopped and turned to face Tempy. "One final point, Miss Bliss. I am giving you my time, and in return, I expect hard work and strict obedience from you. I am providing my assistance to you as a favor to Mr. Hamlin, so don't abuse my good will. If you do as I say, you should have this young man of yours falling over himself to get back into your good graces. Once he's there, you can decide what you want to do with him."

For the first time in days, hope lifted its forlorn head, like a tired old dog hearing its master's return after a long absence.

This might actually work. She might finally have a real chance at winning Ernest back.

13

AN ERNEST ENCOUNTER

Nearly a week later, Mr. Hamlin's normally tidy office was strewn with items from Tempy's wardrobe, and it looked as though a disorganized dressmaker had taken up residence in the room.

At Mme Le Clair's request, Tempy had sent most of her dresses to the casino so that they could examine them together. When Tempy had suggested that Mme Le Clair simply come to her house, the woman had just sighed her annoyance at the suggestion and then ignored it.

Now, Tempy gazed into the tall mirror next to the office door that Mr. Hamlin had added for her use. After a week of lessons with the demanding Mme Le Clair, Tempy already noticed a difference in the reflection facing her. Gone was the simple hair style she'd had for years. At Madame's insistence, Tempy had hired Mary, a highly recommended lady's maid, through a London employment agency. Mary was particularly adept at arranging Tempy's hair.

In the past, Tempy would typically run her brush through her hair and pull it back, pinning the locks up in a simple bun. But over the past three days, her routine had changed. Now she sat at her vanity each morning and allowed Mary to tease, braid, and curl her hair into one of many new, more fashionable styles.

On their first day together, Mary had demonstrated a few different ways she could arrange Tempy's hair, trying out various looks to see what they both found pleasing. Experimenting had taken some time, but Mary assured her that it was essential. She'd also used some sort of special rinse on Tempy's hair. It had smelled horrible at the time, but now when Tempy looked in the mirror, her hair seemed to have more depth and a variety of subtle shadings of color. Who knew something that smelled so vile could have such a transformative effect upon her appearance?

This morning, Mary had plaited two sections of Tempy's hair starting at her temples and then pulled them back to encircle a bun at the back of Tempy's head. Mary's fingers were deft, and she was finished within two minutes. It would have taken Tempy just as long to create her simple bun that shed loose hairpins all day.

Now, Tempy shifted her weight so that she could see Mr. Hamlin's reflection in the mirror. He sat at his desk, and the rather sour expression he had been wearing all morning was still in place. For some reason, he'd decided to stay in his office to review some ledgers, but she'd noticed that he was having some difficulty keeping his attention from wandering. She frequently caught him watching them.

Mme Le Clair raised her chin, looking down her nose at Tempy's wardrobe. "Although the quality is excellent, these dresses are all much too frilly. Perhaps if we were to adjust the necklines a bit, some of them might do, but really, you need some new gowns."

Mr. Hamlin threw his pen onto his desktop and shoved back his chair as he rose to his feet. "I must protest. I find Miss Bliss's gowns to be quite attractive. I've seen her in a number of them, and I can find no fault."

Mme Le Clair shot him a stony glare. "I hardly think that you, with your limited knowledge of the subject, are in the position to be judging women's attire, but that's beside the point. We are attempting a transformation, and one of the speediest ways to accomplish it is through a new wardrobe."

Mr. Hamlin strode around his desk to stand face-to-face with Mme Le Clair, and Tempy continued to watch the exchange, wide-eyed, from across the room. "It may merely be my own *limited* opinion," he said, "but I believe that Miss Bliss possesses qualities that are rare in a woman and quite desirable. It's an enormous mistake for her to paint over an original work of art simply to replace it with something else that is more commonplace. She doesn't need to pretend to be like you. She already has assets that can't be duplicated."

Tempy blushed deeply at those words. Assets? What on earth was he talking about? Her money?

"Mr. Hamlin!" Mme Le Clair's voice swelled with indignation.

"I was referring to her youth and her belief that she can conquer the world," he said, holding his hands up to ward off her wrath. Unfortunately, he smiled, ruining any possibility that Mme Le Clair wouldn't take offense. "Why must young women always be completely unaware of the attraction these simple things hold for men?" He rounded on Tempy. "Why do you want to pretend to be jaded by the world? You need to revel in your wholehearted enjoyment of new experiences. Wear it like a flag. Don't pretend to be yet one more bored young aristocrat. Hamlin House is full of those."

"I beg to differ, Mr. Hamlin," Tempy said, striding across the room to face him. "If youth and an unjaded attitude toward life are so desirable, then why do men seek the company of courtesans? Hmm? Why don't they simply stand outside the doors of a finishing school and whisk away the first girl who walks through them?"

"That would be rather crass, wouldn't it?" His eyes caught Tempy's for a moment, but then he looked away.

Mme Le Clair laughed. "But that's simply the nature of men. They have an angel on one shoulder and a devil on the other. The angel guides the man to marry one type of woman, and the devil entices him to desire the other. If he can ever find that one unique woman both his angel and his devil agree upon, then he will be content."

Tempy stifled a snort of laughter. "You're telling me that what men really want is to find an innocent seductress?"

"That's ridiculous," Mr. Hamlin said, losing some of his aplomb. "Of course they don't."

Mme Le Clair ignored him. "Yes. Exactly that. Yet they deceive even themselves. I think all of the rules the modern Englishman must follow in this age have only served to repress his passions, leaving him in a sort of perpetual torment."

Mr. Hamlin snorted. "I can't believe you are teaching her such drivel. I can't listen to any more of this." He shook his head as he stormed from the room, slamming the door behind him.

Mme Le Clair smiled. "You are already beginning to elicit a reaction in men."

Tempy's eyes widened and she glanced at the office door. "You mean..."

"Yes. Mr. Hamlin. I think he finds you intriguing. And that's exactly the effect we want you to have upon men. I think it's time to reveal you to your Ernest. But only a peek. Just enough to make him curious. In fact, we need to make him burn with curiosity. It will be essential for us to keep the meeting brief."

Tempy glanced at the closed door, thinking about Mme Le Clair's offhand comment. Was she right? Was Mr. Hamlin intrigued by her?

"What do you think of the idea?" Mme Le Clair prompted.

Tempy glanced back at her and noted a curious expression on the woman's face. "About having Ernest see me?" She shook her head. "I don't know. Do you really think I'm ready?"

"Most certainly."

Tempy's chest tightened at the thought, but she nodded anyway. "Then I'll rely on your judgment. I just hope I don't do anything foolish."

With a satisfied smile, Mme Le Clair nodded. "You'll be fine. Here," she said, and then picked up one of Tempy's dresses. "This one should do." She took advantage of Mr. Hamlin's departure and draped the dress over the surface of his desk. It was pale pink with rows of rosettes along the neckline and dotting the skirt. "Lucien does, however, make a good point about appearing innocent and unjaded. It can be quite enticing."

Mme Le Clair took a pair of sewing scissors and began snipping away the satin roses dotting the neckline. "Yes. Much better." By the time she was done, she had also removed some of the ruffles and flounces, giving the dress a more elegant look.

"Let's discuss cosmetics," Madame said. "Too much is worse than none at all. You only need a touch."

Apparently, she had arrived that day armed with a variety of bottles and jars, all in slightly different shades. First she put a touch of pink on Tempy's cheeks. Next, she chose a color just a shade darker than that of Tempy's lips and applied it with a small brush. As the final touch, she used a short, stiff brush to darken Tempy's eyelashes.

"There," Madame said, stepping back to examine her handiwork. "One last thing." She turned away to search through her containers, opening and closing them as she searched for the item she wanted.

Tempy took the opportunity to look at her face in the mirror and was startled. It was her, but not quite her. She still looked like herself, yes, but it was as though someone had created a new, crisper version of her face. She thought of the photos she'd seen, by that photographer, Lady Clementina Hawarden, and of her examples of both sharp and blurred images. Somehow, Mme Le Clair had merged those two ideas and had created a version of her face that looked both softer and clearer.

"Here we go," Mme Le Clair said, approaching Tempy with a large, soft-bristled brush. It was about an inch in diameter, and the soft bristles were about two inches long. There was powder on it, and before Tempy realized what Madame was doing, she had plunged the brush into Tempy's cleavage.

"Oh!" Tempy jumped.

"I'm sorry," Madame said, grinning, "but I couldn't think of a good way to tell you what I intended to do. You'll notice that the slightly darker powder helps to deepen your cleavage just a bit without being obvious."

Tempy did see. "It all comes down to choosing the right colors, doesn't it?" She glanced at the clock. "We need to leave and let Mr. Hamlin have his office back. It's getting late."

Mary, Tempy's new maid, began to bustle around the room, packing the dresses back in the trunks so that they could be sent home.

"Why don't you leave now," Mme Le Clair suggested, "and I'll follow along later."

Tempy nodded and hurried toward the door. She had her head down as she swung it open, and when she stepped through it she walked straight into Mr. Hamlin.

Tempy stumbled back, and Mr. Hamlin grabbed her by her elbows to steady her. When she looked up at him, her face was inches from his. She inhaled the pleasant aroma of his soap and cologne.

He froze in place and stared at her with a bemused expression.

"I'm sorry," she said. Her voice sounded slightly husky, so she swallowed before trying to speak again. "I was just leaving. We ran a little late today." She breathed in deeply, feeling momentarily engulfed by Mr. Hamlin, and was surprised that she enjoyed the sensation.

He cleared his throat, still staring at her. "That's not a problem," he said.

"Well, then," she said "I should be going." She pulled her arms from his grasp and took a small step away from him.

He pulled his hands back as though he'd forgotten he still held her. "Good day, Miss Bliss."

"Good day, Mr. Hamlin."

As she crossed the foyer toward the main exit, she could feel his eyes on her.

She rode home feeling quite uplifted by the day's events.

She spent an hour working on her article for Mr. Dickens. She liked the direction, but something was missing from it. It needed a sharper focus, but she wasn't certain which particular lens she should use. There were a number of aspects that deserved more attention, but she knew that the article would be stronger if she chose a single focal point.

As she stared at her pages, a thought struck her. If she wanted to "accidentally" meet Ernest, she'd need to arrange a meeting. She smacked herself in the forehead with the palm of her hand. How could she be so foolish?

Tempy pulled out a fresh sheet of paper and immediately penned a note to Ernest's sister, Emily, asking to meet her for tea the following day. She glanced out the window and saw the postman approaching her door on one of his eight daily mail deliveries. How did people manage to live in the country with only one mail delivery daily? London was much more civilized.

She hurriedly stuffed the note into an envelope and affixed postage. When she flung the door open, the postman was obviously startled to see her. When she shoved the envelope in his hand, he smiled and handed her the two letters he was holding. One was from her lawyers, and the other was from Millicent.

Millicent would be returning from her travels in a few days, and the railroad's board of directors was again pressuring her to sell the railroad. She penned her reply, as she always did, emphatically rejecting their request. Father would rise from the dead if she ever sold Bliss Railways.

A couple of hours later, Tempy received a reply from Emily in which she agreed to rendezvous with Tempy at Pink's Tea Room.

The next day, Tempy used one of her many circuitous routes to meet Emily. It would ruin her plans if Earl E. Byrd decided to inform all of London about her meeting with Emily. When Tempy arrived at the appointed time, she looked in through the red-mullioned window panes of Pink's Tea Room and saw that Emily was already seated at a table for two.

"Tempy," Emily said, rising to her feet as Tempy joined her at the table. "It's so good to see you. I've missed you terribly." She gave a sisterly embrace, pressing her cheek against Tempy's.

After they'd ordered tea, they chatted about a few inconsequential things. Tempy waited for their order to arrive before she broached the subject of Ernest. "I heard that your brother went to a casino last week."

"Oh, I know. Isn't it terrible? Mother was so upset, especially because he won."

"Why is winning so bad?" Tempy asked, lifting her teacup.

"Because now he's keen to return and win again. He calls it easy money."

"What about your father?"

"He says it's important for a young man to see more of the world. *I* think he's just worried about Ernest moving to Paris."

"What?" Tempy asked, almost spilling her tea. She quickly set it down. "When did he decide to do that?"

Emily smirked. "Apparently Clarisse's father offered him a position in his bank. Mother's beside herself."

"And your father wants him to go?"

"No. I don't believe so. But I think he's wondering if he should have allowed Ernest to have more experiences on his own.

He even suggested that Ernest go back to the casino again on Friday night."

Clarisse would have helped him celebrate his good fortune on that first night. They must have been so excited. Tempy frowned as she imagined them together. "Will he go back to the same casino or try a different one?"

"Oh, the same one, most certainly. He says he's lucky there. He's quite looking forward to it."

"And what about you? How do you feel about all of this?"

"Oh, Tempy. I hate it all. I don't want our family torn apart this way." She let out a deep sigh. "I just wish we had you back and that Ernest would come to his senses."

She reached out and covered Emily's hand with her own. "So do I. Please tell your parents I miss them."

On Friday evening, Tempy's own carriage carried her to Hamlin House for a change of pace, and it dropped her off directly in front of the main entrance. She'd been hesitant to take the chance that Byrd would follow her, but tonight she couldn't risk relying on a cab. She could've very well spend her life trying to avoid being written about. If she did, she might never leave her house.

One of her footmen opened the carriage door and assisted her as she exited the conveyance. "We'll be waiting just there, miss," her footman said, indicating the space that was being held for her coach. Her quick departure was an important element of the plan, because they needed to ensure that Ernest didn't have the opportunity to waylay her. In order to facilitate that aspect of the evening, Mr. Hamlin had arranged for her carriage to have a spot near the casino entrance.

Mr. Hamlin had also volunteered to help them with another important part of their plan. Since Ernest needed to believe that other men also found Tempy desirable, Mr. Hamlin had offered to play the role of an enamored suitor.

A tremor of anticipation ran through Tempy at the thought of having Mr. Hamlin at her side. He was so handsome and worldly. Any woman would be proud to be with him. She'd never seen him with any particular woman, but she could only imagine him with someone sophisticated, like that woman in red.

Over the past couple of days, Mr. Hamlin had become more intense and brooding, and that made her a little uneasy. Especially when he pinned her with that piercing gaze of his. It had become worse since the discussion about altering her dresses, and she frequently found herself blushing under his examination. He'd quickly look away, leaving her uncertain as to whether or not he'd really been staring at her, but it still caused her to feel self-conscious.

She'd need to be more in control of her emotions tonight.

When Tempy entered the casino, she didn't go to the gaming floor. Instead, she headed directly for Mr. Hamlin's private office.

Mme Le Clair turned to greet Tempy as she entered the room. The woman examined her from head to toe, finally nodding her approval. "You look marvelous, Temperance. You'll create just the right impression." For some reason, Mme Le Clair had taken to calling her Temperance and refused to use the name Tempy.

Tempy's tension eased at hearing those words. She hadn't realized how much she'd needed Mme Le Clair's approval.

"Confidence is what will carry you through this," Mme Le Clair said. "It's the key to your success. You look the part, which is half the battle, but you must also act the part."

Tempy nodded and then squared her shoulders.

The door knob rattled, causing Tempy to start. She glanced at Mme Le Clair in embarrassment, wondering if the woman had noticed that she wasn't quite as confident as she was pretending to be. Fortunately, her attention was focused on the opening door. Tempy followed her gaze.

As Mr. Hamlin swept into the room, his elegant black frock coat opened slightly to reveal an indigo satin waistcoat with slightly paler swirls of purple dancing across it. The sight of it brought a smile to Tempy's lips.

Upon seeing the unconventional waistcoat, Mme Le Clair pursed her lips into a moue. She gave it a pointed stare but refrained from commenting. "I'm glad you were able to join us. I wanted to see the two of you together before your little performance begins."

Mr. Hamlin bowed his head in reply. "Always at your service."

"Come closer. I want you to stand next to each other," she commanded.

Mr. Hamlin crossed the room in long strides as he complied with her request, and Tempy took a step back from his sudden approach.

Mme Le Clair turned a look of censure on Tempy. "Just as I feared. You're quite nervous around the man. How will you convince this Ernest person that your affections belong to Lucien if you behave in such a skittish manner toward him?"

"I am most certainly *not* skittish," Tempy said, embarrassed to have Mme Le Clair see through her so easily. "It's simply that Mr. Hamlin is a rather large man. I wanted to give him some room."

Mme Le Clair's head tilted to one side. "I believe I have identified the root of the problem. Your relationship with Lucien is much too formal. In order for your ruse to work, you must relax around him. Let's begin by having you call him Lucien."

"Lucien?" Tempy said, feeling the soft word slide from her lips. There was something quite seductive about that name. Something luscious. She smiled at that.

"Ah, yes. See? This less formal mode of address begins to work its magic already. And you, *monsieur*, must address her as Tempy. Not Temperance or Miss Bliss. This is very important. You must show the man that your relationship with her is stronger than his."

"Of course. It will be my pleasure to address her as Tempy."

He stressed the 'm' in her name, making it sound more like a caress, and Tempy felt the hairs on the back of her neck rise up in response. She glanced into his eyes, but when a rush of heat pooled in her belly, she quickly looked away. How could hearing him say her name have such an alarming effect on her?

"Temperance, you haven't practiced taking a man's arm. Let's take a moment to do that, shall we? Watch." Mme Le Clair stepped closer to Lucien and brushed his forearm with the back of her fingers. He lifted his arm and offered it to her. Her hand slid through the crook of his arm in a smooth, languid motion and then rested lightly on his forearm. "There. An elegant movement with no fumbling or bumping of body parts. Your hand must be as light as a hummingbird on his sleeve." She released her hold on him and stepped away. "You try."

Tempy had become used to Mme Le Clair's precise instructions, but being this close to Mr. Hamlin...or rather, *Lucien*, made her self-conscious. As she reached for the arm he offered, she rushed the movement and bumped his arm with her hand, fumbling as she slid it into place on his forearm.

"Again," said Madame. "And with a bit more grace."

Tempy dropped her hand away, earning a disapproving look from Mme Le Clair. With an apologetic twitch of her shoulder, she reached for Lucien's arm again, this time managing to make her movement appear much more natural and graceful.

"Better. Now, try it again, but this time, look up at Lucien with affection. It should appear as though placing your hand on his arm is the thing which you *most* want to do at that moment."

Tempy raised her brow at that.

"Don't look at me that way," Mme Le Clair scolded. "You are playing a role. Do it well."

Tempy tilted her head as she accepted the good sense of the advice, and then looked up at Lucien as she tried to throw herself into her role. She slid her hand into place and kept her gaze locked on his.

For a moment, the playacting seemed to fade, and the moment felt real. Right now, she truly *wanted* to feel his arm under her hand more than anything else in the world. When she realized that she wasn't acting, a chill crossed her shoulders and her hand trembled very slightly on his sleeve.

"Perfect," Mme Le Clair sighed. "You're quite the clever student."

Before Tempy could respond, she heard a knock at the door. Boothby opened it.

"Sir," he said, "the gentleman you asked me to watch for is arriving in his carriage. He should be in the casino momentarily."

Mme Le Clair took a small step away from them. "It's time. Go. Just as we planned."

Tempy nodded and took leave of the pair. Outside the office door, she took a deep breath, raised her chin slightly, and glided through the entrance of the glittering casino.

A shadow followed her. And when she looked back, she saw that Boothby hovered at her elbow.

He smiled at her. "Good evening, Miss Bliss. If you will permit me, I'll collect your chips from the cashier and bring them to you."

"Yes, thank you," she said as she continued toward the roulette table. She remembered not to simply walk, but to insinuate herself, just as Mme Le Clair had taught her. In doing so, she was aware that a number of gentlemen watched her openly, and she smiled in satisfaction.

She stopped at the same spot at the roulette table where she'd stood a week ago. Tonight required that she choose a casino game where she could be noticed and then quickly abandon. Roulette suited her needs perfectly.

She watched some other patrons gamble for a minute, and then Boothby slid her rack of chips in front of her. She turned to smile her thanks to the young man and was startled to discover she'd been mistaken.

"Mr. Hamlin," she said in a flustered tone. "Are you in the habit of bringing your patrons their chips?"

"Lucien," he corrected. "And, no I don't usually take on that task. But in your case, I'm happy to."

He smiled down at her, and Tempy felt her toes curl in her shoes. My, but that man's smile was devastating. Why hadn't she ever noticed that before? His lips were full and curving, and his teeth were even and straight, except for that one tooth, right next to the front one, that tilted slightly to one side with a rakish air.

She gave herself a mental shake. It wouldn't do to be staring at the man like this when Ernest walked into the casino. He might think she was infatuated with the illustrious Lucien Hamlin.

But wait a minute, that was her goal, wasn't it? After all, Tempy's sense of competition had peaked once she'd had a rival for Ernest's affections. Wasn't that the reason Mr. Hamlin...Lucien, was standing next to her?

Suddenly, Lucien's charismatic smile no longer seemed to belong to her. After all, he was simply playacting for the benefit of an audience. This wasn't real.

Not real at all.

She smiled brightly at him. "How shall I place my bet? Do you have any advice?"

"I'll give you the same advice that has always worked well for me. I find I win every time I follow it."

She raised her eyebrows and looked up at him expectantly.

He leaned down so that his mouth was close to her ear, and she felt his breath on her neck. In a quiet rumble, he murmured in her ear, just loud enough for her to hear. "Always remember," he said, his low voice sending vibrations down her spine, "to place your bet on the winning number."

She inhaled his scent of crisply bleached cotton, men's cologne, and the lingering aroma of cognac. For a moment she felt trapped in a web-thin cocoon by his nearness, unable to move or respond, but then she broke free. His words sank in. "Bet on the winning number? That's your sage advice?" she quipped, wondering if her voice sounded as breathless as she felt.

"Works every time," he said, in tones still pitched so low that only she could hear him.

She smiled, still feeling the tendrils of that web of intimacy he'd spun around her. When she glanced away shyly, searching for a safe landing for her gaze, it fell upon Ernest. His mouth was agape as he stared at her.

"Temperance. What on earth are you doing here?" Ernest demanded.

Tempy smiled serenely, just the way Mme Le Clair had taught her. She tilted her head to one side and said, "Mr. Lipscomb. How pleasant to see you here. Is this your new fiancée?" She was surprised at how calm she felt. It was as though a languid haze surrounded her.

Ernest's gaze flew from Tempy to Clarisse and back again, not quite knowing where to stop. Apparently, he either chose to return his gaze to Tempy or his eyes simply got tired of rattling around in his head. But he didn't seem capable of speaking quite yet, so Tempy decided to fill the silence.

"You must be Miss Clarisse Beaumont." Tempy paused for a moment, but the young woman didn't reply. Tempy glanced back at Ernest. "I can see why she stole your heart, Mr. Lipscomb. She's quite beautiful."

"I cannot steal something which is given to me freely," Clarisse said in a clear, French accent. Her stinging words were softened by her beautiful voice and practiced smile.

"Oh. And she has her wits about her too. I'm impressed," Tempy said.

"Please, Temperance. Don't make a scene," Ernest said. His eyes were wide and round, as though he expected Tempy to lose control at any moment.

Tempy waved away his fears with a graceful fluttering of her hand. "I wouldn't dream of it. But please, for your fiancée's sake, don't you think you should refrain from calling me Temperance? I'm afraid it gives the wrong impression."

Ernest blushed. "I..., I mean..., but of course." He glanced in embarrassment at Mr. Hamlin, clearly unhappy at being reprimanded in front of a stranger.

Tempy glanced up at Lucien. "Do you two know each other? No? This is Mr. Hamlin. Of Hamlin House."

If possible, Ernest managed to flush even more deeply.

"Mr. Hamlin, this is Mr. Lipscomb, a childhood friend of mine, and his charming fiancée, Miss Clarisse Beaumont."

"*Enchanté*," Lucien said, lifting the young woman's gloved fingertips to his lips.

The young woman's eyes glowed. "*Vous êtes Français?*"

"*Oui. Demi-français.*"

"Half French?" Tempy asked, feeling somehow betrayed. "You never mentioned that."

"I didn't? My mother was French."

Tempy wasn't certain how she felt about that. After losing Ernest to that little French tart, Tempy had decided to abhor all things French. Of course, Mme Le Clair had begun to sway her opinion. But Madame was only one person. Discovering that Lucien was half French was more than a little disconcerting.

Tempy sighed, remembering to use the practiced pout that Mme Le Clair had taught her. "I suppose this will force me to reexamine my opinion regarding all things French. Perhaps they have some merit to them after all."

Lucien's eyes twinkled at her back-handed compliment, but Miss Beaumont's eyes narrowed at the slight.

Lucien cleared his throat. "Tempy, there's someone I'd very much like you to meet. If you'll do me the favor of accompanying me, I'd like to introduce you to the Earl of Penworth."

This had been their prearranged signal to leave. Mme Le Clair had been worried that Tempy might overstay the moment once she had the upper hand, and she had insisted that Lucien remove her from the situation at the appropriate time. Tempy nodded very slightly to let him know she recognized the signal and then smiled broadly to Ernest. "I do hope you'll excuse us."

"Certainly," Ernest said, looking appropriately impressed at the mention of the influential young earl.

Lucien held out his arm and Tempy slipped her fingers around it, gazing up into his eyes as she did so. Her hand rested delicately upon his arm, and she allowed him to escort her away from the stunned couple. Tempy glided as she moved. She did not saunter or rush. She insinuated. But inside, it was all she could do not to howl her triumph at that moment.

Even though Tempy didn't glance back, she could easily overhear Clarisse's hissing, scolding tones and Ernest's murmured sounds of protest. A slow smile of satisfaction spread across her face. What she'd give to hear the tongue-lashing Ernest must be receiving right now.

14

MORE LESSONS?

L ucien glanced down at Tempy and liked what he saw. Especially the smile on her face. It was slow and seductive and eminently satisfied. Even though she maintained a sedate and steady pace as she crossed the casino, he could feel the exhilaration radiating from her. It almost made her float across the room. Lucien wondered if her feather-light hold on his arm was the only thing that kept her tethered to the ground.

"Try to contain your jubilation," Lucien murmured. "You're vibrating with it." He glanced back at the couple. "They're watching us."

"Then I'll turn that to our advantage," she said, beaming up at him.

The jolt that hit Lucien took him by surprise, but he was even more startled by the surge of envy he felt for that pretty-boy, Ernest Lipscomb.

Suddenly, they were standing directly in front of the Earl of Penworth. Lucien greeted him with a smile and introduced

Tempy, but then he dropped out of the conversation and used the moment to observe Mr. Lipscomb.

Lucien had to admit, Lipscomb had a style about him that certain women preferred. That combination of an athletic build and glossy blond hair often attracted women like bees to clover, and apparently Tempy had developed a fondness for that man's variety of honey. But there was something about him that Lucien didn't like. Some weakness of will that showed in his overly pretty features.

Or perhaps the twinge of envy he'd felt a few moments ago was affecting his judgment. Either way, he no longer wanted to be in the same room with the man.

At an appropriate lull in Tempy's conversation with the earl, Lucien made their excuses and led her away. She never looked back at Ernest Lipscomb and his detestable "French tart," but Lucien could sense that her attention was focused on the couple.

"Our friend will be anxious to hear about what just transpired," Lucien said as he made his way toward his office door.

Tempy nodded and looked up at him again, delivering another one of those gazes that hit him like a thunderbolt. If Mme Le Clair could see her now, she'd be proud of what she'd created.

As they crossed the casino floor, Lucien took one last opportunity to glance back at Mr. Lipscomb. The man was watching their progress across the room with a strange expression on his face. He appeared both confused and deflated, and his attention was fixed upon Tempy.

Just as he knew she'd hoped.

So why couldn't he feel more pleased with her success?

Lucien turned the cool brass knob of his office door and pushed his way inside. Mme Le Clair awaited them, looking triumphant. Her telltale flush and broad grin were dead giveaways.

"I couldn't resist. I watched it all from the doorway," she

announced. She took both of Tempy's hands in hers. "You were perfect. I couldn't be more proud of you."

Tempy appeared to glow under her praise. "Do you really think so? That's what I thought too, but I wasn't certain."

"A complete triumph. You have him so off balance he has no idea what's happening to him. He's exactly where you want him." Madame tilted her head to one side in a contemplative gesture and gave Lucien a conspiratorial look. "We should celebrate. Whiskey?"

"No," Lucien said. "Champagne." He called for a bottle and was pleased when Boothby returned within moments, carrying a silver tray. On it were three champagne flutes and a rather large silver wine cooler. The wine cooler was a tall, urn-shaped container with two ornate side handles, and it was filled with ice. Nestled in its embrace was a dark green champagne bottle.

Boothby offered to pop the cork, but Lucien shook his head and began twisting the wire holding the cork in place.

"Will you be needing anything else?" Boothby asked.

Lucien grinned at him as the cork popped from the bottle and went flying toward the ceiling. It bounced off with a soft sound and fell to the carpet where it rolled to a stop at Tempy's feet. "We'll be fine. Don't worry about us," he said, and waved Boothby from the room.

Lucien poured champagne into the glasses and passed them to the ladies.

He watched as Tempy held her glass up to the light, examining the lines of bubbles rising to the top of the glass. Had she never had champagne before this? He cleared his throat. "We should toast."

Tempy's face brightened. "Yes. A toast. But to what?"

Madame raised her glass. "To success."

"Success," Lucien repeated, and touched the rim of his glass against the others. The crystal emitted a bright ringing sound as the champagne flutes bumped against each other.

Both he and Mme Le Clair took sips from their glasses, but Tempy quickly drained hers.

"There's a lesson we never addressed," Madame said tartly. "*Ma petite*, you must *sip* champagne. Never drain the glass that way. Lucien, refill her glass so that she can try again."

Tempy held out her champagne flute and Lucien refilled it.

"First, you must hold your glass at the stem. The heat of your hand on the glass will warm the wine, and you want to avoid that."

Tempy nodded pleasantly and adjusted her grip on the glass.

"Good. Now, I'd like you to take a small sip. Taste the wine. This is an excellent bottle, and you need to learn to savor the flavors."

Tempy nodded again, and took a liberal swallow.

"No, no, dear. I said a sip."

"I'm so sorry. It's just that this is so delicious."

"Of course it is," Madame said. "Lucien has always kept an excellent cellar." She turned her attention back to her lesson. "Now let's try that again. Take a sip. A small one. What's happened to your wine? Lucien? Refill her glass."

Lucien chuckled. "You need to slow down a bit, Tempy, or you'll wind up with quite a headache." Despite his words, he filled her champagne flute for a third time.

She sighed. "Two glasses of champagne can't be so terrible. I see people drinking it all the time in the casino."

"Yes," said Mme Le Clair. "But not an entire bottle within the space of ten minutes. Moderation is the key." She sighed. "I think we should stop this particular lesson now. We can try again another time."

"That's probably wise," Lucien commented. Tempy grinned at him like a naughty child who had just escaped from her governess, and then finished off another glass of wine. "Perhaps we've had enough lessons for today."

Mme Le Clair gave a disappointed sigh. "That's too bad.

Tonight would have been perfect for a particular lesson I had in mind." She frowned. "I'm afraid that given the circumstances, we'll need to reschedule it for a time when the three of us can meet again."

Lucien tightened his grip on the stem of his wine glass. "The three of us? Why would the lesson require my presence?"

"Because it requires a kiss."

Lucien felt his smile freeze on his face. "What are you proposing?"

Mme Le Clair lifted her hand with her palm up. "Nothing life-shattering, I assure you. I simply wanted to ensure that our young friend understands the difference between the peck on the cheek a daughter gives her father and the kind of kiss a woman bestows upon a man."

Lucien glanced at Tempy, wondering what she thought about the proposed lesson, and what he saw surprised him. She wasn't blushing or looking away. No. Tempy's eyes were wide and wondering, as though Mme Le Clair's words were making her think of things she'd never before considered.

As he watched, her gaze flitted toward him. When she began examining his mouth as though she were considering kissing it, he felt a rush of warmth radiate outward from his chest. She lifted her glass to her lips and sipped, staring at him all the while. When had she refilled it again?

Lucien cleared his throat. "Miss Bliss seems to have had entirely too much...excitement tonight." Upon seeing Tempy's disappointed pout, he couldn't repress the teasing smile that twitched the corners of his mouth. A few glasses of champagne made her positively incorrigible.

"In that case, I hope you won't mind if I leave you now. My friend has already sent his carriage to collect me, and I'm sure he's becoming impatient." She set her champagne glass on the silver serving tray on Lucien's desk. "*Au revoir.*"

"Thank you for your help," Tempy said.

Mme Le Clair dipped her head in acknowledgment and then took her leave.

Lucien cleared his throat again. It was as though Mme Le Clair had just fired off a starting pistol and then suddenly departed, leaving them standing at the gates. Should he pretend he'd never heard her mention a kiss, or address the subject openly?

He needn't have worried, because Tempy took matters into her own hands. "I wouldn't mind just one more lesson tonight," she murmured. She drained her wine glass and then ran her tongue across her lips, causing the warmth in Lucien's chest to move lower.

"I'm not certain that would be wise, given the circumstances."

"But if we wait until a more appropriate time, Mme Le Clair might insist on watching us kiss and then critiquing us," she said, and stopped. "Me."

"No. It wouldn't happen that way. I can assure you of that. Kissing requires some privacy, and an audience would make anyone self-conscious."

"Then you agree with me," she said, and let out a huge breath. "Thank goodness. I was afraid it was me."

"You?"

She blushed. "That you didn't want to kiss me. I was afraid that you...that you might find me...you know." She looked down for a moment, but then she smiled and looked into his eyes. "But you don't."

She stepped closer.

The scent of her perfume--something floral and light--wafted toward him. He blinked slowly. Could this be happening? Could the single-minded Miss Bliss be focusing her sights on him? But what of Ernest Lipscomb?

To hell with Ernest Lipscomb.

Lucien closed the distance between them, keeping his gaze locked on Tempy's. Her eyes widened slightly as he slid his hand around her waist, pulling her against him. The length of her body pressed against his and her full skirts surrounded his legs in an embrace. She sighed softly and tilted her head back, closing her eyes.

He lowered his head slowly, wanting this moment to last. Her lips were pressed closed as she waited for his kiss. That, if nothing else, told him that she'd never been properly kissed.

He touched his lips to hers briefly, softly, letting her adjust to the feel of them, and then he kissed her again. A little more firmly.

Her lips parted slightly under his pressure, and his followed suit. He deepened the kiss, flitting his tongue against her lower lip. She jerked slightly in surprise, but then she relaxed and responded in kind. Her warm tongue tested his lip in a tentative taste. He darted his tongue against hers, and she responded by pressing her body closer.

He splayed his hand on her back and held her more firmly against him.

Tempy slid her hand behind his neck and entwined her fingers in his hair. The entire length of her body melted into his.

Holding her close with one arm, Lucien took a short step back, groping for the edge of his desk as he pulled her with him. He leaned back slightly, sitting on the edge of his desk, and then he pulled her between his legs. Having her pressed against his groin, even with those layers of petticoats between them, was an exquisite form of agony. If she were more experienced, he'd guide her hand down...but no. That would shock her. And this moment needed to be special.

He gently cupped her face in his hand and began tracing kisses along her cheek until he reached the hollow under her ear. She let out a soft sound of pleasure and tilted her head away from him, granting his lips access to that tender spot.

Tempy's breath quickened against his skin, and Lucien wanted to feel her heart racing as well. He slid his hand from the back of her waist and up along her ribcage, resting it just below her breast. He could feel her heart thumping against her corset, and a feeling of possessiveness washed over him.

He'd caused her to respond this way. Not her Ernest.

Never her Ernest.

He was certain of that.

Lucien wrapped his other arm more firmly around her and pulled her closer again, moving his mouth back to hers. Their lips and tongues met again as he slid his hand upward, tugging down the top of her bodice so that he could touch the soft, rounded mound beneath it.

At his touch on the top of her breast, Tempy gasped and pulled away. At first, Lucien's head followed her as he tried to maintain contact with her lips, instinctively needing that connection, but then he came back to himself, opened his eyes, and focused on her face.

Tempy stared back at him with wide, round eyes and parted lips. He gazed into her large pupils, mesmerized by them, and he wanted to fall into their depths. He tried to pull her closer, wanting her back in his arms, wanting her pressed against his body again, but she resisted.

Her mouth clamped shut in a frown, and she tugged at the top of her bodice, hiding her soft flesh away from him. "That lesson was quite edifying," she said in husky tones. "I'm afraid I learned more than I expected." A flush began to creep over her skin. "What would Mme Le Clair think? And Father?" Then she paled. "Oh, no. What would Ernest say?" Her hand flew to her face, covering her mouth. She turned away from him and hurried to the mirror next to the door.

Her words hit him like a slap to the face, and for a heartbeat he couldn't speak. He just gaped at her as she examined her reflection. He could see her face in the mirror, and the look self-reproach he saw on it made him wince. Then she hung her head.

Lucien pushed himself away from the desk and turned his

back to her. The pain from her rejection swelled in his chest like a living thing and it wanted to howl. He could feel its hot, slavering breath as it opened its mouth to release its lament in a wail of loss.

But he wouldn't let it. He wouldn't give it voice. Instead, he pressed the beast back, forcing it into a corner of his soul until it had no place to go but into the box. He slammed the door shut on the pain, locking it away where it couldn't hurt him.

Behind him, he heard Tempy move. "I'm sorry," she murmured. "I had no idea..." Her voice trailed off.

Lucien turned to one side, not quite facing her, but still, he could see her. The push and pull of his emotions kept him fixed in place, unable to approach her but also unable to turn away.

She was staring down at her hands, clenched tightly together like a sailor's knot. "I mean, I...I was taken by surprise," she said, stumbling over her words. "I d-didn't mean to put you in such an awkward position. It w-won't happen again."

He turned his head to stare at her fully as he tried to decipher the meaning of her words. Was she actually apologizing to him? For responding to their kiss?

Without looking at him, Tempy suddenly turned and fled through the door next to her and out into the casino's foyer.

Her action took him by surprise, and for an instant, he stood there, unmoving. Not quite comprehending what was happening. But at the click of the closing door, Lucien suddenly broke free of his lassitude and lurched forward, crossing the length of the room in four long strides.

He had to stop her. Had to speak to her. He couldn't let her leave thinking that she'd done something wrong. He yanked open the door, but she was already hurrying toward the exit. A large group of casino patrons who must have just arrived moved across his path, blocking his progress. He pushed his way forward, bumping shoulders as he wove through the crowd.

"Mr. Hamlin." Boothby seemed to appear out of nowhere at his elbow. The young man put his hand on Lucien's arm.

Lucien shook free. "Later," he said tersely. Every second counted. Every tick of the clock took Tempy farther away from him.

"I'm sorry, sir, but the Earl of Sherwood needs a word with you. He's quite insistent. I've been putting him off, but I dare not any longer."

"Sherwood?" Lucien puffed out an breath. "Tell him...I don't care what you tell him. I don't have time for this," he said as he continued pushing his way through the crowded foyer toward the door, and Tempy.

But now, directly in his path, stood John Snowden. Lucien looked over the man's shoulder, and caught sight of Tempy's skirts disappearing out the main doors as she fled to the street.

Lucien stopped short and let out a frustrated sigh. Her coach would be waiting, as planned, and she'd be driving away within seconds. Even if he ran after her now, pushing everyone from his path, he still wouldn't be able to reach her in time.

And John Snowden was staring at him oddly.

Lucien tamped down on his frustration. He could still fix this. They'd simply had a misunderstanding. All he needed to do was come up with a new plan.

But for now, he offered John Snowden a smile of greeting and reached out to shake his hand.

John's handshake was quick and firm. "Is anything wrong? You look harried."

Lucien smoothed his features, masking any signs of stress. "It's been a busy night. As a matter of fact," he said, as an idea came to him, "Lord Sherwood has requested my attention. Why don't you join me, just to learn a bit more about how I manage the casino?"

"That's an excellent suggestion. I'd like to see you in action. Young Miss Bliss seems quite enamored of you."

Lucien's eyes widened, his mask of equanimity slipping briefly before he was able to put it back into place. How on earth could Snowden be so confident about Tempy's feelings toward him when he'd only begun to suspect them in the last few minutes? Had she confided in him? "I don't think I'd put it that way," he said, stumbling to find the right words.

"I see her here every time I visit. I've never seen her take to one of her research projects with quite this much gusto. But perhaps that's not fair. She always did throw herself into a task. She's never been one to hold anything back."

The tension eased from Lucien's body. Snowden hadn't been talking about Tempy's feelings, but about her work. That made more sense.

Something must have shown on his face, because Snowden stared at him more intently. "Is there something I'm missing?"

"No, nothing at all. It's just that I was unaware of her whole-hearted commitment to her projects."

But Snowden's words continued to resonate, their vibrations shaking out new ideas, new paths of thought. Could Snowden's description of Tempy's character explain her behavior in his office? Could she have been *throwing herself into a task?*

From that angle, his view of what had just transpired in his office suddenly altered. It no longer seemed like a moment of passion between two people discovering one another for the first time. It transformed, instead, into an experiment that had had a more potent reaction than expected, but an experiment nonetheless.

Lucien's ego deflated, flattened by a diligent, hardworking young woman who threw herself into every goal she set for herself.

Especially the goal of winning back her fiancé's love.

15

A SPINNING HEAD

Tempy rushed down the steps of the casino, and her carriage immediately lurched forward from its spot near the entrance. Her footman jumped down to open the door, and the carriage swept her away within seconds.

Within the darkened confines of her carriage, Tempy moved her hand to her mouth. Her lips didn't feel swollen to her touch, but she could have sworn they were. Lucien's mouth had been tender at first, but then things had changed. She realized now that she'd been playing with fire when she'd decided to kiss the man. But how could she have predicted she'd react the way she had?

She suddenly realized that she was quite thirsty. Could it be from the wine?

She'd never felt this way when she'd kissed Ernest. Those kisses had always been temperate. Proper. She'd had no idea kisses could be so...so...wanton. Did the combination of wine and kissing have this effect on all women?

Her hand dropped to her breast as she checked to make sure

the bodice of her dress was properly in place. She could still feel Lucien's hand there.

"Lucien," she murmured. Drawing out the soft "sh" sound. She liked saying his name.

What would have happened if she hadn't pulled away from him? She blushed, confused both by her lack of knowledge about the details of intimacy between men and women and by the sensations coursing through her body.

Tempy rested her woozy head against the seat back and closed her eyes. This was one of those moments when she most missed having a mother. She felt entirely unprepared for the world in which she found herself. And she hated feeling unprepared. If her relationship with Mrs. Lipscomb hadn't been destroyed by Ernest, she'd speak with her. But perhaps not. How could she discuss kissing Lucien with Ernest's mother?

She needed some guidance. Mme Le Clair would probably give her the most practical advice, but Tempy immediately dismissed that idea. She sensed that the demimondaine was not the best person to approach regarding matters of the heart. Although she was certain that the woman would be full of practical advice, that wasn't what Tempy needed to help her come to terms with what had just taken place. She wanted to understand the emotions involved, and she sensed that Mme Le Clair would be uncomfortable with discussing that aspect of relationships.

She needed someone with more delicate sensibilities. Perhaps Millicent would help her.

Tempy opened her eyes and had trouble focusing on the interior of the carriage. It made her dizzy, so she closed them again.

Lucien had a similar effect on her. He had made her feel slightly off balance ever since she'd met him. So why had she responded to his kisses that way?

And why had something like that never happened with Ernest?

But, then again, she'd never kissed Ernest this way, so perhaps the comparison wasn't fair.

Did Ernest's new fiancée kiss him like that? A wave of distaste ran through Tempy as she imagined the two of them together. Could that be why Clarisse had won him away from her? Because Tempy had never kissed him the way a woman kisses a man, instead of the way a sister kisses a brother?

Well, there was only one way to find out. A sense of resolution descended upon her. She'd have to kiss Ernest again. It was the only way she'd know for sure.

But even as she made the decision, doubt niggled at her. After all, she and Ernest had spent years together. Shouldn't they have already discovered this sort of passion? If Ernest had never made her feel this way before now, maybe he never could.

The rocking and jostling of the carriage were beginning to make her feel queasy. Or perhaps it was her tight corset in combination with the three...no, four glasses of champagne she'd consumed. She gritted her teeth and tried to ignore her growing discomfort.

What if she decided not to find out if Ernest's kisses would move her? What if she abandoned this plan to win back his love? What if she simply let him go? What then?

As the carriage rolled to a halt, Tempy pressed her hand to her stomach and sighed resignedly. She already knew "what if." She knew herself well enough to realize that she'd always be plagued by those questions. She had to find out.

The door snapped open, and Tempy stumbled out of the carriage's stuffy confines. As she stepped onto the paving stones in front of her house, the cool night air helped clear her head and settle her stomach.

Tempy lifted the hem of her skirts and began climbing the front steps to her home. When she wobbled slightly, the footman hurried forward and took her elbow, escorting her safely to her front door.

Perhaps she could blame tonight on the champagne.

🙦 16 🙤

MILLICENT'S ADVICE

*A*s always, Tempy rushed toward the docks, but she arrived too late.

As she stood on the shore and watched the ship grow smaller and smaller in the distance, she became aware of someone standing next to her. A man.

"They've abandoned you," the man said.

"No! They simply forgot me. I'll find my way back to them."

"I'm here. Now."

"But we're alone," she said, looking around the deserted island. "How can we survive this way?"

"We can take care of each other." He wrapped his arms around her and pressed his mouth against hers.

She wanted to sink into him and let him surround her senses, but she couldn't make herself do it. Instead, she pulled away. "But what happens when you leave me too?"

And he vanished.

TEMPY SLEPT LATE THE FOLLOWING MORNING. WHEN SHE HAD arrived home, her lady's maid, Mary, had tut-tutted over her, cajoled her into eating some bread with water, and then had tucked her into bed. Whether it was due to Mary's ministrations or not, Tempy found that she didn't feel the lingering after effects she'd dreaded from overindulging in champagne. She'd seen them in her father only once or twice, and they'd never looked pleasant.

She couldn't say the same about the aftereffects of that kiss. She felt certain that she'd had a dream about it last night, but she couldn't remember any details.

Millicent would arrive soon. Tempy had been pacing through the drawing room for the past fifteen minutes, and the odor of father's pipes seemed stronger than usual today.

She glanced out the window again, and stared for a moment at the train statue in the grassy area directly across the street from her front door. Some boys had climbed onto it and sat straddling it. Their bodies bounced up and down from what must have been a very rough train ride in their game. Father always hated it when children climbed on his statue, but Tempy never minded. They looked like they were having fun.

After another minute passed, Tempy dragged one of the heavy chairs over to the front window and sat down. After all, if she planned to continue peering through the glass to watch for Millicent's arrival, she might as well be comfortable. And anyway, she would be less obvious from the street if she sat, and it would be easier for her to watch the children play.

Millicent wasn't late, of course, but Tempy was too anxious to wait calmly. She and Millicent usually met at restaurants or museums, or occasionally for some shopping. Calling upon one another at their homes had never been their habit. They were both much too active to be content with chatting over tea in the drawing room. The upper class might enjoy making formal calls as part of their daily routine, but Tempy could never understand why. The activity of a tea room, restaurant, or shopping district seemed vastly preferable to anything a drawing room had to offer.

But Tempy had sent the invitation to Millicent in the midmorning post, and Millicent's acceptance had arrived just past noon.

As a carriage rattled across the cobblestones toward the entrance of Tempy's townhouse, she sat up straighter. Yes. That was Millicent. She'd recognize that ostrich feather hat anywhere.

Tempy lurched to her feet and saw Millicent's eyes track her movement in the window. Tempy hurried toward the door, but paused when she saw that her butler, Royce, was already there with his hand on the doorknob. Apparently, he, too, was aware that Millicent's carriage had arrived and was simply waiting for her to come to the door.

Tempy took a step back, allowing Royce to perform his job. It would be unkind to prevent him from doing so. The man could be quite proper and rigid, but he kept the household running smoothly, much like a yardmaster in a train yard. He examined every aspect of the household daily, making certain that everything ran smoothly and on schedule.

The bell rang, and a heartbeat later, Royce swung open the door. "Good afternoon, Mrs. Kidman," he said, stepping back from the open door to allow her to enter the house.

Tempy moved forward, extending both hands in greeting. "Millicent. How good of you to come." She embraced her friend and they brushed cheeks. She led the way to the sitting room.

She glanced at Royce. "Please send in the tea."

"Yes, miss," he said with a nod and then hurried off.

She had thought that her anxiety would ease once Millicent arrived, but it hadn't. If anything, it had grown worse.

Millicent pulled off her gloves and removed her hat, eying Tempy the entire time. "You seem tense. Are you still pining away over Ernest?"

"What? No, not that. I think I'm making some progress on that front."

Millicent arched her eyebrows. "Then what's this about?" she asked, coming directly to the point, as usual.

Tempy was grateful for the interruption when the door opened and one of the maids came in, carrying the tea tray. She set it on the table in front of the sofa and departed.

Tempy gestured toward the tray and moved to take her seat on the overstuffed sofa, sitting carefully so she didn't slip to the floor. Perhaps she should replace the thing, now that Father was gone. She'd always detested it. Millicent sat next to her.

Tempy lifted the teapot and china cup simultaneously, just as Mme Le Clair had taught her, and poured a cup for Millicent. Steam rose, carrying with it the faint citrus aroma of Darjeeling oolong tea, Millicent's favorite. "One lump?"

Millicent looked at her strangely, but nodded. "Have you been taking comportment lessons? I thought you hated it when your governess tried to teach you trivial things like the proper way to pour a cup of tea."

Tempy's hand, clenching the tongs with the lump of sugar, paused, and then she dropped the lump into Millicent's cup. She didn't reply as she set aside the tongs and placed a small teaspoon on the saucer, but then she smiled, offering the teacup to her friend. "I decided that the lessons had some merit, after all."

"Humph. This is because of him, isn't it? You've decided to change, simply to please a man."

Tempy felt the heat rush to her face. "That's not fair. You've been urging me to behave in a more ladylike manner for years. I've simply decided to follow your advice and buff off some of my rougher edges."

Millicent looked unconvinced. "Why now?"

"Because now I'm reevaluating my past decisions and making some changes." When Millicent opened her mouth to comment,

Tempy rushed on. "I promise I'm not changing who I am. I'm just polishing what's there."

"You're not doing something foolish, like giving up on writing, are you?"

"Oh, heavens no. Never. Didn't Mr. Hamlin tell you? He's allowing me to do my research at his casino."

Millicent's mouth dropped open slightly. "I thought he'd only allow you to visit after hours."

"I was able to convince him to change his mind."

"Then you have me at a loss. I know you have some sort of purpose in inviting me here, otherwise we'd currently be viewing that new exhibit at the Royal Gallery."

Tempy sighed. "You do love to get to the point. I usually like that, but today, the subject is a bit delicate. I hope you'll be patient with me."

Millicent tilted her head to one side, intense curiosity causing her to narrow her eyes. "All right," she said, surprising Tempy. "Take whatever time you need."

Tempy chuckled. "It's your advice I need. And a little bit of wisdom."

Millicent smiled back. "That I have in spades." She set her teacup on the low table in front of the sofa and then faced Tempy, folding her hands on her lap as she settled in to wait.

Tempy bit her bottom lip, not meeting Millicent's gaze. "You've been married." She paused, but Millicent said nothing. "I'm trying to understand more about marriage. About closer relationships between men and women."

Millicent reddened. "Oh, my. Are you asking about the mechanics of how men and women...? Oh, my." She reached for her teacup, and then drew her hands back without touching it. "Of course, your mother would have been the one...Oh, my." She began carefully arranging her teacup and saucer on the low table.

"I didn't mean to upset you. I'm so sorry." Tempy's heart sank. Perhaps this wasn't a good idea. "I didn't want to ask you about the actual mechanics, as you put it. I wanted to know more about the emotions involved."

Millicent stopped her fussing and turned to face Tempy. "Are you saying you want me to explain *love* to you?" Millicent asked, looking taken aback. "You'd be better off studying poetry than asking me."

"No, that's not it. I'm not expressing myself well." Tempy sighed and started over. "When a woman kisses a man she finds attractive...I mean, *really kisses* him...is the response always the same? Does she always feel...well...the same rush of emotion, no matter who the man is?"

"Are you trying to understand the distinction between love and pure animal attraction? Is that it? Are you wondering if a woman can respond to a man's kisses even if she doesn't love him?"

Tempy thought about it. "Yes, I suppose that's partly what I'm asking."

"Well," Millicent said, relaxing slightly, "despite what you may have read in novels, the answer is yes, a woman can most certainly experience pleasure without love, but physical pleasure is only a small part of the relationship between a man and a woman."

Tempy nodded. So her response to Lucien could have been "pure animal attraction." The knot of tension in her stomach loosened fractionally. "Then those base attractions aren't necessarily important in a marriage?"

"Oh, no. I wouldn't say that at all. I believe that the physical connection in a marriage is critical to the overall health of the union. It provides the mortar that holds the pair together when problems arise. And problems always arise."

Tempy's clenched her hands together. "But what of mutual respect? What of common goals for the future?"

"Oh, I'm not saying it's impossible to have a successful marriage without that physical attraction, but it's more difficult to maintain. And you are correct in thinking that common goals and mutual respect are essential elements to a good marriage. I just don't want you to underestimate the importance of basic attraction. Without that spark, few marriages can be truly happy. I've seen too many couples who live separate existences, sometimes even maintaining separate households."

Tempy didn't respond. She stared vacantly down at her hands in her lap, pondering Millicent's words.

Millicent cleared her throat, paused, and then said, "These questions you've been asking, do they pertain to Ernest Lipscomb?"

Tempy flinched, and her ears began to feel a bit warm. "We've never shared a truly passionate kiss. Someone was always with us. My governess or his sister or mother...someone was always there. Our parents were quite insistent on that point, and we were always circumspect." Tempy's voice seemed to fade. "And now I can't help but wonder. How might things be different now if we'd only--" she broke off, embarrassment choking off her words.

"If you'd only stolen away together?"

Tempy felt her face flame. "Yes. I can only wonder how things might be different if we'd only had a few moments of privacy to find out." She had to force the words from her lips.

"'Where there's a will, there's a way,'" Millicent muttered. And then she said, more clearly, "If you'd wanted those moments, you would have found them."

Tempy's head popped up at those words. "But they watched us constantly."

"No. You frequently came out with me, and you know me well enough to realize that I wouldn't begrudge you a few moments of privacy. You could have ducked into an empty drawing room together, or into his father's study when the man was out. There must have been plenty of opportunities for you to steal away for a kiss."

"It never entered my mind."

"Which says a great deal."

Tempy lurched to her feet, bumping her knees against the low table as she did so and causing the tea tray to clatter. "Well, it's entered my mind now," she said. "I believe a kiss should be my litmus test."

Millicent shook her head. "Can't you simply let him go?"

"Let him go?" she repeated. "Why can't you understand? If I let him go, I'll be alone. I won't just lose him, I'll lose my family. I'll have no one left."

"You'll have me," Millicent said, rising to her feet. "You know I'll always be here for you."

Tempy closed her eyes and shook her head, and then she met Millicent's gaze. "If you really want to be here for me, then please support me in this. I need you, Millicent."

Millicent's shoulders sagged. "I'll always support you. Even when I don't agree with you."

"Thank you. That means everything to me." She reached out a hand and took Millicent's. "Come on. Let's go to the Royal Gallery. I think it will do us both some good to have an outing. And on the way, you can listen while I tell you about my article. I could use your advice regarding that as well."

17

A WELL-TIMED
SPOT OF TROUBLE

Lucien prowled the floor of his vacant casino, clutching a letter in his hand as he listened for Tempy's arrival. Many matters weighed heavily upon him today, but until he could see Tempy for himself and read her response to last night's events, he couldn't focus his attention on anything but her. He'd come to expect punctuality in her regular visits with Mme Le Clair, but even so, he let out a sigh of relief when Tempy arrived promptly for her scheduled appointment.

He shifted his weight from one foot to another so his movement would catch her eye even though he stood on the far side of the large casino floor. If she wanted to speak with him, it would be easy enough for her to do so, but if she didn't, then he'd keep his distance.

Her gaze immediately flicked toward him, but then her eyes widened and she hurriedly looked away as a bright pink wash of color suffused her cheeks. Even from this distance, it was impossible not to see her mortification. She spun away, providing him with an excellent view of her back. Her spine stiffened so that it became ramrod straight, and then she rushed past the doorway, heading toward his office and her meeting with Mme Le Clair.

A sharp pang of disappointment pierced Lucien as he dropped his chin. Would anything take place during Tempy's lesson with Mme Le Clair to alleviate her embarrassment?

Perhaps, but unlikely.

He sighed and looked again at the letter still clutched in his hand. Leaving now felt like cowardice, but he had little choice in the matter. This summons saw to that. Perhaps spending some time away from Tempy would help ease her discomfiture. He could only hope it would. He didn't want to think about her reaction to their kiss right now. The inadvertent pain she'd caused him was too raw, too new.

With a sense of resignation and perhaps a bit of relief, Lucien turned to the task of making arrangements for a short and inconvenient trip to Porlock, a town a few hours outside Bath. He'd be damned if he'd stay there one minute longer than necessary. But he'd be double-damned if he'd give Formsworth the satisfaction of knowing the inconvenience he'd caused.

One of the estates Lucien had inherited, the one in Somerset, had been his grandfather's favorite, and now it was the focus of a land dispute with his neighbor, Squire Formsworth, a despicable man. Lucien had hoped his estate manager would be able to resolve the conflict so that Lucien wouldn't even need to speak to Formsworth, let alone breathe the same air as him, but negotiations had rapidly deteriorated and now Lucien's presence was required in court.

Marcus Formsworth must have realized that Lucien had inherited the land. Why else would he have chosen this moment to press a lawsuit?

Despite himself, Lucien's thoughts scurried back to the moment when Tempy saw him across the casino and blushed with shame. The pain her natural response had inflicted upon him now seemed to be settling more deeply in his heart. How much of her reaction came from a sense of shame at kissing the owner of a casino? He knew he was the sort of man from whom most respectable fathers would hide their daughters. According to what Millicent had said at the tea room, even Tempy's rather negligent father had been no different.

The letter in Lucien's hand crackled as he clenched his fist, drawing his attention back to the missive. Despite his animosity toward Squire Formsworth, at least one good thing would come of this dreaded visit to Porlock. He'd be able to avoid seeing that look of shame on Miss Bliss's face for a few days. Perhaps by the time he returned, she'd have more control over her emotions.

Lucien spotted Boothby, and waved the man over to him. "I'd like you to join me on a trip to Bath and then on to my grandfather's estate near Porlock." He paused and pressed his lips together. "*My* estate," he corrected. "My valet hasn't been well for a while, and I need someone to accompany me in his place. You're the perfect choice, since you have a knack for picking up useful bits of information. I need to know how things stand in my households, and I'll depend on you to see what you can learn from the other servants while we're there."

Boothby's eyes lit up. "Most certainly, sir. I'd be honored. How soon do you plan to leave?"

"Later this afternoon. I'll take the four o'clock train. Stop at my residence and pack my things for me. I plan to be gone for three or four days." He paused, eyeing the young man thoughtfully. After all, Boothby had never performed this task before. "Make sure you include day clothes, riding attire, and something appropriate for the evening. And don't forget my toiletries."

"Yes, sir," Boothby replied, his gap-toothed grin revealing his enthusiasm for the trip. "And may I say, I think this is an excellent plan. Just the thing." Then he turned and hurried away.

Lucien furrowed his brow as he watched the young man leave. Did Boothby know more about Lucien's personal life than he'd realized? He shook his head in a bemused manner. That young man was more well-informed than an oddsmaker at a racetrack.

Lucien needed to send a couple of letters, but since his office was occupied, he'd need to find another location where he could write them. In the past he'd always felt free to use his desk in the office during Tempy's lessons, but today he wanted to avoid going in there.

He headed toward the cashiers' office, pulling his key from his pocket. Once inside, he quickly found a stack of paper. He sat and jotted notes to John Snowden and a couple of regular casino guests, informing them of his planned absence over the next three days. After addressing them, he exited the caged area and waved over one of the footmen.

Lucien didn't recognize the young man. He must be new. All these footmen tended to look alike after a while. This one fitted the basic physical requirements of the job: tall, slim, young, and fairly good looking. "Make sure these go out immediately," he told the dark-haired young man. "What's your name?"

"Tines, sir." The young man rocked back and forth on the balls of his feet, obviously eager to please.

"Take these to the post office," Lucien said. "I want them delivered as quickly as possible." He pulled a few coins from his pocket and handed them to the young man. "This should cover the postage."

"I could deliver them myself, if you prefer."

"Don't be daft," Lucien said, surprised by the suggestion. "Look at those addresses. Do you want to run all over London? The post office will deliver them much more quickly than you could."

The young man's face reddened and he glanced at the envelopes. He held them upside down as he pretended to read the addresses and then nodded. "Oh, yes. I see, sir."

Lucien closed his eyes for a moment as he mentally berated himself for his own insensitivity. It was obvious Tines couldn't read, and Lucien had just embarrassed him about the fact by calling him daft. "No. No need to apologize." He didn't embarrass the young man by commenting on his reading deficit, but instead made a mental note to discuss the problem with Boothby. Between them, they'd find a way to help the footman learn the needed skill without embarrassing him. "Thank you, Tines," his said.

The young man took his words as a dismissal, and with a dip of his head, he hurried off with the letters.

Lucien kept checking the clock as he quickly discussed the menu offerings for the next few evenings with the chef, and then he headed back to the spot on the casino floor where he'd stood an hour ago when he'd watched Tempy arrive.

He both dreaded and craved seeing her again. What if she couldn't meet his gaze? Then again, what if she did? He couldn't make himself stay away from her, no matter what the risk. If she wanted to speak with him, then he'd offer her the opportunity to do so.

He heard the click of his office door as it opened and busied himself with sorting through a sheaf of papers he'd brought along as a prop. After all, he couldn't just stand there looking like a wayward schoolboy who was waiting for the headmaster to haul him into his office.

Heels clattered on the marble floor and then the two women appeared at the doorway. Tempy glanced toward him, apparently looking for him, because this time she didn't turn away, but met his gaze. As she crossed the casino floor toward him wearing a self-deprecating smile, the sense of rejection that had been suffocating him evaporated. Even that fact that Mme Le Clair trailed behind her did little to diminish Lucien's elation.

"Good day, ladies," he said, tipping his head to them both. "I hope you had a productive morning."

"Yes," Tempy said, still watching him.

"More productive than you might think," Mme Le Clair added. "I understand that you'll be leaving today to visit Bath. Your timing couldn't be more perfect."

Had Boothby told her? Lucien raised his eyebrows at her, waiting for her to elaborate.

"It has come to our attention that Mr. Lipscomb and his young fiancée will also be leaving for Bath today, in the company of her parents. Apparently he wants her to enjoy some of the pleasures of England during her visit. Tempy and I have taken the liberty of sending a message to your mutual acquaintance, Mrs. Millicent Kidman, to ask her to accompany Tempy as her chaperone for the trip."

"Chaperone?" Lucien parroted the word. What on earth was Madame talking about? "Why does Tempy need a chaperone?"

"How else could she accompany you to Bath? It would be quite improper otherwise." Mme Le Clair looked at him as though she thought him rather slow-witted. "If Mrs. Kidman agrees, she'll make the perfect escort. She knows you both and is aware of the predicament Mr. Lipscomb has created."

"I'm certain she'll want to help. She'll see it as a lark." Tempy said. Her eyes seemed to sparkle with excitement at the prospect of the trip, but she glanced away shyly. "I've always wanted to visit Bath. Father was always working and didn't have time to take me there."

"Didn't he ever take a holiday?"

Tempy shook her head. "He didn't believe in such extravagances. He always said," she paused to raise one finger in a dramatic gesture, and her voice dropped to mimic a man's voice, "'work is the foundation of society'." She dropped her pose and one corner of her mouth turned upward as though she wasn't quite sure if she wanted to smile. When she opened her mouth again, her normal, feminine tones emerged. "But I'm certain even he would have approved of this trip, given the circumstances." She bounced slightly on her toes.

Poor little rich girl. She'd never even been to Bath? Lucien wished the excitement in her eyes was for him, rather than for the opportunity to chase down that dolt, Ernest, but how could he turn her down? How could he extinguish that spark? And how could he refuse her request to travel with him? "It sounds like an excellent strategy. And while you're doing whatever it is you propose to do to further your plan with your *sweetheart*," he said, trying not to overly stress the distasteful word, "I will do what I can to help distract his new fiancée."

Tempy's smile faltered, and she finally looked at him. "Distract her? How?"

Was that a spark of irritation he detected? Something within him crowed at seeing it. "I don't know her well enough yet, but perhaps I can help drive a wedge between them. It will depend on how the hand plays out. We shall see."

Mme Le Clair's gaze darted back and forth between them, and then she stared at Lucien as she narrowed her eyes in dawning comprehension. "Yes, I believe we shall."

Mme Le Clair shifted her feet so she faced Lucien, and it was as though she pinned him in place with her gaze. What did she want? "I'd like a private word with you."

Lucien wanted to say no, but with a sigh of resignation, he watched Tempy walk away. He turned his attention back to Mme Le Clair.

"What's going on between you and Temperance? Don't bother to deny it. I know you too well. It's obvious you're smitten with her."

"You're imagining things. And even if I were *smitten*, as you say, what difference would it make? She's in love with Ernest."

"No, she isn't. She's simply afraid to be alone."

"And she's chosen him, along with his entire family, to be her companion in life."

"For now."

"What's that supposed to mean?"

She waived her hand in dismissal. "Nothing. I'm allowing myself to be sidetracked. That's not what I wanted to discuss with you." Her normally smooth forehead showed signs of worry. "Are you certain that Boothby is the best person to take with you, considering your destination?"

"What do you mean? He's perfect."

"I'm worried that he might come in contact with his father."

"Would that be so bad?" Lucien asked, but then paused. "What are you saying? You *did* tell him who his father is, didn't you?"

She pressed her lips together for a moment, as though she didn't want to answer him, and then she let out a frustrated sigh. "I never thought it was necessary. It's not as though the man ever comes to London. I thought they'd never lay eyes on one another."

"But Boothby has a right to know," Lucien insisted.

"A right? Who has a right? The father who denied his son, or the boy who I tried to protect from that humiliation? Where is the 'right' that makes that knowledge of any benefit to Marcus?"

"Considering he was named for his father, I think his mother must have had a different opinion."

She shook her head in denial. "She only named him that in the hope that his father would accept him. But it didn't work." She looked down at her clenched hands. "I can only wonder how many more sons named 'Marcus' the man has discarded over the years."

"Boothby has a right to know."

"Fine. But I want to be the one who tells him. As his mother's closest friend, it's my obligation, not yours."

Lucien shook his head. "He's not here right now, and I don't think this can wait. I can tell him."

"I'll do everything I can to make sure I tell him before he

leaves, but you must promise me that you won't tell him. This is important. It needs to come from me."

Lucien sighed. "Fine. I won't tell him. But you must talk to him today."

She nodded. "Yes. It's for the best."

18

BATH

Something interrupted Tempy's snooze, and she sat with her eyes closed for a moment, wondering what had awakened her. It didn't take her long to realize that the train was slowing. She opened her eyes and blinked against the sunlight streaming through the train window as she leaned forward to look outside.

The Georgian facades of buildings seemed to roll past, but, of course, it was she who was moving, not the buildings. Each building had its own symmetry and balance and Tempy found their order to be soothing, especially when compared to the more riotous architecture of London.

She could feel the rattle of the car continue to slow as they lost speed. They'd stop soon, and she'd finally be in Bath.

She glanced at her traveling companions. They were waking up as well. All except for Lucien, who appeared completely alert. He gathered together some papers and ledgers and slid them into a satchel.

The train lurched to a stop at the platform. Once she was

certain that it wouldn't jerk forward again, she rose to her feet. When she glanced at Lucien, he looked away.

That kiss had changed things. She wanted to go back to the comfortable camaraderie they'd developed over the past week, but didn't know how.

Lucien lifted his arm toward the door of the compartment, ushering Tempy and Millicent ahead of him. Her skirts brushed against the sides of the narrow, paneled corridor as she moved toward the exit.

The train was high above the platform, and Tempy grabbed hold of the handrail as she negotiated the steep steps leading from the train car. A uniformed porter assisted her as she stepped off the last tread, smiling and nodding as he welcomed her to Bath.

Tempy looked at the faces of the men around her, wondering if Mr. Byrd had followed her here to Bath. She recognized some of them as being fellow passengers, but none of them paid her any particular attention. A moment later she gave up. She was no good at this sort of thing. How could she expect herself to spot one unknown man in this throng?

She spotted Boothby and her maid, Mary, hurrying toward them through the press of passengers. Once they were all together, Lucien led the way toward the front of the station.

After only a few moments, Boothby procured a hackney and a wagon. He supervised as their bags were loaded into the wagon, and Lucien led Tempy and Millicent toward the waiting hackney.

It was at that moment that Tempy realized that she didn't know where they were going. "I never asked, but where will we be staying tonight?"

"I have a house at the top of the hill." Lucien tilted his head back as he walked and looked up at the sky. Could he be searching for signs of rain in the cloudless sky, or was he simply trying to avoid looking at her? "We'll stay there tonight," he continued, "and tomorrow we'll leave for Exmoor. It's at the opposite end of

Somerset, so it will take us some time to reach it. I have an estate there with a problem that needs sorting out."

Tempy's steps faltered. "I had no idea you owned so much property."

Lucien didn't say anything, but just tugged open the door of the carriage and waited for the two ladies to enter.

Millicent snorted. "I'm not surprised. Up until last week he hadn't even decided whether or not to accept it."

Tempy looked from Millicent back to Lucien. "What is she talking about?"

Lucien shot Millicent an irritated frown.

"Don't look at me that way," Millicent said, obviously nonplussed by his ire. "You had plenty of time to tell her on the train. She's bound to figure it out on her own soon enough."

He glanced over his shoulder at the crowded station and said, "If you'll kindly enter the carriage, I'll explain en route."

Tempy hesitated and then acquiesced. The carriage was open, and as it sprang forward onto the street, the cool breeze against her face was pleasant change from the stuffy air of the train car.

For a moment, she lost herself in her enjoyment of the city as she took in the bright blue skies above the perfectly sculpted architecture of Bath. Each front door was centered with precision, anchoring the symmetry of its edifice. The honey-colored stone facades and the nearly identical mansard roofs made the buildings seem as though they were standing at attention, or perhaps in a slightly relaxed military parade rest. She'd heard that Bath was beautiful, but this was beyond her expectations. As the carriage moved north along the road, she could only catch glimpses of a river off in the distance to her right. A number of hotels blocked her view, but then they came upon an open park, which finally provided her with a clear view to the river. "It's so pleasant here," she murmured.

"Perhaps that's why it has endured so long," Lucien replied. "When the Romans found that the ancient Celts had discovered hot springs here, they dubbed the city Aquae Sulis and built elaborate baths. The city has been continuously inhabited ever since then. The entire town exists because of a geological curiosity," Lucien said.

Tempy remembered the question she'd asked and turned away from the view to glance over at Lucien. "You put me off earlier. Why are you being so enigmatic? I'm beginning to suspect that someone gave you property here."

"In a manner of speaking, yes. I inherited it from my uncle. He passed away about a month ago."

"I'm sorry for your loss," Tempy said automatically.

Lucien shrugged one shoulder. "We weren't close. I hadn't seen him in years."

"Look over to the right," Millicent said, gesturing. "This is the Parade Park. There's a nice view of the river from here."

Tempy glanced over politely, but the conversation inside the carriage was much more interesting than the view out there. She turned back to Lucien. "He left you a house here in Bath and an estate in Exmoor?"

He nodded.

Millicent chuckled and then cleared her throat. "Along with a title."

Lucien shot Millicent an annoyed glare.

"Don't look at me that way," Millicent scolded. "She'll find out soon enough when you arrive in Exmoor tomorrow and everyone starts *my lord*ing you."

"What title?" Tempy asked, startled by the revelation.

"Earl of Cavendish," Millicent said, not without glee.

The carriage turned onto a new road, and they began heading away from the river.

"You're the new earl everyone's been speculating about?" Tempy asked, confused by the news. "But I thought his last name was Prescot, not Hamlin."

"I took a different name when I decided to open a casino," he said, "in deference to my father's wishes."

"That explains why no one's been able to identify you yet," Tempy said, almost to herself. This was quite the story. "When do you plan to announce your identity?"

That put a sour expression on Lucien's face. "I've been delaying that for as long as possible. At first, I wasn't even certain I wanted to accept it. And now, I'd prefer completing the sale of my casino before word gets out. John sent a message that he'll have his offer ready by the time I return from this trip."

He looked conflicted. There must be more to the story of how he'd come to be the Earl of Cavendish than he was revealing. Considering that he'd wanted to reject his inheritance, whatever it was must be significant. And to think he'd been dealing with all of this while she'd pushed her own personal problems onto his plate. How could she have been so oblivious? She should have realized that something was troubling him.

Tempy shot Lucien a sympathetic look. "I hope you know that I'd never reveal something like that."

When some of the tension eased from his face, she realized he'd been afraid of just that. He'd actually thought she might betray him. It hurt to know he'd trusted her so little. She turned away to hide how deeply this slight cut her.

In an effort to distract herself, Tempy focused on the world outside the carriage and noticed that they had moved into a residential area. In the nearby park, little girls pranced around in their pinafores while a group of boys used sticks to roll their hoops along the side of the street. When the carriage turned onto Gay Street and headed up a hill, some women pushing prams along the paved sidewalk greeted one another and stopped to chat.

Millicent cleared her throat. "Are we expected at your house in Somerset, or will it be a surprise visit?"

"We're expected. To my knowledge, it's been some time since

either of the last two Earls of Cavendish visited there. I'm sure there's work they postponed. And anyway," Lucien said, "I'd prefer sleeping in a room that's been properly aired out."

The road they were on curved around a large grassy circle at the top of the hill and continued on toward their destination. The pale buildings facing the street had a curved, uniform façade that cupped around the small park as though holding it in a great stone hand. Their smoking chimneys thrust skyward at neat and orderly intervals.

Tempy was disappointed when they left the circle behind them. "That was such a lovely area," she commented.

"If you like that, just wait until you see the area they call the Royal Crescent," Millicent said.

"It's not much farther," Lucien added.

They continued down a street lined with identical townhouses until they came upon an enormous open common.

"This is it," Millicent said. "The Royal Crescent. I like to think of it as the crown jewel of Bath. What do you think?"

The road curved around a large, crescent-shaped grassy area that descended toward a stand of trees, and along the right side of the road rose a curved building. At least, Tempy *thought* it was a single building until she realized that it was made up of individual homes, all with nearly identical facades. Only the precise shade of the golden limestone varied from one home to the next.

Tempy turned to face the large common. "What a spectacular view. I can see all the way down the hillside to the river. Can you imagine waking up each morning to such a sight?"

"I'm trying to," Lucien said in an enigmatic tone.

The carriage pulled to a stop in front of one of the entrances, and Lucien leaned forward to release the catch on the carriage door.

Tempy looked at his back with surprise as he exited the carriage. "We're getting out?"

"Yes," he said patiently. "Unless you want to take a tour of Bath right now. I thought you'd prefer to be shown to your room."

Tempy's jaw dropped as she looked up at the imposing building. "*This* is one of your properties?" She took his proffered hand as she stepped out of the carriage.

"Yes," he said. "I assume it meets with your approval?"

Tempy grinned at him. "How could it not, with a view like this?"

There was a general flurry once they entered the house. The servants seemed both excited and nervous that Lucien had arrived. The housekeeper showed Tempy and Millicent to their adjoining rooms, while Lucien remained downstairs, conferring with the butler.

The deep-gold curtains at the floor-to-ceiling windows of Tempy's bedroom were thrown wide, letting the sunshine stream into the room, and someone had set a cheery fire in the limestone fireplace to drive the chill from the room.

Tempy rested her hand on the burnt-orange fringe at the edge of the curtains and peered out over the common, soaking in the view of the open, grassy area and the trees and city beyond it that seemed to fall away into to the river below.

At the soft knock at the door, Tempy turned away from the window. "Come in," she said.

Millicent entered the room, smiling broadly at Tempy. "I'm so glad we came. I think we'll have a wonderful time. But we need to remember that this trip *does* have a purpose."

Tempy looked at her blankly. Between Lucien's revelation about his title and the opulence of this house, everything else had been driven from her mind. But now she remembered. "Of course. Ernest."

"Yes. There was a message waiting for me in my room. I asked a friend to send me news regarding Ernest's accommodations here in Bath. It seems that he arrived last night with Clarisse's family, and they are staying at a house near the circle we passed through.

Unless their plans change, Ernest and Clarisse will be walking right past Lucien's house this evening on their way to dinner at an address over in the Marlborough building."

"Walking?" Tempy smiled indulgently. "That sounds like my Ernest. He loves to walk whenever he's able. But how can you be so sure they'll be on foot?"

"I can't, but even if they take a carriage, they're certain to drive past here."

Tempy nodded. "Who would want to miss this view? I think we can count on them taking this route."

After they freshened up, Tempy and Millicent located Lucien and outlined their plan.

Lucien sent Boothby to reconnoiter, and presently a message arrived from him. Yes, Mr. Lipscomb would be leaving at precisely seven o'clock that evening, and yes, he and his fiancée planned to walk to their dinner engagement.

"How does he do that?" Tempy asked, not really expecting an answer.

Lucien chuckled. "That's why I wanted to bring him with us. That young man has a talent for this sort of thing. Sometimes I think he knows what people will do even before they've decided to do it. It's uncanny."

Millicent looked startled. "You aren't suggesting he reads minds, are you?"

Lucien laughed. "No, nothing like that. He's simply observant, and he's also quite good at chatting up other people's servants."

Tempy tucked that bit of information away to use later. A man like Boothby could be quite useful in certain situations. Such as the one she found herself in right now.

Rather than positioning herself to watch the street on the ground floor, Tempy chose to move upstairs, which afforded her a better view. Since the road was curved, it was easy to see all the way to the spot where Ernest would appear. Shortly after seven, she spotted him as he and that horrid French woman turned onto the Royal Crescent. Tempy did a little jig and then sped down the stairs toward the marble entry hall.

In her rush, Tempy turned on the slick marble floor a bit too quickly, and her heel nearly slid out from under her. Fortunately, she still had hold of the banister, and she kept herself from falling, but the incident reminded her to slow down. How did that saying go again? *For want of a shoe, the horse was lost, for want of a rider, the kingdom was lost?* It would be foolish to lose Ernest over something so trivial. She slowed her pace and entered the main salon, where Ernest and Millicent awaited.

"They're on the street," she announced. "They should be here within a couple of minutes."

They had debated over the precise location of the *accidental* meeting, and they finally agreed that it would be best to have Ernest see them exiting the house. That way, he would be unlikely to think Tempy had followed him to Bath. But the plan required precise timing.

Millicent stood and donned her ostrich feather hat. "This should help him identify us," she commented. Apparently she was aware of how distinctive her hat made her. Tempy had wondered about that.

A moment later, they heard a sharp knock on the front door. It was Boothby's signal that the couple was nearing the entrance.

Millicent took the lead, with her ostrich feather fluttering as she moved. Tempy and Lucien followed her out the door. Tempy slid her hand around Lucien's arm as they moved out onto the sidewalk. She carefully kept her gaze directed toward the ground because she wanted Ernest to find her, and not vice versa.

She wasn't disappointed.

"Mrs. Kidman?" Ernest asked. "Is that you?"

Tempy held her breath.

"Mr. Lipscomb!" Millicent cried, evidently delighted to see him. Tempy fervently hoped her friend didn't ruin everything by overacting. "What a pleasant surprise to see you here. I had no idea you were in Bath."

"Nor I you. What brings you here?"

"I'm escorting Miss Bliss," she said, stepping aside so that Tempy was now face-to-face with Ernest.

When Ernest's gaze met hers, his jaw dropped. "Tempy?"

"Mr. Lipscomb? What on earth are you doing in Bath?" She shot him a look filled with suspicion. "This is quite a coincidence. First Hamlin House and now this? If I didn't know better, I'd think you were..." She left the words "following me" unsaid, but nonetheless, Ernest turned a bright shade of red.

"Uh, yes. I mean, I see."

"And I must remind you, please remember to call me Miss Bliss. I believe your fiancée might also prefer that you do so."

Ernest glanced at Clarisse, and although the woman continued to smile, her eyes narrowed fractionally as she examined Tempy.

Lucien must have noticed as well, because he smiled at Clarisse and bowed slightly. "Enchanté, mademoiselle."

Tempy glanced up at Lucien and was startled by the admiring look he was giving Clarisse. He was throwing himself into the role with entirely too much enthusiasm. Surely everyone would see through his ruse, wouldn't they? And that Clarisse person! Tempy could swear the woman was simpering at him. Between Millicent's reaction at seeing Ernest and Lucien fawning over Clarisse, Ernest was certain to see through their little scene.

Tempy clenched her teeth and smiled. "How pleasant to see you, Miss Beaumont. Are you touring our country?" she asked, hoping to underscore the other woman's foreignness.

"But it will soon be my country too," she replied. Her sharp little teeth were bright when she smiled.

Detestable woman.

"There's nothing quite like England," Lucien said, saving Tempy from saying something she might regret. "Of course, there's also nothing quite like France. I love them both."

"When you return to London," Clarisse said, "you'll find some news waiting for you. But it will keep." She smiled at that, looking entirely too pleased with herself.

"What brings you to Bath?" Ernest asked.

Tempy dragged her thoughts away from the self-satisfied expression Clarisse wore to reply to Ernest. "Lucien invited me and Millicent for a visit. It was very kind of him, wasn't it? I've never been to Bath before." Why on earth did Clarisse look so smug?

"I didn't know you wanted to come here," Ernest said, sounding defensive. He cast Lucien a peevish look. "I would have been happy to bring you."

"Would you?" Tempy cocked her head to one side. "How odd that you never offered."

"I-I suppose I always thought of you as a Londoner," Ernest stammered, "like your father. He hated to travel."

"Yes. Strange for a man who owned railroads, wasn't it?" She locked gazes with him, almost daring him to glance away as the seconds ticked by.

Lucien cleared his throat. "I can't tell you how pleased I am to be able to introduce you to more of England," he commented. Ernest glanced at him with a slightly bemused expression "It's a joy to travel with someone who is uninhibited in showing their delight with the world." Lucien took her hand and tucked it around his arm, giving it a possessive squeeze as he gazed down at her.

A small thrill of pleasure traveled through her at his words of approval. Lucien always knew exactly what to say.

"Miss Bliss, whatever are you doing in Bath?" a man said.

Tempy glanced down the street to see who was speaking and spied a heavyset older man with a full white beard bearing down on them. "Mr. Trevor," she said, startled to see the president of the Bliss Railways' board of directors. She automatically tightened her grip on Lucien's arm, but then forced herself to relax it. "I must say, I'm surprised to see you as well. Are you here on holiday?"

"No. I'm here on business. I assume that means you didn't read the memo I sent out two days ago." He looked irritated with her, which was typical. "We're having some problems with our Bath line and I've come to oversee things personally."

Tempy frowned. "But Mr. Shane is in charge of the Bath office. He's handling negotiations. I've always found him to be extremely competent."

Mr. Trevor let out a harrumph of annoyance. "I suppose that means you plan to interfere."

"I beg your pardon, Mr. Trevor, but it appears that you are the one planning to interfere. I may only be a shareholder..."

"Let's not mince words, Miss Bliss. As the majority shareholder, your influence is significant."

"I was attempting to be diplomatic, Mr. Trevor. But in response to your earlier statement, yes, I read your memo. I responded as well. Did you not read it?"

Trevor flushed. "And did you read the additional memo I sent out regarding the issue of your notoriety? These newspaper articles about you must end. They reflect poorly on Bliss Railways."

"What's this?" Ernest interrupted. "You know those articles are filled with nothing but half-truths and conjecture. Our Miss Bliss is nothing like the person Earl E. Byrd portrays in his articles."

"Our Miss Bliss?" Clarisse repeated in an icy tone.

Ernest frowned at her. "Tempy has been like a member of my family for years."

"Mr. Trevor," Lucien interrupted, "are you suggesting that you believe Miss Bliss is to blame for what Mr. Byrd is writing? Because that strikes me as a rather harsh point of view. Anyone who knows her realizes that his stories are false."

Bright patches of color crept up from beneath Mr. Trevor's

white beard. He might have looked jolly if not for the anger darkening his eyes. "My primary concern is for Bliss Railways."

Lucien narrowed his eyes. "But since Miss Bliss owns the majority of shares, shouldn't her well-being also be your concern?"

Mr. Trevor froze for a moment and then smiled tightly, looking as though his face might crack from the strain. "Of course you are right. Please accept my apologies, Miss Bliss." He took her hand briefly and dipped his head in a movement that resembled a bow.

Tempy nodded, feeling slightly bemused by Mr. Trevor's sudden capitulation. She was so used to being at odds with the man that she wasn't quite sure what to say.

"If you'll excuse me," Mr. Trevor said, "I have an engagement to keep. Good day."

He hurried off down the street without a backward glance.

"I never liked that man," Ernest muttered as he stepped forward, casually pushing his way between Tempy and Lucien.

"Truly?" Clarisse commented. "I found him rather sensible." The look she pinned Tempy with was pointed. Clarisse ignored the looks of surprise the others sent her way. She focused only only on Tempy, and her cool gaze seemed to take in Tempy's growing irritation with satisfaction.

Ernest didn't comment, but instead turned his back on Lucien and peered intently down at Tempy.

As if on cue, Lucien and Millicent both began speaking with Clarisse. It was difficult to tune out their conversations and focus on Ernest.

Millicent said, "Surely you found him a bit overbearing."

Tempy's chest tightened as Ernest leaned closer to her. "You seem different these days," he murmured into her ear. "Entrancing. There's a fire in you I've never seen before. What happened to you?"

Tempy glanced at Clarisse and wasn't surprised to see the woman glaring back. Clarice flushed with anger and then turned her attention back to Millicent. "Not at all," Clarisse said. "I found him most level-headed."

Tempy gave Ernest a coy look and spoke softly as she replied, "Am I really different, or are you just looking at me with fresh eyes?"

"Didn't you find his attack on Miss Bliss a bit harsh?" Lucien asked Clarisse.

Ernest reached out and took Tempy's hand. "Why do I keep seeing you with this Hamlin character? I don't think I approve of him."

Apparently Clarisse noticed them holding hands because her eyes flew wide and she looked as though one of her corset strings had just broken. "Ernest, we must be going." Clarisse darted forward and wrapped her hand around his arm, tugging him closer. "We'll be late."

Ernest snapped his head toward Clarisse in surprise. It was almost as though he'd forgotten she was there. He dropped Tempy's hand as he stepped away from her. "I'm sorry to hurry off, but we have an engagement we must keep."

"And it's always important to keep one's engagements." The words were out of Tempy's mouth before she could stop them, and she wished she could snatch them out of the air and shove them back into that deep hole of resentment from which they'd been born. But it was too late for that.

Lucien propelled her forward as he tipped his hat. He kept his head upright and facing forward, but under his breath he said, "Are you trying to sabotage yourself?"

"I know," she muttered. "The words just popped out before I could stop them." Then, she felt the quick surge of anger. "But what about you? What was that?"

"What was what?"

"You and Clarisse. I thought you were about to swoon at her feet."

"I'm trying to build a rapport with her, just as I said I would.

How can I drive a wedge between them if I haven't stirred her interest?"

He might sound logical, but that didn't mean Tempy had to accept such a weak excuse. "Well, stop being so overt about it. You'll scare her off."

Tempy heard footsteps hurrying up behind her, and then Millicent was at her elbow.

"It worked perfectly," she said, her voice breathless with excitement. "He kept looking back at you as you walked away, and Miss Beaumont was quite annoyed with him."

Tempy knew she should feel pleased with the outcome, but rather than feeling elated by the day's success, she could only feel her resentment toward Clarisse growing.

☙❧

"ARE YOU CERTAIN I SHOULD LEAVE NOW?" TEMPY ASKED Millicent as they joined Lucien for breakfast. "Shouldn't I push even harder now that I have him off balance?"

"Better to disappear and let his paranoia work against him. He'll be expecting to see you again in Bath, so let him keep waiting and wondering."

"I agree," said Lucien. "It will eat at him, and the lovely Clarisse will grow more and more frustrated with his distracted state."

Tempy's mood grew even more sour. The lovely Clarisse? "It seems she's gathering quite a few admirers."

"You mean me? That's ludicrous. I see women like her at the casino every day. They're nothing special, except perhaps to sheltered men like your Ernest."

"Then why are you and Ernest so enchanted with her?"

He paused in the act of raising a piece of toast to his mouth. "I can't speak for Ernest, but I am most definitely not enchanted with her. I prefer a woman more like you. Someone who is more straightforward and forthright. Someone who says what she means."

"Yes. That's me. Forthright. See how forthright I am in my pursuit of Ernest?"

He paused at that. "I think your behavior of late in your dealings with Ernest doesn't show the real you. It's simply a role you're playing. In fact, you might want to put some thought into how you will maintain this façade once Ernest comes crawling back to you. Because he will. Mark my words, he will."

Tempy shrugged. "I can keep Mary to help me with my hair, and now that I've learned these skills, they won't simply disappear. I'm certain I'll be able to keep most of the polish I've worked so hard to develop."

Lucien shrugged. "I'm certain you can, if that's the life you want. If that's the man you want."

"What's that supposed to mean?"

"Exactly what it sounds like. Perhaps you and Clarisse have more in common than I realized, because you both seem to want a weak-willed man to control."

"Ernest is not weak-willed." How could Lucien make such a quick judgment about him? They'd hardly spoken.

"No? Then why did he lose so much at my casino on his last visit?"

"What?"

"I extended him credit that evening. He even used your name to try to persuade me to offer it to him. He promised to pay me the next day, and he didn't. If he can't afford to lose money, he shouldn't gamble."

"Of course he can't afford to lose the money." Tempy could feel a deep flush suffuse her face and she wasn't sure if it was from anger with Lucien or embarrassment for Ernest. Perhaps it was both. "His father's a doctor, not some peer of the realm."

Lucien's face fell. "What? He's a doctor's son?"

Seeing his surprise mollified her somewhat, and her embarrassment for Ernest began to win out. "How is he supposed to pay you back?"

"I'm sorry, Tempy. I had no idea." He pressed his napkin to his lips. "How would you like to handle this? I only extended credit because I believed he was wealthy and because he said you'd vouch for him. I have no interest in becoming part of a conflict that will complicate your relationship with him. Nor do I want to fleece the man. If you like, I can forgive the debt and ban him from my casino."

Tempy shook her head. "Ban him from the casino? That seems extreme. He'd be humiliated. And I can't let you take over his debt. You've already done so much to help me. I wouldn't want his gambling losses on my conscience as well. Let me discuss it with his family first. I'm certain we'll come up with a solution."

"Then I'll leave it in your hands. I trust your judgment in this."

Tempy nodded, pleased by his confidence in her.

But what would she do about Ernest?

Perhaps it was just as well that she wouldn't see him for a few days. It would give her time to find a solution to this sticky problem.

Perhaps the trip to Exmoor was for the best after all.

❦ 19 ❦

AN INAUSPICIOUS DAY

໒໒ৎ

Or perhaps they'd both die of exposure. Tempy pushed a dripping strand of wet hair behind her ear and glared moodily at the dark sky.

FREAK RAINSTORM BANISHES BLISS

She shivered and leaned closer to Lucien.

The clear day that had greeted them that morning had lulled them into a false sense of complacency as they left Bath. Riding in a carriage with the top folded down had seemed like a grand idea.

But once they were away from the city, the day had turned on them with a vengeance. Clouds blew in from the coast, carrying rain.

Lots and lots of rain.

Every inch of Tempy, from her scalp down to her undergarments, was soaked. She shivered as water trailed from her sodden hair and down her back.

The pretty little cabriolet no longer held the same appeal that it had when Lucien had suggested he drive the two-seater to

Exmoor. Tempy shifted to glare over her shoulder at the unmoving convertible top, which was furled behind her and provided no protection from the heavy downpour.

BROKEN CARRIAGE DAMPENS BLISS

"'Let's ride on ahead of the others. It'll be fun,'" Tempy muttered, mocking her earlier words. Right now, she wished she were curled up, dry and warm, next to Millicent in the slow, plodding carriage. The one with four wheels and a fixed top that kept out the rain. She could even be using the time productively, working on her article.

Tempy sighed.

"What did you say?" Lucien asked loudly, competing with the sound of the rain.

"Nothing," she shouted back, letting some of her irritation seep into her voice.

He shot her an inquisitive look, but she glanced away, ignoring him.

At first the drive in the jaunty, two-wheeled little cabriolet had been glorious. She'd rejoiced in the unobstructed view it provided with its top down.

Well, she'd had her fill of that view.

When the rain had threatened, Lucien had stopped to pull up the collapsible top, but the folding mechanism remained stubbornly immobile. No matter how hard he pulled and pried, it refused to move.

She'd tried pulling as well. She didn't care if it didn't look ladylike. Anything would be better than just sitting there getting wet. But the top was rusted firmly in place.

"I think I see lights up ahead," Lucien shouted to her now. "I think it's a town."

Tempy squinted, trying to make anything out in the heavy downpour. She thought she saw a dim light in the distance. "Maybe they'll have an inn or a pub where we can stop," she shouted back. "And if they don't, I'll bang on someone's door and beg for help."

Pressed next to Lucien to keep warm, she felt his laugh rather than hearing it. She thought he muttered, "I'm sure you would," but she couldn't hear him clearly and decided not to ask him to repeat himself.

Fortunately, she didn't have to resort to begging for shelter since the first two structures she spotted were an inn and its stables.

At least *something* was in their favor.

Lucien helped her jump down from the cabriolet. She landed solidly, but her first step landed her in a puddle that went halfway up her ankle. *It doesn't matter*, she told herself as her shoes squelched with every step. *It's not as though I can get any wetter.*

Lucien shouldered open the door of the inn, letting in a gust of wind as they both stumbled through it. The air inside was warm against her skin, but the feeling of welcome was shattered by a startled shriek.

"Ahh!" a woman squealed.

Tempy's gaze flew toward the source of the sound, and she saw a serving girl near the fireplace with both hands over her mouth. Her eyes were round.

The two men sitting next to the fire burst out in guffaws. "That'll teach ya ta listen ta ghost stories on a stormy afternoon," one of them said in a mock-scolding tone.

"Fetch some blankets," the man behind the bar shouted at her. "And be quick about it. These two are soaked through."

The girl scurried through a door and returned quickly with the blankets. She handed one to Lucien and helped drape the other one around Tempy's shoulders. Her eyes were wide as she watched them, as if she still wasn't quite certain that they were real. Tempy was tempted to say "boo" just to test her theory, but she managed to refrain.

The two men sitting next to the fire vacated their seats and offered them to the sodden pair. Tempy smiled gratefully and squished across the floor, drawn by the flames and their promise of warmth. Lucien and the barman followed, but the girl scurried away and disappeared through the door again. Given her propensity for screaming, that was probably for the best.

"My boy is stabling your horse." The man wiped his hands on his apron. "I'm Sanders, Will Sanders, and this is my place. We don't have any rooms right now, but you're welcome to sit by the fire as long as you like."

Tempy and Lucien both sat, and with Mr. Sanders's help, she scooted her chair as close to the hearth as she dared. She held her hands out toward the flames, fingers splayed to soak up the heat.

Mr. Sanders seemed like a genial host, despite the shrill reception they'd received from his serving girl. Tempy sensed that making them feel welcome was very important to him. That was always a good attitude for an innkeeper to hold.

"You look familiar to me," Sanders said. "I'm usually good with faces. Do I know you?"

Tempy glanced up and saw that he was looking at Lucien.

"No," Lucien said without bothering to break the gaze he kept locked on the flames.

Tempy noticed the muscles of Lucien's jaw tightening. This had all the appearances of being one of those moments when it would be best for her to change the subject. She gazed up at Sanders, doing her best to look wistful, and asked, "Do you think you could bring us a pot of tea," she glanced at Lucien and decide he looked as though he could use something a bit stronger, "and some whiskey?"

Sanders furrowed his brow. His renewed concern for the welfare of his guests seemed to push all other thoughts from his mind. "I'll add some water to the kettle. T'won't take long." But before he turned away, he gave Lucien's profile one last look. Then he left, rubbing his chin.

"What was that about?" she asked.

"What? Him?" Lucien shrugged. "He's just mistaken. That's all."

"You've never met him before?"

Lucien shrugged, but didn't respond.

Tempy narrowed her eyes. She didn't like the evasion. "You're hiding something. I can tell."

"Can you also tell that I don't want to discuss it?" he snapped.

Tempy jerked her head back in surprise. Fine. If that's the way he wanted to act, then so be it. She returned her gaze to the fire and studiously ignored him. He didn't have to confide in her. After all, what was she to him? Just an inconvenience, nothing more.

Still, his tone stung. Apparently her growing affection toward him was more one-sided than she'd realized.

The silence stretched between them, and Tempy noticed that the sound of the storm outside had altered. The worst of the rain seemed to have passed, and it had settled into a slow, steady drizzle.

Lucien cleared his throat, but didn't speak. Finally he glanced up. "Where is that innkeeper?"

As if on cue, Sanders pushed through the door leading to what must be the kitchen. He carried a tray laden with teapot, teacups, and two short glasses holding an amber liquid--whiskey.

Sanders set the tray down on a nearby table and then adjusted another small table so that it sat between Lucien and Tempy.

"The blacksmith looked at your carriage," Sanders said as he finished making his adjustments to the furniture. "He said it's a fine one, but hasn't been maintained in a while. He was able to loosen the accordion hinges on the collapsible top and clear away a great deal of the rust, but he recommends having it maintained more frequently." He sounded reproachful. Or, at least, as reproachful as an innkeeper dared to be toward a patron.

"I inherited it only recently," Lucien said. "It's been in storage."

"Well, if he left you anything else, you might want to check it over before you use it."

"That's excellent advice. I'll certainly follow it."

The innkeeper looked pleased with himself and returned to the bar.

The heat from the fire seeped its way into Tempy's flesh, and the tea worked its magic as well. Soon, she felt much better. Her voluminous skirts soaked up the heat, and she could see tendrils of steam rising from the hem closest to the fire. The only thing that would help more than sitting next to a hot fire would be to change out of her wet clothes. But that would have to wait until Millicent and the others arrived with the trunks. Of course, with their delay here at the inn, they might all arrive at Lucien's Exmoor estate at the same time.

Lucien cleared his throat, startling Tempy. He hadn't spoken to her since he'd scolded her for prying into his life. "Since the rain has let up and we now have a roof for the cabriolet, would you be willing to continue on our journey? We're nearly there."

"We are?" It seemed as if they'd been traveling all day, but when she checked the clock on the wall, she realized they had only spent a little over four hours on the road. "I'm in favor of leaving now. I'm looking forward to being completely dry again."

Lucien signaled to Sanders that they were ready to depart. After throwing a few coins on the table, Lucien picked up his whiskey, tipped his head back and tossed it down his throat in a fluid motion. He jutted his chin toward the tray. "Finish up your whiskey."

She glanced at the remaining still-full glass on the tray. Father had often imbibed in a bit of whiskey on a cold, damp evening, but she'd never tried it. She hadn't really intended to order one for herself, but perhaps she could give it a try. After all, this was a bit of a holiday, wasn't it? She picked it up and took a sniff. Its sharp, smoky scent seemed specifically designed for her current surroundings.

She glanced at Lucien. He was watching her, and the ghost of a smile tugged at the corner of his mouth. Did he think she wouldn't drink it? She raised her chin at the challenge. If he thought she'd be too missish, he didn't know her very well.

Tempy brought the glass to her lips and tipped back her head, swallowing half of the liquid in a gulp, mimicking the motion Lucien had made.

She immediately regretted it. The whiskey burned, and liquid fire ran down her throat. Tears welled up in her eyes and a hacking cough burst from her mouth. She covered her lips with the back of the hand that still held the whiskey glass, and as she continued to cough, Lucien began thumping on her back with the flat of his hand.

"Have a sip of tea," he said, pulling the whiskey glass from her grip and replacing it with her half-empty teacup.

She followed his advice, and the tepid liquid soothed the fire in her throat.

"I see you've never drunk whiskey before. It seems that I'm introducing you to a number of firsts. Wasn't that your first glass of champagne as well?"

First champagne.

First whiskey.

First real kiss.

Tempy's throat tightened, and she set down her teacup with clatter. The kiss. Was that why he'd been staring at her so intently before she drank the whiskey? Was he remembering what had happened the last time he'd offered her something containing alcohol?

Instead of answering him, she stood and yanked the blanket from her shoulders. She couldn't trust herself to look at Lucien, so she busied herself with folding the blanket as neatly as possible.

Tempy knew that if she looked at him, she'd end up staring at his mouth. Even now, she wondered how it would feel to press her lips against his again. To have those sensations course through her body like tendrils of fire. Warmth began to grow in her that she couldn't attribute to the whiskey.

Perhaps another ride in the rain would cool her off.

She hurried back toward the entrance and Lucien followed. Sanders met them at the door and pressed a bundle into Lucien's hands. "For the young lady," he said, smiling at her.

Lucien murmured his thanks and ushered Tempy outside where they ducked into the cabriolet. Now its roof was up and she could only hope it would keep off the worst of the rain for the remainder of the trip.

Lucien shook open the bundle Mr. Sanders had given him, and Tempy realized it was a large piece of oilcloth. She grinned at the man in gratitude, and then she snapped it open and spread the cloth over her skirts. It smelled sharply of linseed oil, but that didn't bother her as long as it helped keep the water off.

"Thank you," she said to Sanders. "We don't have much farther to go, so this should keep me dry for the rest of our drive."

Sanders smiled and nodded at her, but then froze. Just as Lucien flicked the horse's reins, Sanders said, "I knew it. I knew I recognized you. You're the new earl, what's come back to Exmoor."

Lucien shrugged, as usual. "Might be."

The man chuckled. "This should be an interesting few days. I'd like to be around when news of your arrival reaches certain ears. Just as long as I'm not *too* close. I'd hate to get in the way of any stray blows."

Lucien grimaced. "Then you might want to keep your distance." He flicked the reins and the cabriolet lurched forward, leaving the innkeeper standing in the drizzle and wearing an expression of delighted anticipation.

Tempy peered around the edge of the cabriolet's top, trying to watch the innkeeper, and saw him spin on his heel and hurry into the door of the building. She could hear him shouting, "He's back! Formsworth's bane is back!"

Lucien ignored the man and kept driving.

Tempy watched Lucien's profile. "I see you've been here before. Why didn't you tell him who you were when he first asked?"

"Once that man knows I'm here, so will everyone else in the county, and I was hoping news of my arrival wouldn't precede me."

"He called you Formsworth's bane. What's that all about?"

Lucien shrugged, but said nothing.

Annoying, taciturn man.

But she'd been right about one thing. The rain successfully dampened her ardor.

20

NEWS TRAVELS FAST

Lucien felt like a dolt. What kind of person rides off in a carriage without making sure that it's in good working order?

A dolt.

But when he'd seen Tempy's excitement at the prospect of making their journey in the cabriolet, he'd never paused to wonder if it had been well maintained.

In retrospect, he really should have known better. Especially considering the lackadaisical attitudes both of his uncles had had toward their inheritance. They never took care of their toys, no matter how much they cost. And his grandfather had been no better.

As they crested a rise, Lucien caught sight of the large, fortress-like estate he'd inherited. His surge of relief at the thought of being dry was mingled with tension. His memories associated with that place were all from long ago, and just now he couldn't think of a single good one.

The reddish stone building rose up from the emerald-green

grass like a fist. It was strong and imposing, just like his grandfather had been. Lucien's entire body tensed as he allowed the image of it to sink in, and he worked to alter his perception of the place.

A wing extended to one side. A wing he'd somehow forgotten about over time. It was made of glass, but it didn't glitter in the rain and drizzle, it merely looked flat and gray in the dim half-light. Despite that, his spirits lifted, just a little, at the sight of it. He'd always been intrigued by the estate's conservatory, and now it was his.

So, with slightly improved spirits, Lucien pulled the cabriolet in front of the main entrance of his estate. Just a few minutes later, the coach bearing Millicent, Boothby, and Mary arrived.

Boothby quickly assessed the bedraggled state of his employer and had all of the baggage delivered to the appropriate rooms within minutes. Mary made sure that Tempy's trunk was the first item to be unloaded, and she escorted it upstairs herself.

Fortunately, the staff at the estate was efficient, and they rushed to bring the bedraggled travelers hot water in their respective rooms. It didn't take long for Lucien to change into dry clothes, run a comb through his damp hair, and then set off to begin investigating the current state of the household.

Lucien trotted down the broad main staircase, his mood lighter than he'd anticipated. It was all due to the competency of the staff, he mentally acknowledged. Despite the lack of attention by the former Earls of Cavendish, the building and grounds had been well maintained. After questioning the butler, Barberry, Lucien discovered that there'd been little turnover among the household staff and the gardeners. Their meticulous attention to detail, even without the presence of an owner, should be commended. And would be. This estate, at least, could be removed from Lucien's list of potential problems.

The only thing that still appeared to require his immediate attention was the land dispute with his neighbor. After all, it was what had brought him here. He'd hoped it wouldn't come to this. He'd had a bad relationship with Squire Marcus Formsworth for as long as he could remember, and the upcoming court case between them was certain to be contentious.

Lucien moved toward the southern wing of the building, intent on his plan to explore the conservatory.

He pushed open the glass doors and breathed in the rich aroma of a well-tended garden. The groundskeepers had outdone themselves. The orangery was filled with citrus trees and was dotted throughout with fountains and grottoes. If Lucien recalled correctly, some of those trees were more than one hundred years old.

Lucien walked through the warm, humid space. It was enormous. Once could easily lose one's way inside it. The gnarled roots of the older citrus trees pushed up through the brick pavers of the walkway, and their heavy branches created lush archways that invited further exploration.

When he was a boy, his father had brought him to the estate for a brief visit. Back then, he hadn't been permitted to enter the conservatory for fear he'd damage the plants. If he'd realized what he'd been missing at the time, he'd have found a way to sneak in, no matter what the consequences. Even now, he could imagine discovering King Arthur's sword in one of the grottoes or fighting a dragon bearing down on him from the tops of the lime trees.

It would be a wonderful, magical place for entertaining when the weather turned bad.

Like now.

Inspiration smacked him between the eyes. It would be a shame not to enjoy the space during the short time they were here. He'd instruct the butler, Barberry, to have dinner served in the conservatory this evening. He imagined Tempy's delight at exploring the space and smiled in anticipation.

Lucien was lost in thought as he reached for the doorknob. When he glanced up to look through one of the panes of glass in the door, he was startled to see Tempy peering back at him. A relaxed smile softened her face. It was a vast improvement over the pinched expression she'd worn since they'd left the inn, and Lucien felt himself smiling back.

He opened the door.

"Why weren't you more excited to arrive here when you knew that this gloriously magical spot was waiting for you?" she asked with mock severity.

He shrugged. In the distance, he heard a loud bang, like the slam of a door. "I haven't spent much time here."

"That's a shame," Tempy said.

He heard a shout, and this time, Tempy seemed to hear something as well.

"Did someone just shout your name? I could have sworn I heard a man yell 'Hamlin.'"

Lucien's stomach sank. "This might turn ugly. Perhaps you should stay here," Lucien said, and turned toward the main entrance of the house.

Of course, Tempy ignored him. She seemed to do that frequently. The silk of her skirts rustled as she followed him through the maze of rooms as he headed toward the main foyer.

"Hamlin! I know you're here!" shouted the man.

Lucien rounded a corner and entered the foyer, coming face to face with the man who had forced him to travel here.

Formsworth's normally ruddy complexion was red with anger. He was just as muscular as Lucien remembered, and had gained only a few pounds in the past fifteen or so years since they'd last spoken.

"Formsworth. What a surprise. By your tone of voice, I take it you haven't arrived to wish me luck in my new role as Earl of Cavendish," Lucien said in a falsely friendly tone, unable to prevent himself from goading the man. How bright a shade of red could Formsworth's face produce without causing steam to spout from his ears?

From the corner of his vision, he could see Tempy frowning at the scene.

Some of Lucien's servants began to gather in the hallway behind Formsworth. The housemaids hung back, but Boothby and the butler, Barberry, were whispering with one another, and Lucien saw them separate and position themselves at Formsworth's flanks. Their protective attitudes came as a surprise to him, but he felt heartened as well. He wasn't used to people taking his side against the squire. Especially if the altercation turned physical.

It certainly hadn't happened that way the last time Formsworth and his thugs had come after him.

Boothby's face looked flushed as well, although it wasn't as red as Formsworth's. The young man remained focused and kept his gaze trained on Formsworth.

"Hamlin or Cavendish, it doesn't matter what name you use now. Don't think you can just come strolling back here and have us accept you with open arms. You should leave while you can. You're no more welcome now than you were as a boy."

"Do you mean to suggest that everyone plans to rise up against the new earl and drive him from their midst?" Lucien said, his tone oozing with sarcasm. "I think you're overestimating your pull around here. Do you believe I'm like Mary Shelly's monster in *Frankenstein*, to be reviled wherever I go? I can assure you, I'm not. Although I think they long ago came to recognize the *true* monster in their midst."

"Lucien, stop goading the man," Tempy murmured just loud enough for him to hear as she sidled away from the pair.

Steam didn't burst from Formsworth's ears, but it might as well have. Lucien's words served to ignite the man's barely contained fury, and he lurched forward, clenching his hands into fists. "You scoundrel! You blackened my name all through London." Formsworth crossed the foyer in two long strides and swung his arm in an arcing blow aimed directly at Lucien's chin.

Lucien stepped back, easily avoiding the blow, and he was relieved when Tempy took shelter by stepping through a doorway and ducking around the corner.

Formsworth continued trying to rain blows upon Lucien, but the majority of them missed. Lucien ducked from side to side, his fists raised in a boxing stance. For a few moments, the only sounds in the large foyer were of leather soles sliding against the marble floor and of faint exhalations of exertion that were sprinkled with occasional sharp intakes of breath by one of the onlookers. Most of Lucien's own carefully placed jabs hit their mark, and Formsworth's onslaught began to waver.

Formsworth took a step backwards and Lucien risked a quick glance over his shoulder. Tempy was still safely hidden around the corner. Only the top of her head and her eyes could be seen as she peeked around the corner to watch the fight.

Lucien turned his attention back to Formsworth and wiped the back of his hand across his upper lip to remove the faint sheen of perspiration that had formed. Formsworth's brow was beaded with sweat, and it dripped down the sides of his face like tears.

"If you'd paid me the money you owed me," Lucien said, "you'd still be able to hold your chin up in the city. You knew as well as I did that it was a legitimate bet. You never should have tried to hide behind my grandfather."

Formsworth stepped forward, ready to renew his onslaught, but at the same moment Boothby and Barberry darted forward, each grabbing one of Formsworth's arms and wrestling them behind his back.

Formsworth tried to jerk free but couldn't, so instead he glared at the butler. Barberry didn't seem fazed, and his face remained impassive.

Formsworth turned his attention back to Lucien. "You cheated me," he insisted, his impotent anger ringing through the marble foyer. "You've always been a cheat and always will be."

Lucien shook his head. "It was a fair race. You were simply angry because you lost. I didn't own either of the horses that raced that day, and I didn't wager any of my own money. You always conveniently forget that you insisted that I take your bet. In fact, you begged me to accept your marker."

"You manipulated me. How was I to know the horse would break his leg and have to be put down? That was *your* friend on his back. You stood to make quite a bit of money when the favorite went down in that race. It was supposed to be a sure thing."

Lucien shrugged. "Lots of other people were certain that horse would win too. But they still covered their losses. And I used those funds to pay the winners."

"And kept a tidy sum for yourself. Your grandfather knew you were a cheat and a liar. He knew you'd paid the rider to take a fall. That's what counts."

Lucien snorted. "My grandfather made good on your debt to me. You never knew that, did you? He sent me the money along with a note asking that I ignore all of your accusations because you were his neighbor. He couldn't side with me publicly because he knew you'd make life difficult for him. He always *was* one to take the easy route when possible. But there's one thing I know for sure--if he'd really believed your accusations, he never would've sent me that money."

Formsworth went red in the face again and renewed his struggle to escape from Boothby and Barberry, but failed. "Let go of me!" he shouted, his frustration ringing through the large, echoing foyer.

"Not with the way you're swinging those fists," Boothby said, wrenching Formsworth's arm farther back to underscore the fact that the man was under his control.

When Squire Formsworth heard Boothby's voice, his entire body went rigid for a moment. He slowly swiveled around as far as possible to stare into Boothby's eyes. Then he turned a baleful gaze back on Lucien.

"You...you...," he sputtered. "Why did you bring that man here?"

"Leave him out of this," Lucien said, standing a bit straighter. "Let's stay focused on one outrage at a time, shall we?"

If possible, Formsworth managed to turn an even more livid shade of red. "I've had just about enough of this," Formsworth said, his voice shaking with anger.

"And so have I." Lucien suddenly realized it was true. He focused his eyes just past Formsworth's shoulder and met Boothby's gaze. "Please show this *gentleman* to the door."

Boothby grinned and began hustling Formsworth through the foyer, ignoring both his struggling and his angry protestations of "I'm not done here yet" and "You can't treat me this way."

Boothby and Barberry refrained from literally pushing the man down the single front step of the house, but the unintentional consequences of them suddenly and simultaneously releasing his arms resulted in much the same effect. With his arms abruptly free, Formsworth lost his balance, stumbled forward, and tripped down the step, falling onto his hands and knees in the gravel.

Unperturbed, Barberry gently closed the door on the scene. His calm gaze sought out Lucien's. "Would you like me to serve tea now?"

"Tea sounds like an excellent suggestion, Mr. Barberry," Lucien said.

Tempy let out a snort. "Nothing tea can't cure, right?" she asked.

Lucien glanced at her, surprised by her tart tone, but she wouldn't meet his gaze. Even so, he could see that she was irate. But why?

Millicent hurried down the staircase, a broad smile on her face. "Formsworth looked like a red bantam rooster," she said.

"He kept chasing after you, getting angrier and angrier that he couldn't hit you. If I weren't so annoyed with him for all the trouble he caused, I'd feel sorry for him."

"No need to waste any sympathy on him. His problem is that he's used to hitting people who don't hit back."

Millicent's eyes widened. "What do you mean?"

What on earth had he been thinking? He hadn't meant to say anything. At least, not right now. But by the shocked expressions on both Millicent's and Tempy's faces, they wouldn't be easily put off. "Let's have that tea, shall we?"

Tempy's eyes narrowed, but she nodded and followed Lucien and Millicent into the drawing room. As soon as they settled into chairs, Barberry set the tea tray on the low table by the sofa.

Millicent poured the tea. As soon as everyone had a cup in hand, Tempy rose to her feet and pinned Lucien with a stare.

"Can you explain that to me? Because it appeared to me that you and that man are carrying on a vendetta. I watched you manipulate him in order to fuel his anger. I've seen you diffuse situations like that at your casino, but you didn't do that here. Instead you goaded him into that brawl."

If she'd slapped him, he wouldn't have been more surprised. "That man doesn't deserve your pity. He's a snake."

"Why?"

"Does it even matter? You've already passed judgment."

"You need to explain this to me, because I don't like the side of you I just saw. I don't like seeing people resort to solving problems with their fists."

He said nothing.

"Tell me. I need to understand."

"Life isn't as simple and perfect as you seem to believe, Miss Bliss, and justice isn't equal for all. That man's a murderer. He abused his wife and then murdered her. He even bragged to me about it at her funeral."

He'd clearly shocked Tempy, because she suddenly sat back down.

Millicent clattered her teacup as she set it on the table. "That makes no sense. If that's true, why wasn't he hanged?"

"Because my grandfather backed him rather than me. As usual." Lucien sighed and scrubbed at his face with one hand. "It's an old story, but its aftereffects still linger."

"Tell us." Tempy pressed, but her voice was softer now, and not so angry. A long lock of her hair had come lose, and it curved inwardly, framing her face like a parenthesis.

"What you just saw isn't unusual for Formsworth. He's an abusive man who likes hitting people." Lucien paused. "Especially women."

Millicent gasped, but Tempy pressed her lips together. She didn't look surprised. She looked grim.

"And how is it that you know about it?" Tempy asked.

This was the part he didn't like to think about. The part that still haunted him. "I knew two of the women. One quite well, and the other only slightly." He took a breath and held it for a moment, then let it out in a loud sigh. "They're both dead now, and I believe their deaths can be attributed to his mistreatment. One was his wife; the other was his mistress."

"Are you saying he killed them both?" Millicent's hand trembled as she picked up her teacup. She steadied it with her other hand, but other than that, she seemed to ignore the cup.

"Yes. No." He shook his head. "I'm certain that he killed his wife, and he indirectly caused his mistress's death." At their confused expressions, Lucien stopped to collect his thoughts. "He was a cruel husband. He made Rebecca's life miserable—he'd say hateful things to her in front of friends and then pretend it was all in jest, and later he'd scream at her in private, calling her an ingrate and an imbecile. After he found out that her family was becoming upset with his behavior, he began controlling her communication with her family and cut her off from her friends.

He deliberately isolated her so that he was all that was left. It chipped away at her, stealing bits of her soul." His bitterness at himself rose up. "I wish I'd been here to help her, but I wasn't. I was in London, and had no notion what was happening.

"It wasn't until I spoke to her brother while he was visiting London that I learned she might have a problem. He was worried, of course, but nobody guessed the extent to which her husband's love for her had transformed into such an obsessive need to control her."

"That's not love," Tempy burst out vehemently. "That's ownership. Possession. Love should lift people up, not tear them down."

"Some people have a warped understanding of the emotion," Lucien said. "Formsworth claimed that he loved her and couldn't live without her. But that obviously wasn't true."

Millicent shook her head. "Legally, it would have been difficult for you to do anything. After all, men are allowed to discipline their wives as they see fit."

Lucien shook his head, rejecting her words. "It was cruelty hiding behind the mask of discipline." He closed his eyes for a moment, recalling memories he hadn't paused to dwell upon in years.

"I was able to contact her and offer my help. She smuggled out a reply to me through a servant. We arranged to meet in secret so that she could go into hiding, but when I arrived at our rendezvous location, she wasn't there. I waited all through the night, but she never appeared. The next day I learned she'd died in a riding accident. Supposedly, she'd been thrown from her horse and had broken her neck." He shook his head. "I had a hard time believing it. She'd been a good horsewoman, and the timing of her accident seemed all too coincidental. I remember wondering if she could have fallen as she hurried to meet me." He clenched his jaw. "But when I attended her funeral, I found out the truth. Formsworth made certain I knew exactly what had happened."

Lucien remained silent for a moment, remembering that day by her graveside. Formsworth had sought him out, staying behind to speak to him. No one else had been nearby to overhear their conversation. Lucien could still see Formsworth stalking toward him, eyes narrowed in anger and an envelope clutched in his hand.

Lucien cleared his throat. "Formsworth found my letter and discovered her plans to escape. He told me that he killed her while she sat doing her needlework. He crept up behind her and with a quick twist, he broke her neck."

Tempy gasped and reached out to touch Lucien's hand, but apparently she had second thoughts, because she drew it back. He wished she hadn't pulled away. Her touch would have been comforting.

"For years, that image haunted me," Lucien continued, staring at Tempy's clenched hand as she focused her gaze on the fireplace. "I would imagine Rebecca sitting quietly, perhaps lost in her thoughts and dreaming of escape, and then feeling his hands on her. Did she experience the horror of knowing he was about to kill her? Or did she die dreaming of a life without him?"

"But why isn't he in prison?" Millicent asked. "I know you must have told someone."

"Of course I did, but it didn't do any good. Rebecca's body was found out on the moor, and her horse was saddled and running loose. Formsworth accused me of making it all up. Nobody believed me."

Millicent's teacup clattered against the saucer again as she set it on the tray. She gave the nearly full cup an irritated glance and pushed it away from her, as though to remind herself not to pick it up again. "You mustn't torture yourself over what happened. You're not the one who killed her. If fact, you're the only one who made any attempt to save her."

"That's no comfort," Lucien said in a flat tone. "She's still dead."

"What of the other woman?" Tempy asked, still staring into

the flames. Her voice sounded hollow and distant. "You mentioned a mistress."

Lucien took a deep breath. "After my friend's death, I arranged to have someone keep watch on Formsworth. I didn't want anyone else to suffer the same fate as Rebecca."

Tempy must have noticed the long lock of hair that had come loose, because she reached up and tucked it behind her ear. "That sounds like an excellent idea."

"Formsworth never remarried. Instead, he kept a series of mistresses. Perhaps he decided that marriage was too messy. Or perhaps he didn't want to have to explain another dead bride. His first mistress lived with him for months before leaving him, and after that, few stayed for long. I think they left when he became abusive. But that first one lasted longer than the rest. It wasn't until she discovered she was pregnant that she broke things off."

"Do you think he struck her?" Tempy asked.

"I know he did. She told me so when I went to speak to her."

"Did you contact all of his former mistresses?" Millicent asked. She raised a handkerchief to her mouth and coughed into it.

"Only those I believed were in danger or needed my help. The man I hired to watch him was to contact me if he believed Formsworth might hurt someone again. He also made sure that Formsworth knew he was being watched, and that if anyone went missing, he'd be held accountable."

"And the man you hired believed this woman needed your help?" Tempy asked.

Lucien nodded. "She loved him. It was only because of her concern for her unborn child that she left Formsworth. After the birth, she tried one last time to convince him to recognize the child as his son, but he refused. She gave up on the man after that, and planned to raise her baby alone, but she developed childbed fever and died a little over a week after giving birth."

"That's all so sad," Millicent said. "What became of the child?"

"A friend of the mother's took him in and raised him. She said she couldn't bear the idea of handing him over to an orphanage where he'd probably die. Over the years, I helped where I could. He's doing very well now."

"I've heard too many stories like that in my life to be surprised by this one," Millicent said. "Life is already hard enough, but when a woman falls victim to an abusive man, her life becomes unbearable."

"Do these women know you're watching out for them?" Tempy asked, glancing over at him.

Lucien shrugged. "Very few of them."

"I'm sorry I doubted you." Tempy said. "I never imagined the kind of man he really was. He looked so normal." She shook her head and sighed. "He's a monster hiding in plain sight." She turned her attention back the fire.

Lucien followed her gaze and became mesmerized as he watched flames swirling around the logs in a loving embrace. As he watched, the flames became Formsworth, consuming and laying waste to everything he touched. The room fell silent except for the sound of the hissing flames and the collapsing logs.

21

DINNER IN THE CONSERVATORY

Warm air, redolent with the rich scents of fruit trees, enveloped Tempy as she entered the conservatory. At first, the sound of rain hitting the glass panels of the building and the low murmur of running water muffled any other noise, but as she followed the path toward the center of the conservatory, she detected the low murmur of voices.

She followed the sound. Delicate gas torches lined the gravel walkway, lighting her way like fairy lights. When she passed a bushy tropical plant and rounded a bend, she found herself in a large open area. Lucien and Millicent were already there, seated at a dining table in the center of the space.

Lucien stood as soon as he saw Tempy, his large form in the black frock coat making an inky blot of darkness against the shiny green foliage. Tonight, he wore a rich purple waistcoat that seemed to drink in the light.

"Welcome," he said. "Did you have any trouble finding us?" His gaze scanned her from head to toe, causing her to warm slightly.

What did he see when he looked at her that way? She glanced down at her white dress, wondering if it was an appropriate choice for dinner in an indoor garden. When she glanced back up at Lucien, his expression remained impassive. That was fortunate; otherwise she was certain she would have blushed even more. Something seemed different about the man. Or perhaps it was simply that she was learning more about him. He was more complex than she'd imagined. And perhaps a bit more dangerous. At least, dangerous to his enemies.

The tension in her shoulders eased a bit. "I had no trouble all," Tempy replied as she moved toward her seat at the table. "I simply followed the torches."

A silver charger plate was set in front of each of the three chairs at the small table, and the crystal wine glasses glittered in the torchlight. Tempy took her seat.

Millicent cleared her throat. "You had an inspired idea to have us dine in the conservatory this evening, Lucien. This room feels so lush and primal. We really should be reclining on couches while someone feeds us grapes, just like in ancient Rome." She touched a handkerchief to her upper lip.

One of the young footmen lost his stoic expression, showing momentary shock at hearing her words before restoring his face to its formerly impassive state. The poor man must actually think Millicent wanted him to feed her. Tempy couldn't stop herself from grinning at his discomfort. "I can't imagine living such a decadent lifestyle," she said, in an attempt to put the young man at ease. "Having someone feed me that way would make me quite self-conscious."

Millicent's gaze flickered toward the now-composed footman, and Tempy realized that she had noted his reaction as well. "I've always thought that in one of my former lives I must have been a pampered citizen of Rome. I can easily see myself being carried about in a sedan chair and wearing a toga, although how they managed to keep all that draped fabric from falling off their bodies, I'll never know."

The group of footmen worked silently through dinner. As each small course of the meal arrived, one of the footmen would whisk away the last dish while a second footman set a plate bearing another tempting dish in the center of Tempy's charger plate.

Toward the end of the meal, Millicent suddenly turned her head to one side and let out an odd little chirping sound three times in quick succession. "Chew-chew-chew."

Tempy stared at her for a moment, startled, and then comprehension dawned on her. "Bless you," she said.

"Thank you, dear," Millicent said. "It must be the rich air in here."

Tempy inhaled deeply, breathing in the floral and citrus aromas as she watched the footmen noiselessly clearing away the remaining dishes. "It's a shame that it doesn't agree with you." She turned her gaze to Lucien. "This conservatory must have been a wonderful place to explore as a child."

Lucien looked at Tempy blankly for a moment, and then nodded. "Yes, it must."

His face revealed nothing, but that very lack of expression made Tempy look at him more closely. "But you didn't do any exploring here, did you?" Her words contained a note of sadness, and she immediately regretted speaking them.

A footman set a small dish of raspberry trifle in the center of Tempy's charger plate. Topped with fresh raspberries, it looked too tempting to resist.

"Growing up, I was never allowed in here," Lucien replied, his voice sounding tight. "My grandfather was protective of this place. Children were prohibited."

Judging by Lucien's clipped tones, there was something more to this story. Of that, Tempy was certain. She put a small spoonful of trifle into her mouth, savoring the taste, but that small distraction did nothing to keep her from asking more questions as she searched for an answer to this new puzzle. "You don't seem the type of man to be dissuaded by a grandfather's tight rein."

The corner of his mouth twitched in a smile, and his gaze flashed toward her. "Normally you'd be right, but on our visit I made an effort to refrain from disgracing my father."

Tempy pressed her lips together. That comment raised so many questions, she couldn't decide which to pursue first. "You mean before today, you've only been here once?"

That Gallic shrug rippled across his shoulders. "Only once to this house, but we visited the nearby village more frequently." He scooped up a fresh raspberry with his spoon and popped it into his mouth. "How did you enjoy your meal?"

"It was excellent," Tempy replied. "Why did you visit the village so often?" she continued, unwilling to be sidetracked.

Millicent interrupted with another of her triple-sneezes, and Tempy repeated a "God bless you."

Lucien settled back in his chair. "There are always maintenance tasks that need to be performed around an estate such as this. My father liked for us to be here to help with the swaling each year." He pronounced the strange word as though it rhymed with *whaling*.

"Swaling?" Tempy parroted. "I've never heard that word before. What does it mean?"

Lucien sipped from his glass of red wine. "After we left the inn, did you notice some of the burned areas on the moor?"

Tempy gave a nod. "Yes. I thought perhaps lightning had struck. The areas seemed to have burned recently."

"It wasn't lightning. The fires were intentionally set. It's important to keep the heath and furze under control in the common, so we regularly burn it off. It's a process called swaling. For a number of years, my father and I helped the villagers swale. Our job was to ensure that the fire didn't jump out of control and threaten any homes."

"It sounds exciting. And dangerous."

"And hard work. But you're right about it being exciting."

She noticed he didn't comment on the danger. "How old were you when your father first had you help?"

"About ten or so. I took part in the swaling over the next four years."

Tempy tried to picture him as a boy, his dark hair tousled and unruly, trudging through the heath and digging firebreaks to inhibit the spread of the fire.

"We'd keep the fires small so they couldn't escape our control. They couldn't burn too hot or too long, or they would've killed the plant roots rather than simply keeping the gorse under control." He sipped his wine. "A quick, sharp fire is what's needed. It keeps the land strong and healthy, and helps prevent fires that might take homes or lives."

"It sounds like important work," Millicent said, her voice cracking on the words. She cleared her throat and winced slightly.

Tempy noticed that Millicent hadn't touched her raspberry trifle, and recalled that she'd only picked at each course that had been served. "Are you well? Your voice sounds slightly husky."

Millicent cleared her throat and then grimaced. "Perhaps some tea would help."

One of the footmen gave a slight nod and slipped around a tree, presumably intent upon fetching tea for Millicent.

"Perhaps you caught a chill in the rainstorm," Tempy said.

"Perhaps," Millicent agreed. She pressed the back of her hand to her forehead. "My head has been aching all day, but now it's getting worse. I believe I'd prefer taking my tea up in my bedchamber. Can you have it sent up?" She pushed back her chair and stood, perhaps too abruptly, because she gripped the seat back and wobbled slightly. She glared at Lucien and Tempy. "Why is it that the two of you were drenched to the skin and are entirely sound, whereas I stayed dry and am now feeling wretched? It is quite unfair." She tried to smile at them, but instead she sneezed again. This time, her ladylike little *chew-chew-chew* repeated itself twice. Millicent glared at them balefully, as though annoyed with them for their apparent good health.

"Goodnight." Millicent moved toward the path as she sneezed once again, and one of the footmen hurried to join her. Tempy could just overhear his murmured offer to escort Millicent to her room. She nodded and took the young man's arm.

"She'll feel better once she's slept," Lucien commented. "It's been a busy day." He pushed back his chair and rose to his feet. "Would you care to walk with me? I wanted to explore the conservatory."

Tempy tilted her head back to look up at him. "Now that it's yours?"

Lucien arched his eyebrows in surprise, and then he grinned sheepishly. "I think you're right. I need to stake my claim on a place that used to be forbidden to me." His gaze lingered on her face for a moment, but she couldn't decipher his expression. He moved closer and then stepped behind her chair. He pulled it back as she rose to her feet, and then he pushed it back in place.

For a moment, Tempy simply looked at his proffered arm. The memory of that night in the casino when she'd taken Lucien's arm and had gazed up into his eyes engulfed her, and she remembered how the jolt of emotion she'd felt had startled her. Now she tucked her hand around his arm and noticed, again, that it felt much more substantial than Ernest's arm had ever felt. More solid and muscular. Her hand tightened slightly, and she felt his muscles flex under the fabric in response to her pressure.

He glanced down at her, but she wouldn't meet his gaze. She knew better. He was too attractive, and she couldn't risk a repeat of that kiss they'd shared. "I can hear running water over there," she said, pointing with her free hand. "I'd love to investigate."

He said nothing, but turned and escorted her in the direction she'd indicated.

"Tell me what it was like when you'd visit the village as a boy," she asked, hoping the question would distract them both.

He made that dismissive shrug again, and she knew she had blundered into something important to him. She no longer interpreted his shrug as indicating a lack of interest, as he intended it to. Rather, she now saw it as a cue that she'd somehow stumbled upon a delicate subject area. And that made her curious.

"It was easy there," he said. "Not the work, of course, but the way people treated me. Us," he corrected. "Here at the estate, we were in the way. My grandfather didn't want us here. But in the village, everyone seemed happy to see us."

Tempy's heel slid to one side as a piece of gravel under it shifted, and she clutched a little more tightly to Lucien's arm as she caught her balance. "Millicent told me you didn't want the title. Is that why? Because your grandfather was such a..." Tempy couldn't figure out how to finish that sentence. Such a cold monster? Such a short-sighted man? Such an imbecile? But it didn't seem to matter, because Lucien already understood.

"I suppose so," he said, holding her hand more securely against his side.

Tempy felt a surge of protection at his movement, and hated herself for it. She pulled away slightly.

"I would have loved throwing the title back in his face just to see his expression, but since he's dead, that's really not an option."

He tilted his head to one side to avoid a low-lying branch, but his head still grazed it, and to Tempy's surprise, drops of water splashed down on both of them. Had the gardeners recently watered everything? Lucien glanced down at her and brushed a droplet of water from her cheek with the side of his thumb. The gesture was completely natural, but the heat of his hand left an imprint on her cheek that lingered.

She touched her face as she tried to ignore the way her heart beat faster than normal. "Formsworth seems to have a vendetta against you."

"It isn't just me. He always took my grandfather's side against my father, too, and I never understood why."

"Really? That's curious. Perhaps there was some personal animosity between them." One of the water droplets from the branch must have landed on her head, because she could feel it sliding along her scalp. She rubbed at the spot.

"I've wondered that myself." He took a deep breath and released it slowly, shaking his head. "It's hard to accept the role of Earl of Cavendish when people like Formsworth come with it. He'll stop at nothing to turn the people here against me."

"Could there be some reason other than personal animosity that makes him want to make life here in Porlock difficult for you?" she asked. "As I see it, the only way driving you away would benefit him would be if you were to sell off sections of your land."

The gravel crunched as Lucien came to a sudden stop. He looked down at Tempy. "I'd never sell to Formsworth."

"Perhaps not." She shrugged. "But you'd no longer have control of the property once you sold it. Formsworth might decide to purchase a piece of it, or even all of it, from whomever you'd sold it to just to spite you."

Lucien glanced away and stared at the small fountain ahead of them. Following his gaze, Tempy noticed that the path ended here, and a bed of white gravel encircled the fountain. The fountain was low and round, with a scalloped edge and a jet of water in the center. "I hadn't thought of that," he said. The fresh citrus scent of orange blossoms was strong in this section of the conservatory. His expression changed as he shifted his gaze to look up at the flower-laden branches above their heads and then at the stream meandering alongside the gravel walkway. It was almost as though he were weighing and measuring. Or was he simply trying to imagine Formsworth in here?

Tempy stared at Lucien, trying to understand him. What

drove this man? Or more to the point, what motivated him? Apparently it wasn't money or a title, or they wouldn't be having this conversation. So, what mattered to him?

"Hmm," he said, speaking more to himself than to her. "I'm fairly certain he'd even purchase this estate, if only to spite me."

"But that would only cause you pain if you actually cared about this place," she said, keeping her gaze fixed on his. "And I suspect that you care more than you like to admit."

He looked away and started to shrug, but halfway through the gesture, his shoulders froze and then slumped, as if he were acknowledging the truth of her words. After a moment, he slowly raised his gaze to hers and stared into her eyes. Seconds ticked by, stretching the moment like an elastic band, and then he spoke. "You see a great deal, don't you, Miss Bliss? You are extraordinarily perceptive. Is that what makes you a good journalist? I've read some of your articles, and you have keen insight."

Startled by his observation, Tempy glanced away. It was her turn to stare at the fountain. He'd turned the tables on her. She wasn't used to being the focus of someone else's scrutiny. Recreating herself under Mme Le Clair's tutelage and responding to her criticism had been different. All of those changes had been external. But Lucien's comment struck straight at the most important part of her. It was as though he could actually see *her*. All the way into her soul. The thought left Tempy feeling exposed, but also truly known, and this shook her. She wavered between fear and exhilaration.

So Tempy shrugged, mimicking Lucien's telltale movement. She tried to ignore the unfamiliar sensation of being seen when she'd thought herself safely hidden. Then, in a flash of self-awareness, the movement of her shoulders registered with her, and she smiled at her unintentional communion with him.

When she glanced at Lucien, a smile teased the corners of his mouth. Had he recognized her shrug? Yes. She could read it in his face, and that turned her smile into a grin.

"I think some of my habits might be rubbing off on you," he said. "I'm not certain that's such a good thing. If we keep this up, soon you'll be habitually drinking whiskey and engaging in fisticuffs."

Grinning, she rounded on him and jabbed playfully at his ribs.

Her sudden movement must have taken him by surprise, because he lifted his arm and brushed her blow to one side.

"Ow!" she cried, more in surprise than in pain.

Lucien's lighthearted mood fell away. "Did I hurt you? I'm sorry. I didn't even think." He reached out to take her forearm and gently lifted it to examine the spot where his hand had connected with it.

"It's fine. Really. You just startled me."

He looked doubtfully at the faint red mark on her pale skin. His thumb brushed across it, but his touch didn't hurt. "I don't feel a welt," he murmured, leaning over to examine it more closely.

She could feel his breath against her skin, and the warmth from his hands began to spread through her body.

Or perhaps that was her embarrassment.

She pulled her arm away, but she regretted it as soon as they broke contact. "I'm fine," she insisted. "Really." She turned around to retrace their steps, moving swiftly away from the fountain, and Lucien kept pace with her.

"I regret causing you any pain," he said. He took her hand and slid it back around his arm. "If it helps, you can hit me again. I promise not to move."

Tempy slowed her pace and lowered her brows at him in mock reproach. "I don't think so. Where's the challenge in that? It would be like punching a cow."

"Done a lot of cow punching, have you?"

She pushed at his arm, feeling his muscles bunch under his jacket. "Don't tease. You know what I mean."

They rounded a bend in the path, and Tempy realized they

were back in the clearing where they'd eaten dinner. The dishes had been cleared away while they were gone, and the candles guttered.

"I hadn't realized it was so late," Tempy said. "I should check on Millicent." But she didn't want to leave. Not yet.

He wore a contemplative expression as he let his gaze wander over the conservatory.

Tempy took a step closer to him. "If it means anything, I think you made the right decision when you accepted your inheritance. This place suits you. You might not consider yourself the Earl of Cavendish yet, but I think that it won't be long before you find that you're quite comfortable in the role."

"Perhaps. This should help me adjust," he said, his gesture encompassing the conservatory. "But I don't think I'll ever get used to being addressed as 'my lord.' That seems worlds away from who I am. The upper circles of London society won't readily accept a former casino owner in their midst. Especially since some of them have frequented my establishment for years."

"Perhaps with the right wife..." She didn't want to continue that thought. She didn't like thinking of him with a perfect young bride on his arm. Would she be an English version of Clarisse?

"Perhaps." He looked thoughtful.

She gasped slightly. Had she planted the idea of searching for an appropriate bride in his mind? Someone respectable and from a family that could trace its lineage back generation after generation? Someone who could bring him the connections he needed? And why not? After all, that was the type of wife he needed. "I need to go," she said. "Thank you again."

She turned and hurried away without giving him a chance to say anything more.

❦ 22 ❦

A TRIP BACK IN TIME

The skies were clear when Lucien trotted downstairs the following morning. Pleasant aromas met him as he entered the breakfast room, enticing him to lift the lids of the silver serving trays and sample their contents. He chose ham, toast, and an interesting-looking concoction of egg, mushroom, and cheese and then turned toward the breakfast table.

The table was large enough to accommodate many house guests, but Lucien had never sat at it before. After only a brief pause, he took a seat at its head.

Upon a silver tray sat an envelope with "Lucien" scrawled on the front. He examined it for a moment and then tore it open. He read through the brief note from Millicent. Apparently, she wouldn't be joining them for breakfast. That wasn't good. He needed her to serve as a buffer between him and Tempy.

Tempy walked in just as he finished reading and he handed her the note. She quickly scanned it. "I stopped by her room," Tempy said. "She's developed a bad head cold, but your housekeeper seems to have things well in hand. She has Millicent on strict bed rest and has prepared a rather pungent-smelling poultice. It's really a shame."

Lucien frowned. Was she was referring to Millicent's illness or the poultice as a 'shame'? He was about to ask when she continued.

"I hope she feels better soon." Tempy handed the note back to him and began filling her plate.

He watched her quick movements as she examined the selection of food. She seemed full of energy this morning. "With Millicent sick, I'm afraid you'll be on your own today. I have an appointment in the village. I'd take you with me, but I'm certain you'd be bored. The meeting should be dull."

She turned back to the table with a full plate, seemingly unaffected by his comment. "There's no need to worry that I'll be bored in the village. I'm certain I can visit some of the shops or simply look around the area."

Lucien paused with his forkful of ham halfway to his mouth. He'd wanted her to stay here. Having her along was certain to complicate things. "Are you sure?"

"I always enjoy exploring new places and meeting new people. In fact, the more I think about it, the more I love the idea."

Lucien continued to eat as he made adjustments to his plans for the day. He'd hoped to remain anonymous while in Porlock. Would he still be able to do so with Tempy at his side? But then he realized that it didn't matter. He'd much prefer go to the village with Tempy than without her. "We'll take the carriage. Boothby has some errands to run and you, my dear, need to bring Mary along as your chaperone. It wouldn't do for you to be seen in the village alone with me."

Tempy nodded agreeably.

"My appointment isn't until one o'clock. If you like, we can leave early so that I can show you around the village first. It will help orient you." He watched her face, waiting to see the pleased expression he anticipated, and she didn't disappoint him.

"Thank you. I'd appreciate that. Perhaps you can show me where you and your father stayed when you visited."

Lucien suddenly remembered one of the reasons he hadn't wanted her to come along. He pressed his lips together to keep from frowning at her. "Perhaps. If there's enough time."

At Tempy's urging, they left within the hour. Her enthusiasm was contagious, and Lucien's anticipation grew.

The drive to the village took more than a half hour. Lucien sat in the carriage across from Tempy and her maid, and young Boothby sat up top with the driver. On their way, they crossed a low stone bridge. Moss dotted with spring flowers grew both above and below it along the banks of the stream. Tempy looked over the side at the little waterfall that cascaded down the hill toward them. "It's beautiful here. This bridge is quite old, isn't it?"

"It's known as Robber's Bridge. This area used to have roving bandits. It was dangerous for travelers to come this way."

"And now?" She glanced suspiciously at the banks of the river, but it was plain that no thieves lurked in the sun-dappled carpet of primroses and bluebells or behind the moss-covered stones.

"I think we're safe enough," he said, smiling wryly.

She glanced toward him and caught sight of his smile. "Don't laugh at me," she said in mock offense, grinning. "You know this area better than I do. What was I to think when you called this the Robber's Bridge?"

Lucien shrugged. The carriage lurched up the hill on the far side of the stream, and Lucien braced his body so he wouldn't topple forward onto Tempy. Not that it might not be pleasant. He glanced at Mary. But it probably wouldn't have a very gratifying result.

Lucien relaxed, allowing his body to roll with the motion of the carriage as it climbed up the hillside.

When they arrived in Porlock, Lucien headed for the shops he remembered on High Street. He hoped Tempy would find them so distracting that she'd forget about her desire to learn more about his visits there as a boy.

Lucien strolled down High Street with Tempy's hand resting on his arm and with Mary trailing behind them. He liked the weight of her hand there. When he glanced over, he saw that Tempy's gaze was darting around as she tried to take in everything.

Tempy noticed him looking at her. "I had no idea this town would be so pretty," she murmured. "When you called it a village, I expected something quite different. Porlock reminds me of a precious box of chocolates, full of delights."

He liked her way with words, and he suddenly found himself looking around at the village as well. As they passed a window box full of hyacinths, Lucien inhaled deeply.

He was immediately transported back to a similar moment twenty years ago when he'd walked this same street with his father. The memory fell upon him complete, and he recalled his enjoyment at spending time with his father and how much he looked forward to seeing the new friends he'd made.

Most of the boys in the village helped with the swaling as the girls watched from a safe distance. Their full skirts made it too dangerous for them to come near the fire. Even one errant spark could set the fabric ablaze, and with the thick petticoats they all wore, a girl might not realize she was on fire until it was much too late.

Lucien had made friends with a few of the girls, Rebecca among them. Just like all of the other boys, he'd shown off to the onlookers, moving a bit too close to the fire until one of the men shouted at them to back away. The girls laughed at them when they were scolded, but he could also see that they loved the excitement of watching them dodge the flames.

Not all of the girls felt that way, of course, but enough did that it encouraged the boys to take foolish chances. Rebecca had been one of the few who didn't approve of the game.

Lucien tensed, as he always did when he thought of Rebecca. There was too much regret in those memories, so he thrust them aside for now.

"Here's a likely shop," he said, indicating a glass door that had the name *No Common Scents* painted on it in gold letters. As they entered, a bell jingled to announce them.

Lucien scanned the store, but saw no one he recognized. He let out a breath he hadn't realized he'd been holding. He knew he'd eventually meet someone today who knew him, but he'd prefer the moment not take him by surprise.

Tempy took a deep breath and her face transformed with delight. "It smells heavenly."

A shopgirl approached them, and Lucien stepped back to allow Tempy to explore the store on her own. The shopgirl showed Tempy where the bottles of scent were located and also pointed out the large glass jars that contained various blends of flower petals and herbs.

Tempy drifted slowly past the jars of potpourri as she read the labels, occasionally lifting the glass lid of a jar that intrigued her so that she could take a deep whiff. She seemed to like most of them, although there were a couple that caused her to put the lid back on rather quickly. He noticed her lingering over one in particular before she eventually moved on down the row. After a while, she returned to it again. She motioned Lucien over.

"Do you like this one?" she asked, raising the lid.

He leaned toward it, wondering what the mixture of dried flower petals might include. The flowers looked much different in this state than when they were still alive. He sniffed. Lavender? And roses? And what was that spicy note? It reminded him of...cloves. Yes, that was it. It was faint, but he was certain the mixture contained just a hint of cloves. He smiled. The scent Tempy had chosen reminded him of her. Soft, but with a sharp hint of spice. "I like it," he said. "It suits you."

"You think so?" she asked, and then blushed slightly.

Both spicy and reserved. "Yes. Most certainly."

She raised her chin and met his eyes. "Good," she said, as she overcame her brief moment of shyness, "because I believe I'll make some sachets with the potpourri. And I'll purchase some scented oil as well. You'll encounter this aroma frequently while we're on this trip." She turned and caught the eye of the shopgirl, who had been watching them for just such a signal.

They strolled down the street, wandering into whichever shop struck Tempy's fancy. Mary managed the packages, making sure that they were safely stowed in the carriage.

As noontime approached, Lucien grew hungry. He glanced up and down the street and then steered them toward a restaurant he remembered.

Even from outside, delicious aromas of food greeted Lucien. "Would you care for something to eat?"

Tempy's gaze was already fixed on the entrance, and she nodded as she moved toward it.

"This is the Three Horseshoes," he said. "My father brought me here years ago." He immediately regretted mentioning his father. He didn't want her to remember her plan to learn more about his visits. He escorted her into the building.

The dining room was moderately full, which Lucien took as a good sign. It looked much as he remembered, with whitewashed walls, dark floors, and wooden tables arranged in rows. One pinch-faced man sat alone, sipping at his beer, but most people were there in couples or small groups. No one seemed to pay much notice to him and Tempy, and Lucien found himself relaxing.

Their food arrived promptly and was as delicious as he'd remembered. At the end of their meal, Lucien pulled his pocket watch from his gray waistcoat and checked the time. His meeting would take place in a half hour, so they were on schedule.

Tempy cleared her throat. "I see you're wearing a more conservative waistcoat today."

He glanced down at the gray wool. The color wasn't a typical choice for him. He usually preferred something that both drew the eye and kept the observer off balance. "Dressing more conservatively today makes it more likely that I'll achieve my goals."

She raised her eyebrows. "Now you've made me quite curious about this mysterious appointment of yours. What goals might those be?"

Lucien puffed out a sigh. "It has to do with Formsworth. He's claiming that some of my land is rightfully his, so I'm required to meet with the magistrate to clear this up."

Her face screwed up as though she'd tasted something bitter. The mention of Formsworth had that effect on many people. "Does he have a valid claim?"

"Of course not. He's trying to goad me, as usual. It's one of the many reasons I prefer avoiding the man."

"Is there any chance you'll lose?"

"I don't know. He's lived here his entire life, and the last time I came to Porlock I accused him of murdering his wife. I was invited *not* to return." He decided not to mention the part where Formsworth had had him attacked by a group of men and beaten. It was one of those memories he preferred not to share.

"And now you're back, as the Earl of Cavendish," she said, cocking an eyebrow at him. "Won't that work in your favor?"

"Perhaps. But as a longstanding member of the community, Formsworth is bound to have a strong reputation here."

"Strong doesn't necessarily mean good," Tempy said. "Based on his behavior yesterday, I wager it wasn't the first time he's come to blows with someone."

"Hm," Lucien said, but it came out more as a grunt than he'd intended. "You'd win that bet."

She looked at him curiously, but Lucien didn't elaborate. What man likes to admit to being soundly thrashed?

After they finished eating, Lucien and Tempy stepped out to High Street, where the bright sunlight made Lucien squint. A pair of women engrossed in conversation strolled past, followed by a man in a top hat and frock coat who glanced at Lucien, looked away, and then stopped mid-step. He turned back and examined Lucien more closely.

"Lord Cavendish? Is that you?" The man's smile was growing as he peered into Lucien's face.

Lucien returned the gaze, perplexed for a moment. Then he, too, examined the other man's face more closely. It was his dark blond hair that had thrown Lucien. As he recalled, the man's hair had been much lighter as a boy. "As I live and breathe. Is that you? Henry Conner?"

"Judge Conner now," he said, shifting his weight slightly, "but yes, it's me. It's wonderful to see you again, my lord."

Lucien frowned and shook his head with a jerk. "You must call me Lucien. I insist. After all, we've known each other since we were children." Someone brushed past Lucien and bumped against his shoulder, so he moved closer to one of the storefronts. He stood so that Tempy was protected from any buffeting as well.

"It's a shame you had to return here under duress," Henry said, "but I can't say I'm sorry. It's been entirely too long since you've visited Porlock."

Lucien couldn't help smiling at the man. "I'm glad someone has found some good in it, although I must admit, I'm enjoying my day here more than I had expected."

Henry's eyes flickered toward Tempy and then back to Lucien.

"I'm sorry. I've been amiss. I'd like to introduce you to Miss Bliss. She accompanied me to Porlock for the day."

Tempy offered a small curtsy.

Henry arched his eyebrows and smiled. "I can see why your day's been so pleasant. You're a lucky man."

Tempy blushed.

Clearly, Henry thought they were a couple. Lucien wished he could correct the misunderstanding, but couldn't think of how to do it without causing her even more embarrassment.

"You shouldn't be in court for long," Henry said. "He's simply harassing you."

Lucien's surprise must have shown.

"Did you think I wasn't aware of your history with the man? He's always been one to hold a grudge, even for the smallest slight. And since you offended him on a grand scale, well...," Henry waved his hand, "let's just say he's happiest when he's being a thorn in someone's side."

Tempy glanced up at Lucien. "Is he referring to the same man who, ah..., visited yesterday?"

Lucien's jaw tightened.

Henry chortled. "So, that explains his bruise. He'd said he'd fallen from a horse. Those beasts have caused him no end of trouble over the years." He paused and then grimaced in apology at the tactlessness of his joke. "But I must admit that it looked more like someone had blackened his eye."

Tempy flashed a grin and then tried to suppress it.

Henry shot her an assessing gaze. "It appears I was correct. Well then, we'll have to do our best to keep the two of you on opposite sides of the courtroom. Hmm?"

An image of Formsworth launching himself across the room flashed into Lucien's mind, and he nodded. "That's probably wise."

Judge Conner turned his attention back to Tempy again. "Something about you seems familiar. Have we met before?"

She shook her head. "I don't believe so. This is my first time in this part of England. I rarely leave London."

"London. That's it. Someone pointed you out to me the last time I was there. You're the 'poor little rich girl,' aren't you?

Heiress to Bliss Railways? I met your father a few years ago. He was quite the businessman. I'm sorry for your loss."

Tempy's hand on Lucien's arm tensed. "Thank you," she said.

Henry seemed unaware that he'd made Tempy uncomfortable, and he pulled a watch from his pocket to check the time. "I'll see you shortly. Good day," he said. Then he tipped his top hat to them and continued on down the street.

Lucien felt her relax as Henry Conner walked away.

Lucien watched Henry for a moment as he let Tempy come to terms with being recognized. She didn't say anything about it, so neither did he. "That wasn't what I expected," Lucien murmured.

"What wasn't?" Tempy asked.

Lucien gazed down at her, collecting his thoughts. "I haven't seen Henry Conner since I was eighteen. I hadn't realized he'd become a judge."

"Is that a good thing? Him being the judge in your case, I mean."

Lucien looked at the man's receding back and smiled. "Yes, I believe it is." He and Tempy began strolling down the street in the direction of the courthouse. Tempy slid her hand around his arm and tucked it next to his elbow, as though it were a bird settling onto its nest. It was a completely natural and common-place gesture that ignited the slow, steady warmth of contentment deep within him.

She tightened her grip on his arm. "Look," she said.

Lucien followed her gaze and saw two men arguing. Although they were dressed quite differently, they had similar builds. The one with his back to them seemed young, and the other was...Squire Formsworth. In an instant, Lucien realized who the younger man must be.

Boothby.

"Wait here," he told Tempy. He hurried toward the pair. Maybe he could stop them before they came to blows.

"Lucien," Tempy called. He heard the soles of her shoes hitting the pavement as she hurried after him.

Formsworth clenched his fists and his eyes narrowed in anger.

"Stop!" Lucien shouted. But it was too late. Formsworth was fast, and he threw a punch with all of his weight behind it.

But Boothby bobbed to one side, easily avoiding the blow.

Lucien sped forward. He wrapped one arm around Formsworth's neck from behind, and with the other, he grabbed the man's arm, twisting it behind his back. He yanked it up with a forceful jerk, and Formsworth let out an explosive grunt of pain.

"Blast you! Let go of me." Formsworth surged forward, trying to break Lucien's hold on him.

Lucien twisted the struggling man's arm even farther up his back, torquing his shoulder into what must have been an extremely painful position.

"Ahh!" Formsworth stopped struggling.

Lucien waited to see if the man would continue to struggle, but when he felt some of the coiled tension leave Formsworth's body, he eased up on the pressure on his elbow.

"What's the problem here?" Lucien asked.

"It's none of your affair," Formsworth hissed.

Boothby spoke up. "Of course it is. I work for him." He met Lucien's gaze. "This one," he said, jerking his chin toward Formsworth, "decided to take offense when I asked him about me mum."

People were stopping to stare.

"You dare to speak to me!" Formsworth shouted at Boothby. "I want nothing to do with you. I made that clear when you were born." He tried to break free of Lucien's hold, but Lucien pushed the man's elbow up again, and Formsworth stopped his struggling.

"Try to keep a civil tongue in your head." Lucien said. "Things will progress more smoothly if you can manage to draw less of a crowd."

Formsworth jerked his head from side to side, looking up and down the street, and then glared at the group of onlookers. "Let me go," he hissed. When Lucien didn't immediately comply, he added, "I won't fight him. Just let me go."

Lucien relaxed his hold on Formsworth, and the man yanked his arm to the front of his body and began massaging it. "You nearly broke my arm," he muttered, turning to face Lucien. "Are you so enamored of your low connections that you'd side with the likes of them against your own people?"

Contempt flooded him. "My own people? Can you possibly be counting yourself in that group? How can you imagine that I owe you any allegiance? You attacked me yesterday, and not for the first time. It was Boothby who came to my aid, so if that's what you mean by my 'own people,' then you're right. I choose to take the side of an honorable man I've known since his birth over one who thrives on intimidation."

"How dare you!" Formsworth puffed up his chest. "I'll have you know that my family has lived in Somerset for generations."

"As has mine. But that doesn't mean I have the right to abuse the people around me."

"Then you're more of a fool than I'd thought. People like him," Formsworth said, indicating Boothby, "are the worst of them. Always after something. Money. A handout. Special favors. You'll never shake yourself free once they sink their teeth into your flesh."

Bright, hot anger sparked in Lucien. "He's nothing like that. He's worth more than a hundred of you." He stepped forward threateningly, but then stopped himself.

Tempy was watching.

Formsworth took a step back, fear showing in his eyes as his gaze darted from Boothby to Lucien. "I've had just about enough of this." He sidled away, keeping his gaze pinned on Lucien. "I'll see you in court." He pressed his top hat more firmly onto his head and then turned on his heel and strode down the street.

Lucien watched him depart, a little stunned. After all of the buildup, the altercation had ended abruptly, leaving Lucien feeling as though things were still unsettled. He held out his arm to Tempy, and when she slid her fingers back around it, he nearly sighed with relief. The last thing he wanted was to renew the argument they'd had yesterday.

Boothby and Mary followed them as they departed. When Lucien glanced down the street, he could still see Formsworth hurrying away in the distance.

"I'm sorry, sir," Boothby said. "I never should have approached him. I was hoping he might be able to tell me something more about my mother."

"I'm glad you didn't dignify that man by referring to him as your father. He's the most bitter and manipulative man I've ever met," Lucien replied.

Tempy stopped, and turned to look at Boothby. "Mr. Formsworth is your father?"

Boothby nodded. "Quite a surprise, isn't it? No one ever told me much about him, but based on small things people let slip, I knew he was a wealthy squire. I also heard someone say that I looked exactly like him. When Squire Formsworth became so angry with me yesterday, I realized who he must be. Even then, I wasn't completely certain until I came into the village today. Can you believe it? People here in Porlock began asking me if I was his son. That removed the last of my doubts, so I decided to approach him and ask him about my mother." He grimaced. "You saw the rest. You'd think I'd asked him to welcome me into his home, when all I did was ask him where my mother came from. I've always hoped to find her family."

"You shouldn't have found out this way. Mme Le Clair said she'd tell you before we left London. I didn't realize that you still didn't know. She begged me to let her be the one to tell you. If it's any consolation, she regretted not telling you sooner."

"If by sooner, you mean ten years ago, then yes. Sooner would have been much better. How could she keep my own history from me for so many years?"

"I think she was worried you'd try to confront Formsworth."

Boothby reddened. "Perhaps I would have. But that decision should have been mine to make."

"I don't necessarily agree. You mother left you in Mme Le Clair's care. Hasn't Madame protected you? Prepared you for the world? Helped you find employment?"

"I should have been told," Boothby insisted. "I had a right to know."

"And she meant to tell you."

"So you say. But that's only words. Empty promises. All I know is that she didn't do it."

"Actually," Tempy said, "I think you were probably better off not knowing about that man. It must be difficult to grow up not knowing who your father is, but I imagine it would have been even worse to suffer a father's loathing. That type of disdain would certainly have affected you. It might have altered the course of your life."

Boothby's expression became thoughtful.

They had left most of the shops behind as they walked, and the street was much less busy here. Lucien could now see Formsworth far ahead of them, entering the town hall.

Lucien glanced at Tempy and then back at Boothby. "I've never mentioned this, but my father was aware of my grandfather's low opinion of him, and I'm certain it affected him. It was hard for him to face that sort of loathing every day. I'm certain he would have had a better life if that man hadn't continually berated him. As it was, he always felt as though he had to prove himself."

"Thank you for telling me that, m'lord," Boothby said. "Fortunately, I've already come to realize that Formsworth means nothing to me. I only approached him today to see if I could learn something about my mother. Can you tell me anything more about her?"

Lucien frowned slightly. "I know little of her. I only met her once, while she was carrying you. She was a demimondaine, much like Mme Le Clair, but not as lucky."

"Why," Boothby asked, "because she met Formsworth?" Although the young man's tone was belligerent, Lucien knew his anger wasn't directed at Lucien, but at the man who had caused his mother so much pain.

"She left him because he hit her. She said she didn't want to risk losing her unborn child to one of his rages. Formsworth refused to believe the child was his, despite the fact that he'd kept her isolated at his home here in Somerset for months. His jealousy was like poison to the women he claimed to love. But your mother escaped, unlike his wife. After you were born, she sent a message to Formsworth to let him know he had a son. She hoped that his love for her would transfer to his newborn child, but Formsworth insisted he had no child."

"But Boothby is the image of him," Tempy said. "How can he continue to deny it?"

"He didn't deny it just now," Boothby said. "He accused me of wanting money. But he's wrong. I want nothing from that man. I wish I could strip away any resemblance we share."

As they paused in the shadow of the town hall, Lucien turned to look squarely at Boothby. "Any resemblance you share is superficial. I've known you for years. In every way that matters, you are nothing like him. I admire the man you've become."

The clock in the tower above the town hall began to chime.

Boothby glanced at it guiltily. "You need to go inside. I'm sorry I delayed you. Thank you, m'lord."

"I'm glad I could be of help."

Boothby nodded. "Yes, sir." He hurried away and then turned down a side street.

"Formsworth's been your bane for years," Tempy murmured.

He frowned. "And this court case is simply his way of trying to irritate me."

"At least the judge already recognizes that."

"Yes. At least there's that."

He turned to enter the town hall, and Tempy turned back toward the area with the shops. Suddenly he realized he *wanted* to face Formsworth in court. The man had gotten away with running roughshod over everyone for years. Even Grandfather had bowed to the man's will simply because he hadn't wanted to rile him.

Lucien walked through the town hall doors with a lightness in his step that formerly hadn't been there.

❦ 23 ❦

CAVENDISH TAKES STAND

※

Tempy paused and turned to watch Lucien enter the town hall. Something was different about him. His chin was higher and his shoulders were thrown back, like a man preparing for a battle.

But this would be a legal battle.

CAVENDISH TAKES STAND

She loved that double play on the word *stand*.

She smiled. The new Earl of Cavendish was obviously feeling confident. The court case should be an interesting one.

So why was she standing here on High Street rather than watching the proceedings? What had she been thinking?

Tempy quickly retraced her steps and entered the town hall less than a minute behind Lucien. She'd been neglecting her role as a journalist on this trip, and it had left her feeling unanchored. She wasn't cut out for an aimless life of ease. Making the decision to throw herself into her role as a reporter immediately released the floodgates on a dam of tension that had been building, leaving her energized.

A few other people were milling around in the main foyer, but it didn't take long to find the room where Lucien's case was being heard. Quite a few locals were already filling the rows of seats at the back of the room, so it was easy for her to find a seat where Lucien was unlikely to spot her.

She didn't want to distract him. Of course, there was always the chance that he'd be annoyed at seeing her here. She certainly hoped not. But it was an open court, so she had just as much of a right to be there as anyone else.

Tempy dug around in her reticule and found the small wooden box containing a dip pen and a pot of ink. She wondered, yet again, if she should switch to a fountain pen. Her frustration, however, was that she found them to be more temperamental than a traditional dip pen and inkwell. And she simply detested pencils. The always managed to break at the most inopportune moment.

Paper. What about paper?

Tempy shoved her hand back into her reticule and was relieved when she closed her fingers around her slim bound notebook.

She checked her inkwell and discovered that the ink was too thick, so she exited the court room and walked down the hallway, searching for an open office where she might find a bit of water.

She caught sight of a man leaning on a cane as he walked through the nearest doorway, so she followed him to look for some assistance.

There was nobody in the room. There was another door on the far side of the room. Perhaps the man was in an interior office. "Hello?" she called, hoping that someone would appear who could help her. She glanced around and spied a pitcher of water on a side table.

She waited a moment, but nobody responded to her call. Why didn't the man reply? "Do you mind if I take a small bit of water?" she asked, feeling a bit foolish. There was still no answer.

With a sigh, Tempy crossed the room to the pitcher and dribbled a few drops of water into her ink pot. She closed it and shook it, then opened it again to examine it. Perfect. After stoppering the inkwell, she hurried back to the courtroom.

It was even more crowded now, and she ended up sitting closer to the front than she would have preferred. Fortunately, a rather tall man sat in front of her, blocking her from view.

But that also meant that *her* view was blocked. She set her pen kit on a small wooden block affixed to the seat in front of her that was probably meant for that purpose, opened the lid of the inkwell, and readied her pen.

She heard someone, most likely the clerk to the court, announce the judge.

She leaned to one side and caught sight of Judge Conner entering the room. She easily recognized him despite the white wig and black robes he wore. It occurred to her that his short hair must make the wig a bit more comfortable to wear.

Chancery court was now in session.

Judge Conner spoke first, and Tempy leaned to one side to observe him. "I've read the Bill of Complaint submitted on behalf of Squire Formsworth. In essence, he disputes the ownership of a piece of property. He claims that the late Earl of Cavendish erected a fence and that part of that fence intrudes upon his property. The fence was constructed twenty years ago, but Squire Formsworth only recently discovered the error." He glanced at Formsworth's barrister. "Is this correct?"

"Yes, your honor," the barrister replied.

Tempy quickly scrawled notes regarding the initial complaint.

"Mr. Severson, how does your client respond?" Judge Conner asked, glancing at the man sitting next to Lucien.

"We formally reject this bill, your honor. As you already mentioned, the fence has been there for twenty years and it is clearly well within the boundaries of the Cavendish land."

Tempy leaned to one side to watch Mr. Formsworth while Mr.

Severson spoke. He was speaking with his own barrister. Even from her distant vantage point, she could hear Formsworth's hisses of anger.

Judge Conner nodded. "Thank you, Mr. Severson." He glanced at Formsworth's barrister. "Mr. Aikley, I see you have something to say. What is it?"

Formsworth's white-wigged barrister stood, a peeved expression on his face. "It is my client's contention that various pieces of land have been in dispute over many, many years. He believed that the issue concerning this particular piece of property had already been resolved and only recently discovered he'd been mistaken. He begs the court's pardon in waiting so long to begin these proceedings, but he is confident that his rights in this matter will be upheld."

Tempy took a moment to jot down brief descriptions of the men in the courtroom.

Mr. Aikley presented evidence showing that, indeed, these sorts of disputes had been dealt with in Chancery Court for a number of years. Apparently, the bad blood between the two families could be traced back over at least four generations. That would probably explain the ongoing animosity between Lucien and Formsworth. Tempy had felt certain that there was more to it than was on the surface. She'd been right.

Mr. Severson stood, letting out a deep, long-suffering sigh. "I admit, your honor, that these land disputes began over a hundred years ago. Fortunately, however, we have not seen any new claims made by the Formsworth family in about thirty years. Not since the Tithe map was updated in 1820. The map is detailed and accurate, and shows all structures in the region. These include the rectory, mills, gardens, common areas, woods, boundary posts, trees used to mark boundaries, and every disputed boundary. You will note that this particular fence is not among those listed as being under dispute. The map also shows hedge and fence owner-ship, field gates, hill-drawings, footpaths, bridleways, bridges, embankments, and streams. If you examine the map, you will discover that the fence in dispute is shown as belonging to the Earl of Cavendish, and that it is well within the boundary of his property. I am prepared to offer witnesses who have walked the entire length of the fence while consulting this map, and they can attest that the map is accurate with regard to this particular fence. I beg of you, your honor, that you not only settle this dispute in favor of my client, but that you also reprimand Mr. Formsworth for wasting the court's time in such a frivolous manner."

Tempy wrote as quickly as she could, but she paused a moment to lean to one side and glance at Formsworth. She could see his face turning that deep shade of red that had presaged yesterday's angry outburst.

"I object," Formsworth shouted. "This man isn't even the acknowledged heir. He's a usurper."

"Please be seated, Mr. Formsworth, and refrain from speaking in this court. It is your barrister's role to speak for you, and if you cannot control yourself, I will take measures to *ensure* that you do not address this court again. Do I make myself understood?"

Formsworth sputtered and fumed for a moment, but then he nodded to the judge and sat back down.

"It is the opinion of this court that Mr. Formsworth's case is without merit, and I hereby dismiss it. Furthermore, Mr. Formsworth is heavily cautioned against presenting any more of these frivolous suits. Should another one as baseless as this appear in my docket, I'll be forced to deal more sternly with him. Have I made myself clear?"

"Yes, your honor," Formsworth's barrister replied. "And thank you for your leniency in this matter."

Tempy hurriedly transcribed the judge's ruling before his words could fade or become jumbled in her memory. She was so busy that she barely took note of the people around her exiting the room. When she looked up, she found herself staring directly into Lucien's eyes.

He raised one eyebrow sardonically and she lifted her notebook to display it to him. He looked quite happy as he crossed the courtroom to stand closer to her. They were separated by the low railing surrounding the visitor's area and a row of seats. "Taking notes?" he asked.

"I thought I might get a story out of this."

"And did you?"

"Certainly. But I'm not certain it's one that the London papers would find of interest. Perhaps Porlock's paper is looking for an article."

Lucien shook his head in mock reproach. "You're a journalist to the core, aren't you? I'll introduce you to the editor tomorrow night while we're at Judge Conner's house. He's hosting a dinner party, and we're invited."

Tempy stared down at her notebook for a moment and then glanced back up at Lucien. His offer of an introduction was more than either Father or Ernest had ever done to further her career. "You'd do that for me?"

Lucien shrugged one shoulder. It wasn't that Gallic shrug that he used to disguise his real feelings. This was his natural one. "Of course. I'm happy to help."

Those simple words struck deep into Tempy's heart. She'd faced so many people in the past who wanted to dissuade her from following her passion that she'd come to expect a negative reaction whenever she mentioned her writing. Lucien's casual support of it meant more to her than all the forced praise she'd received over the years.

She felt tears welling and glanced down at her notebook as she closed it so that he wouldn't see them. "Thank you," she murmured as she busied herself with putting away her pen and ink. She tucked everything safely away in her reticule.

Had Ernest ever accepted her writing so freely and easily?

She'd always thought there'd been a vague assumption on his part that her interest would fade over time. When she'd tried to discuss her love of writing with him, he'd never truly comprehended it.

But somehow Lucien already knew. She'd never needed to explain it to him. He simply knew.

24

WOULD YOU LIKE SOME
CHOCOLATE TART?

The following evening, as the carriage bumped down the country lane toward Judge Conner's house, Tempy's stomach quivered with nervous tension. She slid her hand down the front of her cloak just below the two satin frog fasteners. Mary was with them, serving as chaperone in Millicent's absence.

Tempy had kept her plan for tonight a secret from Lucien. She needed to do this as a sort of test, away from London and Mme Le Clair's guardianship. Lucien had already helped a great deal, and she was afraid that she'd come to rely on him. She needed to do this on her own. Lucien certainly wouldn't be there when she finally used her newly developed womanly wiles on Ernest. She needed to test the extent of her new abilities now, before she confronted Ernest.

BLISS SHINES BRIGHTLY

If she could manage to live up to *that* headline, she could hold her head high with the knowledge that she was ready to overthrow Clarisse and win back Ernest's love. She just hoped the headline shouldn't instead read

BLISS BOMBS

or something else equally dismal.

Her stomach knotted.

"We're nearly there," Lucien said. "You've hardly spoken a word all the way here. Are you well?"

"I'm fine," Tempy said, flashing him a bright smile while clutching at the front of her cloak. This was the first time she'd worn the gown hidden beneath its dark folds, and she wanted the unveiling to be a surprise. "It's just that I feel a bit guilty about Millicent. If I hadn't asked her to accompany me on this trip and exposed her to that rainstorm, she wouldn't be sick and miserable right now." She glanced at her lady's maid. Mary hadn't said so, but Tempy could tell that she was excited to be brought along on the outing. Once Lucien and Tempy were inside, Mary would join the other servants and have the opportunity to socialize.

"You can hardly blame yourself for her illness. And my housekeeper seems to enjoy coddling her. Didn't Millicent mention having a sore throat while we were on the train from London?" At her nod, Lucien continued. "Then the rainstorm didn't cause her illness. She already had it." He paused. "Is something else troubling you?"

She noticed him looking at her hand and noting the way she gripped her cloak. She relaxed her fist. "I'm a bit nervous about meeting all of these people." The carriage stopped in front of what she assumed was the judge's home.

"My intrepid journalist? Nervous?" Lucien reached out and lifted her hand that wasn't currently engaged in mangling the front of her cloak and gave it a comforting squeeze. "Simply don the armor that Mme Le Clair helped you craft. I'm certain you'll be fine."

Tempy nearly jumped at his words. It was as though he'd read her mind. But at least he was encouraging her on her chosen path. Even if he didn't know it. "That's an excellent idea," she murmured.

He helped her down from the carriage and escorted her to the front door.

As they swept inside, Tempy saw a number of guests in a large room to the left of the foyer. Butterflies of panic began slamming against the inside of her stomach, so she took a deep breath to calm them.

She glanced at Lucien. Perhaps she should have let him see her dress before now so she'd know how he'd react. What if he thought it was inappropriate? If she saw a look of disapproval on his face right now, she knew she wouldn't be able to let anyone else see her.

She needed to stick to her plan. It was a good one, and she couldn't let this sudden bout of nerves ruin it.

She turned her back to Lucien so she couldn't see his reaction once her dress was revealed. The butler helped her with her cloak, revealing the low-cut pale aqua lace gown. The layer of fabric beneath the lace was flesh colored, giving the impression of bare skin. Tempy's shoulders were bare, and the simply cut gown revealed much more skin than she'd ever been comfortable with showing in the past. Mme Le Clair had been quite insistent, telling her that she made a devastating impression in it, so despite her reservations, she'd decided to trust the demimondaine's opinion.

But she still kept her back to Lucien and entered the salon ahead of him.

The first reaction to her gown and her artfully applied makeup came from the guests who would be dining with them that evening.

One elderly gentleman's monocle popped from his eye and fell to dangle from a string around his neck. Another man stopped mid-sentence and stared openly for a moment before resuming his conversation with the woman with whom he had been speaking. A third gaped openmouthed at her before snapping his mouth shut with an audible click.

Tempy's stomach tightened. This was a much stronger reaction than she'd anticipated. Was this an enormous mistake? She took a step back, wondering if she could still flee, and stumbled into Lucien.

He steadied her by taking her elbow and moving to stand next to her. Then he glanced down at her, taking in the low-cut bodice of her dress for the first time.

She blushed, but watched him to gauge his reaction. His eyes widened ever so slightly, and then he smiled. "*Brava*, Miss Bliss. I see my advice wasn't needed. Your armor is quite disarming."

She smiled up at him as her confidence began to swell. She hadn't even modeled the dress for Millicent for fear that she'd try to talk Tempy out of wearing it. But wasn't it creating precisely the reaction she'd hoped it would?

Judge Conner moved to greet them, his wife following with alacrity. Although Tempy couldn't be certain, she believed Mrs. Conner shot her an irritated look. The expression disappeared from her face so quickly that Tempy couldn't be sure she'd even seen it. But a moment later, Henry Conner winced and moved his foot out from under his wife's skirts. If Tempy wasn't mistaken, the woman had just stomped on his toes.

This wasn't the reaction she'd intended to elicit from her hostess, and Tempy felt a renewed twinge of doubt at her choice of attire. Perhaps her gown would have been more appropriate for London than for a dinner party in the country.

But Lucien had liked it. That bit of knowledge allowed her to keep her chin held high rather than ducking it in embarrassment.

She met Mrs. Conner's gaze and offered her a sincere smile. "Thank you so very much for inviting us to your home. It's quite lovely."

The woman's face looked as though it might crack as she

forced it to smile. It was amazing to see how unwelcoming the woman could look while still going through the motions of inviting them into her home. "It is a pleasure to offer our hospitality to an old friend. And just imagine our delight that he's the new Earl of Cavendish."

Tempy didn't fail to notice that Mrs. Conner's "pleasure" only extended to Lucien, but before she could decide how to respond, they were interrupted.

"Henry, you rapscallion," an older man said, clapping Judge Conner on the shoulder. When Tempy noticed the monocle dangling from a piece of ribbon, she recalled his reaction when she'd entered the room. "Who are your friends?" he asked, turning his gaze on her. "You *must* introduce me to this delightful young woman."

Judge Conner made the introductions, informing them that the older man was his father, Squire Conner.

Squire Conner kept his attention fixed upon Tempy, his eyes seeming to miss no detail in her attire. She wondered for a moment if he could see all the way through her corset. It certainly felt like it.

She smiled politely at him. The older man's eyes seemed to dance with delight as he smiled back.

"It isn't often that I get the opportunity to talk with such an attractive young woman," Squire Conner said. "Most of the people I see every day are closer to my own age." He glanced at Lucien and a confused look crossed his face. "Do I know you? You seem familiar to me."

"We met when I was a boy," Lucien replied. "My father was the youngest of Lord Cavendish's three sons."

"Ah, yes. You helped with the swaling. I remember you now." His gaze flicked to Tempy before returning to Lucien. "And is this lovely young lady your fiancée?"

"No. This is Miss Temperance Bliss," Lucien said, without elaborating further.

Squire Conner smiled broadly and opened his mouth to speak, but he never had a chance to say anything. Instead, a younger man who had been standing on the fringe of the group, holding a glass of whiskey, spoke up.

"Lucien. It's been years. I doubt you'll remember me. I'm Charles Conner, Henry's brother."

Squire Conner shot his younger son a stony glare, and the Judge and his wife used the opportunity to excuse themselves to speak with some other guests.

Lucien arched his eyebrows in surprise. "Charles. I wouldn't have recognized you. The last time I saw you, you had blond hair and were about four feet tall."

Charles ran his hand through his wavy light brown hair. "That was years ago. But you look much the same." He glanced at his father, and then back at Lucien again.

Lucien shrugged. "I'll always remember how conscientious and hardworking you were as you hauled all of those pails of water."

Charles grimaced. "I always hated that job. By the end of the day, my clothes were soaked and my shoes squirted water with every step."

Squire Conner snorted as he slid his monocle in place over his eye.

Tempy sensed an odd undercurrent between father and son that she couldn't quite identify.

Squire Conner turned his attention back to Tempy and Lucien with a delighted expression. "It's nice to see some fresh new faces here tonight," he said. He smiled up at Lucien. "You look familiar, young man. Have we met before?"

Charles tensed.

Lucien looked confused for a moment and glanced at Charles, apparently looking for some sort of cue before replying. "Yes. We met many years ago when I was here with my father to help with the swaling."

Squire Conner's monocle dropped from his eye again. "You're the Earl's grandson? Henry will be so pleased you could come tonight." He turned and walked a few paces toward Judge Conner.

Charles grimaced. "Please excuse my father. He tends to forget things, including people he's only just met. You get used to it. Gatherings like this one seem to make it worse, but he loves this sort of thing."

Tempy watched as Squire Conner plucked at his eldest son's sleeve. The two men spoke briefly, and then returned to their group. Squire Conner grinned broadly as he rejoined them. It was obvious he was enjoying himself immensely. "Henry, do you recall that the old earl had a grandson? Here he is."

"Actually, I had business with the earl earlier today and invited him to join us for dinner this evening," the judge said. He glanced at his brother sharply. "Do you have everything in hand?"

Charles shrugged, lifting his glass in a gesture that resembled a toast. "I do what I can."

Henry narrowed his eyes. "See that you do *everything* you can."

Mrs. Conner returned to their group. "Henry, please come greet our neighbors. They've only just arrived," she said. She wrapped her arm around her husband's and shot Tempy a dismissive glance. Squire Conner followed them, leaving Tempy with Lucien and Charles.

"What was that all about?" Lucien asked.

Charles shrugged. "With the state of my father's memory, Henry asked me to keep an eye on him tonight. Just to make sure he stays out of mischief."

"Mischief?" Tempy asked.

Charles shrugged. "Sometimes when he gets muddled he also gets a bit angry. He doesn't like being confused, and he hates what's happening to him."

Tempy remembered another of Mme Le Clair's lessons. A light touch to the arm or hand was supposed to help forge a connection with a man. Charles struck her as someone who needed some emotional support. She reached out and rested her hand on Charles's forearm, giving it a squeeze. "You're a good son to be so supportive."

Charles patted her hand where it rested on his arm and looked into her eyes. "You are a very sympathetic young woman. Thank you." His smile was a few degrees warmer than it had been.

When Tempy glanced over to where Squire Conner was standing with his older son, she noticed that the judge was glaring at his younger brother. She glanced up at Charles to see if he noticed the glare as well, and saw his jaw clench. Yes, he'd noticed, and it was obvious that he didn't like it. But that was often the way with brothers, wasn't it? They knew each other too well, judged each other too harshly, and jumped to conclusions too quickly.

"If you'll excuse me," Charles said, giving her hand a pat, "I need to collect my charge." He sauntered toward Squire Conner and caught his attention with what must have been a witty comment or jest, because the squire laughed rather loudly and walked away with him. The next time she noticed father and son, they were holding drinks and chatting with another group of guests.

Lucien introduced her to the man who ran the Porlock newspaper. He had kind eyes. During the course of their conversation, he mentioned that he'd attended Lucien's court case and had written an article about it for his paper.

At dinner, Tempy didn't sit near Lucien. At an event such as this, it was customary to seat couples apart from one another so that they'd have the opportunity to socialize with others. Tempy found herself next to Charles and across from Squire Conner. She didn't recognize the gentleman sitting to her right, but he seemed engrossed in a conversation about horses and steadily ignored her.

Charles handed his empty whiskey tumbler to one of the servers as he sat down, and then gestured for his wine glass to be filled.

"What brings you here to Somerset?" Charles asked Tempy abruptly, fixing his gaze on her.

Tempy sighed. "It's all rather complicated, and not very interesting, but suffice it to say that I'm mixing business with a little sight-seeing. Porlock is a gem of a village."

Charles didn't comment, but simply shrugged. His bones seemed loosely jointed under his frock coat, giving Tempy the distinct impression that he'd imbibed too much.

Dinner was excellent, and Tempy spent most of the meal chatting with Squire Conner. Charles remained silent on her left, drinking steadily. From time to time, she'd hear his silverware clatter noisily, or his arm would bump against hers. He seemed unaware of it, and she noticed that his eyes became more unfocused as the evening progressed.

The man to Tempy's right moved on to a discussion of pheasant hunting, not bothering to engage Tempy in conversation. The only person interested in speaking with her was Squire Conner. Fortunately, he was entertaining, even if he did tend to repeat his witticisms.

At the end of the meal, servants brought in individual chocolate-filled tarts for dessert. The golden crust was flaky and buttery, and the warm chocolate filling was thick and rich. Tempy finished hers rather quickly, and she distractedly slid her fork along her plate to chase down the last few flakes of crust that remained.

Charles hadn't touched his tart, nor had he eaten much dinner at all. When she glanced over at him, his bleary eyes tried to focus on her and then on her plate. "Liked it, did you? My sister-in-law will be delighted. She's quite proud of that tart." He glanced at his own untouched dessert. "Have a bit of mine," he said, reaching for his fork and cutting off a morsel. "If I send it back uneaten, she'll be offended."

Before Tempy could decline his offer, Charles leaned toward her, brushing his upper arm against her breast as he raised the fork toward her face. "Sweets for the sweet?" he murmured, trying to put a bite of his chocolate tart into her mouth.

Tempy jerked her head back. What on earth was the man thinking? Why would he try to feed her?

His fork wobbled, and Tempy felt a thick, warm blob of chocolate strike her on the chest and then drip down between her breasts.

This couldn't be happening.

"Oh, my," Charles said. "Sorry 'bout that." He looked confused for a moment, and then directed the tines of his fork toward her cleavage. "Let me just..."

Good lord, the man wanted to poke his fork down her dress?

On the other side of the table, the squire pushed his chair back with a clatter and bolted to his feet. "I think NOT. Have you no decency? Stop it this instant, Charles."

Charles looked up from her cleavage and glanced down the length of the dining table. Tempy followed his gaze and saw the row of dumbstruck guests, their mouths gaping in shock. Her cheeks burned with embarrassment. The only person who didn't look dumbstruck was Lucien. Judging by the grin on his face, he was tremendously entertained by the scene.

"It seems I misjudged who needed a keeper tonight," Judge Conner said from his vantage point at the head of the table. "Father," he added, addressing the squire, "would you be so kind as to escort Charles from the room? I believe he needs a turn outside in the fresh air."

The elderly gentleman darted around the table much more quickly than Tempy would ever have guessed possible. He took Charles by the elbow and hustled him through the door.

Mrs. Conner tut-tutted. "Oh, my. And it's such a lovely dress, too. Come with me, dear." Apparently the woman's former feelings of rivalry had dissipated. Now she oozed concern as she escorted Tempy through the door and into the kitchen. There, she laid out some clean cloths Tempy could use to wipe away the chocolaty blob.

The gooey mess had slid down the inside of Tempy's corset. Although she was able to wipe off her exposed skin, she could still feel the sticky wetness spreading against her chest. She wouldn't be able to clean off the rest of it until she was home and could remove her corset.

"I've read about you in the papers, you know," Mrs. Conner said. Her gaze was cunning, and when Tempy flinched at her words, she gave a satisfied smile. "You're London's 'poor little rich girl.' People talk. People ask questions too."

Tempy didn't trust herself to respond in a civil manner, so she ignored the comment and continued to work at removing the chocolate that had dripped down her cleavage.

Mrs. Conner smirked. "I suppose it's a good thing your gown is so low cut. Otherwise the chocolate would have ended up all over it."

Tempy tensed. "I suppose London's latest fashions haven't made their way here yet."

The woman bristled. "Are you calling me provincial? I'll have you know I visit London every year during the Season."

"Then I'm sure you know what I mean about the speed at which fashions change. Now, if you'll excuse me." Tempy didn't wait for a response, but stepped past the woman to return to the dining room.

Mrs. Conner wrapped her fingers around Tempy's arm. Tempy ignored it at first, but Mrs. Conner tightened her grip.

Tempy whirled on her. "Let go of me."

Mrs. Conner's mouth was pinched. "Did the 'poor little rich girl' decide that she wanted to buy herself a title? The 'Countess of Cavendish' is a rather impressive one, isn't it?"

The words stung. "You don't know what you're talking about," Tempy said hotly. "You would do best to keep such ridiculous conjectures to yourself."

"Ridiculous?" Mrs. Conner seemed to puff up, like an annoyed pigeon with ruffled feathers. "Are you calling me ridiculous? You dare to say that after behaving like a common tart?" She snorted derisively. "Chocolate tart for the London tart. It suits you."

Tempy pressed her lips together, biting back a scathing retort, and instead tried to keep her voice calm. "I've been confronted by people like you for the past year, Mrs. Conner. People who believe that because they've read about me in the newspaper, they have the right to invade my privacy and comment on my life. I'll tell you now, you are not. And unless you wish to have me turn my critical eye upon you in turn, you'll keep your opinions to yourself."

This time, when Tempy tried to break free from the woman's grip, she succeeded. Tempy turned her back on Mrs. Conner and walked back in the dining room.

Lucien waited there for her, sitting alone at the dining table. Tempy'd never been more relieved to see him than at that moment. The other guests must have retired to the drawing room.

Mrs. Conner burst through the door behind Tempy, apparently intending to continue berating her, but when she saw Lucien there, she paused. Then she gave Tempy a look of contempt and, without a word, changed course to hurry on through the door and into the adjoining drawing room.

Lucien rose to his feet to stare at the woman through the open door. "What was that about?"

"I don't think Mrs. Conner likes me."

Lucien chuckled. "From what I recall, she doesn't like most people."

"What?"

"I remember her as a little girl. She was always trying to order people around and make them do her bidding. Henry was her closest neighbor, but he never catered to her the way the others did."

The tension in Tempy's shoulders eased. At least she hadn't been singled out by the woman. That made her feel slightly better. "Is that why she married him? Because he stood up to her?"

Lucien shrugged. "Who knows? Her parents died when she was just a girl and she married Henry as soon as she was able. It was an arranged marriage, and they were both rather young at the time."

Tempy watched Mrs. Conner though the open door. If Lucien had known her as a boy then she must be around his age, but the woman wore a pinched expression that added years to her face. She certainly didn't appear very happy. "She has no other family?"

"No. She was an only child," Lucien said. "I recall that she had a baby brother, but he died as an infant."

The woman's story was similar to her own. They'd both lost their parents. And Mrs. Conner had married into a family. Now she had a husband, a brother-in-law, and a father-in-law. "Do they have any children?"

"No."

Tempy watched Mrs. Conner for a moment and then suddenly didn't want to look at the woman any longer. She seemed like a warped reflection of Tempy, and the woman's unhappiness made her uneasy. Instead, she smiled as she turned to face Lucien.

"Shall we rejoin the others?" she asked, gesturing toward the other room.

He nodded.

Tempy rested her hand on his arm and they passed through the drawing room door. Despite being nervous about how she'd be received after the incident at the dinner table, not to mention Mrs. Conner's rude comments, nobody looked at her twice. She didn't sense resentment from anyone except her hostess. Tempy and Lucien joined another group of guests as far away from Mrs. Conner as possible.

Lucien became embroiled in a conversation about some local

issues, and Tempy slipped away, chatting with various guests as she wandered through the room. The gentleman who had been sitting to the right of Tempy and had ignored her throughout dinner now smiled warmly in greeting as he approached her. Tempy could see Lucien on the far side of the room, still deep in conversation with Judge Conner.

The man introduced himself as Major Payne. Despite having ignored her all through dinner in favor of discussing horses and hunting, he now seemed eager to talk with her. Major Payne explained that he was a local landowner and a former military man.

"Do you ride, Miss Bliss?" he asked. "You have the bearing of a rider."

"I'm a writer, not a rider," she quipped. When he looked at her blankly, she explained. "I write newspaper articles. I'm currently working on one for *All the Year Round*, and if it's successful, I hope Mr. Dickens will ask me to write for him again."

Major Payne waved his hand dismissively. "That seems like quite a lot of bother. I never understood writers. All pensive and solitary. I'd take a good fox hunt any time over sitting inside all day and scribbling on paper. But it takes all kinds."

"Yes, it does. From writers, to industrialists, to fox hunters, and everything in between."

"Still, do you think you'll continue writing once you're married? After all, won't being a wife and mother take up most of your time?"

"Not necessarily. Lady Harwarden has ten children, but that doesn't stop her from being a photographer. She set up her own studio in her home in South Kensington."

The man frowned, but didn't comment. "How are you enjoying your visit to Porlock?"

"It's a lovely village. Have you lived here all your life?"

"Except for my time in the military, yes. The place seeps into your bones and it makes it hard to leave. I was exceedingly grateful when I was able to return."

Tempy glanced at the bowl of punch sitting on a table along the wall.

"Can I offer you some punch?" the major asked.

"Thank you. I'd be exceedingly grateful. It's rather warm in here."

He returned shortly with two glasses and handed one to her. "Would you care to take a brief turn outside?" he asked. "It should be much cooler there."

Tempy glanced toward the open door leading onto the lawn and nodded. She could see a number of torches lighting the way along a path leading to a flower garden a short distance away.

When they stepped outside, the air was cooler than Tempy expected. But even so, the damp chill in the air felt refreshing after the heat of the drawing room. A scent, both floral and loamy, surrounded her as she moved down the path in the spring night. Tempy inhaled deeply, feeling invigorated by the cool air.

The flower garden was delightful in the moonlight. Someone had planted a variety of white flowers, and they seemed to glow from the reflected light. Beds of little white daffodils flanked the path.

When she glanced at Major Payne, his eyes looked like round saucers in the flickering torchlight. But what Tempy found disturbing was that his gaze seemed firmly fixed at the cleft between her breasts, as though trying to examine the spot where the glob of chocolate had landed.

"You are quite a healthy young woman," he muttered, jerking his gaze up to meet hers.

With some embarrassment, Tempy realized his mind was on something other than the glob of chocolate. She felt herself redden and turned abruptly, intending to walk back toward the open doors.

As she took her first step toward the house, Major Payne put a restraining hand on her arm.

"Wait a moment," he said. "There's no need to play the innocent." He pulled her closer and wrapped an arm around her waist. "I simply wanted to speak with you alone." He jutted his chin toward a path leading into the trees. "There's a bench just through there where we won't be disturbed. I'm certain I won't disappoint you if you choose to join me."

Tempy jerked away. "You've misjudged me, sir." As she turned away from him, she could hear her heart pounding in her ears. She barely kept from breaking into a run as she hurried toward the doors.

"If that's the case," he called after her, "you might want to reconsider some of the choices you made this evening."

Tempy paused just outside the drawing room door to compose herself. She didn't want anyone to think she'd been fleeing from the man. She closed her eyes for a moment and breathed more slowly as she tried to slow her heart rate.

"Is everything all right?" Lucien asked from behind her.

She jumped and whirled around. Had she walked right past him without seeing him? She'd been so intent on returning to the safety of the house that she must not have noticed him in the darkness. "You startled me. What are you doing out here?"

"Making sure you're safe," he said in a low voice. His deep bass rumbled, striking a chord that resonated within her.

Tempy leaned toward him, drawn to his strength and solidity. "You followed me?"

"I saw you leave. I was concerned about the intentions of your escort, but I see you kept him in hand and didn't need my help."

It came as a surprise to know that he'd been watching over her. She'd become so used to doing things on her own over the past year that having someone want to protect her seemed strange. But he hadn't interfered or tried to control her, and she realized that she liked the sense of security that his presence engendered. She hadn't often felt that way in the past.

"Some of the guests are going home. Would you like to leave as well? We have a long drive back to my estate."

She nodded. "And thank you. For watching over me."

He shrugged that Gallic shrug again, and her gaze focused on his lower lip as it jutted out ever so slightly.

That kiss in his office had been unforgettable.

She really needed to get back to London. And quickly.

After one more day in Exmoor, they began their return trip to Bath.

For Lucien, ending this little holiday would be both a torment and a relief. A torment, because with the success Tempy had achieved in so short a time in reinventing herself, it was obvious that her lessons would soon come to an end. And a relief, because his acting abilities were being stretched to their limits.

Sooner or later he knew he'd slip. In fact, if Mary hadn't been with them during the long ride home from the dinner party, he was certain he'd have lost his battle against temptation. Tempy's dress had nearly done him in. But he had to admit that he'd enjoyed watching the various reactions she'd elicited by wearing it.

But being around her so much during this trip was its own special kind of torment, and the tension was beginning to wear on him. To have her so close and then pretend that she meant nothing to him was torture.

Tempy pulled all of his attention all the time, but it wasn't anything she did intentionally. In fact, when she was around him like this, she didn't use any of the tricks that Mme Le Clair had taught her.

She was just Tempy.

Pretending he didn't notice everything she did, every move she made, exhausted him.

It was nearing twilight when they walked into his home along the Royal Crescent. Lucien retired to his bed chamber for a short time to change his clothes and wash up before returning to the drawing room. He was a bit surprised when Tempy and Millicent arrived just moments later. They both looked a bit weary.

"I think I'll get some fresh air," Millicent said. "We've been cooped up in that carriage for hours." She gave Tempy a critical gaze. "You look a bit peaked, dear. Would you like to rest?"

Tempy sighed, sounding annoyed. "Thank you, Millicent, but as I keep saying, I'm fine. What would I ever do without your constant concern?"

Millicent chuckled. "Was that sarcasm I detected, darling? You really must be tired. I won't be long." She was on her feet and out the door before anyone could react.

Tempy let out a heavy sigh as soon as Millicent was gone. "With the many little comments Millicent's been making all day, I'm nearly convinced she wishes for me to be sick too. I think she resents that she's the only one who was ill on this trip."

Lucien pushed himself from his chair. The idea of staying alone in the drawing room with Tempy was more than he could bear. Millicent was right. She did look tired. And vulnerable.

It wasn't a good idea to be with her right now. She didn't want him. Not really. She wanted Ernest. Lucien knew he'd end up making a fool of himself if he stayed with her this evening. "Far be it from me to comment on a lady's state of exhaustion, but Millicent may have a point. We've had a busy few days. Would you like to relax and have a quiet evening?"

Tempy's smile held a tinge of relief. "That would be lovely."

"How about a light dinner then? I can arrange for the cook to send something up to your room if you like. Or, if you prefer, you can dine with Millicent." He cleared his throat, uncomfortable with the lie he was about to utter. "I need to go out for a while. I have some things I need to take care of." It was only a small lie. One that had her best interests at heart. Along with his. All he knew was that he couldn't stay here alone with her any longer.

She seemed to deflate, as though his lie had pricked her and drained away her last reserves of energy. "We head back tomorrow, is that the plan?"

He nodded. "There's a train that leaves Bath at noon. That would put us back in London by early afternoon. Is that agreeable?" He avoided her gaze as he reached out to pull the velvet cord that would call one of the servants. He wasn't even sure if she responded. But did it matter? Either way, he still had to leave.

Lucien was out the door and on his way to a nearby restaurant within the next five minutes. He'd never spent much time in Bath before this, and he had to admit that it was a beautiful town, especially now, at sunset.

But he wasn't in the mood to appreciate such beauty alone.

He made his way toward Wrightson's, a restaurant he'd noticed during his last visit. The place was pleasant enough. It was clean and comfortable, and the food was good. And best of all, no one looked at him twice for sitting alone. He wasn't the only solitary diner. He noticed two others. One was an older man who contented himself with reading a book while he waited for his food. The other was a middle-aged man with sharp features. Lucien had noticed him when he'd entered because of the cane he leaned upon. Rather than reading, this man chose to write, scribbling away in a small bound book using the stub of a pencil.

Lucien lingered over the meal, finishing a bottle of red wine with it. He normally didn't drink alone, but tonight seemed like the perfect occasion for it.

He stepped back outside into the damp night air. It was early.

Tempy and Millicent would probably still be awake, so he couldn't go home yet. Lucien glanced up and down the road. There were a few pedestrians strolling along it, so he decided to join them in their pastime. As he meandered his way through the streets of Bath, he moved steadily downhill, making his way toward the river.

To him, the river had always meant people and life and activity. It was a place where a person could mingle with others and yet still remain anonymous. And anonymity meant freedom. When Lucien was in his casino, he was at the beck and call of every patron who passed through the doors. He was the face of Hamlin House. Normally he embraced the role willingly. But tonight he craved something different. And Bath opened her arms and offered it to him.

He could see why so many people found this place appealing. There was a serenity about it. A healing peace.

A door opened and a burst of laughter interrupted that peace. He turned his head and peered toward the glow of light shining through the open door. The pub was a cheerful one, and suddenly the warmth and camaraderie it offered beckoned to him. He moved toward the light.

As he shouldered his way through the door, he paused for a moment to allow his eyes to adjust to the brightness of the room. There were a few open places at the bar, but he noticed an empty table near the back wall and moved toward it. The bar was perfect for a person who wanted to socialize and be seen, but if one preferred the role of observer, then a table at the back was far better suited to that purpose.

Lucien settled into a spot with his back to the wall, watching the room while sipping whiskey. He was surprised when the pinch-faced man from Wrightson's entered the bar. The man seemed to be leaning more heavily on his cane than he had been earlier in the evening as edged closer to a vacant stool at the bar. Lucien observed him closely. Seeing the man twice in one night was beyond pure chance. Was he being followed?

Another man approached Lucien. "Mind if I take this chair?"

Lucien waved his acceptance, and watched as the man dragged the chair across the room toward a large group of men. They appeared to be celebrating something. There was a lot of smiling and patting of backs. Based on the snippets he heard, Lucien was fairly certain that someone had just become engaged.

Even though his awareness was focused on the man sitting alone at the bar, Lucien examined the young man everyone was congratulating. And "young" he was. He must be only about twenty-three or so. Lucien had been almost exactly that age when Rebecca Formsworth had died. But even so, he wasn't sure that he'd ever been quite as callow as the young man across the room. He'd never had that luxury.

The vagaries of heredity that had created such different character traits in his uncles and in his father had come together in an unusual combination within Lucien. In him, his uncles' ease at making quick calculations had merged with his father's sense of responsibility. It made him perfectly suited to running a casino. And from what he could tell so far, he also seemed well suited to assume the new role of the Earl of Cavendish.

As the evening wore on, the group of young revelers began to absorb the other small knots of patrons in the pub. A few people appeared to attempt to include the loner sitting at the bar and scribbling in his journal, but the man rebuffed them all.

It wasn't long before the merrymakers absorbed Lucien into their group. He was willing. They shared drinks and stories and jokes. It was one of the most fun and relaxing nights he'd had in a long time. And he'd probably never see these people again.

As the young groom's friends plied him with spirits, he spoke more and more about his bride.

"What does she look like?" asked one of the men who'd been absorbed into the group. "Is she pretty?"

"She's as beautiful as...as a spring day," the young man said, as he groped for words to describe her. "Her hair's black. As black as Lord Witton's stallion, and she's prettier than any other girl in town."

"We get it. She's beautiful," someone else said in a bantering tone.

"He's just besotted with her," another man said. "Has been for years. He can't help himself."

"You're lucky your family likes her. I remember how upset they got when your brother started chasing after that serving maid. They were none too pleased with him when he brought her home to meet them."

The groom shifted his weight as he pulled back his shoulders and thrust out his chest. "Don't you go comparing my Lily with the likes of her. Of course they didn't like her. She's a church-bell. Chiming all day long. She never would shut up. And the things she'd say. The sauce-box on that one would drive a man to drink."

Lucien suppressed a chuckle. The young man was much more colorful when it came to describing the woman he despised than he'd been when describing his own bride. Perhaps love had made him unable to find the words to use.

"Well, you're lucky they approve of Lily," someone said. "I've known your parents long enough to tell that they would have made your life nigh impossible if they hadn't."

Lucien's thoughts turned inward as he considered those prophetic words. Hadn't that been what his grandfather had done to his father...made his life impossible? His father's decision to marry a Frenchwoman who had no family or status had only served to ostracize him from his family. Once they'd married, they'd never found a place where they truly belonged. Father didn't have the funds to socialize with those peers who would accept his marriage, and he was never completely accepted by their working-class neighbors either. Everyone was polite, but there was never that warm camaraderie that spoke of true friendship.

But Tempy's situation was completely different from that of his father's. She was alone, yes, but she wasn't penniless. And she obviously never thought about the whims of society. She'd already proven she didn't care a whit about them by ignoring their condemnation and becoming a journalist worthy of the attention of Charles Dickens. So why was she so determined to become part of Ernest's family? It made no sense.

Perhaps she was simply driven by momentum, like a freight train barreling down a hill. What if he were to divert her onto a different track? One that led her to him?

As the crowd began to dwindle, Lucien glanced over at the bar again to locate the pinch-faced man, but couldn't find him. Had he left? It must be quite late. Tempy must certainly be asleep. Perhaps this was the perfect moment to head home. He needed a good night's sleep before he decided on what course of action to take with Tempy.

Once outside, Lucien began walking toward the Royal Crescent. Remembering the pinch-faced man, he carefully surveyed his surroundings, but he saw no sign of the man. Even so, he couldn't shake the feeling that someone was watching him. Fortunately, an empty hansom cab came lumbering past. At his wave, it pulled to a stop. He climbed aboard and was home within ten minutes.

There were no lights burning upstairs in the bedrooms. Tempy must be asleep.

Would he be able to sleep soundly tonight? That was more than he could say for any other night since he'd left London. He sighed, his mind turning toward thoughts of Tempy again, just as they had almost every night since he'd met her. No, tonight would be another sleepless one. Of that he was certain.

As he awoke the next morning, the gloom of the overcast day kept Lucien's eyes from being pierced by sunlight. He'd need to have a chat with Boothby about adjusting the curtains at night. Fortunately, however, this was one of the few flaws that he'd found in Boothby's performance as a valet during this trip. He glanced at the bedside clock. It was already ten thirty. He'd need to move quickly if he wanted to eat and be aboard the train by noon.

Feet on floor, he thought to himself. Feet on floor.

Lucien only groaned a little as he forced his body to move and planted both feet on the thick rug that covered nearly the entire floor of his bedroom.

After pouring tepid water into a bowl, Lucien soaped up and rinsed off and then carelessly dropped the damp towels to the floor. He pulled on the clothes that Boothby had carefully laid out for him, pausing only to choose which waistcoat he wanted to wear.

Blue. Today seemed like a blue day. He selected a waistcoat of cobalt blue with a tone-on-tone windowpane print and shrugged into it. He draped his frock coat over his arm and then hurried downstairs to join the ladies and make his apologies.

The breakfast room was empty. In fact, from what he could see, there were no signs of movement from either of the ladies.

"Boothby," he called as he reached toward the bell cord. He gave it a sharp yank. "Boothby."

Boothby hurried into the room, a newspaper folded in half and tucked under his arm.

"Oh, good, you're here. I'm surprised the others aren't up and about yet. We need to leave within the hour if we want to catch that twelve o'clock train. Will they be ready in time?"

Boothby didn't speak. Instead, he held out the folded newspaper. Lucien froze for a moment. This couldn't possibly be good.

He hated being right. Especially this time. His mouth thinned as he read the headline.

BEAU BEGUILES BLISS
By Earl E. Byrd

Temperance Bliss, sole heiress of the estate of Herbert Bliss, the founder of Bliss Railways, has recently been associating with Lucien Hamlin, the proprietor of the popular casino Hamlin House. Sources close to Miss Bliss indicate that she has been a frequent visitor to his gambling establishment. Should this be a cause of concern?

Has Miss Bliss been busily losing her fortune in one of London's most notorious casinos?

Others have noticed a marked change in Miss Bliss's behavior of late. Could this account for the sudden change in the affections of her longtime friend?

Not only were Miss Bliss and her chaperone recently seen in Mr. Hamlin's company in Bath, our "poor little rich girl" also accompanied him to a dinner party held at the home of Judge and Mrs. Conner in the town of Porlock. One guest commented cryptically that Miss Bliss's scandalous choice of attire that evening had been fortuitous, because any other dress would have been ruined by an unfortunate accident that took place following the meal.

LUCIEN CLENCHED HIS JAW AS HE GLANCED TOWARD THE staircase. No wonder Tempy was still upstairs. She must have already read this and had decided to avoid him for as long as possible. Millicent must be with her. He scanned the rest of the article. It went on to make suggestions about Lucien's past with regard to Rebecca. They sounded startlingly similar to the accusations Formsworth had made back in Porlock. Apparently Formsworth and the reporter had spoken. Lucien could spot Formsworth's twisted version of the past from a mile away.

He should have known better than to bring Tempy with him. The trip had been a mistake.

In fact, all of it had been a mistake.

He never should have agreed to this ridiculous plan. Wasn't this exactly the sort of bad press he'd feared? Not that he blamed

Tempy. This wasn't her fault. But the timing couldn't be much worse.

A new thought struck him. How on earth would he explain this to Snowden? The man would have his hide.

And what about the casino?

"Get her. Tell her I need to speak with her."

Boothby shook his head. "I'm sorry, sir, but she's not here. She and Mrs. Kidman left early this morning to return to London."

"What? Are you telling me she ran off without saying a word to me?"

"Mrs. Kidman returned from her walk yesterday evening with this newspaper. Miss Bliss waited up for you to come home yesterday evening, but you were very late."

Lucien shook his head vehemently, and then ripped the article from the newspaper, shoving the scrap into his trouser pocket as he tossed the rest of the paper onto the table. He yanked on his frock coat, grabbed his top hat from the table in the front hall, and yanked open the front door of his house.

"Pack my things and meet me in London as fast as you can get there," he said over his shoulder to Boothby. "I'm heading to the station." And he slammed the door shut behind him.

26

TEMPY TRIES TO FIX THINGS

❧

Tempy had forgotten her hat.

Again.

And, based on the scandalous looks everyone on the street kept shooting in her direction, being hatless was by far the most egregious sin she could possibly commit. Unfortunately, she didn't have time to run back home to get it. Why did people have to wear hats all the time, anyway? They were a blasted nuisance.

Tempy blushed as yet another woman openly stared at her with a shocked expression.

A scattering of raindrops blew across her face. Tempy glanced skyward and noticed that the clouds had grown much thicker and darker in the past few minutes. She sighed. Today would have been a good day to remember that hat.

Tempy raised her arm, hailing the driver of a passing hansom cab. She let out a sigh of relief as he stopped for her. He helped her inside, and soon the cab was bouncing her along the rain-slickened street. Tempy was irritated with herself. Would she ever learn to make a plan instead of rushing headlong into situations?

Once the carriage rolled to a stop, Tempy paid the driver and then hurried up the front steps of John Snowden's townhouse. Perhaps he hadn't read the newspaper. There was a chance, wasn't there? Admittedly a slim one, but what was life without hope?

After opening the door to her, the butler immediately ushered her into the morning room. The moment she saw John Snowden's face, her hopes scattered to the winds, racing along after some stray cherry blossom petals that blew past the townhouse door. The man's face looked as ominous as the London sky.

Tempy took an involuntary step back from the imposing man. "It's not what you think. That reporter has it all wrong," she said, trying to ward off a storm of recriminations.

The furrows in John's brow deepened. "Does that even matter? The idea that you would even *put* yourself in such a situation is beyond belief. Is it true that you've been at that casino almost daily?"

"But I already explained that to you," Tempy said, her tone pleading.

He shook his head vehemently. "You did no such thing."

"Yes," she said, taking a step closer to him. "On that first night you saw me in Mr. Hamlin's office. Remember? I told you I was doing research?" A scattering of raindrops hit hard against the window, like a handful of pebbles, and the sound startled her.

The furrow between John's brows eased a little. "Of course, but according to this article you are in a relationship with Mr. Hamlin. You even traveled with him. I can't countenance such behavior. I must say, I'm extremely disappointed to learn that you both deceived me. I must be slipping. It's troubling to learn that you were able to completely mislead me." He shook his head as if in frustration.

"But I already told you. I'm doing research about gambling. I never deceived you about that."

John's brows rose in surprise and he snatched the newspaper off the table and shook it at her. "According to this article, what you're doing with Mr. Hamlin could hardly be called *research*."

What? "That's entirely unfair," she snapped at him, unable to keep her annoyance from coloring her voice. "You know quite well that I've been the target of that odious Earl E. Byrd in the newspapers for the past year. You've always believed my version of events in the past. Why doubt me now?"

"But what else am I to think? If I'm wrong, then tell me. Why are you spending so much time at Hamlin House, and why are you researching gambling?"

Tempy pressed her lips together. She wasn't normally superstitious, but what if she told him about her opportunity to write for Mr. Dickens only to have him decide her article wasn't good enough? She closed her eyes and huffed out a sigh of frustration. John Snowden wasn't leaving her with any other choice. She'd have to tell him. She opened her eyes and pinned him with her gaze. "As a matter of fact, Mr. Charles Dickens has requested that I write an article for his newspaper."

Judging by the stunned look on John's face, she'd managed surprise him. "Charles Dickens? *The* Charles Dickens?"

She stared at him coldly. "Is that so hard to believe?"

"That's, that's..." His face reddened. "That's stupendous news. Charles Dickens. Just imagine that."

"Yes," she said in a tight voice. "And, as you can also imagine, I'm taking this opportunity very seriously--" She stopped short. Had she truly taken it seriously? She felt a blush rise in her cheeks. She hadn't worked on the article in days, so how could she stand here claiming that she'd been taking it seriously? Her shoulders slumped. "I'm not being entirely honest with you," she said, shaking her head. "Ever since I received that letter from Ernest, I haven't been myself."

John looked perplexed. "Dr. Lipscomb's son? What does he have to do with this?" He scrubbed his hand across his face, as though trying to rub away his confusion. "I'm afraid I'm not following you."

"That makes two of us," Tempy mumbled. How had her life become so convoluted?

"What was that?"

"Nothing," she said, irritated with herself for speaking the words aloud. "It's just that everything has been terribly confusing lately. Ernest and I were supposed to be married. At least that's what I always thought would happen. But he's decided he wants to marry someone else."

John kept his face blank and didn't say a word. Even so, she had the impression that she'd surprised him. Poor man. She must have completely confused him by now. "I've been trying to win him back. I'm certain he'll get over this infatuation, and when he does he'll come back to me."

John cleared his throat as he picked up the newspaper. "I'm not sure how any of that relates to this article," he said, pointing at the offending bit of newsprint.

Tempy let out a deep sigh. "Neither am I. In fact, I'm not sure how anything relates to *anything*. I have no idea where Earl E. Byrd came up with his newspaper article. It's largely based on rumor and speculation. There's nothing between me and Lucien. He's simply been helping me, both with my research and with trying to win back Ernest. That's all there is to it."

He narrowed his eyes. "You're telling me the two of you aren't romantically involved?"

"That's exactly what I'm telling you. I hope you understand that Lucien's been hurt by this article too. He was extremely kind to allow me to conduct my research at his casino. I can't tell you how much it pains me to know that I am repaying him by ruining his good name."

At that, John Snowden snorted and then grinned. "Humph! Wouldn't he need to have a good name in order for you to ruin in the first place?" He shook his head. "Ah, that's not fair of me. It's just that I don't think this article damaged his reputation." He paused and fixed her with a stare. "It's yours I'm worried about." His brow furrowed again as he frowned. "So what are we going to do about that?"

Tempy smiled. "I have a plan."

27

A MEETING ON THE STEPS

John Snowden's letter was folded into thirds and rested in the breast pocket of Lucien's frock coat.

It felt heavy resting there, despite the fact that it weighed no more than a feather. It was the letter's contents that made it feel like a lump of cold lead in his pocket.

It was raining heavily as his carriage stopped in front of John Snowden's townhouse. Lucien snapped open an umbrella as he stepped out of his carriage. At the same moment, the front door of the townhouse opened and a figure stepped outside. A woman scurried down the front steps, almost colliding with him as she ran through the rain.

"Tempy. Is that you?" Of course it was. Who else would be running out into a rainstorm without a hat?

Lucien tilted his umbrella so that it sheltered both of them, and Tempy moved closer to him to avoid the rain. It beat down heavily, and nobody else was on the street. The weather provided them with a momentary cocoon of privacy.

He breathed in her scent. Lavender and roses with a hint of

cloves. A wave of longing and loss washed over him, threatening to overwhelm him. But he refused to give in. He pushed it away. He needed to remain calm.

"You left," he said, keeping his tone level. "You left without saying a word." He managed to hide the pain she'd caused him. Barely.

Her smile of greeting disappeared as her jaw dropped. "I left a note. I slid it under your door."

Lucien thought of that morning, and of his bedroom in Bath where he'd woken up. He fixed that waking image of the bedroom in his mind, and then he shook his head. "There was nothing there. No note. Nothing."

"I'm...I'm so sorry, Lucien. You must have thought..."

"That you'd abandoned me? That you left at the first sign of trouble?" He had to speak loudly to be heard over the rain, but that suited him well. He *wanted* to shout at her. "I should have known better. This is exactly what I was afraid would happen. John's pulling out of the deal," he said, pulling the letter from his pocket. "This letter from him was waiting for me when I arrived back in town. In a few days all of London will know I'm the new earl, and all of my plans will come crashing down around me. How will I be able to sell my casino?" He shook his head. "I should have kept my distance from the 'poor little rich girl.'"

Tempy jerked her head back as though he'd slapped her. "You can't mean that."

"Can't I?" He moved past her and began to walk up the steps, but then he paused.

Lucien turned and put one foot back down the steps so that he faced Tempy again. He stared at her for a moment, taking in her bedraggled condition. She looked pitiful, and a knot of sympathy twisted inside Lucien to see her this way. She must be cold, standing in the rain. He sighed and handed her his umbrella. "Take my carriage. Otherwise, you'll end up looking like a drowned rat."

She refused to meet his gaze. Her lips were pressed into a thin line. She looked furious, but what did she have to be angry about?

Tempy hesitated a moment, clearly considering refusing his offer, but then she yanked the umbrella from his grasp. "You're wrong about me, Lucien," she said, her face damp with rain, "but I *am* sorry I've caused you so much trouble." Then she turned and hurried toward the carriage.

Unable to watch her any longer, Lucien whirled and hurried back up the steps. There was a slight overhang above the door, but it did little to keep away the rain.

Lucien pounded at Snowden's door so that his knock could be heard over the sound of the downpour. He refused to look back and watch as his carriage left with Tempy. Thankfully, the door opened and he was able to slip inside.

"What's all that commotion?" Snowden asked, entering the foyer from an adjoining drawing room. He grabbed the temple of his reading glasses and pulled them from his face, letting them dangle from his fingers. "Lucien, is that you? You just missed Miss Bliss."

Lucien removed his dripping top hat and handed it to the butler, and then he wiped his hand on his frock coat before holding it out to shake John's. "I saw her as she was leaving."

John nodded, and Lucien fell in step next to him as he headed back toward the drawing room. "She seemed quite anxious to correct any misconceptions I might have about the two of you after reading that article," John said. He glanced sideways at Lucien, leaving him with the distinct impression that John was trying to scrutinize his reaction. Did John believe there was more between him and Tempy? Perhaps he hoped Lucien would give himself away and show that he cared about the girl.

"Was she?" Lucien asked. "That article contained a great many errors." He cleared his throat. "I'd like to assure you that I've never taken advantage of Miss Bliss."

"And I'd like to assure you that if I thought you had, I never would have shaken your hand just now." John managed to make his tone both genial and menacing. How he managed that, Lucien wasn't sure, but he was impressed.

Lucien nodded. Then he reached into his breast pocket and pulled out the letter John had sent him that morning.

John's face fell as he caught sight of it. "Ah, yes. About that. I believe I acted hastily in sending it to you. I should have spoken to both of you first. I deeply regret writing it."

Hope flared in Lucien. "Does your offer for the casino still stand?"

"Yes. It still stands."

"Then, if you don't mind, given the circumstances, I'd like to expedite the transaction. Do you think we could complete it by the end of this week?"

John raised his eyebrows and then nodded. "I suppose that's possible. In fact, I probably owe you that, given the fact that I tried to break our agreement."

"Good. Let's finalize things so that the casino is yours no later than this coming Monday."

"I'll speak to my lawyers. We can sign on Saturday."

Lucien nodded. "Saturday it is."

28

THE PLAN COMES TOGETHER

Tempy returned home, sodden and uncomfortable.

Again.

That was twice in one week, and she wasn't eager to repeat it anytime soon.

She hurried up the steps, and then paused to glance over her shoulder. Lucien's coachman was climbing back on his perch, and beyond it she could see Father's train statue in the park across the street. Lucien's carriage pulled away with a jerk, and she presumed that the coachman would return to John's house to collect his employer.

As Tempy stepped inside the house, Royce hurried into the foyer. When he saw her state, he pursed his lips into a rare frown.

She fumbled with the button holding her cloak closed, but the leather covering of the button was swollen with water, and it wouldn't slide through the buttonhole. Royce made quick work of it, and when a footman hurried into the foyer, Royce handed him the wet garment.

While all of this was taking place, Tempy glanced down at the silver tray near the front door. Royce had sorted the correspondence, as usual, but there was a letter he'd placed prominently on top of everything else.

Could it be from Lucien? Did he regret what he'd said? But that didn't make sense. She'd only just left him. A letter couldn't possibly have arrived before she did. She snatched it up and tore it open with her cold, damp fingers.

Inside was a sheet of paper, and folded inside that was a neatly clipped bit of newspaper. She recognized it immediately as coming from a column that posted the banns.

A chill deepened within her as her eyes scanned the page. There it was. Ernest and Clarisse's banns, plain for all to see.

The letter said, "I thought you would be interested in seeing this," and was unsigned. But when Tempy recalled Clarisse's irritating smile from that day in Bath, she knew it could only have come from her.

The engagement was real. She couldn't deny it. Posting the banns proved it. She checked the date on the piece of rough newsprint and saw the notice had been posted just over a week ago. How had she missed it?

She slowly lowered herself to sit on the slippery sofa, hardly aware of her surroundings. The second posting had probably been in yesterday's newspaper. That meant that their wedding could take place in less than two weeks. If she really meant to go through with her plan to win back Ernest, she needed it to happen quickly. Otherwise it might be too late.

Tempy forced herself to ignore the niggling sense of doubt that had invaded her over the past few days regarding her current path. It was now or never, and she wasn't ready to let go of her dream of a life with Ernest.

Was she?

An hour later, after drying off and changing into warmer clothes, Tempy entered her office so she could write.

It was a restful space. The walls were pale yellow, and if it had been a sunny day, the view out her tall windows would have been appealing, but instead it was dismal. The rainstorm had passed, and now the world outside was gray and foggy. Even the spring flowers in the beds outside looked beaten down.

Tempy could identify with them.

She was tempted to close the yellow-and-blue floral curtains, but knew it would make her feel too cut off from the world. She didn't want to reinforce that sense of isolation, so she left them open.

She'd already sorted through the rest of her correspondence and had come across a letter from the board of directors of Bliss Railways. They'd seen the article as well and were back to pressuring her to sell her controlling interest in the company. They always jumped at any excuse to manipulate her into giving up her father's legacy, but she wouldn't do it. She couldn't.

One of the servants had started a fire in the fireplace, and it had already driven the chill from the room. Tempy picked up the neatly folded pale blue lap blanket from the sofa and wrapped it around her shoulders. She rubbed her cheek against the soft wool as she sat down at her delicate writing desk.

Tempy kept her workspace clear, so the only things on her desk blotter were her ink pot, her pen, and a stack of paper. At the rear of her desk was a stack of little drawers containing more writing supplies, and on top of that sat a bud vase containing a single yellow daffodil.

Tempy pulled out a fresh sheet of paper from the stack and her notebook from one of the drawers. She pushed her personal problems aside as she focused on writing her article, but it was difficult.

She wrote for a few minutes, making good progress on the first part of her article. For a while, the only sound in the room came from the scratch of her pen against the paper and the crackling of the fire in the hearth.

Tempy dipped her pen in the pot of ink and then held it poised over her paper. Lucien had been right. Her notoriety had nearly derailed the sale of his casino, just as he'd feared. Even though the article had obviously been written by the same person who'd been harassing her ever since her father died, she could see Mrs. Conner's fingerprints all over it, and if Tempy hadn't lost her temper and goaded the woman, the parts that incriminated Lucien might never have been written. It was clearly intended to cast her in a bad light. Mrs. Conner might not even have considered the effect it could have upon Lucien.

A drop of ink dripped from her pen, landing on the paper with a plop.

Blast.

She yanked open one of the drawers and pulled out a small square of blotting paper that she used to wick up the worst of the stain, but her mistake was still obvious. With a sigh, she decided to ignore it for now. Given her state, it wouldn't be the last blot today, and she couldn't afford to take the time to start over and rewrite her page every time she made a mistake.

She glanced up. When her gaze immediately landed on Clarisse's letter, she regretted looking up at all. She stood to move it. She couldn't let it sit there within her eyesight, ready to pounce on her again and distract her.

She didn't want it in her pocket, nor anyplace within her sight, so she looked around her cozy office to find a place to hide it away. Ah, there. In that book, *Wuthering Heights*. Ernest had always hated it. She opened the book and placed the letter inside, and then slid it back onto the shelf.

Unfortunately, hiding the letter out of sight didn't stop her from worrying about it. Ernest and Clarisse would be married soon, and she needed to move quickly if she had any hope of preventing it.

Thinking about it made her shoulders tense. She needed to seduce him away from Clarisse, and she needed to do it soon.

Her last attempt at seduction had led to some unexpected results. Had she been responsible for both Charles's and Major Payne's behavior? Had she overdone it at the dinner party? Obviously Mrs. Conner thought so.

She needed to formulate a plan. And for that, she needed Mme Le Clair.

Tempy sat back down at her desk, determined to work on her article. As she dipped her pen in the pot of ink, she thought about the row of quill pens on Mr. Dickens's desk. Perhaps he preferred to be obliged to sharpen them in order to give himself something to do with his hands while he was deciding what to write next. Tempy always used a desk blotter to clean her pen and draw random designs. Doing so often helped her focus her thoughts. When she was done writing each day, she'd tear off the top sheet on the blotter, revealing a fresh, clean one.

But scribbling on her blotter wouldn't solve her problem this time. Her article was challenging, and she sensed she'd left out something. It needed balance. Perhaps if she spoke with people who no longer visited casinos, she could figure out what was missing. After all, if she wanted to understand how gambling impacted families, she should also look at some people who had turned their backs on the pastime.

With her new goals firmly in mind, Tempy set aside her article and penned a couple of brief notes. Then she put the cap on her inkwell and cleaned off the pen nib before putting everything away.

Tempy received replies to her notes a couple of hours later, but when she collected her mail, she was startled to discover a letter from Mrs. Lipscomb. What on earth had caused the woman to break her silence?

With a frown, Tempy set aside the one from Ernest's mother for the moment and opened the other two first. Mme Le Clair would meet her tomorrow morning at the casino, and Millicent wanted Tempy to stop by her home today at five o'clock to meet "the perfect interviewee" for her article.

With both of those problems firmly in hand, Tempy's sense of looming disaster eased, but only slightly.

With some trepidation, she tore open the envelope from Ernest's mother.

My dearest Temperance,

First, I must apologize to you for what must seem like a callous desertion of affection. I have no excuse for my behavior. Both Ernest and Mr. Lipscomb thought it best to sever our relationship with you after his engagement, and I abided by their wishes, but I most fervently regret that decision.

I miss you, Tempy. And I'm worried about you.

As I'm sure you must have guessed, I read the article about you in this morning's newspaper. Of course, I realize that you have frequently been the target of unscrupulous journalists, and with that in mind, I initially dismissed it out of hand. But then Ernest told me that he'd seen you both at Hamlin House and in Bath in the company of Mr. Hamlin, and this news troubled me greatly.

I realize I am not your mother. No mother would have abandoned her child the way I did, and for such trivial reasons. Again, I sorely regret my actions. But I feel I must caution you in regard to your continued acquaintance with Mr. Hamlin. There are things you do not know about him.

Ernest has been to his establishment twice. On the first occasion, he won a great deal of money, but on his second visit, he lost all of it! To make matters worse, Mr. Hamlin extended credit to our Dear Ernest, so now he is in debt to the man. I am quite upset by this, as you can well imagine. Hamlin House has a reputation for not advancing credit to its patrons, so I can only assume that he did this in order to put Ernest, a former rival for your affections, into debt with him, thereby gaining some control over both him and you. This is quite upsetting.

Please be assured that Mr. Lipscomb will pay Ernest's debt so that Mr. Hamlin will not be able to use it to manipulate either you or Ernest.

I fervently hope that this financial indiscretion has not caused you any heartache. The thought of this man taking advantage of you is like a knife to my heart.

Please know that I am here for you now, just as I should have been all along. You may never be Ernest's wife, but you will always have a place in my heart.

My most sincere apologies and heartfelt love,
Doris Lipscomb

Tempy felt a tear slide down her cheek. It had been difficult to make the mental transition to calling this dear woman "Mrs. Lipscomb" rather than "Mother," but now it seemed more natural. Even so, Mrs. Lipscomb was still the closest thing she had to a mother.

Poor, sweet Mrs. Lipscomb. No wonder Tempy hadn't heard from her in nearly two weeks. Even though the letter was laced with misunderstandings, at least Tempy was assured of the woman's continuing affection.

She needed to reply. And she needed to explain that Mr. Hamlin had only extended the credit because Ernest had used his friendship with Tempy to ask for it. Tempy was certain that this would come as a surprise to Mrs. Lipscomb.

She pulled out a fresh piece of paper and began writing.

Precisely at five o'clock, Millicent's butler escorted Tempy into her drawing room.

Millicent rose to greet her. She had been sitting and chatting with a conservatively dressed man who appeared to be in his early thirties. His hair was sleek and dark, thinning just above the temples, and he had thick sideburns that seemed to emphasize his hair loss.

As Millicent brushed her cheek against Tempy's in an embrace, Millicent murmured, "Treat him gently," so that only Tempy could hear. As she stepped away, she said, "Tempy, I'd like to introduce you to Harlan Mall. He graciously consented to allow you to interview him for your article."

"But I told you that I wished to remain anonymous," Mr. Mall said, his voice querulous as he rose to his feet from the sofa.

"And so you shall be," Tempy reassured him. "I won't divulge your name or any other information that might allow people to identify you. I promise."

The man still sent Millicent a peevish look, but when he turned his gaze to Tempy, his expression softened a little.

"I can't afford to have my reputation damaged. I'm only beginning to recover from my youthful excesses, and to have you shine a public light on my life could bring me even more shame."

"I understand, Mr. Mall. Again, I promise that I'll never use any personal information about you. Would you like to have the opportunity to see what I write before it's published?" She paused to watch his reaction. He seemed intrigued by the idea, and that was good. "I can offer to remove anything that you believe would cause you or your family harm. But that's an easy promise to make since I don't intend to include information of that nature. My goal is to warn others so they don't travel down the same dangerous path you did."

She could tell he was wavering. She nearly had him. "Wouldn't you like to know that your example helped save others from experiencing the same pain and anguish you did?"

Finally, the man's shoulders relaxed. He nodded. "Little good has come from all of my mistakes, but if I can help someone else...well, maybe that would help balance the scales." He lifted his chin and looked at her steadily. "How can I help?"

Tempy chose a spot on the pink sofa and Harlan Mall sat back down next to her. "Just tell me your story," she said. "I'll make sure I gloss over any details that might make you identifiable."

Mr. Mall drummed his fingers on his leg for a moment and then looked at Tempy. "I suppose I should begin at the beginning, back when I first started gambling. You see, when my father died, he left all of his property to my older brother and three thousand pounds a year to me. My brother doled out the money from the income of his estate. At first, I was satisfied with things as they stood, but having so much money to spend at my own discretion was a heady experience. I went from living with a small allowance to having ample funds at my disposal. I'm afraid I let it get the better of me."

Tempy kept her gaze focused on Harlan while she pulled her notebook from her satchel along with her pen-and-ink set. Perhaps if she were discreet in taking her notes, he might even relax enough to forget that she was taking them.

"I frequented the casinos in London, betting on whatever took my fancy." Harlan rose to his feet and pushed past Tempy's skirt to begin pacing.

She discretely slid her notebook on the low table in front of the sofa. Harlan didn't even glance at it.

"It didn't take long for me to burn through my ready cash, and then through all the money I'd planned to live on for the rest of the year. I'd become used to going to my father for money whenever I ran low, but I knew my brother wouldn't be so understanding."

Tempy dipped her ink in the pot, not worrying about leaving spots on her paper. These were just notes, after all, and only she would see them.

"Rather than going to him, I ended up taking out a sort of 'gentleman's loan' from a lawyer I'd met." Harlan stopped pacing and slid his hands into his trouser pockets. "Some friends of mine had also borrowed from him in the past, and he was quite accommodating. He seemed to understand my embarrassment. It was a simple matter to borrow the cash by signing a piece of paper."

One of Millicent's maids entered the room and set a tea tray on the table by the sofa, and then she left. Millicent poured cups for each of them. However, Mr. Mall hardly seemed aware of the activity around him, engrossed as he was in telling his tale. When Millicent handed him his tea, he took it absently and resumed his pacing.

"With my gambling debts paid off, I went back to my brother's home in the country. I was convinced that the lawyer had saved me from a terrible fate, and thankful that I had a place to live until I received my annual allowance. I stayed there all summer and into the fall, but once the Season began, all of my friends returned to London. A couple of them wrote to invite me to stay with them at their club. It was a generous offer, and I decided to join them for a month or two.

"Unfortunately, it didn't take long for me to fall back into my old habits. I tagged along with my friends when they went to a casino one night, and my resolve to never gamble again broke within an hour. Watching other men win money while I stood there with my hands in my pockets was torment. I convinced myself that I'd be able to win back everything I'd lost the year before.

"I was wrong.

"I bet ever larger amounts, and much more recklessly than before. Within a week, I had lost all of my money for a second time. Fortunately, my annual allowance arrived a week after that, so I was able to pay off my loan to the lawyer from the previous year, but between paying him and covering all of my new losses, I was again left with nothing."

Harlan paused in his pacing, which prompted Tempy to glance away from her notes to look at him. He frowned as he looked down at the teacup in his hands, as though surprised to see it there. He took a small sip and grimaced. "Needs sugar," he muttered. He looked around, and Tempy was afraid he might become aware of her note-taking, but instead his gaze focused on the tea tray. He was next to it in a couple of strides and added four spoons of sugar to his cup. After stirring it vigorously, he took another sip and nodded.

"I approached my lawyer friend again," he said, and then licked his lips. "He was happy to offer me terms to borrow more money since I had paid back the first loan as agreed. But this time, I needed much more than before. The first loan was for fifteen hundred pounds, but the new loan was for the full three thousand. I didn't know what else to do. If I didn't borrow from him, I would have nothing to live on for an entire year." Tempy could hear him swallow as he took a large gulp of tea. He smacked his lips in satisfaction.

Tempy dipped her pen in the little pot of ink and hurried to continue taking notes.

"I attempted to avoid the casinos by leaving town again," he said, waving his nearly empty teacup in a broad gesture toward the world outside of London. "But even after I returned to the country, I couldn't stop placing wagers. When my friends visited, we'd gamble on everything, from a race down the lane to which cow would drop the next cow patty." He reddened. "Begging your pardon, miss."

"That's quite all right. Cow patties happen," Tempy murmured. She tried not to smile since she didn't want to interrupt his flow of words, but it was difficult. The soft scratching sound of her pen nib against the paper was the only sound for a moment.

Harlan scrubbed his fingers through his hair, leaving it tousled, but he didn't seem to notice. "When I lost all my money for the third time, I felt as though I'd hit the bottom. I couldn't go to the lawyer because I hadn't paid back the last loan, so I was forced to go to my brother and ask him for money." Harlan's face reddened at this part of the story, but he continued on, despite his embarrassment. "When he refused, I had to confess to him what I'd done. After all, I owed three thousand pounds and had no means to repay it. My brother finally relented and loaned me what I needed to pay off the lawyer, but he said it would come out of my income for the next two years, reducing it to only fifteen hundred." Harlan stopped pacing and grimaced. "And can you believe it?" Harlan asked, locking gazes with Tempy. "I gambled it all away again."

He shook his head in disbelief. "I couldn't stop myself. I kept going deeper and deeper in debt. It wasn't until the lawyer had some men threaten to thrash me and have me thrown into debtors' prison that I finally stopped gambling."

Tempy stifled a sharp intake of breath at the threat of violence. She needed to tighten her grip on her pen before she was able to continue writing down his story.

The teacup and saucer clattered as Harlan set them down too forcefully on the end table. "I had to lose it all," he said. "Even my fiancée. She left when she discovered that I would have no income at all for the next ten years. Nothing except what I could earn through my own labor."

Harlan hung his head and shook it slowly, then let out a deep sigh. "I ended up finding a position with a shipping company. I worked for them for five years to make enough money to pay back my brother. They sent me to their India office, and I found it much easier to live on a small income there. I was able to turn a profit with some shipping ventures of my own, but I missed England. Last fall, when I was offered the chance to return, I took it. I haven't laid a single bet ever since I left for India," he said, raising his chin, "and I don't plan to. It's obvious that I'm not constitutionally suited for it. I have bad luck at it, and my pockets aren't deep enough. I've learned to leave that pastime to the extravagantly wealthy. They're the only ones who can afford it."

Tempy glanced through her papers, searching for the questions she'd noted. "How many loans did the lawyer arrange for you over the years?" Tempy asked.

"I'm not sure," Harlan said, and began pacing again. "At least five. And each time the interest rate was higher. He knew what he was doing. I'm certain of it. He presented himself as a kindly man who only wanted to help young gentlemen who were in over their heads. We just kept handing him our money, happy to get loans when we needed them. I don't know of a single one of those young men who didn't go broke."

"He introduced you to one another?" That made sense, because if they all became friends, then taking a loan from the same man would then seem like the normal way of things.

Harlan nodded. "He regularly hosted social events so that we could meet."

"How do you avoid gambling now that you're back in town?" That was the key to everything, wasn't it?

He stopped pacing for a moment and paused to look out Millicent's front window facing the street. A carriage rolled past, and his head turned as he tracked its progress. "Mostly, I avoid associating with my former friends. Of course, when I began working in the shipping business, most of them dropped me anyway." He turned to face the room again, and a mournful smile tugged at the corner of his mouth.

Harlan returned to sit next to Tempy on the sofa, and then he leaned back to relax against the cushions. "They found me socially acceptable when I was heavily in debt, but I was beneath their contempt when I began to earn a wage to climb out of the financial hole I'd dug for myself." He laughed under his breath, but it was a grim sort of laugh. "I have to admit, I felt the same disdain for myself when I first took that position, but that changed. Paying back the debt I owed with money I earned felt good. Now, I'm a respected member of my community, and none of my new associates are aware of my feckless past. That's why I was hesitant about this interview." His gaze fixed on hers, but he was much more relaxed now.

"Was? Does that mean that you no longer are worried about it?"

"Not so much. Odd, isn't it? But now I agree with you. If I can help someone avoid making the same mistakes I did, it will make this interview worth the risk."

A thought struck Tempy, and she closed her eyes for a moment to consider it. Harlan had led a sheltered life. He'd been weak and had never developed the kind of self-control he needed. Not until he'd been forced to.

What struck Tempy was that Harlan and Ernest shared a few too many personality traits. After only two nights at Hamlin House, Ernest was already in debt.

Once they married, it would be best to keep him away from casinos. But that probably wouldn't be a problem since he wouldn't feel as tempted to gamble once they were married. After all, she had money enough for both of them.

THE FOLLOWING MORNING, TEMPY ARRIVED AT THE CASINO A few minutes late for her meeting with Mme Le Clair and found the woman already waiting for her in Lucien's office.

The courtesan's back was to Tempy when she entered the room, and Tempy noticed that she wore a simple navy skirt and a crisp white blouse and navy jacket. Very conservative, as usual. Tempy had been surprised to learn that Mme Le Clair only wore her daring fashion choices in the evening and preferred to dress the part of the modest London lady during the day.

At the sound of the door, Mme Le Clair turned to face Tempy and looked surprised as she caught sight of her. "Just look at you, *ma chère*," she said. "Your cheeks are pink and you are brimming with confidence. How could any man resist?"

Tempy paused as she closed the office door, her hand still on the doorknob, and raised her eyebrows in surprise. "Confidence is irresistible?"

"Did you think that men find timid women attractive? Don't be foolish." Mme Le Clair said, and gave a dismissive flick of her hand. "I don't know of a single successful courtesan or demi-mondaine who is *timid*." Her skirts swished with the sound of rustling satin as she crossed the room toward the door.

Tempy stepped out of her way and moved toward Lucien's desk as she contemplated those words. "Perhaps that says more about the profession and less about what men like."

Mme Le Clair examined her face in the tall mirror next to the door. "Not in my experience. But don't take offense," she said, glancing over her shoulder at Tempy. "My comment was meant as a compliment."

Tempy turned away as she removed her gloves and then extracted the long pin affixing her hat to her hair. Mme Le Clair would have been apoplectic if she'd arrived hatless, which was why she'd been late. After seeing her coachman's look of surprise at her hatless state, she'd hurried back inside to put a hat on. She jabbed the long hat pin into the side of the hat and set the annoying concoction of pink silk, wire, and ribbon on Lucien's desk. "I wasn't offended. Just surprised." She tossed her gloves on top of her hat.

"Tell me about your trip to Bath. Were you successful?"

"Yes," Tempy said, turning to smile at Mme Le Clair. "I believe I accomplished everything I hoped for. Ernest was star-tled to see me, and Clarisse was obviously put out. It was all quite satisfying."

"Tell me all about it. I need details."

Tempy described the meeting on the Royal Crescent, not even leaving out the snide comment she had made.

"Perfect," Mme Le Clair said, smiling her catlike smile. "I'm glad you let your claws show. I believe we can proceed according to plan."

"There's something more." Tempy took a deep breath. Now that the moment had arrived to tell Mme Le Clair about the dinner in Porlock and the newspaper article, all of her self-confidence fled. Was that really the secret? Confidence? Is that all she needed right now? She lifted her chin and gave the demimondaine a level gaze. "We were invited to a small dinner party, and I used the occasion to try a few of the lessons you taught me."

"C'est magnifique," Mme Le Clair said, her eyes lighting up. "Tell me more."

"It worked," she said. She had trouble maintaining her steady gaze, so she glanced down at her hands and examined the nail on her left index finger. It felt rough. She needed to run a file across the edge of it. "Perhaps a little too well." She brushed her thumb against the broken edge of her nail, testing it.

"But that's wonderful," Mme said, causing Tempy to glance back up at her. Mme Le Clair arched her brows and gave a knowing smile. "Ah, the errors a woman can make when underestimating her power over men. Did you cause them to fight?"

"Oh my, no." Tempy said, but then she paused and tilted her head to one side as she thought about the entire incident surrounding the chocolate tart. "Well, almost. A man became exceedingly intoxicated and had to be escorted outside after behaving inappropriately. And later that evening another one made overt advances."

Madame tilted her head to one side, mirroring Tempy, and a smile tugged at the corners of her mouth. "What did the inappropriate one do?"

Tempy felt the flush rise on her face. "He, ah, tried to eat something off my...uh...off my chest."

Madame's eyes widened, and then a burst of laughter escaped

from her tightly pressed lips, making a 'pffft' sound. "It sounds as though you were most successful. I think you are ready, *ma chère*."

A cord of dread tightened around Tempy's chest, making it difficult to take a deep breath. She was ready? How *could* she be? She'd been certain that Mme Le Clair would declare the dinner a failure. "But that's not all," she added, trying to keep a note of panic from invading her voice. "There was an article in a London paper describing some of the events that took place at that dinner, and it accused Lucien of taking advantage of me."

Madame tilted her head to one side. "I *do* read the newspapers, you know. I was wondering if you'd mention it."

Tempy closed her eyes and shook her head tersely. "It wasn't fair. Those things they accused him of weren't true."

"I wouldn't worry about Lucien. He'll be fine. I'm more concerned about your reputation."

"I'll be fine. It's not as if I'm one of those society ladies who worries about being snubbed by the Countess of Whozit. The newspapers have been writing about me for years. I'm used to it." Tempy frowned as she glanced down and rubbed at her rough fingernail again. "It's not as if I have any family to offend." Her throat tightened. The Lipscombs had always welcomed her, despite her undeserved notoriety.

"The article is of no importance. At least, not with regard to what we are planning. From what you've told me, Ernest has come to expect these sorts of articles to appear from time to time, so he shouldn't be troubled by this one. And Lucien has weathered worse storms in the past. I think you are ready. It is time for you to win back your Ernest."

The loop of dread drew more tightly around Tempy's chest, causing her breathing to become shallow. But this couldn't be dread she was feeling. It had to be something else. Nervous tension, perhaps. Yes, that's what it had to be.

At the thought of seducing Ernest, so many emotions came welling up within her that she became confused. Perhaps there was a touch of dread, but mostly she was nervous, so that must be the source of her dread. After all, what if she failed?

Tempy cleared her throat. "We'll need to move more quickly than we'd planned. Clarisse sent me an anonymous letter with a newspaper clipping. I'm certain it was her. She wasn't very subtle when she hinted about it in Bath. They've already published the banns once."

"Oh my. Then Clarisse will be able to marry him after they've been posted two more times. So that's what? In two weeks? Yes, I can see why you want to accelerate things."

"I'll make arrangements to meet with him. I'll tell him that I want to give him back some letters he wrote to me, along with his grandmother's brooch. He gave it to me a few months ago. He never stated it as such, but I believed it represented a promise of marriage. I'm certain he'll want it back."

"That's an excellent plan." Mme Le Clair's dark eyes held a devilish glint. "You should have him meet you here, this Saturday night. He'll see it as a more neutral location since you first encountered each other here well *after* Clarisse entered his life. The timing will work out well, since Lucien is finalizing the sale of his casino that evening. Saturday night will be the last night he owns it."

"I hadn't realized that things had been finalized. Good for him." He and Mr. Snowden must have come to an agreement yesterday. That was a relief.

"Clarisse is likely to accompany him here," Mme Le Clair said, looking pensive.

"I'm sure you're right," Tempy said, and stroked the side of her thumb against her lower lip. "That poses a problem. I'll need a way to keep her occupied."

The door to the office opened.

"We'll ask Lucien to help with that," Mme Le Clair said.

Lucien entered and closed the door behind him. "Help with what?" He crossed the room in long strides and picked up a sheaf of papers from the desk. Tempy's stomach tightened as she watched him, but he didn't even glance at her, which she found quite annoying.

"With keeping Clarisse occupied this Saturday night. Temperance will need your help while she meets with her darling Ernest."

Tempy contorted her mouth as though she tasted something sour. She didn't like hearing her former fiancé described as "her darling Ernest."

Lucien frowned at the papers.

"Is there a problem?" Tempy asked, unaccountably irritated with him.

His frown disappeared, and he glanced up at her. "No. Not at all. I was just wondering how long you might need me to keep her distracted," he asked, returning to his task of shuffling through the papers. He seemed to be paying scant attention to their conversation.

"You should plan to keep her occupied for at least an hour," Mme Le Clair said.

"An hour?" Tempy said, her voice rising almost to a squeak. Had she heard right?

"*Mais bien sûr*. If you are able to win back his interest, you will want to be certain he is firmly back in your grasp. In fact, I think it would be best if Lucien were to *seduce* Clarisse."

"I don't think that's a good idea," Tempy said hastily. "I don't want her compromised. I only want to keep her out of the way for a while." An image of Lucien kissing Clarisse burst into her mind, and it wasn't a pleasant one.

"Then an incomplete seduction," Mme Le Clair said with a careless flick of her wrist. "Either way will work."

"Don't worry. It shouldn't be a problem," Lucien said.

"I wouldn't want to inconvenience you," Tempy said, her voice a bit sharper than she'd intended.

"Isn't this what I promised?" There was his damned Gallic shrug again. "We made a deal." He still refused to meet her gaze.

Well, if that's the way he wanted to be, who was she to argue with him? "Fine. Saturday it is."

Lucien finally stopped riffling through the papers and plucked one from the stack. "Saturday. Fine." He stalked out of the office without another word, closing the door quietly behind him.

But he might as well have slammed it.

29

DREAM A LITTLE DREAM

***

*T*empy ran down the hill, trying to reach the ship, but also knowing that she wouldn't. No matter how fast she ran, the shore remained just as far away.

She abruptly arrived on the beach. The ship was in the distance, and she could barely make out the figures of Ernest and her father on the deck. They waved to her as always. Melancholy figures disappearing in the distance.

This time, she tried to transform herself into a dolphin. She stepped into the ocean, splashing water over her skin, the same way she'd splashed water over that dolphin she'd tried to save so many years ago. It had lost its way, swimming up the Thames, until it finally beached itself on the river bank.

She willed herself to grow fins and a tail.

For a moment, she could feel her face lengthening; could feel a blow hole opening on the back of her neck; could feel her skin becoming rubbery and slick. Just like the dolphin she'd tried to help. She remembered seeing her reflection in those liquid black eyes as she helped it back into the water.

And now, suddenly, that dolphin was here with her. Bumping up against her. It lifted its head and stared at her with one liquid eye.

But why did it look so sad?

The dolphin slowly swung its head from side to side, and Tempy felt her transformation halt. Then it began to fade, her face resuming its normal shape, her skin pinkening, the blow hole disappearing from her neck. She was Tempy again. Not a dolphin.

She wailed in frustration as the ship disappeared in the distance.

The dolphin disappeared under the water, and she heard a splash behind her. Her head jerked around and she spotted a rowboat moving swiftly toward her.

"Need a lift?" the man in the boat shouted. "I can only offer rides to women, not dolphins. I never much cared for dolphins in boats. They tend to swamp them." He looked at her skeptically. "You aren't a dolphin in disguise, are you?"

"No! I'm human. I was simply pretending to be a dolphin."

"Why on earth would you want to be a dolphin? That's madness. All they eat is fish, and they can't even play the piano." His boat began to drift away.

"But I am a woman. Truly."

"That's a relief."

The boat moved closer, and Tempy scrambled aboard, taking care not to capsize it. When she faced the man, she recognized him. It was Lucien.

"Thank you. I don't know what I would have done without your help," she said.

Lucien stowed the oars and then dug around behind him. After a moment, he produced a blanket and draped it over her shoulders. "Are you certain you aren't a dolphin?" he asked, looking at her dubiously.

At a loss, Tempy stared at him for a moment. "Can't you tell?"

He shrugged.

Tempy sighed. "Don't you remember this?" she asked, wrapping her arms around his neck and pressing her body against his. "And this?" she said, kissing the corner of his mouth.

"It all seems familiar, but rather dolphin-like. Not at all Tempy-like."

"BLISS BOMBS," she muttered, taking refuge in one of her newspaper headlines.

"Ah! It is you," he said, wrapping his arms around her and pulling her close. "I thought for a moment that you'd truly become a dolphin. But you're still you, after all." His head lowered and his lips pressed against hers.

A flood of warmth and acceptance heated her from within, drying her hair and clothes, and she pulled him closer as their bodies entwined.

Suddenly they were standing on a sandy beach, not in the rowboat. The sun shone down upon them, and when Lucien lifted his head, he grinned down at her in delight. She cupped his cheek.

❦

A clatter of noise woke Tempy. It was followed by the sharp intake of breath. "Oh, dear," said a woman's voice.

Tempy opened her eyes. Her maid stood next to the window and the breakfast tray rested on the low table. On the floor, Tempy spied her inkwell, pen, and pen rest. Fortunately, the lid hadn't fallen off the ink; otherwise the rug would have been ruined.

"It's all right. No harm done," Tempy said, and then yawned and stretched.

She felt a profound sense of contentment. It was a feeling she hadn't experienced in a very, very long time.

She'd been dreaming something quite pleasant. She tried to recall it, but even as she did so, its tendrils slipped from her mind, disappearing to wherever dreams go upon wakening.

Her contentment must be rooted in her plan to see Ernest tonight. She'd win him back. Of course she would. And then they'd be together. Just as they always were fated to be.

But if dreaming about her plan for tonight was what had made her feel so contented upon waking, then why was that feeling of contentment slipping away?

No, she was certain that she'd dreamt the same dream that had been plaguing her almost every night. The one about the ship setting sail without her aboard. But something had been different this time. She just wished she could remember what it had been.

It must have been important.

30

LUCIEN IS RELUCTANT

L ucien found himself slamming quite a few doors over the next couple of days. It wasn't as though Tempy's plan for Saturday night came as a surprise, but he still didn't like it.

And there was that debt that *dear Ernest* still hadn't repaid. Lucien didn't want to mention it, but normally he'd never allow a patron to return to the casino with an unpaid debt still lingering on his books. He'd make the exception this time, for Tempy, but he didn't like it.

He'd avoided announcing the sale of his casino to his staff, which was unlike him. Normally he preferred being direct with them, but with everything being so unsettled this week, he wanted one thing in his life to remain the same. At least, for a little while longer. But that would end soon.

He also had to admit that he felt an impending sense of doom about tonight, as though everything was about to fall apart. The idea of announcing the casino's sale seemed like tempting fate.

He focused again on reviewing the tally of the take from the night before, but thoughts of Tempy kept intruding, forcing him to restart his work more than once. That was an unusual occurrence. Normally numbers came easily to him, but today they didn't offer him their usual calming influence.

Why on earth Tempy still wanted to win the love of such a weak-willed man, Lucien had no idea. Those sums simply wouldn't add up either.

With force of will, Lucien finished his final review of the books, and then, with a sigh, he placed the ledger in the cash box. Closing out the books had been one last task he'd wanted to complete himself, but it had taken him longer than anticipated.

Lucien slammed closed the lid of the cash box and then frowned at it. He was frowning quite a lot lately too. That woman made no sense.

But he'd promised to help her. And he would, even if it broke him.

Lucien spun the dial on his office safe to reset the tumblers, focusing his attention on turning the correct sequence of numbers. When he heard the last tumbler click into place, he yanked down the handle and pulled open the safe door. He crammed the cash box inside, but it caught on something. He pulled the metal box back out and reached into the safe to move a smaller, velvety object that must have fallen to one side.

The rectangular velvet box had belonged to his mother, and he hadn't opened it in years. Lucien let out a grunt of surprise at seeing it. He couldn't believe he'd nearly forgotten about it. He withdrew it, clearing a space into which he thrust the cash box. Then he paused.

Instead of closing the safe, he examined the velvet case.

Lucien slid his fingers across its lid and then released the catch. The lid sprang open, revealing glittering jewelry. Things that had belonged to his mother. Even when Father had faced debtors' prison, he hadn't been willing to part with them. After paying back all of his debts, he'd kept the jewels as Lucien's inheritance.

The necklace, earrings, and rings sparkled in the overhead gaslight, reflecting a warm glow as though lit from within. He lifted out his mother's ring to examine it more closely. It had a round diamond with three smaller marquise-cut emeralds on each side, arranged so that they resembled leaves. Father had worked with a jeweler to design the ring, and then he had given it to Mother as her wedding gift. It had meant the world to her.

Lucien slid the ring onto the tip of his index finger. The band was tiny. He had such large hands that it barely slid past the base of his fingernail. Someday, he knew, he'd give this same ring to his own bride. Would it fit her?

He imagined Tempy's small hands and realized that yes, the ring would probably fit. He smiled, pleased at the thought. As he pushed the ring back into its cushioned slot in the case, he froze.

Why had his thoughts immediately flown to Tempy when he contemplated his future wife? That was absurd.

Or was it?

He felt a flash of annoyance with himself. Of course it was. She obviously wanted Ernest. She'd wanted him her entire adult life. Surely that alone should convince Lucien to keep his distance.

But why? Hadn't the man already cast Tempy aside for Clarisse? That voided any claim he might have had upon Tempy's affections.

But there was also the sad truth that Tempy still wanted Ernest, despite his defection. She wanted that stupid, arrogant man who preferred form over substance. Lucien shook his head in disbelief.

Ernest was an imbecile.

But Tempy still wanted him. She wanted everything he represented. His family, his ties to her past, and, yes, even him. What right did Lucien have to deny her that? She was right. She had nobody else left in her life. She'd lost her mother as an infant and her father only a year ago. Even her governess had died unexpectedly in a train wreck. That left her with no one else but the Lipscombs. How could he take that away from her?

Yes, Lucien now had a title, but obviously she cared nothing for that. He had money, but that, too, held no appeal for Tempy since she'd already inherited vast wealth from her father. And Lucien would never be able to compete with Ernest when it came to family or a shared history.

And those things meant everything to her.

Lucien snapped the case closed, cutting the glittering diamonds off from their source of light. While still holding the case, he closed the door of the safe, spinning the lock to scramble the tumblers. Then he placed the velvet box in his carpetbag along with a few other important personal items he'd already packed. He would take his mother's box home and place it in his personal safe. The jewels would remain locked away.

He wondered if they'd ever feel the warmth of a woman's skin in his lifetime.

There was a knock at the door. Boothby pushed it open a crack and stuck his head inside the room. "Mr. Snowden is here. Shall I send him in?"

Lucien nodded as he closed his carpetbag, then stood.

The door opened fully and Boothby ushered John inside. It was hard to resist the man's beaming smile, and Lucien felt the corners of his mouth tug upward despite his foul mood.

"I don't think I've often seen you looking so happy," Lucien said, offering his hand.

John gripped it briefly before releasing it, and then he lifted his walking stick. "I even bought a new cane for the occasion." He twirled the long black walking stick around his fingers.

"Elegant. I like the silver handle and tip."

"And it holds a secret." John stopped his twirling and twisted the knob on the top, unscrewing it. He then upended the cane, and a glass vial slid from within a hollow interior space. "It has a steel tube inside that holds four glass vials."

"Don't tell me you have whiskey in there." Lucien chuckled. "Is that to celebrate your purchase of my casino?"

"You can't call it 'your casino' for much longer. It will be mine after tonight."

"Most certainly," Lucien replied. He'd been both anticipating and dreading this moment all day. Of course, selling was what he'd wanted, but once he signed the papers, there would be no turning back. He'd be stepping off a precipice into a new life, with no real ties to the past. "Have you had your lawyer review everything? Are you ready to sign?"

John nodded. "And more importantly, I'm convinced that there's nothing to that newspaper's allegations about you and your relationship with Miss Bliss. I investigated the man who wrote that article, and I'm not even willing to call him a journalist. He styles himself 'Earl E. Byrd', but its obviously a pseudonym. He's been making a living spreading baseless rumors and gossip for years now. Miss Bliss has been the focus of his scrutiny many times in the past, and his stories seem only loosely based on fact."

Lucien raised his brows. "Really? Do you think there's anything personal behind it?"

"Perhaps. He worked for Bliss Railways for a couple of years, so perhaps he holds some sort of grudge." John's gaze traveled around the room as he spoke, examining everything. "If that's the case, he's kept it well hidden, because I could find no evidence of it. But that's my theory. And I think his grudge has transferred over to Miss Bliss."

Lucien didn't like the idea that someone was intentionally targeting Tempy this way. "When did she become the target of all these articles?"

"Shortly after her father died. That supports my theory that the journalist transferred his vendetta from her father to her."

"Perhaps," Lucien said. "Or perhaps she she's been the target all along. Could someone be trying to make her stop writing?"

John shook his head doubtfully. "None of the articles have mentioned it. Byrd seems to focus more on her status as the 'poor little rich girl'. I'd swear the man never met her. He makes her seem feckless and spoiled. You know Tempy. She's nothing like that."

Lucien scratched the back of his head, perplexed. "It's quite the mystery. You've given me some clues to ponder. I'll look into it further. Perhaps I'll be able to see some clue that's been overlooked."

"Does that mean you're planning to stay here longer?" John glanced around the office. "It doesn't look as though you're ready to vacate the premises. You haven't even packed away any of your personal items."

"There's very little I plan to take with me. Only what's inside that," Lucien said, gesturing toward the carpetbag. "As I said, I'm selling you everything."

John frowned at the bag. "That's not much for a lifetime's work."

Lucien shrugged. "I have a great deal of work waiting for me. I intend to make each of my estates completely self-sustaining. I also have some plans to help improve the surrounding regions. I can't cling to my past. If I do that, I'll never be able to embrace my future."

"You've always had a glib way of speaking, I'll grant you that. You go ahead and *embrace your future*. I suppose I'm doing the same thing, leaving my time in the military behind. It just sounds better the way you say it."

They sat at the desk, and Lucien claimed his customary chair. As he stared at his old friend, he was hit with the sudden realization that the next time they sat across from each other in this room, their positions would be reversed. He also realized that he didn't mind.

Not in the least.

Lucien smiled. "Let's start signing." Now that the moment was upon him, he was eager to conclude business. Once the papers were signed, he could focus on his role in tonight's...well, he could only think of it as a farce. But he had a role to play. He'd be Clarisse's suitor for the evening, leaving Tempy free to pursue Ernest.

And tomorrow, he'd be off to his estate in Somerset, and Tempy would be back in the arms of the man of her dreams.

Just the way she wanted it.

31

TEMPY SEDUCES ERNEST...

☙

The carriage was ready.

She was ready.

Now she just needed to leave.

Tempy adjusted the low-cut bodice on her ice-blue dress. The sparkling rhinestones sewn onto the fabric made her glitter like an ice princess. She rubbed her cold fingers together to try to generate some warmth, but it felt like a fruitless exercise. After all, weren't ice princesses supposed to be cold?

At least her wrap and mantle were warm. Her wrap was of the same ice-blue satin, with a heavy, clattering fringe of rhinestones that moved like an effervescent liquid. Her dark blue velvet mantle covered her from shoulder to toe and hid the glittering ice of her dress from view.

She glanced at herself in the mirror. Had the rhinestone pins she'd placed in her hair been too much? Mme Le Clair had been quite insistent about them, so she would bow to the woman's vast knowledge and experience in this area.

She had set herself on this track only a few short weeks ago, rushing headlong on a collision course toward tonight's encounter with Ernest. Millicent was right about her. Once she set her mind to a task, she was determined to complete it. Headstrong. That's what Father had called her. And stubborn to a fault.

Tempy hurried down the front steps of her home and climbed into her carriage. As she settled onto the cushions, she let out a frustrated sigh, irritated with herself for being so nervous. But everything depended on tonight. Her entire future would be determined based on how well she performed over the next few hours. On how well she'd learned to be a glittering, entrancing seductress.

Well, perhaps not her *entire* future. There was, of course, the newspaper article she'd completed and sent to Mr. Dickens that afternoon. No matter what happened tonight with Ernest, she could still be proud of the article published in Dickens's prestigious paper.

Her research had taken her in a different direction than she'd anticipated, but it was a direction that provided an even deeper insight into the problem of gambling than she'd first anticipated. She'd even been able to track down poor Mr. Mall's former fiancée. And, wonder of wonders, the woman had agreed to speak with her, as long as her name wasn't used, of course. No true lady would want her name mentioned in the newspaper.

Tempy smiled as she remembered her governess's admonition. "A gently bred woman should only have her name in the paper on three occasions: at her birth, upon her marriage, and at her death." Tempy had broken that old maxim so many times by using her real name in her newspaper byline that the warning had nearly faded away into dim memory. Mr. Mall's former fiancée's comment had brought the rule rushing back.

For some reason, tonight she wasn't in the mood to compose newspaper headlines, even though they normally helped calm her nerves. Why was that? Usually, creating headlines helped her relax, but tonight's endeavor seemed different.

Then she realized that this plan wasn't something she'd ever want printed below the banner of a newspaper.

Tempy pushed the worry from her mind and tried to focus on something that would help distract her. Her thoughts returned to her trip to Bath and Porlock.

And to Lucien.

She felt a twinge of excitement. He'd be there tonight. At the casino.

Distracting Clarisse.

Tempy frowned. She wished she hadn't needed to pull him into this. She knew he'd help, of course. After all, he'd promised. But even so, seducing a woman he hardly knew must be...be what? Distasteful? Difficult?

She tried to imagine him with Clarisse, but she simply couldn't. Her mind wouldn't allow her to picture them together. Her fists clenched, and she realized that her train of thought was making her feel worse.

The carriage pulled to a halt in front of the casino. Relieved at the chance to escape her musings, Tempy flung open the door before anyone could assist her and hurried inside the casino.

Although she was greeted warmly by the staff, she sensed an undercurrent of tension. Something was definitely wrong. At first, Boothby wouldn't meet her gaze as he escorted her to Lucien's office, and she could see the tension in his jawline as he clenched his teeth. He pushed open the office door and ushered her inside.

"Is something wrong?" she asked, turning to face him in the empty room.

"Did you know?" he murmured without looking at her.

"Know what?"

He turned his gaze to her now. "Did you know that Mr. Hamlin was selling Hamlin House? The new owner takes over tomorrow." When she didn't answer, he nodded and looked away. "You did. I can see that. Why didn't he tell any of us?"

"I'm sorry. My guess is that if he didn't tell you, it was because he didn't want to worry any of you in case nothing came of it."

"So, instead he catches all of us off guard? How is that supposed to be better? Everyone here feels betrayed by his announcement. This is just like what happened with Squire Formsworth. He kept information from me that I had a right to know."

Tempy touched his forearm. "I'm sorry to hear that. I suppose that means that he finalized the sale?"

Boothby gave a terse nod. "He announced it just an hour ago. After tonight, Mr. Snowden will be running the place. Does he even know the first thing about running a casino?"

"I've known Mr. Snowden for a number of years, and he's a good man. He was an army colonel, and from what I hear, his men had a great deal of respect for him."

"Well, that's something, I suppose," Boothby said, sounding slightly mollified. "But he'd better not come in here and order us about as though he's still in the army, that's all I can say."

Tempy felt a pang of sympathy. It must be terrible to be caught by surprise by such a fundamental change. After all, Lucien had been the heart and soul of Hamlin House since he'd founded it. "Mr. Snowden is a very nice man. It's hard for me to imagine that he would make this a difficult place to work." Tempy wondered briefly about Boothby's hopes of becoming a valet, but decided that this wasn't the moment to broach the subject. He was already so upset by what he saw as a breach of trust that she didn't want to raise such a sensitive subject. She hoped Lucien and Boothby could resolve the rift between them.

Boothby said nothing, but simply gave her a brief nod before he left the room, closing the door behind him.

Tempy glanced around Lucien's office, wondering if she'd notice any changes, but everything looked exactly the same. You'd never know that someone else would be using this office after tonight.

The door opened behind her, and as she turned at the sound, Lucien walked in. He must have already known she was there, because he didn't seem surprised by her presence, but he didn't really look at her either. He kept his gaze averted.

Tempy took a sharp breath at the sight of him in his crisp, black frock coat and gray trousers, and she felt her pulse quicken.

Nerves. She hadn't been alone with him since that day on the steps outside John Snowden's home.

She watched him as he crossed the room, noting his smooth and graceful stride and the glass of amber liquid in one hand. Whiskey, she assumed. Tonight his waistcoat was an elegant silvery gray. It was more subdued than usual, but it still had that personal flair that distinguished him. But there was something in his eyes that caught her attention. He seemed troubled. Could it be because of the casino? Was he regretting his decision?

"Is everything all right?" she asked, crossing the room to move closer to him.

He glanced at her, finally focusing his attention on her, and he took a sip of whiskey. His eyes seemed to light up at the sight of her, and his tension eased. "You look lovely tonight. A sophisticated, graceful lady. He won't know what hit him." The smile that followed seemed forced.

"You like it?" she asked.

He tilted his head to one side and examined her a little more closely. "You shine like an evening star. But something's missing."

"Missing? What's missing?"

Lucien moved around to the far side of his desk and set down his whiskey glass before he leaned over. When he stood back up, he was holding a carpetbag. After he set it on his desk and opened the catch, he dug through it, searching for something. He extracted a dark blue velvet box, and set it on his desk with a flourish.

Curious, Tempy moved closer. "What's that?"

"Just the thing." He released the catch, allowing the spring lid to pop open, and lifted a glittering object that moved like liquid ice in his hands. "It was my mother's," he said, "and I'd like you to wear it tonight. For luck."

Tempy's breath caught at the sight of the necklace and her hand flew to cover her throat. "I couldn't possibly. What if something were to happen to it? What if I lost it?"

"It's a necklace. It's meant to be worn. It deserves to have an evening out after being hidden away in this box for so many years."

Silly man. Tempy smiled at him. "It deserves a night out? Do you often believe that inanimate objects have rights and feelings?"

"I tend to reserve those for people, but it seems such a shame for you not to wear this." He moved around the desk to come closer. "Perhaps it isn't the necklace I'm speaking of, but you. Perhaps you are the one who deserves to wear this necklace."

There was an intensity in Lucien's gaze that made Tempy tremble. She had to look away.

Lucien stepped behind her and draped the diamond necklace around her neck. The metal of the setting was cool against her skin, but Lucien's hands were warm as he worked the catch. He seemed to be having trouble because she could feel his touch linger for a few seconds. The warmth he radiated swept through her. Just as her skin began to tingle from the prolonged contact with his hands, Lucien stepped away.

He spun her around to face him. "Perfect," he said.

Tempy's smile trembled on her lips. What was happening to her? A sudden and intense sense of doubt swept over her. How could she be feeling such strong emotions for Lucien while planning to seduce Ernest? What was she thinking?

Lucien stared at her mouth for a moment, but then he abruptly looked away. He took her by the hand and led her across the room toward the mirror by the door. "Look for yourself. You're beautiful."

The diamond necklace glittered against her throat. Tiny

stones were set in oval links, each link surrounding a large, round diamond. It shimmered with every breath she took, and the necklace almost looked alive. In that moment, she understood why Lucien had said that the necklace deserved to be worn. Shutting it away in that box seemed almost cruel.

"Thank you, Lucien. It's perfect." Not wanting to meet his gaze, she instead looked around the room as she tried to think of an innocuous subject to discuss. The carpetbag on his desk caught her eye. "I understand that you've sold the casino. Is that all you plan to take with you?"

"I keep few personal items here. And anyway, it's time to move on. I leave for Somerset tomorrow."

Her stomach sank. "I won't see you again?"

"Invite me to your wedding. I promise to be there."

Tempy felt a little sick to her stomach. "About tonight. I feel terrible about using you to distract Clarisse."

"No need. I made a promise to help, and I intend to keep it. After all, you've already kept your promise to me. The sale of my casino is complete, and I'm now free to pursue my new life."

"Are you certain you want to do this?" Tempy asked. Her hand went to her neck, and she traced the necklace with her fingertips. It now felt warm to the touch.

When she noticed that he was watching her hand, she dropped it to her side.

He looked away. "I'm certain," he said. "In fact, I think that it will serve as a sort of tonic. I need to move on and make a break from this life, and spending time with Clarisse will be a change of pace for me." He shrugged. "Plus, I very much want to help you recapture the life you always dreamt of. I know how much Ernest means to you, and how close your ties are to his family. I don't want you to lose that."

At that moment, Tempy envied Lucien. Envied his ability to face his future and let go of the past. It certainly would make her life simpler if she could do that as well. But she also knew what it was like to be alone. To have nobody. No family. She couldn't face that. Therefore, she needed Ernest, didn't she?

A knock interrupted her thoughts. Boothby opened the door just far enough to stick his head into the room. "It's time," he said curtly, and then shut the door with a click.

"It's time," Tempy echoed. She bounced on her toes a couple of times as she tried to generate some enthusiasm for what she was about to do, and then she moved toward the door. She and Lucien had planned to separate Ernest from Clarisse as quickly as possible so that Tempy would have as much time as she needed with Ernest. As long as Clarisse didn't insist upon staying by Ernest's side, things should go smoothly.

Lucien followed her out the door, and they quickly spotted the other couple.

Ernest stood next to the roulette table and when he caught sight of Tempy in her ice-blue gown, his jaw fell slack. He scanned her from head to toe, pausing briefly on the glittering necklace. She could swear that his eyes lingered for a moment on her cleavage. She'd used a slightly darker shade of powder, just as Mme Le Clair had shown her, to enhance the V, so she was pleased that her efforts hadn't gone unnoticed.

She was surprised, however, when a chip slipped from his fingers and fell to the floor. She knew from his sister, Emily, that he'd promised his parents that he wouldn't gamble tonight, and it irritated her to see him breaking that vow.

Clarisse noticed his clumsiness and glanced around to see what had startled him. When she spotted Tempy, her smile froze.

Tempy smiled back. In fact, she beamed. With Lucien by her side, she headed directly for the couple. "Miss Beaumont, what a pleasure it is to see you again."

Clarisse smiled in return, but it didn't reach her eyes. "You must come here frequently."

Tempy glanced at Lucien and smiled at him before returning

her attention to Clarisse. "So it would seem," she said, keeping her response intentionally cryptic.

"I read about you in the papers," Clarisse pressed.

"That happens to Tempy all the time," Ernest said. "There's never anything to those stories." But he glanced at Lucien. "Is there?"

"Of course not," Lucien said, almost dismissively. He smiled at Ernest, but then focused his attention on Clarisse. "One of my little informers tells me that you haven't been able to find a decent *terrine de pâté de campagne* since coming to England. Can I tempt you to try mine? It's a specialty of Hamlin House."

"One of your informers?"

"I'm afraid that's my fault," Tempy said. "Emily mentioned it to me, and since I knew Lucien prides himself on that particular dish here at Hamlin House, I mentioned it to him. I hope you don't mind."

"Not at all," Clarisse said, her lips tight.

"I've arranged for our chef to make it tonight, in your honor," Lucien said.

Clarisse tipped her chin down slightly and then glanced up at Lucien. Tempy recognized the move as one Mme Le Clair had taught her. It made one's eyes appear larger. *Brava, Clarisse.*

Separating Clarisse from Ernest was easier than Tempy had expected. It all went perfectly, in steps that almost seemed to mirror the dance steps of a quadrille. Tempy and Lucien had arrived in front of Ernest and Clarisse together, but in moments they had danced away with their new partners.

Clarisse willingly allowed Lucien to lead her across the room toward some small tables. At a signal from Lucien, one of the footmen quickly laid a table with a fresh white cloth and set the *terrine de pâté de campagne* on it with a flourish.

Tempy saw that Lucien's admiring glances appeared to salve Clarisse's bruised ego, especially when Tempy, following their plan, cast the couple a look of jealous rage.

When Clarisse noticed Tempy's anger, she preened and redoubled her charm. Poor Lucien wouldn't have stood a chance if the entire scene had been real.

Tempy and Ernest chatted about inconsequential things, but during their entire conversation, he kept his gaze fixed on her, apparently unable to look at anything else. Ernest seemed enthralled by her. It was all going according to plan.

Tempy shot Ernest a slightly embarrassed look. "I have some items I'd like to return to you. They're in my reticule." She glanced around, making her discomfort at talking about this in a public setting obvious.

Fortunately, Ernest picked up on her embarrassment and glanced around for someplace private where they could talk. After a moment, he led her into one of the little niches the casino provided for private *tête-à-têtes*. Long velvet curtains at the entrance to the niche were held back with gold-tasseled cords. Ernest pulled her behind one of the curtains so that her back was against the wall.

The velvet curtains muffled the sounds of the casino, providing them with a modicum of privacy. "I was surprised to see you with a chip in your hand tonight," Tempy said. Then she snapped her mouth shut. Why had she started off by criticizing him?

Ernest smiled. "It was my lucky chip. I saved it from the first night I was here when I won so much. I thought it might bring me luck again tonight."

Tempy decided not to mention the promise he'd made to his family. Instead, she pulled the drawstrings of her reticule loose and extracted Ernest's grandmother's brooch, along with a small packet of letters. She held them out to him.

He accepted the items with hardly a glance, tucking them away in his inner breast pocket. Then, he leaned toward her, placing one hand against the wall just above her shoulder.

"You look luminous tonight," he murmured, his coffee-scented breath warm against her bare shoulder. "Why is that?"

"Could it be the glittering gemstones?" Tempy cast Ernest a sidelong glance. Was this it? Was this the moment when all her work would come to fruition? She needed to be careful, just as Mme Le Clair had warned her. What had she said again? *Having a fish on the hook isn't the same thing as having him on your plate.*

"No, it's not that," he said, waving his hand as though brushing away her prosaic explanation. "It isn't something external. It's something inside you. It's as though you've stoked the fire within your soul and now it burns so brightly it bursts from every pore."

"Ernest," she said, her voice sounding breathy. "You don't usually speak this way."

"You inspire me. I can't imagine my life without you in it." Ernest took her hand in his.

"Me? I inspire you?" These were the words Tempy had wanted to hear from Ernest for so long, but now that he said them, they didn't provide her with the joy she had anticipated.

Instead, they only made her angry. Angry that she'd had to wait so long to hear them. Angry that she'd had to remake herself in order for him to notice her. Angry that she was no longer being true to herself.

The strong surge of emotion startled her, and Tempy tried to master herself. This was her chance, wasn't it? Her chance, finally, to have her old life back?

She should be jubilant.

Not angry. Not bitter. Not annoyed.

But there it was. Not jubilance. Anger.

"Why do I inspire you now, Ernest, when I never did before? And what about the life you envisioned with Clarisse?"

"Clarisse? I don't know." A befuddled expression crept across his face as he drew his brows together. "I suppose I became entranced with her because she was new. I wasn't thinking straight. Blame it on being in Paris." His expression softened, and he seemed to become more caught up in his memories of the other woman. "Clarisse is so different from anyone else I've ever met. She's exciting and interesting. We always have fun together."

"Then why are you here with me?"

He refocused his gaze on her, returning to the present. His eyes seemed to drink her in, savoring every nuance, every measured change she had made to herself. "You're different now. And it isn't just the hair and the way you dress. I do like those changes, but that's not it. It's what I mentioned before. You have a fire within you now. A confidence that wasn't there before. You've been transformed."

Something inside her broke. "But why weren't you here with me? Why is it that you never supported me in my passion for writing? Why haven't you been in my life these past weeks? Why did I go through this transformation without you?"

He gaped at her.

"I'm still the same person. Don't you understand that? I still want to write. I still want a family. I still want all of the things I've always wanted."

"But what about me?" His eyes widened as if the possibility that she might reject him had just dawned on him. "You still want *me*, don't you? Because I'm here for you, Tempy. I know I hurt you, but I'm here for you. You can depend on that."

"Can I? I used to believe that." She looked at his sincere-seeming gaze and recognized the self-delusion behind it. "But how can you cast me aside so easily for Clarisse, and then cast her aside just as easily for me?"

"I...I made a mistake. I see that now. Please, Tempy. I want you back."

But having him say the words she'd longed to hear left her cold. She stared at him, trying to dredge up any feelings of love and warmth, and discovered that they simply weren't there.

She shook her head. "I'm sorry, Ernest, but no."

She pushed away from the wall, planning to move past Ernest so that she could return to the casino floor.

"Wait, Tempy. Please," he said, blocking her way with his arm. Then he wrapped arm around her and pulled her close, pressing his hips against hers.

She tried to lean away from him, but he lifted his other hand and cradled the back of her neck. He lowered his head, aiming his mouth toward hers.

He kissed her.

In a gross reproduction of the kiss she'd shared with Lucien, Ernest's lips pressed against hers. She opened her mouth to protest, but he took the opportunity to slide his tongue against the inside of her upper lip.

She wrenched her head back and her hand flew up, landing a stinging slap against his cheek.

"I said, 'No'."

32

... WHILE LUCIEN
DISTRACTS CLARISSE

From his position across the room, Lucien watched Tempy and Ernest talking together near the roulette table.

"He's unlike most Frenchmen," Clarisse said. "He's sweet. But I must admit, he...how do you say...*Il me fait tellement frustré.*"

"He makes you frustrated." Lucien said, providing her with the translation.

She nodded. "He can't seem to decide where we will live. When we were in Paris, he promised we would live there," she said lifting one hand, "but now that we are in England, he wants to live here," she said, lifting the other. "He says he wants us to live near his family."

"But a man who loves his family, isn't that admirable?"

"Only if he loves me more," she said, lifting both hands and shaking them in frustration. "I don't want to have him care more for his parents' opinions than for mine. He was prepared to live in Paris until his parents voiced their objections. His goal seems to be to please them, not me."

"Don't you like it here?"

"*Bien sûr.* Of course I do, but that isn't the point."

"I understand. But once you are his wife, you will wield a great deal of influence over the man. I've discovered that men who love their wives will do anything to please them. I have no doubt that you'll hold that same power over Ernest. How could any man deny you your heart's desire? He'd have to be made of stone."

Clarisse fluttered her eyelashes in a practiced way that Lucien normally might have found intriguing, but he recognized the move from Mme Le Clair's lessons.

"You flatter me." Clarisse dipped her chin and then looked up at him, widening her eyes. "Certainly you don't find me so attractive. After all, I see the way your Miss Bliss looks at you. Surely she's captured your heart, hasn't she?"

He glanced across the floor at Tempy. When she caught his eye, she shot him an icy glare. It was the perfect expression of jealousy.

Lucien had to suppress his own smile. When he and Tempy had made their plans for the evening, they had choreographed that flash of jealousy. It was meant to goad Clarisse into believing that Tempy saw Clarisse as a rival for Lucien's affections.

Clarisse stepped a little closer to Lucien, and when he glanced down at her, he saw an expression of satisfaction cross her face. The cunning woman had fallen for the bait.

"My heart is my own," he quipped. But was it? He glanced back at Tempy and saw Ernest leading her toward one of the curtained alcoves. A sharp pang of jealousy shot through him. It was happening. He knew it was.

He smiled down at Clarisse, perhaps a little too brightly. "Would you care for some champagne? I have a bottle chilling in my office, if you'd care to join me."

Apparently Clarisse, too, had noticed where the other couple had gone. And she didn't seem pleased. She raised her chin and nodded, a sharp, definite nod. "I'd love to."

She wrapped her arm around Lucien's and he led her off the casino floor. Her hand clutched at his forearm, alerting him to the tension she was trying so hard to conceal.

"I think we are well quit of them for now," Lucien murmured. "Let them resolve whatever it is that lingers between them."

Her steps faltered for a moment.

"He needs to know that he can't take you for granted. After all, you don't want to marry a man easily swayed by other women."

At that, her chin rose and her shoulders straightened. Her grip on his arm loosened slightly, but remained. Lucien continued toward his office, and she readily kept pace with him.

Once they were inside, Lucien popped the cork on a bottle of champagne and poured it into two fluted glasses.

Clarisse drained over half of her glass, and Lucien refilled it promptly. He didn't like the way the scene reminded him of a similar one enacted with Tempy just two short weeks ago. He'd much prefer it if Tempy were here with him rather than Clarisse.

"You are a very understanding man," Clarisse said. She twirled the stem of her glass between her long, slender fingers. "How did you come to know women so well?"

"I've been running this casino for years. To be successful in this business, you must learn human nature. That applies to both men *and* women."

Clarisse sauntered closer to him, the movement of her hips causing her hoopskirts to sway seductively. "Does that mean that you can read my 'human nature?' Tell me then. What is it saying to you?"

Lucien set his champagne glass on the desk as Clarisse moved closer. She stopped when her body was just inches from his. Her skirts pressed against his legs and he caught a whiff of her rose-scented perfume. It was a much softer, simpler scent than the spicy lavender blend that Tempy favored. But he didn't like the way Clarisse's scent invaded his senses. He had to force himself not to back away. After all, he had promised Tempy he would do this.

Clarisse continued to look up at him expectantly, and he realized that he needed to reply. "I think, perhaps," he said silkily, "that your human nature has been overtaken by more, shall we say, animal urges."

Clarisse's face took on a more fervent expression and she pressed closer to him. Lucien raised his hand, not sure whether he was warding her off or pulling her closer. But his intentions didn't matter, because instead of doing either thing, he inadvertently bumped her champagne glass. The golden liquid splashed down the front of her bodice, and Clarisse jumped back with a squeal of surprise.

"I'm terribly sorry," he said. Fumbling in his pocket, he extracted a freshly laundered handkerchief. He held it out to her, the red "H H" Hamlin House monogram on its corner stark against the white fabric.

With an angry huff, Clarisse snatched it from his outstretched hand. "I had no idea you could be so clumsy." She dabbed at the droplets of wine dribbling down the bare skin of her chest, but she was unable to do anything about the darker spots that had soaked into the bodice of her dress. "It was a mistake to come here tonight. Look at me. How can I walk back out there looking like this? I must go home, immediately."

"I'll send for your cloak. Nobody will see the stain."

"And send for my carriage as well. Tell Ernest to find his own way home this evening. That's no more than he deserves."

The sense of relief that filled Lucien was almost overwhelming as he hurried to complete Clarisse's bidding. He was certain that she would have seen through his ruse if he'd tried to kiss her. And he wasn't even sure that he would have been able to bring himself to do it.

Boothby delivered the cloak and promised to pass on her

message to Ernest. Within a matter of minutes, Clarisse was safely ensconced in her carriage and traveling home.

Lucien locked his office door. He was done. He'd fulfilled his commitment to Tempy. He tossed a couple of logs into the fireplace, sending up a flurry of sparks, and then walked back to the bottle of champagne. He lifted it, held it up to the light to check the level of liquid within it. Even though it was still half full, he set it down with a thunk. The thought of finishing this bottle of champagne alone left him feeling empty.

What he needed was something much stronger than champagne. He crossed the room to the side table, where he picked up the whiskey decanter and poured himself a generous serving, sloshing some onto the granite tabletop. Carrying the glass, he took a couple of strides toward the chair by the fireplace, and then stopped and turned around to retrace his steps.

This time, he picked up the decanter as well and carried it with him to the chair.

He planned to get good and drunk.

For a brief moment, he felt a twinge of guilt for his behavior. After all, this was his last night in the casino. He should be spending time with his former employees, assuaging their fears about the new owner of Hamlin House. But he quickly drowned those nobler feelings.

How could he possibly bring himself to walk out there?

Lucien knew what he'd see. Tempy with Ernest. They would be reunited. She would be glowing. Reveling in her success at winning Ernest back.

Draped in his mother's diamonds.

He lifted his tumbler to take another sip of whiskey and realized it was empty already. Good thing he'd brought the decanter with him.

He sloshed more into his glass, clattering the neck of the decanter against his tumbler.

As he set the decanter back on the small side table, he heard something smack against the door.

33

ON SECOND THOUGHT

Tempy hurried back into the casino and glanced over her shoulder, but fortunately, Ernest had the good sense to stay hidden behind the curtain of the alcove.

Her chin held high, Tempy moved toward the roulette table as she scanned the casino floor, searching for Lucien. She didn't know what his plans were for distracting Clarisse, but he couldn't have gone far.

She tried to look casual as she scanned the room, examining each of the alcoves in turn. She caught sight of movement in one of them, but the gentleman who emerged wasn't Lucien.

Ernest slipped out of his alcove after about five minutes, and Tempy turned her back to him.

What if Lucien wasn't in here? What if he'd taken Clarisse to his office?

Anger swept through her as she envisioned Lucien handing Clarisse a glass of champagne. Smiling down at her. Locking gazes with her as his head descended...

No.

Tempy spun on her heel.

Things would *not* happen this way. She would *not* let that witch Clarisse steal another man from her.

Tempy did not glide. She did not insinuate herself across the room. Tempy stormed across the casino floor. People moved to one side when they saw her bearing down on them, startled expressions on their faces. But Tempy didn't care. She had only one goal in mind.

She stalked toward the door to Lucien's office and then grabbed the knob and tried to turn it with a jerk. She pressed her shoulder against the door but stumbled when it wouldn't open.

He'd locked it.

Good Lord, he'd locked it.

Tempy smacked the flat of her palm against the door in frustration. "Lucien," she called. "Lucien, I know you're in there."

A man entering the casino turned to stare at her.

"Lucien, this is embarrassing. Open the door, please."

She heard a click, and when the door opened, she almost fell through it in her rush to enter.

"I want that woman out of here," Tempy demanded. She spun around, searching the room. "Where is she?"

"On her way home," Lucien said. He locked the door again and then turned his back on Tempy as he walked over to his desk. He leaned back on it, his legs wide and his hands curled around the edge, and then stared down at his feet.

Tempy looked around and noticed the open bottle of champagne on the side table. "What's this?" she asked.

He glanced at her and then over at the bottle. "A prop. Every show needs props. How can I play a part without props?"

"So you plied her with champagne and kissed her?" Tempy's throat was tight.

"Wasn't that the plan?"

"Is that your favored method of seduction? Champagne?" Her eyes began to burn, and she knew she would cry soon if she couldn't get her emotions under control.

"Why are you acting this way?" Lucien asked in a cold voice. "Did Ernest reject you?"

"Of course not," she snapped. "I rejected him." She took a couple of steps closer to Lucien. "It worked, just the way we planned, but then when everything was within my grasp, I realized that I couldn't do it. Not like that. Not with tricks and manipulations." And not with Ernest. Not ever.

He smiled half a smile that only lifted one corner of his mouth. "So you came here to rescue me?"

"To stop you. I couldn't bear the thought of the two of you..."

"The two of us...what?"

She blushed.

"Ah," he said. "Shall I tell you what happened?"

He pushed away from his desk and crossed over to the side table. There he poured two fresh glasses of champagne.

He came back to her and handed her one of the flutes. "It went something like this," he said. "I handed her a glass, and she immediately drank half of it." He paused, waiting.

After a moment, Tempy realized that he wouldn't continue unless she played her part in this pantomime. So she lifted the glass and drank half of it. "I refilled it." He frowned. "Let's skip that part. It didn't end well."

She narrowed her eyes at him. "Go on."

"Then she got this look in her eye and came closer." He paused again, so Tempy took a step closer to him.

"Closer than that."

She blushed, but moved closer. He crooked a finger, and she came even closer, so that they stood only a few inches apart. She could smell the whiskey on his breath, but she didn't move.

"That's about right. And then she leaned just a bit closer. I could tell that she wanted me to kiss her."

Tempy closed her eyes, not wanting to see his face when he said the next words.

"And then I bumped her glass and spilled champagne all over her dress."

Her eyes flew open. "You what?"

He reached out, plucking her champagne flute from her hand, and then set it on the desk. "I spilled her champagne. She seemed quite upset, so I'd rather not make that mistake again, even if it did serve to extricate me from a difficult situation."

Tempy stared at him, bemused.

He leaned back against the desk with his legs splayed and reached out to pull her against him. "You came here to save me?"

Lucien slid his fingertips along the diamond necklace, sending a shiver down her spine as his fingertips brushed against her neck. She swallowed, and his fingertips touched the hollow of her throat. "To save you," she echoed.

"That was valiant of you." His hand slid up the side of her neck and cupped her head.

She sighed. Lucien pulled her toward him, and Tempy put the palm of her hand on his chest as she leaned into him. Ever so gently, she pressed her lips against his.

This was what she wanted. This was where she should be. With Lucien. In his arms.

Lucien responded immediately. He wrapped his arms tightly around her waist and kissed her roughly at first, his lips insistent against hers. Their tongues swirled together, and she tasted the smoky liquor he'd consumed.

Tremors of excitement ran through her, making the small hairs on the back of her neck stand on end. She dug her fingers into his thick, dark hair, relishing the silky feel of it as his kisses threaded their way down her neck.

He lifted his head and then pulled her tightly against him. She could feel him fumbling at the ribbons on her back that held her bodice in place. She knew she could pull away, but she didn't want to.

She only wanted Lucien.

In just a moment, the bodice loosened, and Lucien was tugging at it, trying to free her from its confines.

She paused to help him, unfastening the row of silver hooks down the front that held it closed. This might not be the smartest thing she'd ever done, but it was what she wanted more than anything else.

His eyes widened as her breasts fell free. Her half-corset stopped below them, and Lucien reached forward to cup each breast in his hands. He dipped his head and kissed them as his thumbs brushed against her nipples.

They immediately stiffened at his touch, becoming more sensitive than ever before. Tempy gasped sharply at the sensation. He dropped one of his hands to her waist, where he searched for the closure for her skirt. After a few tugs, her skirt and petticoats were falling to the floor.

Tempy stood before him, wearing only her half-corset, pantaloons, and shoes. But the look of awe on Lucien's face made her feel confident, not exposed.

But now, she wanted to see more of him. She slid her hands up, under his jacket and over his shoulders, pushing his frock coat off.

He shrugged out of it and then began tugging at the fabric around his neck while she worked free the buttons on his waistcoat. The only sounds in the room were from the crackling of the fire and their heavy breathing.

Once the buttons were undone, Lucien pulled everything off over his head, leaving his chest bare for her to see.

And for her to touch.

She breathed in as she rested her palm on his smooth chest. His skin felt hot, and his muscles trembled at her touch.

He leaned back against the desk again and pulled her between his thighs. Her bare breasts pressed against his chest, and she tilted her head back in an invitation for a kiss.

He didn't disappoint. Their mouths merged and Tempy slid her hands over his velvety-soft skin. She wanted to touch him everywhere at once, and she hungrily moved her hands over his chest and arms.

She felt his fingers tugging at her waistband once more, and a moment later her pantaloons were falling from her hips. Lucien slid his hand down her back and cupped her bare bottom, causing her to jump in surprise. She leaned into him and felt something hard between his legs. He pressed her hips closer to him and then exhaled as she felt his body tremble against hers.

He took her hand in his and slid it down, between them, and cupped it around the hard length of him. She squeezed slightly, feeling the outlines, and he let out a soft moan.

She pulled her hand away, surprised, but he found it again and put it back.

The next few moments passed in a blur of sensations. They moved from the edge of the desk to the oriental rug in front of the fire, and they both were naked. At some point, Lucien had turned the gaslights down low so that the dim light cast faint shadows onto the floor.

Lying on her back, Tempy watched as Lucien spread her thighs and then centered his hips between them. He lowered his body over hers, supporting his weight with his arms as he gazed down at her.

His eyes were dark, the pupils dilated as he seemed to try to memorize the moment. Tempy lay naked before him except for the diamond necklace.

Lucien lowered his head and nuzzled her breast, kissing it and then taking it into his mouth. He pressed his face between her breasts, and then his mouth moved slowly as it left a line of fire trailing down her body along her belly.

Tempy moaned as he moved his hands between her thighs. He

slid his fingers between the folds of her cleft, and she was surprised by the slick moisture there as his fingers moved inside her.

The sensations he aroused in her made her head feel light, as though all the blood was rushing away from it. She moaned again as his fingers slid deep within her, thrusting in and then sliding out so that she writhed with pleasure under his attentions.

She wanted something more. More of him. She slid her hand between them and cupped the hard length of him, just as he'd shown her. She gave it a light squeeze, and as before, he let out a small moan of pleasure.

"Are you sure this is what you want?" he murmured. Tempy's brain couldn't seem to form the words to say yes, so she nodded. To make sure he understood, she ground her hips against his hand.

He lifted up and away from her, but only for a moment. Then, he was between her thighs. She felt him press into her. She expected pain, but there was none. Only a slick fullness as he slid inside her. The pleasure that he'd already wrought in her began to increase. He slid his hand between their bodies, just above the point where they joined together, and then began making small circles around a nub of intense sensation.

His fingers created spasms of pleasure that pulsed from the nub. Her body rocked with jolts of pleasure, and she wrapped her legs around him, pulling him inside her as far as possible. Throwing back her head, she moaned, and then he kissed her, devouring her lips and tongue with a passion that matched her own.

He pressed into her then and threw his head back as his eyes widened. His body convulsed over her as he shuddered. "Tempy," he said in a moan. "Oh my God. Tempy."

He kept his arms straight as he held his body above her, and then slowly bent his elbows and pressed his body into hers. His skin was like a furnace, and she could feel the heavy beat of his heart against her chest.

After a few moments, their breathing eased. Tempy closed her eyes, and Lucien rolled to one side. Then he lifted her head and wrapped his arm around her so that her head was pillowed on his shoulder.

34

A FEW HOURS LATER

Something woke Tempy up.

One side of her body was quite warm. Almost hot. And the other was chilled. She opened her eyes and lifted her cheek from the firm pillow on which it rested and looked down at Lucien's face. His eyes were closed and he breathed deeply, still asleep. From this angle, it looked as though he might be smiling. Without turning to look, she knew that the fire was out. That was why her backside was feeling so chilly. She must have been asleep for a while.

She heard a knock at the door, and her body jerked in surprise. That must be what had woken her. Lucien's arm tightened around her in his sleep, pulling her closer to him in a protective gesture.

"Mr. Hamlin," she heard Boothby say through the door. The doorknob rattled as someone tried to turn it. Fortunately, it was locked, since she was sprawled naked across Lucien.

She pushed herself up on one arm and shook Lucien with her free hand. He opened his eyes, looking rather bleary-eyed at first, but then his eyes snapped open. "Wake up," she whispered as she climbed to her feet. "Someone's at the door." She moved so quickly that by the time his eyes focused on her, she already had her pantaloons on and was loosening the crisscrossing ties on her corset so that she could put it back on.

He smiled at her. It was a sated, male smile that made her knees weak for a moment as she remembered the cause of it.

And then Boothby knocked again.

"I don't wish to be disturbed," Lucien called out, holding up a hand, indicating that Tempy should be quiet.

She batted his hand away, annoyed with him. What did he think she was doing? Singing opera? Of course she would be quiet.

"I'm sorry, sir," Boothby said. "But it's Miss Bliss. Her carriage is still here, but nobody has seen her in a few hours."

Tempy's eyes widened in horror. She redoubled her efforts to dress, swinging her corset around her body with a practiced hand and fastening the row of steel hooks down the front.

"Give me a moment," Lucien called back to him, "and I'll come sort it out."

Tempy turned so that her loose corset strings faced Lucien. He stepped closer, tightening them until she held up a hand, indicating that he should stop. He was strong and had made quick work of the task.

He dressed quickly, and she envied him the relative simplicity of his clothes.

Lucien tossed a log on the fire while Tempy pulled on her skirt and petticoats. She tied the drawstrings of her petticoats and fastened the hooks on the waistband of her skirt. Then she shrugged into her bodice. She fastened it and then rushed over to the mirror by the door to check her reflection.

Lucien stepped up behind her, glancing at her eyes in the mirror before checking them both for telltale signs of what had just transpired. He tucked one of her sparkling hairpins more firmly in place and then gave a nod of approval. Apparently, he thought they'd both pass muster.

She agreed.

"They must think I'm still in the casino somewhere," she whispered as she turned to face him. "My cloak is in the coatroom and my carriage is out front."

Lucien glanced at the clock and frowned. "It's just past one. I'm sure many of my patrons are still here. You can't leave unnoticed, but you can't stay either."

"Tell Boothby I fell asleep in here."

Lucien shook his head. "He'll never believe that."

"Perhaps not, but I don't think that matters. I'm certain he'll help us."

Lucien buttoned his frock coat, and Tempy reached out to smooth a stray lock of his hair back in place. But before she could touch it, he grabbed hold of her hand to stop her.

He looked troubled. "This should never have happened. I took advantage of you last night when my judgment was clouded with drink. I apologize."

Gentlemanly though his words were, she hated the idea that he regretted what they'd done. She pulled her hand from his grasp. "Don't say that, Lucien. I wanted it as much as you did."

He shook his head. "I'm not sure you did. You left my office last night intent on winning back Ernest, and then returned and gave yourself to me. I find it difficult to accept that you could abandon that dream so easily and so irrevocably. I'm afraid that in the light of day, you'll regret what transpired between us."

She flinched at his words. He sounded angry. Hurt even. "But I want you. Not Ernest. You're the one who helped me and encouraged me. You're the one who likes me exactly as I am. Not Ernest."

"All I have to give you is me," he said, spreading his empty hands before her. "No family. No history. No connection with your father and your past. Are you really willing to give up on all that?"

Someone knocked at the door again, right behind them. This knock sounded much louder than Boothby's had.

"Hamlin! Open this door," John Snowden demanded.

"I know you're in there!" shouted Squire Formsworth.

"What in blazes is Formsworth doing here?" Lucien demanded in a whisper.

Tempy's entire body tensed and her eyes widened. She glanced up at Lucien. "It can't be good," she said, shaking her head. "But you'd better open the door," she muttered. "And quickly, before they make an even bigger scene than they already have."

Lucien waited just a moment, but at Tempy's urging, he opened the door.

Squire Formsworth and John Snowden came barging into the room, and John's gaze immediately locked on Tempy. "Turn up the blasted lights," he demanded, his voice tight with fury.

While keeping his gazed fixed on Formsworth, Lucien closed the door and moved his hand to the control for the gaslights, flooding the room in light.

Mr. Snowden looked her up and down and then turned his scrutiny on Lucien, but he didn't seem to find anything amiss. He stalked into the room, moving closer to the fireplace.

He picked up the tumbler of whiskey from the table next to the armchair. "Were you trying to get her drunk, Mr. Hamlin? Your whiskey decanter is only half full, and an entire bottle of champagne is empty."

"Miss Bliss only had half a glass of champagne."

"Then why are the two of you closeted away together? Nobody has seen either of you for hours."

"He's seduced her, he has. You can see it in their faces."

Tempy cleared her throat and took a step forward. She sent Formsworth a dismissive look and then addressed herself to John

Snowden. "I'm afraid I fell asleep. It was quite foolish of me, I know."

The stern expression on John Snowden's face froze in place.

"And...," she seemed to lose momentum as she met his disbelieving gaze, "and now I don't know what to do to remedy the situation. Won't you please help us?" Her voice trailed off, ending on a pleading note.

His eyes widened in shock. "Good God. Is that the best excuse you can come up with?"

"It's just that. An excuse. Just look at her. He's ruined her, he has. I knew he was set on seducing her when I saw them last week. I should have stopped him them."

Lucien took a threatening step toward Formsworth. "I think you need to be more careful about the aspersions you are casting. Miss Bliss has a reputation to protect, and your shouting is doing her no good."

A moment later, Boothby burst into the room wearing a harried expression. His gaze immediately landed on Formsworth, and he stormed across the room toward him. "I said you weren't permitted to come inside Hamlin House, and I meant it. You're nothing but trouble, you are."

Formsworth backed away from Boothby, sidestepping Lucien as he did so. "You have no right to ban me from this casino. You're nothing but an underling."

"And you're nothing but a murderer. That means that when it comes to who has the right to be here, I win." Boothby glanced at both Lucien and Snowden. "My apologies, but if you'll allow me, I'll ensure that this 'gentleman' leaves the premises. I'll even escort him out personally."

"You can't treat me this way," Formsworth blustered.

"And if you don't go quietly," Boothby said, "I'll be happy to call the constable and make certain that all of your friends back in Porlock know all the details about how you were forcibly ejected from Hamlin House."

Formsworth's face went red. He stood rooted in place for a moment, obviously wanting to ignore the threat, but then he jammed his hat on his head, let out a great huff of frustration, and turned toward the door.

Boothby hurried after him, but paused at the door and gave a brief bow to the three of them before following Formsworth out and closing the door.

"What was that about?" John Snowden asked. "Are your footmen in the habit of ejecting guests from the premises?" He frowned toward the door.

"On occasion, but it's not a common occurrence. That happened to be a peculiar situation," Lucien replied. "I'm afraid Formsworth is someone from my past. My distant past. He's angry because he lost the court case that took me back to Porlock last week. Our families have been squabbling for generations, and now he's decided to continue the fight."

John Snowden glanced at Tempy. "I don't like this. I don't like it at all."

"I think it would be best if I were to go home now," Tempy said softly. "My carriage is waiting and I'm not usually out this late." She stifled a yawn.

"Hmmph." John narrowed his eyes at her.

Lucien stepped forward, earning a scowl from John, but it didn't seem to faze him. "Could you, perhaps, escort her to her carriage?" he asked. "And don't forget to collect her cloak. If nobody finds out that I was alone in this room with her, then her reputation could remain untarnished."

John glared at him. It was obvious that he wanted to argue the point, but then he glanced at Tempy.

She shot him a pleading look. He had to help them. He simply had to.

John's expression shifted, and he nodded. "Quickly then."

Lucien slid his hand into his pocket and removed a key. In three long strides he crossed the room heading toward the private door to the cashiers' area. With practiced ease, he inserted the key and twisted it in the lock. He opened the door just enough so that he could pass through it, but before slipping away, he paused to turn and give Tempy and enigmatic look.

"Let me know what you decide," was all he said.

And he was gone.

35

BEING ERNEST

Tempy waited in Lucien's office for a few minutes so that some of the patrons could make note of his presence in the casino. She certainly didn't want to run the risk of having both of them reappear at almost exactly the same time.

While they waited, John Snowden refused to speak to her or even to meet her eyes. Instead, he wandered through the office, picking up the champagne flutes and the whiskey glass and stashing them neatly on the side table.

Once enough time had passed, Tempy cleared her throat. "Can you escort me to fetch my cloak?"

John nodded and opened the office door. There were a few patrons standing around in the foyer who stared at them openly, so Tempy made a show of it. She left the door of the office open so that if anybody cared to check up on her, they could see that the room was empty.

She quickly collected her cloak, and John escorted her outside and handed her into her carriage.

It was cold inside the dark carriage, and Tempy wrapped the

lap blanket over her legs, tucking it in place. She glanced back at the entrance as John Snowden walked back inside, and was surprised to see another guest being escorted out of the casino.

It was Ernest Lipscomb.

Based on his hangdog expression and Boothby's stern look, she could only assume that his "lucky chip" hadn't been quite so lucky after all.

He kept his eyes focused on the steps as he walked down them like a man heading to prison. He looked as though he'd lost everything.

Tempy called out for her coachman to wait.

Upon hearing her voice, Ernest glanced up, his eyes widening in surprise. He hurried to stand next to her carriage. "I've lost everything," he said.

"Your lucky chip?"

He furrowed his brow. "Well, yes, I lost that, but I lost you as well. And then when I went in search of Clarisse to apologize, I discovered that she'd last been seen entering Hamlin's office. I tried to follow her, but his door was locked." He shook his head. "I know it was foolish, but I listened at the door for a moment, and I'm convinced she was in there with him. He seduced her, I'm certain of it."

Tempy's eyes widened in horror.

"I did what I could to keep anyone from discovering he had someone in there with him, but I never saw her come out. I've lost her, Tempy."

"And you still love her?"

He nodded. "I realize that now. I was a fool tonight. In so many ways. I stayed until that footman made me leave. He knew I'd run out of funds. He was pleasant enough about it, but still, he said I had to leave. Hamlin House policy."

Tempy frowned. "Ernest, Clarisse left hours ago. I'm certain of it."

Ernest shook his head. "No. People saw her go in there with him. I know what I heard through the door."

"No, you don't understand. She left. She may have entered the room, but she didn't stay long. She was gone before--before Lucien let me in."

Ernest stared at her as though he couldn't understand her words.

"You didn't hear Clarisse in there," she said. "You heard me."

His eyes widened in shock. "You? But that means...Clarisse..."

"She left hours ago. Lucien said she took your carriage."

"I didn't lose her after all." A grin broke across Ernest's face and he beamed with relief. Then his eyebrows lowered. "But Tempy. What were you thinking, telling me something like that?"

"I was thinking that I'd done enough harm tonight. I couldn't let you leave imagining the worst about Clarisse."

"So instead you told me the worst about yourself?" He looked at her steadily for a moment. "Don't worry. I'll keep your secret. But I hope you know what you're doing."

"So do I."

Ernest looked at her gravely for a moment and then gave a nod and stepped back. He signaled to her coachman that he could depart, and Tempy's carriage immediately pulled forward.

Her eyes remained focused on Ernest for a moment, but there was only one thought in her mind.

She was a fool. A complete, bloody fool.

How could she not have realized she'd fallen in love with Lucien? He'd been right in front of her the entire time, and she'd taken him for granted.

He'd been right when he'd demanded that she make a decision in the clear light of day. She'd behaved childishly at best. One might even say cruelly. To both Lucien and to Ernest. And to Clarisse as well, for that matter.

Looking back over the past couple of weeks, she now viewed

Lucien's behavior in a new light. His strange insistence on working in his office while she and Mme Le Clair had their lessons. His smoldering looks. His repeated insistence that she didn't need to transform herself. And most especially, those kisses they'd shared on the night of her lesson. They all painted an entirely different picture in light of what had just transpired between them.

Had a bigger fool ever been born?

36

TRAINS, EPHANIES,
AND ROULETTE

I t's strange the way a moment of sharp clarity can strike when one simply stops worrying over a problem. That's exactly what happened the moment Lucien stopped worrying about Tempy and Ernest and the newspaper articles and his casino.

While he was still mired in Tempy's problems, it had been like watching a ball bounce around on a roulette table and trying to figure out what might happen next. It was an impossible task because the little ivory sphere's movements were simply too random. There was no telling where it might land. But once it stopped moving, everything that would unfold next was already determined with a high degree of certainty. For example, if this were his casino, his croupier would rake in the losing chips and then neatly stack up the winnings before sliding the chips to their new owners. By now Lucien knew his customers well enough to know with a fair degree of certainty how they'd respond to either winning or losing.

And now that Tempy had made her decisions and her wheel of

fate had stopped spinning, everything came into focus for Lucien. And one of those things in particular required his immediate action.

While waiting in station for the train to Bath, he wrote three letters; one to Tempy's law firm, a second to her board of directors, and a third to John Snowden. He considered writing a fourth one to Tempy. What would she think if she were to see it? Would she open it? And if she did, would she be disappointed with its contents, or relieved?

No. He wouldn't write to her. He wanted to tell her in person or not at all. Just the three letters would do.

❧ 37 ❧

A PARTICULAR
SHADE OF BLUE INK

❧

The next morning, Tempy's maid carried a silver tray to her bedroom. In the center of it rested an envelope. She picked it up, examining her name scrawled across the front of it. It wasn't Lucien's handwriting. She would have recognized his anywhere.

Suddenly, she recognized the particular shade of blue ink and her stomach flipped over. It was from Mr. Dickens. It must be concerning the article she'd submitted yesterday. That was the only thing that made sense.

Tempy tore the envelope open and quickly scanned its contents, at first not quite comprehending what she read. As she made a second pass, she studied it more carefully and comprehension replaced confusion.

Mr. Dickens was complimenting her article.

According to the letter, Wilkie Collins was in Bath and wanted her to travel there to meet with him. Apparently, after reading her article, he had insisted that he wanted her to write a second one to accompany a later chapter of his manuscript. Since he didn't want to run the risk of allowing information about his upcoming chapters to be leaked to the public, he refused to trust them to a courier. Therefore, he wanted her to come to Bath to read the particular chapter so that she could understand the context for her article. Then she would be able to suggest a topic that could accompany the chapter. Since it would be published in a month, time was of the essence.

Tempy could hardly believe what she was reading, and she had to review it one more time before she'd allow herself to accept what she'd read on the page. Both Mr. Dickens *and* Mr. Collins had liked her article. They had genuinely liked it.

Tempy grinned.

It was fate. It had to be. She had been trying to decide how quickly she should follow Lucien to Bath, but this letter made the decision simple.

She'd leave immediately.

❧ 38 ❧

TO BATH, TO BATH

❦

This time, Tempy didn't bring Millicent with her on her trip to Bath. Yes, she still felt guilty about dragging the poor woman with her the last time. After all, Millicent had been miserably ill nearly the entire time. But that was only a small part of her reasoning.

Because on this trip, the last thing Tempy wanted was a chaperone.

One of two possible outcomes would take place today. Either Lucien would welcome her, or he'd reject her. It was that simple. And in either case, she didn't want Millicent tagging along as a witness.

If Lucien wanted her in his life, then the two of them would make those plans together.

And if he didn't, then Tempy needed to learn how to face life alone.

If she truly planned to become a journalist-- an unmarried journalist--then she needed to begin behaving as one. And that meant that she would need to begin traveling with a companion rather than a chaperone.

If she returned to London without Lucien, she would contact one of the agencies and hire a paid companion. She was certain she could find someone who could accompany her on interviews or when she traveled to research her articles.

Now, as Tempy sat on the train retracing the journey she'd made with Lucien and Millicent, she gazed out the windows. Was she staring at the same cows that had been there on her last trip? Certainly the same trees grew alongside the tracks. Everything around her remained the same.

But not her. She felt like a butterfly recently emerged from its chrysalis. Her wings were still damp and crumpled, but soon she'd be ready to fly.

She stretched her wings, and it felt good.

Tempy would've preferred to go directly to Lucien's home in the Royal Crescent, but Mr. Collins's home was right next to the train station. Despite her impatience to see Lucien again, she forced herself to wait just one more hour. Besides, if she couldn't convince Lucien that she truly wanted him and not Ernest, she knew she'd be too devastated to speak to Mr. Collins. Meeting him now seemed like the wisest plan.

Fortunately, Mr. Collins had received word that she would be arriving on the afternoon train. He grinned as she entered his drawing room, his pleasure at seeing her obvious.

It only took a moment to murmur pleasantries. She asked after his health and he asked about her train trip. Once that was set aside, they were able to move on to the real purpose of their meeting.

"I enjoyed your article, Miss Bliss. It was exactly what I'd hoped for. You did a wonderful job describing both the delights and the dangers of gambling. I especially liked the way you included a personal story from someone who had been able to put it behind him. That's just the sort of thing our subscribers like to read about...overcoming adversity."

A deep-seated sense of satisfaction welled within Tempy. "You have no idea how wonderful it is to hear you say that."

Mr. Collins chuckled. "I know better than you think I might. After all, I'm a writer too."

She blushed. "Of course. What was I thinking?"

"Even after all these years, I often doubt my ability to write anything new. I can't help wondering if all of my success hasn't simply been some enormous cosmic joke." Then he glanced down at the silver-topped cane leaning against his chair. He lifted it up and gazed at it thoughtfully. "It's my pain that keeps me grounded. It helps me remember that there's a constant power struggle taking place in this world. And with every bit of success, there is a price to pay. I try to use my writing to open the eyes of my readers to some of the injustices taking place around them. We become accustomed to them, just as I've been forced to become accustomed to my affliction."

His leg, with its swollen knee, was stretched out in front of him. It had to be terribly painful.

"Do you see your pain as being the price you must pay to be successful in your writing? And if so, has it been worth the trade?"

He tilted his head from side to side as though weighing her questions. "Perhaps. Perhaps not. But it doesn't really matter, does it?" he asked, meeting her eyes. "It's not as though I've been given a choice in the matter."

Tempy nodded, feeling a little foolish for asking.

"I have the chapter here, all ready for you to read. I'm afraid I can't let you take it with you. You'll need to read it here."

Tempy tried to hide her look of dismay, but apparently she was unsuccessful.

"Is that a problem?" he asked, furrowing his brow.

Was it? "It's just that I need to meet someone." It wasn't as though they planned to meet at a specific time, but she didn't think she could sit here and read an entire chapter of *No Name*. It was unlikely that a single word of it would sink in.

Mr. Collins glanced at the clock on the mantle. "How about tomorrow then? Around two?"

She nearly sighed with relief. "Yes, two o'clock would be perfect. Thank you for being so understanding." She stood to leave, and Mr. Collins struggled to his feet.

"I hope you don't mind if I fail to escort you to the door," he said, gesturing to his leg.

"Not all. Goodbye, Mr. Collins. And thank you."

A moment later, Tempy was back in her carriage and wending her way through the streets of Bath toward the Royal Crescent.

And toward Lucien.

This last stage of the trip seemed to take much longer than she remembered. It was strange, the way time had seemed to compress itself while she was on the train, and now it pulled tight, stretched like an elastic band to its breaking point. There were quite a few more carriages traveling along her route than she remembered from the previous visit.

Finally, as the hansom cab moved along the curve of The Circus, Tempy realized that she was only a couple of blocks away from the Royal Crescent.

Tempy's breathing quickened and her blood rushed to her head, leaving her momentarily lightheaded.

It was nerves, she observed with some surprise. She was quite nervous about seeing Lucien, and that frightened her.

Perhaps this wasn't the right thing to do after all.

But it had to be.

Her hand went up to her neck again, finding the necklace that rested there under her dress. No matter what, she needed to give it back to Lucien. She couldn't turn back now.

Love stories didn't work this way, at least not in the novels she'd read. The woman didn't pursue the man only to realize that he was entirely wrong for her.

That would be ludicrous.

Just like her.

No, the heroine was *supposed* to recognize the man of her dreams immediately. She certainly wasn't supposed to chase one man only to catch him and toss him aside for another.

And a proper heroine in a romantic novel most certainly was *not* supposed to pursue the man to his home. In books, it always happened the other way around. The man came to her and swept her off her feet. Then he carried her away so that they could live happily ever after.

Perhaps she wasn't enacting a romance after all. Perhaps she was destined to be alone.

Perhaps this story was a tragedy.

Well, if that was what fate had in store for her, she knew she could face it.

But she certainly hoped that wasn't the case.

❧ 39 ☙

FIRE IN THE ICE

⚭

Lucien knew he'd been in an obnoxious mood for the past two days. Boothby probably regretted his decision to become Lucien's valet. If their roles had been reversed, Lucien would have resigned by now.

He needed to remember to give the man the night off soon.

Lucien had thrown himself into learning about the state of his affairs as the new Earl of Cavendish. The title still sounded stiff, like a new shoe that wasn't broken in. It chafed and pinched, but he knew it would soon feel comfortable.

At least, it had better.

He still wasn't certain how to handle Formsworth. He mulled the problem over for a moment until a thought struck him. Perhaps he should let Boothby handle the problem. After all, he'd already forced Formsworth into full retreat once, and that was more than most people were ever able to accomplish.

That very morning he'd received a letter from the board of directors of Bliss Railways. It had been extremely conciliatory and would have made him laugh if not for the seriousness of the subject.

The front door chime rang. After a steady stream of visitors had dropped off calling cards this afternoon, he'd given Boothby strict instructions to permit no one entrance to his home today. He was to tell anyone who asked that Lord Cavendish was out.

So, it surprised him when he heard a knock on his office door just a moment later.

Boothby opened the door and cleared his throat. "Sir, you have a visitor whom I believe you'll want to see."

"Take their name," he said, waving his hand in dismissal. "Tell them I'll either call on them in two days' time, or they can come back later today. I should be available in a couple of hours."

When Boothby didn't move out of the doorway, Lucien frowned at him. "Why are you still standing there? Go on."

Boothby looked singularly uncomfortable, and he cleared his throat again.

"What is it? Anyone observing you would think you'd been my manservant for years by the way you clear your throat and refuse to do my bidding. Obviously you disapprove of my decision, so out with it. Why should I see this person?"

"It's Miss Bliss, my lord."

Lucien lurched to his feet and nearly knocked over his chair. "Tempy's here?"

"Yes, sir. She's requested a few moments of your time."

"Well, why didn't you say so? Send her in immediately."

Boothby backed out of the room and began to pull the door closed.

"Wait! Is she with anyone? A gentleman perhaps?"

Boothby pushed the door open again. His expression was unreadable. Irritatingly so. Lucien suspected him of enjoying Lucien's discomfort. "Well?" Lucien prompted.

"She's alone, sir."

Relief surged through him.

Boothby continued to stand at the door.

"Well, go on then. Show her in." Lucien plucked his frock coat off the back of his chair and slid it on over his bright green waistcoat.

He glanced at Boothby as the man closed the door and noted the smirk on his face. That was most definitely a smirk.

Dratted little monkey.

Lucien shot his cuffs, making certain that just the right amount of white sleeve emerged from the black frock coat.

He leaned against his desk, trying to look casual. Or was his position too staged? He turned back to his desk and sat back down in the chair. Yes. This appeared more impromptu. As though she were catching him at work.

There was a soft knock at the door, and then it swung open.

There she was. Lovely as ever.

Lucien sprang to his feet, suddenly feeling foolish. "Tempy," he said.

"Lucien." Her voice was like a caress.

He stopped breathing. There was no more in and out of air. In fact, for a moment his heart even skipped a beat. The moment in time froze, and he could only stare at Tempy.

She was here. She had come.

With long strides, he crossed the room, and Tempy hurried toward him, meeting him in his headlong rush toward her.

He wrapped his arms around her, pulling her close. "You're here," he whispered into her hair. "You came to me." He pulled her tighter, pressing her against him.

"In the light of day," she murmured into his chest.

He slid his hands up to her shoulders and leaned back to peer down into her eyes. "Say it."

He needed for her to say the words. He needed to hear her tell him.

"I love you, Lucien."

She said it so simply, so boldly, that his heart soared with joy.

He wrapped his arms around her again, crushing her to his chest, and kissed her. He put every ounce of his love into that kiss, and he could feel her love flowing back into him.

She slid her palms up his back and stopped at his neck. She wove the fingers on one hand into his hair and then curled them, grabbing a fistful of his hair as she pulled him more tightly against her.

A deep wave of lust washed through him, but then he froze. This wasn't what he'd planned to have happen.

He reached his hands behind his neck and took hold of Tempy's, pulling them free. "Wait," he said.

She opened her eyes blearily, and then they widened in surprise. "What is it? What's wrong?"

She suddenly looked nervous. As though she was worried that he might be rejecting her.

"Wait. I need a moment. There's something I want to do first."

He hurried back to his desk and pulled open a drawer. He pushed the letter from Bliss Railways to one side and pulled out the blue velvet case and released its spring catch.

He glanced down at the sparkling jewelry within and selected a piece, sliding it onto the tip of his finger and then closing his hand into a fist.

He crossed back over to Tempy. "I know it's customary to speak to a father or brother, but that won't work for us. We're different. And I think that makes us well suited for one another." He cleared his throat. "Temperance Bliss, will you do me the honor of agreeing to become my wife?"

A smile tugged at the corners of her mouth. "Say it," she demanded.

He was confused for a moment, but then he understood. "I love you, Tempy. Please marry me."

Her smile broadened and she nodded. Then her lower lip

began to tremble and tears began sliding down her cheeks. "Oh Lucien," she said. "I was afraid you might not want me."

He lifted his hand to her cheek, brushing away the tears with his thumb. "I've always wanted you, Tempy. Even when I didn't know it."

He raised his other hand and glanced down, pulling the small ring from the tip of his finger.

He looked into her eyes. "I don't know if this will fit, but we can have it adjusted. I want you to have it as my betrothal gift." He lifted her left hand and slid it onto her ring finger. He had to push just a little to slide it over her knuckle, but it fit perfectly, just as he'd hoped it would.

He watched as she lifted her hand to the collar of her dress. She stared into his eyes as she undid the top button of her blouse, but he couldn't bring himself to lift his gaze from her fingers as they pressed the circle of ivory through the top buttonhole.

As her dress parted, he caught a glitter of fire beneath it.

40. BLISS

Lucien's hands rested on her shoulders. Their bodies were almost brushing against each other, and she could swear she could feel the heat radiating from his body even though they were inches apart. Lucien overwhelmed her senses, making it difficult to breathe, and even more difficult to think clearly.

One of his hands drifted from her shoulder and he ran an index finger across the diamond-encrusted oval links. Tempy could only close her eyes and try not to tremble at his touch.

But then her eyes flew open. She needed to see him.

As soon as their gazes met, Tempy let out a soft sigh that was a mixture of relief and desire. Lucien's hand slid up, cupping the back of her head and sliding into her hair. Then he lowered his mouth to hers, claiming it again.

Lucien's other arm slid around her waist, pulling her tightly against his body. "When you left the casino, I was afraid you might not come back to me, and it nearly killed me."

"This is where I belong." She leaned into his arms and slid her hands under his frock coat, sliding them across the satin of his green waistcoat until she'd encircled his waist. "I know that now."

"As long as we're together. That's all I want. All I need."

Lucien took a couple of shuffling steps forward and she followed along with him by moving backwards. He pressed her body against the closed door and began kissing her again. His lips pressed into hers, and when she opened her mouth to welcome him, his tongue darted against hers. Tendrils of fire began to wend their way through her, but then focused on the V between her legs.

"I want you in my bed, but not like this," he murmured into her ear. "We need to get married right away."

Right away? Tempy knew she should probably speak, but she didn't think her mouth could form words right now. She could barely even comprehend what Lucien was saying. What was this word, married? And how did it apply to her?

"Tempy?" he said. He leaned one elbow on the wall next to her head and looked into her eyes. She focused her gaze on his face, and then noticed the self-satisfied smile on it.

That brought her around.

She pushed away from the wall and stepped around him before facing him again.

"When?"

"As soon as possible." He moved past her to cross to the far side of his desk, and Tempy couldn't help but watch him as he moved.

She sighed.

"I heard that," he said over his shoulder.

She smiled. "I was just thinking about how lucky I am."

Standing on the far side of the desk, he grinned at her and then began flipping through his calendar. "We have three choices. We can wait three weeks for the banns to be read, or we can try for a special license, or we can take a trip up to Gretna Green."

Tempy licked her lips. "I've never been to Scotland. And just imagine the stories we can tell."

A broad grin spread over Lucien's face. "Scotland it is."

"I wonder if Earl E. Byrd will write an article informing the world of our plans even before we manage to leave Bath," she mused. But as soon as the words were out of her mouth, she realized that she really didn't care. She shot Lucien a devilish grin. "Perhaps we'll scandalize all of London."

Lucien moved back to his desk. "I'm sorry to disappoint you," he said, pulling an envelope from his desk. "But I'm afraid you won't be mentioned in the newspapers quite so often anymore."

She shot Lucien a questioning gaze as she accepted the letter and was even more surprised when she saw that it was from Bliss Railways. "What's this?"

"Something John Snowden said helped me figure it out. It turns out that man writing the articles was being paid to do so by your board of directors."

"What! How can you be certain?"

Lucien gestured toward the letter she held. "They've admitted it. I first noticed someone following me in Bath on our return trip, but when I thought about it I recalled seeing him in Porlock as well. John was able to track the man down and, um, *convince* him to help."

Tempy cocked one eyebrow at his choice of words, but didn't say anything. When he paused at though waiting for her to speak, she gestured for him to continue.

"John confronted your board of directors yesterday with his proof." He jutted his chin toward the letter in her hand. "That letter is their response to me. John insisted that if they didn't write it, he'd bring the police into the matter. You'll have to decide how you want to proceed from here."

"You interceded without speaking to me?"

"I'm sorry." His look of remorse seemed genuine. "With what happened at the casino the other night, I didn't think it was wise to wait. After what he did when there was nothing illicit to write about, I could only imagine what he might do if he caught even the hint of real scandal."

Tempy frowned. To avoid speaking, she pulled the letter from the envelope and read through it. There it was. The board's admission that they'd been trying to manipulate her into selling her controlling share of Bliss Railways by paying Byrd to harass her. Apparently, they'd also sent a letter of apology to her home. She must have just missed receiving it.

This meant Byrd was gone from her life. She no longer had to worry about opening the paper and finding yet another article criticizing her. She tried to suppress the smile that wanted to escape her lips, but she couldn't. "You've made things quite difficult for me, Lord Cavendish."

Her smile must have been infectious, because she caught him grinning back at her. "And how is that, Miss Bliss?"

"You've given me two wonderful betrothal gifts. How can I possibly repay you?"

He took a step closer. "I know exactly how."

"Yes?" she asked.

"Come with me to Gretna Green."

"I like the way you think," she said, grinning in delight. "How soon can we leave?"

The End

ALSO BY

Historical romances
By Sheridan Jeane
Gambling On a Scoundrel

Secrets and Seduction series:
It Takes a Spy...
Lady Catherine's Secret
Once Upon a Spy
My Lady, My Spy
Along Came a Spy
Also available:
Lady Cecilia Is Cordially Disinvited for Christmas
(only available via Sheridan's VIP club)
View the full Secrets and Seduction series and leave a review

Duke By Dawn (Novella, part of the anthology *Dukes All Night Long*)

The Shadow of the Black Rose - a Victorian-era Romantic Suspense trilogy
Whispers and Spies
The Spy In Disguise
Protect the Prince

Contemporary Romances
By Sheri Tyler
The Way to a Woman's Heart series - the **Coming Home** trilogy
Slow Simmer
Here's the Scoop
From Bitter to Sweet

The Way to a Woman's Heart series - the **Destination Wedding** trilogy
One Cup of Chemistry
Say Cheese!
Kebabs and Kisses

Scan the QR code to download your free copy of Lady Cecilia Is Cordially Disinvited for Christmas

ACKNOWLEDGMENTS

I want to thank my husband, Bob, and our children for their help, their support, and their understanding. I couldn't have done this without you.

In addition, I want to thank Christy Carlson, Sheila Larkin, Chloe Flowers, and the members of Sunshine Critique Group for everything they did to help make this book a reality.

HISTORICAL NOTES

When I first planned this novel, I wanted Tempy to be a writer working for Mr. Charles Dickens. I researched the time period and chose one that suited my needs with respect to the story I wanted to tell. In doing so, I researched some of the women of the time who were doing notable things. Many of the people who I mention in this book existed, and I'd like to offer some brief notes on the lives of some of the notable women of the time.

I won't bother to outline the life of Mr. Charles Dickens. You've probably read a number of his books and are well acquainted with him. My favorite is "The Tale of Two Cities."

Eliza Lynn Linton (10 February 1822 – 14 July 1898) was more of a "real-life" version of Tempy. She was the first salaried female journalist and was on staff for Charles Dickens when he published "Household Words." I found it quite interesting to discover that she was a critic of "the new woman" and wrote an attack on feminism. She also believed that politics was the natural sphere of men and fought against the vote for women.

According to her obituary in The Times, she held an "animosity towards all, or rather, some of those facets which may be conveniently called the 'New Woman'."

In the 1850's, Lady Clementina Hawarden (Clementina Maude, Viscountess Harwarden 1 June 1822 – 19 January 1865) began taking photographs, first of Ireland's landscape near her home in Dundrum County, Tipperary, Ireland, and later focusing on her ten children (yes, TEN). In 1859, when the family relocated to their London home in South Kensington, she set up a studio there to continue her work.

While many male photographers of the day traveled extensively to photograph foreign lands, Lady Hawarden remained at home, capturing images of her family. It is from these photos that we can have a peek at the life of an upper-class family. Sometimes her daughters wore fashionable Victorian gowns, and at other times they wore costumes from the family's dress-up box. Reenacting historical tableaux was a popular pastime of the day.

Lady Clementina's first public exhibit of her work took place in 1863 in an annual event hosted by the Photographic Society of London, and then again in the following year. She won a silver medal both years. Sadly, she died of pneumonia in January of 1865 at the age 42, leaving behind ten children and a large body of work.

To see many of her photographs, visit the website for the Victoria and Albert Museum.

Another historical figure I used in my story was Wilkie Collins (8 January 1824 – 23 September 1889). He was a longtime friend to Charles Dickens and wrote a number of books. The serialized version of *No Name* (and which inspired my book *Once Upon a Spy*) was his second novel to be published with *All the Year Round*. His first to be serialized, *The Woman in White*, was pivotal in starting a new genre of "sensation novels" (a blend of Gothic horror and domestic realism) and is considered by many to be the first mystery novel. He also wrote more than sixty short stories and fourteen plays, some of which were performed by Mr. Dickens's acting company.

Mr. Collins initially studied to become a lawyer, but after the death of his father he published his first book. He met Dickens in 1851, and following that, he became heavily involved in Dickens's world, performing in his acting company and publishing short stories in Dickens's magazine "*Household Words*." He also began writing essays, dramatic criticisms, and a travel book.

In the late 1850s he began to suffer from "rheumatic gout," which we now call rheumatoid arthritis, and in January 1862 he finally resigned from the staff of *All the Year Round* so that he could spend some time in Bath for his health. In 1863 he traveled to spas in Germany and Italy. Over time, he became addicted to laudanum, and this is thought to have contributed to his death. His book "The Moonstone" was published in 1868, and Dorothy L Sayers described it as "probably the very finest detective story ever written."

I inaccurately promoted the Village Hall in Porlock to a Town Hall, a building which I entirely invented for this story. Most of Porlock, however, is much as described, with the exception of "*No Common Scents*," a store which actually existed at one time in Yellow Springs, Ohio.

ABOUT THE AUTHOR

Sheridan Jeane is an award-winning author of historical romantic suspense, weaving stories of intrigue, danger, and slow-burning romance. She also writes lighthearted contemporary romance under the name Sheri Tyler.

She grew up in Huber Heights, a suburb of Dayton, Ohio, and now lives just outside Pittsburgh. Sheridan holds a bachelor's degree in computer science with a minor in English. She co-founded Three Rivers Romance Writers, a former chapter of Romance Writers of America that supported a vibrant local community of romance writers.

When she's not reading or writing, she can be found learning to salsa dance, tumbling downhill on skis, or volunteering with the Child Health Association of Sewickley to support children in need in southwestern Pennsylvania.

www.SheridanJeane.com